PENGUIN BOOKS

Flesh in Armour

Leonard Mann (1885–1981) served in the Australian Imperial Force during the First World War and with the Department of Aircraft Production in the Second World War. Aside from *Flesh in Armour*, he wrote seven other novels.

T0359156

FLESH IN ARMOUR

LEONARD MANN

PENGUIN BOOKS

PENGUIN BOOKS

Published by the Penguin Group
Penguin Group (Australia)
707 Collins Street, Melbourne, Victoria 3008, Australia
(a division of Penguin Australia Pty Ltd)
Penguin Group (USA) Inc.
375 Hudson Street, New York, New York 10014, USA
Penguin Group (Canada)
90 Eglinton Avenue East, Suite 700, Toronto, Canada ON M4P 2Y3
(a division of Penguin Canada Books Inc.)
Penguin Books Ltd
80 Strand, London WC2R 0RL England
Penguin Ireland
25 St Stephen's Green, Dublin 2, Ireland
(a division of Penguin Books Ltd)
Penguin Books India Pvt Ltd
11 Community Centre, Panchsheel Park, New Delhi – 110 017, India
Penguin Group (NZ)
67 Apollo Drive, Rosedale, Auckland 0632, New Zealand
(a division of Penguin New Zealand Pty Ltd)
Penguin Books (South Africa) (Pty) Ltd
Rosebank Office Park, Block D, 181 Jan Smuts Avenue, Parktown North,
Johannesburg, 2196, South Africa
Penguin (Beijing) Ltd
7F, Tower B, Jiaming Center, 27 East Third Ring Road North, Chaoyang District,
Beijing 100020, China

Penguin Books Ltd, Registered Offices: 80 Strand, London WC2R 0RL, England

This edition published by Penguin Group (Australia), 2014

Printed and bound in Australia by Griffin Press

National Library of Australia Cataloguing-in-Publication data is available.

ISBN: 9780143571742

penguin.com.au

MIX
Paper | Supporting
responsible forestry
FSC® C018684

CONTENTS

FOREWORD

No individual soldier is referred to in this book. Its characters have been created only out of the conglomerate. Their Platoon, Company, Battalion, Brigade or even Division is no particular body and, in spite of the evidence of places and times, exists only in fiction.

IN LONDON TOWN

CHAPTER I.

THROUGH the chill blur of an afternoon early in
August, 1917, the figures of two men in long, tawny
greatcoats, lurched wearily out of the London throng
and seated themselves on the stone railing in Trafalgar
Square with their backs to the classical portico of the
National Gallery and the spire of St. Martin's in the
Fields. Their hats distinguished them as Australians.
The traffic reeled this way and that without cease about
them, beating towards and sheering off and throwing up
now and then such odd bits of human flotsam on to the
staunch atoll in the middle of the square. The figure
of Nelson, small and disproportionate on the top of the
column, was hardly discernible in the dirty mist. Looking up at him perched up there, a sardonic stranger
might be pardoned the thought that the English, unable
to reconcile the hero and his Lady Hamilton, his Copen-
hagen and his "Kiss me, Hardy," with the traditional
newspaper type, had elevated him to that precarious
eminence for their safety's sake. For him there was
no more the hissing and washing of the cold grey seas,
but the deep dull roar of murky London, the hoarse
honking of motor cars and sharp crackling of motor
'bus tyres on wet pavements, and hastening to and fro'
of ant-like people in the bemused dimmed lamplights
down there below him, where he is securely guarded by
the lions of British respectability.

Before he sat down Bill Potter waved a nonchalant
greeting with "Good-day, Nelson."

"Eh?" asked his companion.

"Just passing the day to old Wingie."

Bill eased his six-foot length slowly on the damp stone. The bull-ring had failed to cure the slouch acquired on the heavy soil of his father's farm in the Wimmera, and, once half off the parade ground, he relapsed completely into the old habit with no care for the efforts which had been made to instil into him some semblance of soldierly bearing. The skin of the long horse face under the colourless hair was deeply tanned. Simple in some things and ignorant in many he was yet no fool. The pale washed-blue eyes, which seemed so vacant, had a knack of becoming in a flash cunning, mocking and derisive, as the sergeant in charge of his squad had perceived often enough to his annoyance. Charl Bentley was younger than Bill by three years, being a few months over his nineteenth birthday. In contrast to the boniness of his mate he seemed almost plump, so that his gracefulness had a sleek feline quality about it. He was in fact strong and agile and had been at school in Melbourne, which he had left only to enlist, a footballer of distinction. His colour was rather dark and his eyes were at once shy and intelligent. Both of them belonged to reinforcements of the Nth Battalion on final leave, as that leave was called with some sound of ill omen to the superstitious, which was allowed to troops when their training was deemed sufficient and they were marked down on the list of the next draft for France.

There were others squatted like them on the railings around the basin, most of them soldiers from overseas, and about a third Australians, resting there with sombre, hump-backed stolidity in this last hopping off place

from which they would scatter into the Strand, Picca-
dilly, Leicester Square and Shaftesbury Avenue. Their
immobility in the half light made them appear, like the
sculptured lions, part of the monument's engarniture,
and when one of them rose, stretched and moved slowly
off, an onlooker might have been as startled as if one of
the couchant stones had come to life before his eyes.

All the while London reeled and swayed around them,
a phantasmagoria of crackling, poster-decked buses and
disdainful cars, so disdainful that their expensive occupants were not even likely to notice those statuesque or
gargoylesque figures leaning humped forward with protuberant chins. The pedestrians, too, passed by with
hardly a glance or only a hurried one at the foreign
immobile figures. Slightly hostile instinctively, at the
instant of sidelong perception, under the gaze which
seemed so fixed, for it encompassed their steps only so
far as it might by mere turning of the eyes, they moved
coldly and silently past on the other side of an invisible
barrier, like dark drab little fish in a tank, the glass
sides of which and the water were of the same grey dingy
hue and soupy consistency as the surrounding atmosphere.

Charl, leaning forward with elbows on knees and chin
in cupped hands and eyes turning almost the complete
semi-circle after this and that female form, knew himself
wistfully, but withal a little proudly, an alien there in
spite of a father born not five miles distant.

Bill's words, spoken with a note of enquiry, "Last
leave in the big smoke, boyo," formulated more painfully for Charl the urgency of setting out in quest of
the splendid adventure which surely ought to await him
in those last few days before he departed for France.

The fear that he would not find it was enhanced by the anticipation that, when in France and perhaps destined to die, his recollection of those days would be bitter as for a right denied him.

"You're a gloomy coot," he replied, and continued energetically: "Let's get a place to doss. What about the Strand Palace?"

Bill's reluctance was indicated by his silence and absence of any responsive movement. His father, who was well off, had a farmer's parsimony, or was it instinctive rural economy, towards his children, which kept them at work at home on a niggardly allowance instead of even a labourer's wage. Even when two sons had married and he was forced to do something for them, he held the titles himself of the new small properties he put them on, so that his patriarchal authority might not be impaired. Charl's father, though he was a middle-class civil servant and had little, stinted himself to be lavish in "cables," so Charl was far better off than Bill, who only had his pay to depend on and a little his mother scraped together to send him from time to time. There were other reasons also for Bill's reluctance. He had been uncomfortable at the Strand Palace on their first leave. He had openly avowed his preferment of some small, unostentatious pub more like what he had been used to at Horsham and Murtoa and on his few visits to Melbourne, when he had had to live at an hotel because his city relations in Brunswick could not find room for him. Charl, too, had not been quite at ease; had been indeed rather miserable, but he felt that not to go to the Strand Palace again would have amounted to a confession of social inferiority to the well-dressed men and women and the officers and, at the same time, a denial of his hope of adventure. His envy nourished his contempt of a system which set such a real social difference between officers and men. Such a distinction did not exist in so real a way, though because of British precedent it still lingered in the outward forms, between officers and men in the Australian divisions.

"How could it possibly exist," thought Charl, "when I have an uncle who is a colonel and Bill had a brother who was a lieutenant; when most of our officers now are being promoted from the ranks?"

"I promised to go and see my relations," Bill hurried on to apologise for his desertion. "I'll be along to-morrow though, you bet."

"Let 'em wait." His voice, however, carried no insistence, because in truth he had a vague wish to be alone and was already savouring in advance a comparative pleasure in the loneliness which awaited him. He found himself soon distinctly preferring it to the warm humdrum jollity promised by Bill at Golders Green, a preference which was founded ultimately in the realisation, almost disloyal to Bill, that he would have a better chance without Bill's company of meeting the romantic adventure for which he hungered. And so he was prepared to offer no sustained objection to Bill's leaving him and it was only a sort of shame at disloyalty to their friendship which had caused him to say "Let 'em wait." Bill accepted the position more readily because he was determined on his part not to forgo his visit. Recollections of his call on those relations during his last leave lingered too pleasantly. He had gone merely that he might write truthfully to his mother, to her at any rate the truth being due, that he had looked them up. It had turned out unexpectedly. The two girls

were nice lively sort of girls and the family had given
him a good welcome once they had found him an ordinary sort of bloke, and the family blood unaffected in
any obvious way by a half convict or blackfellow strain.

"That's a fine tabby."

Bill's observation provoked no attention from Charl,
and so far as he himself was concerned denoted no
enthusiastic interest in the particular girl who had
already gone by.   It was only the expression of his
desire to be off.   The girl's figure recalled to him his
own opportunity for feminine companionship which he
was neglecting.   His thought warmed at the memory
of the scuffle he had had with Myrtle in the passage
when she had persisted in her attempts to push his
awkward chuckling bulk before her.   Myrtle was 26,
pale and plumpish.

"Come an 'ave a drink first anyway," he proposed
energetically, becoming still more impatient to get
Charl moving out of that depressing quietude.   The
agreement that they should part had been tacitly concluded.

They found a bar off the Strand and took to a green
marble-topped table the stouts they ordered of the large
female, yellow and red under the electric chandelier,
in the brown polished bar with its brightly coloured
bottles and shining pump handles.   Stout was being
preferred by Bill at that time because of its reputation
as an invigorant of the system.

"Better'n stuff you get in the canteens," he mur-
mured in the pot.

"You bet."

"They say if you go across to Dublin you can go over
Guinness's.   O'Rourke told me."

"Yes."

"Not a bad tabby with the black fur?"

"Her?" Charl's contemptuous monosyllable damped the light in Bill's eyes. Anyway, the other's pretty old, Bill's thoughts continued after a space; so was Hilda, Myrtle's sister, more than thirty and it would hardly be fair for Charl. She was no oil painting either, really.

Drinks finished, they sidled past the two women to the swing door. The one who had caught Bill's eye gave them a smile and—"Won't you sit down, Aussie?"

Bill got past her with a sheepish grin. She looked after them with a less professional, almost whimsically tender, sort of smile for such a retreat, as Bill's and Charl's, could by no manner of means be resented as a rebuff.

"Poor bloody kids," she said slowly.

"They ought to get some sort of a good time before they go out There," agreed her companion, as if she found this vindication that in giving boys good times, she too was doing her bit.

"Wasn't a bad sort of tabby that," Bill argued aloud when the door swung behind them and they were out in the gloom of the street. "She looked all right, too." He felt almost as if he had funked it.

"How could you tell?" Charl still retained a too vivid memory of the warning lecture they had been given by the medical sergeant at Horseferry Road.

CHAPTER II.

"I'LL get along. See you to-morrer," said Bill after a few moments silence. With a nod and grin they separated, Charl continuing slowly at first and then with quicker steps into the Strand towards Fleet Street. He was experiencing again the satisfaction which had possessed him when on his first leave he had entered the Strand from the Square. Though it was not much of a street really with its low, uneven shops and fantastically drab architecture and not to be compared even with Collins Street, which, rising from the gully of Elizabeth and Swanston Streets through the elms and planes to the facade of the Treasury, was far more beautiful as Charl himself perceived, it was not without a special magic of its own. Not only was it for Charl the Empire's centre but out of all that wilderness of streets it peculiarly belonged to it. Australia House was at the end and in it were the offices of some of the States with kangaroos and emus and samples of farm produce on show in their shop windows. As that in which we have a share ourselves comes to possess not only most value for us, but most intrinsic value, so Charl felt more at home there and actually now endowed it in his imagination with a beauty and splendour which it did not really possess. Also there were always diggers about it passing by with "Good day, dig," some of them seeming hardly ever to get away from it, as if they found an ease there, if not of nostalgia altogether, at any rate of absolute loneliness. Most of them were on leave from France and Charl, envious of them, wished he were one such who had already been out and had an honest claim to be reckoned a dinkum soldier. He had been brought up on such stuff as Green's "Short History of the English People," "Westward Ho," Tennyson's "Revenge," and "Deeds that Won the Empire." His father had kept the original "Argus" clippings of the latter and had read them to him when he was quite little. Dear old Dad! Charl had come to smile a little of late years at his father's Empire zeal, but he, too, was proud of the English blood. Since he had been in England, however, the feelings which had been instilled into him by his father had weakened more and more as those of his distinctive Australian nationality were nurtured by his resentment towards this cold alien England.

He stared at a brass-hat and insolently neglected to salute him.

All the time as he threaded his way through the throng his eyes met doglike those of the young women and girls advancing towards him. Unconscious of the attraction of his tanned faunish face and the grace of his own movements, which even the long droop of his light buff Australian greatcoat could not altogether conceal, when he did hold the gaze of one of these swift passers-by it was he who looked away quickly and almost blushingly. Arrived at the hotel he slipped unobstrusively past the gilded commissionaire and diffidently approached the girl at the booking desk. She looked at him dubiously. Knowing at once what was in her mind he flushed angrily and drew himself up straight. She thought better of it and booked him in. You never could tell with these Colonials. Once he was in his room on the fourth floor and had thrown his greatcoat and haversack on the white bed and looked for a few moments into the lane at the back, his loneliness poured down on him, bursting like a deluge from the dark cloud which had hung over him all that day, the unique solitary atom in the heedless swarms of life dancing and revolving in London's lamp lights. All the same he had no regrets for not having accompanied Bill.

It was the thought that he could not sit there moping all night in the cold quiet room which brought him to his feet with a jerk. The luxury of a hot bath, which was one of the real comforts of leave, at any rate could be his and he lay in the steaming water for half an hour before he got out. When with his greatcoat wrapped around his glowing body he slipped swiftly on bare feet along the corridor to his room, a young woman in a crimson and gold dressing gown came out of a room a few doors down and passed him with the tremor of a smile. So quickly did it happen that he was left doubting whether it was really a smile at him and wondering whether, if it was, it held any invitation for him or had been merely one of slight amusement at the figure he made. He became miserable at his lack of wit and initiative. He had never been able to hook a girl easily.

Downstairs he only glanced into the main dining room from which issued the sound of chatter and string music. He was too self-conscious to search out a place for himself in front of all those eyes inside, so many the disdainful eyes of British officers. His detestation and envy of them for their class distinction and ease in those surroundings found meagre assuagement in his pride of being an Australian. So he took himself out into the bleakness of the Strand, again walking inevitably in the direction of Trafalgar Square until he found an ordinary restaurant, a long room with comfortable padded seats against the walls. Treating the restrictions of ration tickets cavalierly as not meant for such

as he, he took his time over a full meal. Not expecting to get it he demanded in conclusion an ice cream.
The girl was doubtful. When at last she came back
with a water ice they smiled together in mutual
triumph. He would have liked to engage her in conversation but could find nothing to say.

Outside, the question of what to do became clamant.
To one alone in a strange city there comes not so much
a sense of isolation but, because of the absence of all
connection with environment, a sense almost of nothingness, of non-humanity. His haste was, therefore, like
that of a man in some desperate search; a search for
himself. He started off towards the Square and continued walking, endlessly walking and walking, peering
at people with anxious eyes, along streets and back
again, turning his head uncomfortably away from
hoarse murmurs now and then of women mingled with
the shadows of doorways, their faces like white discs in
the darkness, until his feet were sore on the pavements.
Approaching once again Leicester Square by one of the
smaller streets he came to a halt at last to watch the
queue waiting patiently for the early doors of
the Prince of Wales Theatre to open. A quick
journey round to the front showed him boards announ-
cing Alice Delysia in Carminetta. When he came back
he took up his stance on the kerb opposite the string of
people, some of them seated on folding stools which they
had brought with them or perhaps hired, to whom, under
the weak lamp light, a thin figure in a long black coat
played a lugubrious flute for coppers. A typical Cockney Pan.

So profound was Charl's melancholy and so certain
had become his hopelessness during his wanderings

through the streets that the sight of a girl's head bent
out of a window over the queue below, which at any other
time in that place would have aroused in him all sorts
of romantic feelings, served only to attract an idle and
casual interest. A mass of curly hair, it looked reddish,
was all he saw of her for some minutes, and then she
lifted her head and let her gaze rest on him, immediately
awakening by that regard a tumult of sensations in his
breast, which, sweeping away all his muddy melancholy
and chagrin, dashed violently through his whole body
so that it set him trembling and shaking. She nodded
and smiled. Emboldened rather by his distance from
her than by this advance on her part to such a show of
courage as may be made when there seemed no likeli-
hood of its being tested, he smiled back and waved his
hand. She smiled and waved her hand in return and
then vanished, leaving him, not disappointed as might
have been imagined but expectant, for there seemed in
her disappearance after those moments of appraisal
something purposeful, implying a request to wait and
see. His eyes fixed on the window beheld her at the
moment of her reappearance. His movement and the
intensity of his attention had attracted a number of
those in the queue who also looked up with the eager
interest which even the slightest thing will arouse in
those who are bored with weary waiting. They saw
the girl's head reappear above them and grinned and
giggled and nudged each other at this little comedy
being staged for their amusement. She thrust her arm
out and threw something white towards him, which fell
near the centre of the roadway. Conscious of, but now
superbly indifferent to, grins and giggles he stepped off
the kerb and picked up a chocolate carton. After a

swift glance of acknowledgment aloft he proceeded slowly to open it. She watched him take out a few chocolates and then a piece of paper on which was scrawled in lead pencil "Meet me after the show at the stage door or better in the front of the house."

When he raised his eyes dizzy with wonderful delight a magical change had come over the world. After he had waved his acceptance, the very gesture stammering with the eagerness of his joy, she with a brief nod withdrew and did not return. Though he waited awhile on the chance of catching another sight of her the very absoluteness of her disappearance carried conviction to him that he was not going to be made a fool. By this time the tail of the queue had disappeared into the dark doorway of the theatre, and when he too went in, the only seat he could get was a poor one towards the back of what he would have called the dress circle. All the rest of the house had been booked out. It was not alone this distance from the stage which annoyed him, but the loss of his own individuality when he sat down and became an indistinct unit in the innumerable hazy white blobs of faces in so many concentric semi-circles about the vast amphitheatre sloping down and breaking into the gulf of the stalls. There was not the faintest hope that she might pick him out. He cursed himself for a fool for having delayed so long outside. When the show at last commenced he paid not the slightest attention to it, being intent only on scanning the characters and chorus for the girl. At last he believed he had identified her and as he gazed and gazed he became sure that one of the four gypsy friends of the heroine was she. Yes, it was she. He had never doubted that she would be on the stage. The thought that she might be some usher, sweet-seller, maid or dresser never entered his head. The play henceforth existed only as an indistinct movement around her. When she was off stage, which was often, it had no rhyme or reason. This fuzzy red-headed gypsy was the real star and heroine; like a prin-cess who, though she is incognito and is dressed insigni-ficantly, is yet, for those aware of her identity, the really important and central figure in a crowd of other women whose splendour for the nonce far outshines her.

He never knew what the play really was about, but the music nourishing his raptures was beautiful beyond words. The interval when it came was only a longer annoying absence of her from his view. His self-satis-faction, however, was too deep to be borne in silence and when the man next to him made an attempt at con-versation he met him with eager affability. His neigh-bour was a Canadian as solitary as himself. With an assumption of almost contemptuous nonchalance Charl mentioned to the Canadian, as soon as he had a chance, that he had not seen the show before but that he knew one of the girls in it, the gypsy with reddish hair, and that he had a meet on with her. They went out and had a couple of whiskies together and another later. The pledging of luck over the glasses which the Cana-dian had hoped might lead to the introduction of him-self to some friend of the gypsy, an idea which he en-deavoured to insinuate, was the very thing which baulked him. Charl was unused to whisky, and when he returned to his seat at the end of the second act, he sank half intoxicated into grandiose and voluptuous dreams of the delights in store for him and almost forgot the existence of his companion.

When at last the finale came and the bouncing bosom

of the Delysia, filled with flowers, had curtsied for
the last time in the centre of the crowded stage Charl,
madly impatient now to get outside, was held stationary
while the patriotic house sang the National Anthem
right through. The result was that he was caught help-
lessly in the movement of the people in the aisles. It
seemed as slow as a glacier's. He squirmed past a few
but still hundreds blocked him. At last he was down
the stairs and out on the dark pavement. On his emer-
gence into the black night air which smote sharply on
the flush of his slight drunkenness, he swayed dizzily.
Alarmed now that the stupor of his brain might lose
him his adventure just when it was really about to begin,
he succeeded by a desperate effort of will in regaining
some control over his wits. What to do now? The
alternative of the note presented itself vividly before
him; the stage door or the front of the house; "or, better
still, the front of the house." That was it. That meant
to him only one place, the street in front of the theatre.
But it was his shyness really which sent him thither
rather than to that other unknown place where it
seemed their meeting would be too obvious and where
he imagined ingenuously it would, perhaps, be as em-
barrassing for her to greet him as it would be for him
to wait for her. He had read of Johnnies waiting at
stage doors; and he was no Johnny. Besides, she had
preferred the front of the house.

It came on to rain, thick dull golden streams under
the dimmed streets and shop lights and lamplights of
the motors sliding past on the shining roadway. He
took up his position fair in the centre of the footpath
so that the crowd of gay people had to veer each side
of him. His eyes eagerly searched the face of each

woman who came around the corner or out of the
theatre's door. At last! Her appearance seemed as
miraculous as the sudden gift of sight to a blind man.
His entire faculty of recognition, stretched too tautly
on the bow of his desire, flew out at the first glimpse of
the girl coming towards him as if it could be retained
by strength of will no longer for the more careful discernment of its mark's identity. Beneath her small hat
burst fuzzy reddish hair, and to set at rest at once the
doubt which had sprung up the moment his mind had
twanged, she greeted him, "Hello, Aussie." Her hand
gripped firmly underneath his arm and they were walking along together. His tremendous good fortune and
the swiftness with which it had all happened quite be-
wildered him. So vast was the hiatus between the opening
of the note and the waiting there outside the theatre that
it seemed the presence of the girl on his arm could be
explained only as sheer magic, and his progress along
the street had become, indeed, a literal illustration of
the Australian adaptation of the music hall song,
"Cheer up Aussie, the Tommies envy you, they don't
know how you do it, but you do, do, do." For how he
had done it or why it had happened to him he most certainly did not know.

Before he quite realised what was happening they
turned as it were instinctively into a cafe, one of the
kind which has imitation marble tables, cast metal
chairs cold as ice, and a counter in front with shelves
of sweets in glass jars behind, and drab tired waitresses
of uncertain age. The girl led the way. They passed
along the passage between the tables to one at the far
end with old tea stains and stale yellow cake crumbs
on its cold, clammy surface. It was then she faced him

and he got his first eye-full of her. He felt that something was wrong. She shouted for a waitress. The hoarse dissonance of her voice gave another shock to the iridescent harmonies of his imagination. To banish that first horrible doubt, as soon as they sat down opposite each other he mentioned the theatre. She paid no attention to him; as if what he said were babblings so foreign to reality as to have no sense at all.

"You're the boy, Aussie," was all she said as she preened herself. She was young and had reddish fuzzy hair certainly, but her flabby, rotten face was crudely powdered and rouged. Impelled by the horror of his increasing doubt, he provoked from her at last, "Theayter, what theayter? A' work on t'munitions at Woolwich."

At the sight of the misery on his face she let out a screech of laughter which, though she had no very clear idea of the reason for his feelings, held a malicious note because she at least apprehended that they contained a reflection against herself. Although his ears must have rung with the pitiful sound of that laughter, he seemed to become aware of it only through recollection when, as he furtively looked around, he saw scornful amusement on the faces of the others in the place and read there the plain comment, "Another of these Orstrilians drunk as usual in the sort of company to be expected, a young trollop off the streets."

Panic possessed him. He searched desperately for an opportunity to escape, but it was become impossible for, as if she guessed what was in mind, she grabbed firmly hold of his hand, "A'll give you a gude time, sonny," she promised.

So he had to give an order for coffee and cakes and

stay there pretending to eat and drink until her suspicions were allayed.

At last he ventured, "I'll just go and get a box of
chocolates."

Even then she was half in the mind to stop him but,
eluding her hand, he got up and walked quickly between the tables up to the counter where he demanded
of the fat Italian, "Coffee and cakes for two, how much
it is? Quick."

"What say?"

A stealthy glance showed her standing up as if to
chase after him. He could not wait for explanations
with any Dago. Throwing down two half-crowns he
bolted into the street and travelled more than two
hundred yards at a half run before he drew breath
with a long sigh of relief. He must have shaken her off
now. For a few minutes he entertained the idea of
returning to his post outside the theatre, but dejectedly
gave it up and turned towards Trafalgar Square and
the Strand, sick and sorry after battering all day on
the unaccustomed pavements. A corn under his left
foot shot pains up his leg like the devil, and he got a
sort of cramp by trying to walk on the side of the foot
with his toes turned in. At last in the security of his
room he crawled between the crisp, cold sheets. Sheets
in the bed, they were one of the great pleasures of leave,
so much so, indeed, that they seemed almost the supreme
achievement of modern civilisation to those who, emerging from camps and trenches, were in a position to
reckon up in anticipation those things in civilised life
which would give them the greatest joy.

CHAPTER III.

THE National Gallery had been one of Charl's own personal discoveries on his first leave. The luck which had led him to it affected his self-satisfaction at his exploit as little as sheer luck has detracted from the pride of many a mariner who has been sent to the discovery of a new land only by the vagaries of a storm. It was to the Gallery he went now on the Sunday afternoon. But it was not art which took him there but the fact that in its halls he could sit and rest in comfort and quiet. The leather cushioned seats were much to be preferred to the hard stone railings set in the midst of the crowd and the noise in the Square outside. After the discomfiture of the night before, he felt now that he needed some such haven. However, it is also due to him to testify that, wandering around the walls after half an hour's ease, he had on his last visits there begun to take a mild interest in the pictures, which especially quickened to something stronger when he stood opposite those with female figures in them, particularly those of the Italian women, whose warm flesh tints are so rich and whose figures are so ripe and voluptuous. Perhaps Charl was going to afford in himself another example of appetite for the sensual becoming the precursor of the pure love of art. So on his last visit Charl might have been found observing with pleasure other pictures, such as one of Turner's Venetian scenes or Titian's portrait of Ariosto, which he was prepared to admit to himself were pretty to look at even though not so interesting as Corregio's Mercury and Venus.

In those days portion of the Gallery was closed, but some of the pictures which were at any one time stored for safety against bombs and fire from heaven were later brought out and changed with others on the walls, so that by this continual movement the persistent visitor, even though he could not see the whole collection, might see something new each time. On the occasion of this visit of Charl's, for instance, there was an alcove of Turner and Constable alongside one of Corot and the Brabazon school, a juxtaposition inspired, no doubt, by the patriotic desire to display an entente cordiale in art as in war. Charl was not alone. That morning he had been over the Tower of London, from which rather remarkably he had derived at first neither historical nor political instruction but ethnological, for he had observed with satisfaction that the men of those olden times for whom the armour had been made must have been considerably smaller than the normally sized modern, the armour seeming, indeed, to have been fitted to mere youths. Such disparity in sizes was like a light which set the days of chivalry in a more accurate perspective, and he could only conclude from it that after all the the knights of old could not have been such marvellous physical champions as the history books made them out. The living model on whom he made a test, unsuccessfully attempting by measurement of the eye to fit the largest of the suits of steel upon him, had turned out to be, when he drew near enough for Charl to perceive the colour of his shoulder patches, a corporal of his own battalion. The corporal gave his name as Frank Jeffreys, of D Company. He was on leave from France.

Jeffreys had showed himself rather pleased at the opportunity of some companionship on the last clear day of his leave, which until the day before he had spent forlornly in the vicinity of Birmingham, where he had some relations. He was one of those men with a perpetually anxious look. When he laughed, as he did at Charl's rough comparison of the old with the new and past with the present, he did so in a spasmodic, painfully self-conscious way. It was the sort of laugh which is a denial of cause for laughter, a complete deadener of fun. In private life he had been a state school teacher with pronounced Labour sympathies. He had been in France a year and was now about to return, with no reservoir of beauty drawn from England's countryside or of pleasure gained in her cities, to be drawn upon through memory in the trenches in France as by one thirsty for life. He was about to return deeply oppressed by the dark squalor of the central industrial cities, and yet haunted by the feeling that he was leaving behind something which was there, easily to be discovered, but which he had missed because of some indefinable fault within himself. He was always feeling that he was missing something, not some other beauty, perhaps, so much as beauty itself, some trace of the truth, which he knew was there, but which, when he turned, had disappeared.

Each of them, as they went about together from prison to tower in the ancient keep, was secretly warmed by the proffer of companionship which the other's sticking along with him tacitly made. To this silent admission of their desires there contributed, in addition to the mutuality of their loneliness, diverse sensations arising from the same fact. Charl's pride in thus becoming the temporary cobber of one of his own battalion, who had already spent a long time in France, displayed itself in an enthusiastic expression of his gratification in being on the next draft, which, in other circumstances.

he would not have dared to admit for fear of ridicule. And just because he had been those long months over there, the corporal was touched to some pity for this mere boy, who was so eager to enter those fields of disillusionment, weariness and death. He was all the more moved because he recalled his own experience. Although he had been single and twenty-eight when war was declared, he had waited for more than a year before he had enlisted, weighing during that time in a torment of conscience the right and wrong of the issue, and whether war was itself any answer to wrong. Even then he had taken the fateful step not so much on account of any self determination of the answers to those momentous questions, but almost impelled by the need for some decisive action to relieve himself of the agonies of doubt and shame he had endured during the preceding months.

Once the decision had been made, it was his admiration of France, the France which had given the world Democracy and the peoples the war cry of Liberty, Equality and Fraternity, to which he had turned for support, and which he had finally nourished to a glowing fire of idealism, so that he had embarked at Port Melbourne as on a Crusade, experiencing, when after tedious months he had at last set foot on French soil at Marseilles, an emotion not less in fervour than that which the soldiers of the Cross had felt suffuse them when they sank down in first fulfilment of their vows to kiss the sands of the Holy Land. But just as the long obstinate sickness of a loved one frets away love's ardour by sheer physical weariness and the constant anxiety of waiting upon her, even though love remains to reproach the weakness of the flesh, so he had come in the terror and drudgery of his service, as no doubt the Crusaders had come also, to a sort of patient endurance, to a pagan stoicism covering taut nerves that vibrated ceaselessly, beyond control at times, a condition in which the semi-automatic endurance required by duty has supplanted the first warmth of a sacrifical love.

Having lunched together at an A.B.C., it was, of course, Charl who led Frank to the asylum of the Gallery. The dull, conscientious thoroughness with which the corporal did the rounds, spending just as much time on one picture as another when Charl had, while in front of one, singled out another a dozen yards away, soon bored Charl, and he was glad enough to flop down purposively on a seat he had selected, because from it he was able to look sidelong at the Bacchus and Ariadne. When, however, he saw himself secure in the corporal's sombre abstraction, he let himself drink in the voluptuous colour of the scene, until at last his eyes concentrated on the glowing flesh of that right leg of the young woman from which she has gathered up, to the thigh almost, her white undergarment, and with which, startled to terror by the drunken, satyr crew, she propels herself to flight from the pursuit of the beautiful god. From these sensations Bill's arrival, which had been arranged by 'phone in the morning, aroused him blushing.

"Here's Bill, the old cow, at last."

Frank felt ill at ease when he saw that Charl's mate was unexpectedly accompanied by two young women.

"With his cousin!" added Charl in explanation hurriedly muttered to forestall any unfortunate conjectures. But he was wrong, for one only was Bill's cousin and she the elder, Hilda, not a beauty, either; frilly and gushing and with a complexion which indicated a bad digestion. The other was a sort of second cousin, Mary Hatton, who had been induced by curiosity to come over that morning from Cricklewood to the Green to inspect this connection from the Antipodes the Carters were exhibiting, of whom notice had been sent to various relations, herself included. Charl, in turn, introduced Frank Jeffreys, who gave an awkward bow and self-conscious little laugh, and mumbled that he would have to be getting along.

"What rot," said Bill.

"O no, you mustn't, you mustn't, really," exclaimed Miss Carter, and hastened on to dispose of any objection which might lie in the disproportion of three men to two girls. "Myrtle, you know, has to work this afternoon—Sunday of all times. She's in the Home Office, but she'll be off at five. There's a war on, you know. You must come along to dinner with us, too; you must, really, mustn't he, Mary?"

She was quite shrill about it, because she foresaw with a pang that if two boys only were left she would be gooseberry. After this, he could not refuse, and it was at once taken as settled. Hilda moved across to his side, advancing her claim to him at once as she felt she was entitled to do because he and she were the eldest.

"Well, let's get a move on," proposed Bill, grinning cheerfully.

To Mary's suggestion that they should first have a look around, Charl replied laconically: "We've seen 'em."

Bill, who had caught sight of Ariadne, was all for it, but Hilda said definitely, "We'll have some tea and then it'll be time to go," and then, "They're really too awful," she simpered, her eyes glancing from the Bacchus to Frank to make sure that he was not unaware of what troubled her maiden modesty. Bill, who was still taking an unashamed look, guffawed, "What O!"

Frank, to whom the possessive air of Hilda was discomforting when he was much more attracted by the neat, quiet form and countenance of Mary Hatton, began again to advance doubts of his ability to accompany them, but he was overruled so decisively that he went along at once with Hilda without further demur.

After tea at Lyons corner shop, they met Myrtle at the entrance to the underground. In the crowded carriage Hilda kept talking to Frank loudly about some cousin who was a Lieutenant in the Durhams, but, indirectly, she talked to the other people in the car in case they should think that she had no better soldier friends than just common soldiers. She did find a little solace, however, in the thought that, anyhow, Australians were a little different to ordinary Tommies, even although, she felt herself tremble rather deliciously, they had such a bad name for wildness. Frank did not mind her talk just then, for it gave him an opportunity to regard Mary Hatton more closely. He marked with approval her neatness, the darkness of her eyes in her rather long, pale face, and the quick occasional nervous movement of her hands in contrast with the stillness with which she sat between Bentley and the other girl. Myrtle was strenuously keeping up her reputation as the merry one of the family, and the little party was quite lively with chatter and giggling, and Bill's "Haw, haw, haws."

When they came out of the station into the street

they fell into pairs, Charl and Mary going first, and Myrtle and Bill, her giggling punctuated by his guffaws, bringing up the rear. Hilda would keep leaning over and looking up into Frank's face, and he was relieved when they turned into a gate with "Holmlea" in large gilt on it, and walked up a short tiled path to the front door of the villa.

Inside, there were introductions; first to Ma, who was fat and important, and then to Pa, an estate agent, a shrewd, sturdy, full-faced little man, who had done pretty well for himself, but not, he felt, as well as he ought, in the new London suburbs. The girls went off to titivate themselves, and he took the three soldiers into the front room for a drink.

When Charl, through inexperience, helped himself too liberally at the whisky, Mr. Carter beamed with delight, "Ah, you Orstrilians like a real taste while you're abaht it," and he nodded his head emphatically as if this was only what might be expected of young men from a wild country.

"Here's luck, Uncle!" cried Bill, whose own ample dose had been deliberately poured, and who, because of his relationship, even though it was only cousinly, applied this title to the elder in accordance with the practice at home, where his mother's and father's more familiar cousins were always by courtesy so addressed.

"The skin off your nose, Mr. Carter!" proposed Charl.

After two rounds, they went into the room, where the ladies awaited them. Dinner consisted of thin soup, boiled mutton and caper sauce and suet pudding. A sort of relation of Mrs. Carter named Ada waited on the table to the extent of fetching each course from the

kitchen; a thin, mousey woman of uncertain age, who
in between times sat at a corner of the table nearest the
door in a state of timid wonderment at these strange
visitors. The whisky had made the men jolly, so that
the dinner went with a bang, and after the girls had
cleared the table, they all, with the exception of Ada,
gathered comfortably together around the coal fire in
the parlour.

It was luck rather than good manoeuvering, for Hilda
was late in coming in, which set Frank next to Mary
Hatton. He had, however, gone no further than to discover that she was a typiste in Smith & Co., a stock-
broking firm in Throgmorton Street and to disclose his
own civil status, when Hilda, resolute in maintaining
her claim as the eldest to the eldest, wedged herself
in between them. She soon put an end to his attempt
at a tripartite conversation, and, a little mortified, he
saw Mary engulfed by the easy loquacity of Charley
Bentley.

The three soldiers were mainly kept answering questions about Australia. Mr. Carter, who had visions of
a lawless place of bushrangers, sheep and cattle, was
particularly curious. He had that vague dissatisfaction
which the presence of the adventurer arouses in even
the tamest male, and which the civilian feels in the presence of the soldier returned from the wars. More
closely sympathetic because he had known the feeling
himself, Charl Bentley, the city bred, began to describe
the few months he had spent as a boy on a Gippsland
farm, as if that had been his whole life. Bill was a
farmer, but it was the country school teacher, Frank
Jeffreys, who was more the bushman of the two.

Excited by the tales his guests were spinning, Mr.

Carter proclaimed at last, "Yes, I've always thought as I'd like to go out to Orstrilia."

The hear, hears, and why don't yous of the three Australians effectively drowned Mrs. Carter's gasping, "Nonsense, Cedric," and quite bucked the little man up, and he stuck his chest out as if to impress them that the stuff which had bred the pioneers was not dead in old England yet.

In such an atmosphere, it was not hard even for Frank Jeffreys to skite a bit, though he was outdone easily by Charley. Bill soon flung all verisimilitude aside, and pulled the legs of his listeners to his great, sly enjoyment, with tales just like those they expected, fights with blacks and chases after bushrangers and snake yarn after snake yarn, until at last he became so preposterous that Charl and Frank began to cackle and then roar with laughter, which put an end to the yarning.

Mrs. Carter at once seized the opportunity of suggesting that Hilda might sing to them. After the due amount of coaxing she sat herself down at the piano and sang in a shrill, brittle voice.

Anticipating their desires, she had already turned to the next in her repertoire, when Bill cried: "Let's all have a sing."

Ignoring Hilda's "don't you think it'll be rather disturbing to the neighbours," he gathered them around the piano. The girls sang as stylishly as they could, especially Hilda. The corporal's voice was a pleasant one which had had a little training. Charl sang what he called seconds. But Bill's cheerful bellow drowned the lot. It was a time for patriotism, and the airs popular with the troops were the favourites, "Good-

by-ee," "There's a girl for every soldier," "There's a
long, long trail," etc., etc. And then Mrs. Carter and
Ada came in with supper.

As soon as it was finished Frank, seeing the inclination of the others to settle down in comfort again, resolutely declared that he must go. He had succeeded
while Hilda was at the piano in obtaining Mary Hatton's permission to write to her, and had made a note
of her address. She felt rather sorry for this ungainly,
nervous man, because she could see that he had not been
really comfortable the whole evening, as if he felt to
some extent an intruder. He blamed himself, if not for
butting in, at least for not having had enough strength
of mind to endure his loneliness.   His rising put a
damper on the spirits of the others. He was going, this
man whose name only they knew, and who, like a strange,
exotic bird, had flown into the light of their warm
hearth, and who had lingered there awhile, and was now
about to plunge into the night outside.   His eyes held
Mary Hatton's awkwardly a moment before she looked
away. The evanescence of that look struck heavy pain
into his heart, for he saw in it a tentative interest,
almost compassionate. In her turning aside there was
merely an acceptance of futility and his total departure.

Bill and Charl and the three girls went with him into
the hall for his hat and greatcoat.   "You must come
again as soon as you can," said Hilda, with a soft,
languishing look. "Yes, all of you," said Myrtle
thoughtlessly. At her words they stood quite still and
silent. The shadow, which hung over the departure
of one, extended its wing over them all. Would they
be able to come? Icy fingers had come in with the

draught to touch them mockingly on their breasts for
remembrance of the odds. Bill broke into an overloud
guffaw, "Apres la guerre finis, you bet your socks."

As if inspired by the bravado of Bill's voice, they all
started laughing, the girls with a touch of hysteria.
They now seemed almost afraid to let Frank go, and
after Frank had bid Mr. and Mrs. Carter and Ada also
goodbye, for she resolutely and almost tearfully stuck
her ground for it, the young people went with him as
far as the station. Charl, having an hour afterwards
magnificently rung for a car, took Mary Hatton home
in some style.

CHAPTER IV.

ON the last night of Charl's leave, he and Mary met a
little later than usual. She had been kept overtime
at the office, and, after they had had tea, it was eight
o'clock when they went walking down the Strand. The
lights dimmed above glinted along the slats of the rain
on to her mackintosh and oil cloth hat. He was buttoned to the throat in his greatcoat. Warmed within by
the steady throb of his own well-being, he was entirely
self-satisfied and sure of himself.

"A girl for every soldier!" No there wasn't, and
looking pityingly at lonely diggers, he realised to the
full his own wonderful luck.

Through the people on the footpaths and criss-cross
about the road, urchins scurried with editions of the
evening papers, with hot accounts from Fleet Street of
slight activity in the Ypres salient, where the haemorr-
hage was threatening to break out afresh and more pro-

fusely. Warnings of what to do during an air raid, for should the gray pall of rain ever rise the moon would shine upon London. There was, too, circulating everywhere, in camps, in clubs and in the streets an amazing story of train loads of soldiers said to have been seen coming down from the North to the Channel posts, soldiers in blowsy uniforms speaking some gibberish—Russians. On the front page of the papers also there was a small paragraph stating it was possible that rationing would have to be enforced more strictly. It appeared just alongside a big heading, ''Destroyer B7 rams submarine.'' The dirty Huns in their submarines —that'd teach 'em.

Mary and Charl were blocked at Charing Cross. Ambulances were coming out of the station—a long line of them, around which swung buses of suburbanites going home and cars with men in white shirts and officers and girls in evening dress. At the sight of the ambulances Mary's grasp on Charl's arm tightened. Puffed with the pride of those hours he gave a short, careless laugh.

The recklessness of life—to-day we live and to-morrow we die being a theorem which had never before been explained by anything like so clear an illustration; images of the wounded in pain and the dead stinking into rottenness and dissolution; the craving to do something and to be something active and forceful, though only atomic in the immense mass; the subtle connection of the passion of sex with all this other lust beat in Mary's temples and wet her lips with a frothy saliva, which had an acrid, intoxicating taste. She had had no soldier lover till this one had come along, and no brothers at the war. Through him she became for the

first time really a part of the struggle. The rapturous
pain of love before death, to clasp someone in the frantic embrace which anticipates the inevitable brutal dis-
ruption, such as was responsible for those couplings in
the prisons of the French Terror, brought thoughts into
her head as she stood there from the fearful madness
of which, half swooning, she only wrenched herself
with an effort. Nine years older than he! Poor boy,
poor boy! She tried to persuade herself that she had
imagined nothing. She tried to dissociate herself from
the horrible wickedness which had possessed her, as a
nun might dissociate herself from responsibility for a
sin committed in a dream.

They went into a cinema, a poor sort of hall of irregular shape off the main thoroughfare. The picture
palace was not yet invented. In the dark Charl took
her hand in his. The night before last, when he had
said good-bye at the iron gates, he had kissed her. She
had seen that he wanted to and had been prepared to
allow him as a big sister might, but when she had half
met his awkwardness, his mouth, once it touched her
own, had seized on it, and did not leave it until it had
drained the strength out of her, and she had fallen back
against the fence gasping. And then last night, when
desirous, though afraid of the passion of it, she had
allowed him again, he had thrust her head back away
from him, and, pushing aside her blouse, he had kissed
her at the commencement of her breast. In the meantime, at work, she had been telling herself that it did
not matter. To-morrow the poor boy would be gone and
she would not see him again. Because, therefore, nothing could really come of it, she could not easily deliver
herself from the danger of recalling the sweetness of

his desire. She had never dared surrender herself so far before. Men had been frightened away from her by her own timidity, which seemed like aversion, and she was not particularly pretty, not pretty enough to induce them to persist. All the sweeter then was the proof that she was not undesirable to Charl, perhaps to the corporal, who had kept looking at her whenever Hilda gave him a chance, and perhaps to other men.

The cone of light spilt through a darkness which was heavy and thick with steam from wet clothing, and the strong, human breath which rose from the parallel lines of pale, vague faces. Charl, though he gazed fixedly with the others, had only an incoherent idea of what was passing on the screen. All his senses seemed to throb in the fingers which stroked her hand in his lap. Slowly he worked his way up under her sleeve, his fingers licking like trembling tongues of flame along the icy flesh of her arm. When he at last touched the moist hair of her arm pit he trembled violently. She was quite still and gazed before her with eyes as sightless as his. A sort of vertigo robbed her of all power and of all sensation, except the response of her nerves to the caresses of his fingers. When she had succeeded after a time in gaining some control of herself, she declared that the pictures were really too silly and she would like to go. So when the interval came they went out into the street again, where it was still softly raining. There was nothing to do now but go home. It would be just as well, too, she thought, for her father and mother would be there and there could be no more of this madness. What had come over her? Tears jumped into her eyes. But as she regained her equanimity it seemed silly to get in such a state. It was nothing,

really. How far did some girls allow men to play with
them, and she in such a condition because he had fondled
her arm! It was ridiculous! To show how silly it was,
she talked away to him in a comradely fashion. When
they walked along Milton Terrace towards No. 154,
with a smile of kindly understanding, she suited herself
to his deliberate tardiness and herself took and pressed
his arm. She felt very tender, protectingly tender for
him.

A dim reflection in the glass panel at the side of the
door indicated a light in the dining-room at the back
beyond the stairs. Charl already knew something of
the plan of the house, for he had been inside twice,
once to tea. First, there was the drawing-room, next,
the dining-room, and then the kitchen and the scul-
lery; upstairs, the first bedroom, and at the back of the
landing, two small bedrooms. Charl tried to kiss her as
she slipped her key into the lock. Because she did not
want to make her father rouse up, who would be asleep
in his chair before the fire, she did not ring the bell.
Mother would be well in bed as usual. She let him just
touch her cheek. Inside, she left him standing in the
hall, and went into the dining-room and then upstairs.

"They are out for a wonder," she said, coming down,
"but they won't be long. They must have slipped over
to father's friend, Mr. Gamage's, just down the street."

She hung their hats and coats on a bracket of pegs
on the passage wall, and he followed her into the dining-room. Embers still glowed sickly in the fireplace in
the wall opposite the door. On the right of the fireplace
was a window which was never opened. The heavy
curtains over it were maroon-coloured, as was the cloth
on the round table in the centre. The escritoire, with

bookcase above, which stood against the wall on the
right, was dark red mahogany. The two easy chairs, one
on each side of the fireplace, and the dining chairs, were
upholstered in black leather. The dark-reddish colour
of the curtains, and the cloth, and the bookcase, and the
backs of the chairs, became warm and glowing when the
coal, which Mary heaped on the fire, began to crackle
and shoot out its flames. While she did it, he stood
with his hands in his pockets nervously inspecting the
things on the mantel-shelf, a couple of china boxes, a
needle case, some photographs, two yellow vases festooned with terrible green leaves, and a couple of Mr.
Hatton's old pipes. Above was hung a large photograph
of a handsome, old woman, in the clear, excellent style
of twenty years ago. On the wall behind him hung a
large engraving in a tarnished gilt frame of a ruined
castle on a cliff above a river. It still stayed there only
because Mrs. Hatton had put her foot down and had
not let Mary remove it with the others. It had been
a gift to Mrs. Hatton from her dead sister, and, though
she never looked at it, she was content with just knowing
that it was there. So as a sort of vague memento mori
this, of all the old pictures, had survived, preserving all
the same its own massive, old-fashioned individuality
alongside the cheap prints: one, Millet's "Angelus,"
and the other, Watt's "Hope," perched on top of a globe
which Mary had hung each side of it.

They were intensely conscious of their being alone
together in the room. They sat down in the arm chairs,
Mary in that nearer the window.

"I'll get a cup of tea when they come in," she said.

"That'll be bonzer!" he said.

The dead stuffiness of the room hung like a dead

weight upon their limbs, but their senses were riotously alive. She could feel the fever of his senses like something palpable. They were both waiting for him to do something. He seemed to be waiting for himself as much as she waited. She kept looking at him with growing pain. The physical beauty of his young body disturbed her. All of a sudden it seized upon her that this night was his last night, and that, soon, perhaps, that beauty would be massacred, torn and battered by the shells, lying in the mud in the trenches. The war demanded its sacrifices. She was a lonely girl of no account to anyone but this boy.

He came over stiffly and sat on the arm of her chair. As he looked down at her with those eyes soon to look daily into the face of death, something cried, "she too, she too." When he went to kiss her, her arm slipped around his neck. She clung to him, while there grew in her a craving for something done, even if it were only her self-immolation, in that wild, dark rush of the world's blood towards the denouement and common cataclysm. She felt his hand close under her blouse on her breast.

"No, no," she muttered, and could not let him go.

He slipped down off the arm of the chair. She started convulsively, but sank back under his leaden weight. It was not that he would not let her escape. She did not have the will to free herself from him. She was like one of those beings who, bound by immemorial law, walk in inward horror and revolt freely to their doom.

Half an hour afterwards Charl strode along the Crescent towards the bus route. He was not only glad to have got away before the others came back, but glad just to have got away. He thrust aside the recollection of her strange, unpleasant quickness when he had said good-bye, or tried to; the picture of her a few moments before that with her head bowed on her arm and her getting him away. The protests of his love had fallen pretty flat. Women had no right to make a man feel such a rotten cad. He wouldn't. After all, he loved her. He felt sure he did. Gradually, he forgot his trouble about her, and his pride and self-satisfaction bubbled to the surface. It had been a spasmodic, fragmentary union which had taken place between those ill-assorted virginities. Soon all that leaped and danced in Charl's mind was that he'd had a girl, he'd had a girl. His inexperience would secretly shame him no more.

When he reached the city road there was no bus in sight. It didn't worry him. He started to march through the iridescent rain as if he could go on and on forever.

A DINKUM DIGGER

CHAPTER V.

THE wheels of the troop train ground slowly and jerked spasmodically onwards. According to the inscription on the side of the truck, 40 hommes, 8 chevaux, which carried an unpleasant suggestion not only that horses were comparable with men, but that, with more decided Houyhnhnmian flavour, one horse was worth five men, the truck did not hold its full complement. Yet it seemed to those inside a sheer impossibility for the most officious red-tabbed transport officer to squeeze in one single man more. The truck contained only 33. The bodies of the 33 tangled in blankets, rifles, packs and webb equipment, made, in the darkness, by which the faint red glow at the brazier from the embers beneath was so heavily circumscribed, a black grotesque unevenness on the floor. Out of this uneven layer issued uneasy snores. Every now and then some part of it would heave gruntingly up, when some one shifted in luckless search of a more comfortable position or tried to wrap a blanket more closely against the frigid stillness of the thick air, and then would subside fretfully into the black inchoate mass again.

Charl lay flat on his back against the planks at the far end from the engine with his head propped on his pack, in which a tin of biscuits and his hold-all made two hard lumps. They resisted his head with a rocky immovability which appeared consciously malignant. With the same impulse which sends the tortured man to seek forgetfulness of his present pains in the conjured vision of the glory which awaits him, and makes the man dying of thirst wilfully imagine the mirage to be a real lake of saving water, Charl had endeavoured to drag his mind off the cold and the aching numbness of his legs by recalling one by one the most pleasurable hours of the past. In a voluptuous reconstruction of that final scene with Mary Hatton, he found greatest efficacy. The love which he had persuaded himself he had for her, seemed to have become a holy thing when he followed himself walking with no shadow of desire after the sergeant from the depot at Havre through the old houses of the Rue de Gallion to the bitter end of that bitter street. It was certainly more romantic to ascribe his cold aloofness to his love rather than to the dreadful oppression with which the long sequence of retail female flesh had benumbed his senses. Yet, there had been one, a young girl, who, for a few moments, had moved mechanically smiling through the tobacco smoke like a wan moon through a bleary sky. She had looked different to the others. She made humankind horrible, monstrous. It could hardly have happened in real life. It was hardly credible that it was she who had gone off up the stairs with a half-drunken man out of the — Division. Her naked legs had been slender and beautiful. She had had a blue bruise on her thigh, and her breasts under the transparent wisp of gauze had been small and firm.

"Well, I've never seen anything like that before," Bill had gasped when they had emerged out of the street on to the road along the Quay.

Edging himself on to his side Charl looked again at the image of Mary. As soon as he got back from leave he had written her a long letter from Larkhill telling that he loved her. Without daring to invite an answer to his declaration, he had told her, also, that he would write once a week and begged a correspondingly regular reply. He got her letter only the day before he left Larkhill. It contained only some slight news of herself and a good deal about Hilda and Myrtle, and made no promise about weekly letters.

The dumb ignorance of cattle, shunted hither and thither by the direction of some inscrutable power, but, nevertheless, approaching irresistibly the slaughter yards, is not very different to the fatalism of the soldier immersed at night in the troop train. Even to the man, Jim Blount, whose head was on Charl's feet and who was returning after recovery of a wound in the head, the scenes of the line to which he had been accustomed were in that dull hour so blurred in his memory that the effort of a lively comprehension of the future was impossible.

At any rate, thought Charl, it was a good thing to be out of Larkhill, that desolate, bleak and abominable weariness and wilderness of huts which overlooked Stonehenge, and which in winter had been almost as murderous to Australians as the Line itself. The short period between his return from leave and the marching out of the draft had been more than ordinarily tedious. There had been no intelligence in the work, only automatism enlivened by funny, clownish episodes.

There was the cursed band which paraded blaring round the huts at 6 a.m. The hut sergeant, who had a small three-ply enclosure to himself near the door, would rouse himself and roar, "Show a leg." The corporal, who slept near the brazier, would commence to climb into his pants, and would yell irritably, "Show a leg—show a leg—five minutes to go."

Then he would pull the blanket off those who were usually late, a little thankful that in the hut just then those who might have displayed more resentment than a few surly oaths were, as a rule, those who got up themselves. Charl had always been one of the bright and early, mainly because he did not wish to suffer this indignity at the hands of the corporal. Once Bill, alongside him, had said to Green, "You pull my blankets off and I'll break your bleedin' jaw." Charl had pacified him. He rather sympathised with the corporal, who would be "roused" if the hut were late. Physical jerks in the cold, half light of the bull ring. All that the exercises did for men, who with empty stomachs shivered in their pants and singlets, was to make them weak and sick. Then there was the bayonet drill under an old regular N.C.O., who faithfully tried to instil into them a fighting spirit which had long died in himself with such approved formula as "In—out—on guard. Now with the short point into his bloody navel—in—twist—out with his guts on the point—in—out—on guard." And then there was the gas drill by numbers, with the long, black-cloth masks you tucked into the top of your tunic. Though still issued for emergency use, these masks had for a long time been superseded in France by the small face mask attached to the container, but most of the drill was with the antiquated equipment. And then to cap it all! The crowning glory! Someone in the war office, someone, the nature of whose intelligence baffles understanding, had seen the completion of a life's work in the new system of drill. After long thwarted brooding over it in the opportuneless times of

peace the war had given him his chance. The damned
Colonials should not escape it. Everyone, even those
who like Charl and Bill were waiting on their draft,
had to put in all of each morning in the bull ring, where
the cadre N.C.O's, who had spent a fortnight at a
special school to learn it, attempted to take the men
in hand. There was a complete new system and style
for platoon, company and battalion drill, and, perhaps,
if the War Office archives were searched, for even brigade and division. The Australians at Larkhill, however, never advanced beyond the novitiate of the squad,
and right, left and about turn. The N.C.O's were in
spirit with the men, whose intelligence stubbornly re-
volted against this annoying nonsense. But they were
kept at it by a heavy lieutenant-colonel, who bumped
about on a sort of half draught, and was, in turn, overlooked by a thin English staff major sent by God knows
whom to see to it that the War should not be lost by any
lack of diligence in the new art. All over the place men
were at it hopping around. To accomplish a simple turn,
one foot had to be brought down smartly as the body
twisted in the new direction, and the other shot out
with a kick.

It was the bodily contortion required by the "about"
which gave the troops their real opportunity. When
away from direct observation, they ridiculed their in-
structors, and when under the eye of fuming superior
authority, became wilfully sullen and stupid. The ex-
asperated non-coms., while the colonel or the sergeant-
major glowered, would explain once more and strut before the squad to illustrate the movement yet again.
Once Darkey Snow tripped himself deliberately and fell
flat on his stomach right before the colonel. The squad,

started off by Bill's Potter's guffaw, broke into a parox-ysm of laughter, from which neither Haig nor King George could have recalled them. And when Darkey, sent off under arrest, performed insolently but superbly in the new style, the colonel, jambing in his spurs so deeply that he nearly unseated himself, galloped away with a curse. For more than a week it was kept up, but the last two days, when the pertinacity of the staff had begun to wilt before that mocking stupidity and clumsi-ness, were absolute idiocy.

When the squad turned to right and left, Jump-to-Glory-Jane had nothing on them. When they turned about they contorted themselves like fiends in torment. The third day of this the colonel and the major did not turn up. The sergeant-major, when the troops appeared before him on the bull ring, gave the command, "Right turn." The men promptly did it with a click in the old way. The sergeant-major grinned, "you win," and left it at that.

Yes, they had had plenty of fun at times, and pleasant days, too. There had been that time they had been half-drunk at Amesbury; and the last visit to Salisbury, with its spire reeling through white clouds over green plashy meadows and immense elms. One day they climbed up to old Sarum.

He tried to put his knee into Bill to stop him grind-ing his teeth. Christ, it was cold, colder than when they had crossed the Channel in the night to the stone wharves of Le Havre. Bill and he had found a warm spot on the plates over the engine room. While their bottoms almost blistered with the heat, their shoulders and heads had just about frozen in the blizzard. But that cold was not such a dead cold as this. Now, there

was nothing but cold, and this interminable creaking
and grinding and bumping slowly in the dark over a
blank, unknown countryside.

"One day, some damned Napoleon will have some
nails put on the walls to hang the damned equipment
and rifles on." The words came from Blount, who was
trying to lever away a rifle, the muzzle of which was
working into his ribs. He went on after a few minutes
to himself again, "And then they'll make it 60 hommes."

Charl was impressed by this man, and particularly
he envied him his savoir faire. It was not that he knew
how to do things like other people did them. He did
them in a cool, sure way of his own. Charl fell into a
stupor, from which he was aroused some indefinite time
afterwards by Bill getting up. A clammy pallor had
succeeded the darkness in the truck. He chuckled as he
saw Bill tramping ruthlessly over squawking bodies with
a desperate intentness which could afford no time for
apologies. The door, opened a foot by Bill, let in a swirl
of fresh, icy air, which cut through the thick atmosphere
in the truck like a knife.

All day they advanced over the swelling Picard plain,
with stops every little while for no particular reason
and at no particular place. The train would give a
whistle and jerk on again, pursued each time by men
caught in disorder. Where villages were centres of
rural aggregation centuries old, the railway line went
its own course, seldom touching one. There were few
people in the fields, but once two laughing mademoiselles
waved to them at a crossing. Finally, they drew into
the edge of a town, where the train stopped some time.
But of more interest to the reinforcements were two
round holes in the chocolate soil of a paddock on the

left of the line. "Ranging." It indicated, some felt, an unpleasant sort of optimism in Fritz. They moved on again, but it was not very long before they came to another halt at a sort of platform near a few houses on a road. Here they detrained and marched stiffly a mile or so to a tent camp in a hedge-enclosed paddock.

CHAPTER VI.

THAT from now on he would be with the battalion was Charl's thrilling thought the day he marched from the detraining depot with the other reinforcements into the camp of bell tents near Vlamertinghe. Uneasily conscious of his rawness, but not without a sort of pride, he returned the glances of the old soldiers, who, with hands thrust into the fronts of their breeches, gathered around and eyed the drafts up and down appraisingly and exchanged greetings with the few old hands who had come back with the reinforcements. He heard such things as—"The new reinforcements, poor bastards!" "Hullo, Geordie, they got you at last?" "Couldn't swing it no longer, Bill?" "Why, here's old Jiggy back again and Jim Blount. How's she goin, Jim?" "Ho, Konkey, you're just back in time for something sweet."

"Dinkum?"

"My oath."

"Christ!" this being Konkey's exclamation, who, returned from a Blighty he got in the last stunt, now lugubriously saw himself about to be pitched straight into another. Such luck as he'd had couldn't last.

It was Jim Blount who saved Charl and Bill from separation by interposing just in time to prevent Sergeant-Major Mahon's hand cutting them apart. "They're cobbers, Paddy." So Bill and Charl found themselves taken off by Blount to his old No. 4 Platoon, of "D" Company, of which Jack Skipton was the sergeant and, as it turned out, Frank Jeffreys the two-stripe corporal. Charl stammered his thanks.

"Oh, Paddy's an old friend of mine," Blount grinned.

Charl looked around him. The camp paddock was surrounded by a high hedge like that at the detraining depot, and the tents were stuck pretty close to the line of the hedge for a reason he as yet did not understand. At the far corner, near the road, the spire of a church could be seen emerging through the foliage of tall elms. They were so tall that a number of the roofs, though they covered some of them two storeys, seemed to be overlaid by an umbrageous second protection.

"The troops must be lying pretty thick at night," remarked Blount. They were, as was discovered later. Not less than sixteen had been allotted to each tent.

This man, Jim Blount, was one of the old originals. Of his three friends of those early days, Horace Calverley was killed, Paddy McMahon was become the company sergeant-major and Gilderoy was now captain of the company. Blount had declined promotion, even when, after he got his M.M., the colonel had himself summoned him to the orderly room and offered him corporal's stripes and a school, with the hint of a lieutenancy quickly to follow. He had refused, not because he was afraid of responsibility, but simply because he did not want it. In the midst of war he had made a discovery. He had discovered himself. And now, he was finding out something else: that life was ductile and could be fashioned into harmony with that new understanding. His eyes were becoming used to a new and appetising world. The life of a private soldier left him free, and his freedom had become essential. He was now thirty-two, a little more than medium height, rather long in the nose, square in the shoulders, toughened and hardened and in good condition, for he looked after himself. Charl and Bill congratulated themselves on having him for a sponsor in their introduction to the platoon. When they had come to a tent pointed out by some acquaintance of Blount's, the five men lounging about inside, who eagerly welcomed the old soldier, seemed to take no notice of Bill and Charl, as though whether the two reinforcements would have to sleep outside was no concern of theirs. It hardly seemed possible to find room for three others in the circle of blankets, which were wrapped around with waterproof capes and had various odd belongings piled on top of them, but Blount said briefly, "Two new chums, Bill Potter and Charl Bentley," and, with a few vigorous kicks, made a space between the packs.

"That makes seventeen," groaned Ted Marshall.

"If there's anyone else, we'll 'ave ter hang 'im up be the slats with the guns." He nodded at the rifles and Webb equipment festooned around the pole.

The next day, which varied sunshine and shower, the battalion moved to Poperinghe, turning to the right out of the ruins and then off the road along a duckboard track over a field, cut into mud by G.S. wagons and other transport, to two lines of Nissen huts. The iron cupolas of the huts were camouflaged with thick, irregular stripes of dirty green and brown. Beyond the camp there was a round hill, pale green with young grass.

During the afternoon, whoever came up the duck board track could see men taking advantage of the sun's warmth to sit at the doors of huts and chat themselves. In the soft field in front, a number were throwing blank Mills bombs, testing their length and accuracy in a game improvised from the old iron quoit game, which was commonly played up till ten years previously in the old midland mining towns and settlements.   You pitched the bomb to a piece of white paper stuck on a ring of mud.   In a firmer paddock on the other side of the huts a football was being kicked about.   Charl, anxious for a part in which he knew he could shine, had gone off there as soon as he could, dragging Bill rather unwillingly with him, for Bill was no footballer.   Down on the road, near where the duckboard track turned in, was a brick cottage where an old Froggie and his Madame still hung on obstinately under a roof which some time or other had been blown half off by a shell, and which had been patched with odd bits of iron and sand bags sewn together. They lived by selling hot baths at a franc per tub.

When darkness began to fall, the rumbling of the thickening traffic on the main road through Poperinghe of wagons, motor lorries and guns, in a continuous stream moving eastward, could be plainly heard by the men coming out of their huts on to the duckboards to clean their plates and dixies.   There was another sound, also, which had power for a moment or to to subdue and quieten; the distant dull boom of the Salient.   It was this which caused Bill and Charl to induce Jim Blount and Frank Jeffreys to plod with them up the

hill to seek there some sign to confirm that dull, moni-
tory sound. From the rounded top, they saw the dark
sweep of the sky changing on its eastern edge to a narrow
curve of yellowish colour, which slowly waxed and
waned, and which now and then flushed up in places a
dirty flame of red into the sky like a mysterious unnatural aurora.

"A dump gone up," said the corporal, seizing the occasion of one of those strange flushes to break the silence
which oppressed them.

"So they say, but, perhaps, it's some heavy battery
letting loose," said Blount slowly.

Charl, though he had a dozen excited questions in
his mouth, could say nothing, for he was too afraid that
his excitement would trouble his speech in a way which
the others might misinterpret. It was not fear, of that
he was certain, which made him tremble. Bill only
grunted and gazed eastward surlily, for the first time
clearly aware of the personal menace of the war. Jim
Blount put a match to his pipe. The flare lit the pro-
file of his strong features as he sheltered the light from
the chill, steady wind, which blew out of the scurrying
sky from the north-east. It became, all of a sudden, too
lonely and eerie up there on the hill, looking silently towards that unearthly glamour whither they were sooner
or later to go, and they were glad to get back to the
hut, which was full of soft, cheerful homely light from
the brazier and a dozen candles, many of which were
stuck in their grease on the top of tin hats.

In the far left corner, four of the battalion sigs, who
had been thrown into the same hut as the platoon, were
playing nap clannishly by themselves. Micky Flynn,
Ted Marshall, Sucker Sykes and Blue McIntosh thumbed

dirty cards at euchre alongside the brazier. The rest of the platoon, with the exception of four who had gone off to try their luck in Poperinghe, were idly dozing, others reading, and a few writing letters. Whereas, at some other time, Charl and Bill might have felt their rawness uncomfortably, now that it was clear that there lay immediately in the future a stunt of some magnitude, the others had at once accepted them as though tacitly admitting that they might as well do it now, as in a few days they would all together enter an experience the endurance of which would, in itself, entitle the new arrivals to an equality with the oldest hands. This identification of the reinforcements with the platoon had also been aided already at Vlamertinghe by a new reallotment into sections, which were now composed as follows:—

Bayonet men—Corporal Frank Jeffreys; Jim Blount, M.M.; Jack Smith, the sniper, nearing the forties, a shambling bushman from the Kelly country; Fred Rogan, a dairy farmer from Warragul, quiet, grey-haired, a devout member of the Church of Christ; Ted Marshall, a brickfaced, good-hearted soul, who had been most kinds of a labourer, but mostly on Sydney wharves; Albie Chomley, a short, cocky, ex-commercial traveller; Bill Potter and Charl Bentley.

Lewis Gunners—Blue McIntosh, No. 1, red in the head, a League footballer; Mick Flynn, withered and saturnine, once a drover; Fatty Gray, a pasty blob of a face over a rotund figure, formerly a grocer's assistant; Sucker Sykes, a nondescript, always chatty; Tug Wilson, a little Pommy, with a very retrousse nose, who had been a skilled hand in a boot factory.

Rifle Grenadiers—Llew Jones, small and nuggety, once a bookmaker's clerk, and now a two-up king; Tom Boyle, big and scraggy, a miner from the Hill; Johnny Wright, a solicitor from a country town, now a bit of a dag, with the habit of going on a real bender now and then; Skinny Paul, very young, a bank clerk of six months' service; Harry Mullane, who had finished his B.A.; Les Henderson, slight and dapper, who had come from a Ballarat draper's counter; Dingo Williams, a station rouseabout.

Bombers—Lance-Corporal Artie Fethers, his father a nob in Toorak; Willy Wallace, sometimes called Weary, who had been in the Lands Department; Pete Hansen, a Norwegian, ex-sailor, and jack of all trades; Ikey Harris, in business with his father as a whitework manufacturer; Sam Kendall, a big, lolloping fellow, usually called Dopey, who was supposed to have been a rabbit trapper; Billy Carter, a clerk; and, finally, Sergeant Jack Skipton, D.C.M., a road construction foreman and small contractor, very broad and tremendously strong, and the new Lieutenant, Mr. Burney, who had been one of the two reinforcement officers who had come over with Bill's and Charl's draft.

The bang of the door when the four came in from the hill knocked down some of the bayonets which had been propped against the wall near it. All the bayonets had been painted that afternoon a light brown in accordance with the battalion order, which had this time re-

quired paint to be used to dull any gleam of steel likely
to attract attention.   The ordinary candle black used
in the past had always rubbed off too easily. Soon, both
Bill and Charlie Bentley were writing letters.

Frank's slow progress with his letter was interrupted
by the sergeant, who appeared in the doorway, and
called his attention.   At the sound of his phlegmatic
voice, everyone looked up with a tense, almost anxious,
expectancy.

"Corporal, the company is going to fall in at 9 in the
morning. Fighting order and rifle inspection. Double
iron rations and oil bottles to be filled. We'll draw ours
at quarter past 8. Everyone's to have hessian around
his tin hat.   If any haven't got it, see they do."

"What's the business, serg.?" asked someone eagerly.

"You'll find out."

One by one the men made their bunks and got into
the blankets, and the number of lights became less. For
awhile Frank worried himself as he always did over
the orders, and then took up his pencil again and finished his writing. He read it over.

Dear Miss Hatton.—I wonder if you'll mind me writing to you. Because you gave me your address and told
me I might come and see you when I'm in London again,
I've persuaded myself you wouldn't. You remember
I met you at your cousin's place, where I went with two
chaps from the battalion. When they joined up, by a
fluke of luck, they were put into the same platoon as
I'm in. That day, which was the last of my leave, was
by far the pleasantest. If you could only know how
much better it feels to have some friend in England
when one's own people are so much further away, so
far that their existence seems to become unreal, I think

you would answer this letter. The weather is showing
signs of breaking up, which is a poor lookout.   One
gets to long for just one hour of real Australian sun.
It's what you get used to, I suppose. This is not much
of a scrawl to ask you to answer, but I hope you will,
and that you won't think it cheek of me. It's not that.
I remember you mentioned your mother had a chill. I
hope that she is all right, and that you are, too. With
best wishes. Yours sincerely, Frank Jeffreys, No. 506,
Nth Battalion, Australian Imperial Force, on active
service.

Relieved now that he had taken the plunge, he resolutely sealed the letter in a green envelope and addressed it after checking the address from his pocket
book.   There were only two candles burning now, his
own and Fred Rogan's, who, without fail each night
when all was quiet, read a chapter of his Bible.

Having got into his blankets, Frank was just about
to dowse his own light when he was arrested by a scuffling at the door. The night shot in Tom Boyle, Skinny
Paul and Artie Fethers. Blinking owlishly, they swayed
about to get their balance. Skinny failed, and sat down
plomp on to the floor.

"What O, she bumps," cried Tom.

"So I say to the Madame," said Artie, earnestly,
bending down to Skinny's insensate ear, "So I say to the
Madame, I say."   He must have forgotten what he
said, because he got no further. He caught sight of his
bunk and pranced towards it. "For God's sake, hit him
with a boot," groaned a muffled voice. Bending down,
Artie pulled out his blankets, and almost with the same
movement, pitched on to them dead to the world. With
Tom Boyle trying to help, Fred Rogan took the boots

off the lance-jack, and wrapped his blankets around him. Skinny was still sitting where he hit, and it took considerable patience from Frank and Rogan to get him into bed, where he was sick. Tom, with a fixed half-moon of a grin, declined all assistance. Long after everyone else was asleep, he was still trying to get off his last boot. He gave it up. Then, with great deliberation, he made his bed, punctilious to the last. The hut became quiet but for the snoring. There was more than one, however, who awoke at times to wonder if it would be to-morrow they'd leave, and whether it'd be the next morning they'd be going over. But it wasn't, after all, to-morrow, for Captain Geoffrey Gilderoy, D.C.M., M.C., whom Charl and Bill saw then for the first time, concluded the company parade; "Mind you, that extra iron ration has to be kept. You needn't fill your water bottles until first thing to-morrow morning. Fill 'em again, and see you do it, because what you get up there will give you a belly ache. Mr. Meadows, see that man Fogarty gets a cover on his dixie. What's he mean by coming on parade without it! Let 'em break off, serg'n. major. O, before you go, you'd better post any letters before tea. Hand 'em in at the orderly room."

"All right." He nodded his big head at Mahon, who gave the order.

That night, the orderly room sergeant, McGill, threw over two green envelopes on to the cartridge box, on which the sergeant-major was laboriously filling in a form.

"Two greenies for the same girl." He giggled.

Mahon cast a whimsical look at them. "Aint Mary Hatton in luck." Then he recognised the writing on one, and looked at the signature. It disturbed him unpleasantly. "Poor Frank, he takes things so hardly."

He tossed them back to the sergeant. "There's one thing," said the latter, "these days, there's a pretty fair chance of solving the triangle. These affairs are so ineffectual. Mostly, too, they're only an aftermath."

"You seem to know all about it?" grinned the sergeant-major, who didn't quite understand what the sergeant meant.

CHAPTER VII.

AT 3.45 the next day the battalion was drawn up in square of companies in the field behind the huts, the men in fighting order, gas masks on their chests and cloth bandoliers with extra ammunition over their shoulders. They stood at ease leaning on their rifles, which were protected by breech cloths and bits of sandbag or rag wrappers over the muzzles. Lieutenant-Colonel William Joyce Bedford, the Adjutant, Captain Crowther and a few other officers attached to the battalion headquarters, and the two padres, one Church of England and the other Roman Catholic, stood in the centre.

The colonel, who was no orator at the best, found words difficult and commenced nervously.

"Er—er, men—comrades. You know a little what sort of job lies er—before us. It is simple. We are to go ahead to our objective and then er—er—we'll stick to it. We will give Fritz a good account of us. Er— the battalion er—it's our battalion. I'm sure er—we won't let it down. I have complete trust in you."

The C. of E. padre, an earnest, solid young man, exhorted them to go in the belief that the God of

Battles and Lord of Hosts was on their side. He felt
rather miserable. His white collar seemed to choke
him. It had been his enthusiasm which had persuaded
the O.C. to allow this service. A touch of the dramatic.
Recollections of the preachers with the Puritan army,
which were hardly reconcilable historically with his
own ecclesiasticism. The image of himself in this
role before these men about to go into battle, and
some—who the Destined Ones—to meet their God,
had tempted him.

His conscience troubled him for a deeper reason.
It was with a bitter pang of jealousy that last night
he had left the tent to the priest and those who came
for confession, whereas none could come to him. He
lifted up his face. Oh God, that he might give himself
in their service, even unto death.

The priest blessed the men. Something held him
silent. If it was the thought that other priests of his
universal church might now be blessing Germans, it
was subconscious, but something it was, and he was
uneasy for fear he had fallen in some way short of
what he might have done.

The men watched the performance, on the whole,
sombrely and patiently. Jim Blount looked round at
their faces, at Frank Jeffreys, who searched his conscience with anxiety for some assurance of a personal contact with Christ—no Lord of Hosts, but an
individual and practical Saviour, Who would walk
with him by his side, to turn aside the splinters of the
shells and the machine gun bullets—at others touched
to solemnity, at others who were uneasy that what
was taking place might bring them bad luck, and
at others who muttered jokes about having a church

parade thrust on them just then. Were they not nine-tenths of them really Pagan?

The mind of the C. of E. padre, fighting to control his emotion, was lost in a turmoil of thoughts. They came, strangely, almost blasphemously, in spite of his will. Where, then, was Christ? Not in the nations, their groups, their parties, or their armies, but, if anywhere, in the hearts of these men. But was He even there, like a ghost pale and sorrowful? Nationality, politics, religion were imposed on each human being like an outer covering, making them seem, for the purposes of the world, in spite of the inner individual man, something which they were not. Just so the flesh of each soldier enarmoured itself, for reasons which he hardly understood, and over which he had no control, with duty and military necessity, fortitude, endurance and courage. And yet, if Christ should exist anywhere, He must exist in that flesh and soul within, be dwelling there in each confronting foeman within the armour, even at the moment of the shot, the bayonet thrust, the bursting of the bomb, the detonation of the gun. There, Christ must be in each; not in nations and sects, parties and armies, but in the breasts of the soldiers, in the flesh within the armour, making war, the general slaughter and the individual killing of shot and shell, bayonet and bomb, immaterial; the soldier — British, German, French, Russian and Australian—not merely forgiven because he knew not what he did; no, not that, but sinless.

The padre's soul cried out in distress: "I was wrong. To serve them, that is the best I can do—the only thing." He determined to attach himself to the foremost first-aid post, and help them there when they brought the wounded in. With that resolution made, he suddenly found some peace. "O Lord, help me," he prayed fervently.

The first thoughts of the colonel had been that he would not let it take place again. And yet, after all, there was something impressive, even—he dared the adjective—magnificent, and he supposed others might feel it now as he did, in that thick set gathering of fighting men about to move up into battle.

"Besides," he considered, with the Church of England chaplain in his eye, "the poor fella's been mad to make himself useful somehow."

Silently the battalion moved off in file, like a curled snake thrusting forth its head, and slowly drawing out its body from the mass of the coil. Only a few of the older men left behind, drivers and odds and ends, gave it good-bye. Soon it was at full length in single file trailing through Poperhinghe out into the soupy rain. As they squelched along by the ditch, they were bespattered every now and then by a despatch rider, or big lorry, bumping past. The grey water trickled down from the low skies upon the humps of dixies, haversacks and rifles under waterproof capes. The trees, which lined the road, became gradually sparser of bough and leaf, and here and there even shattered at their boles.

"How're you going, son?" asked Rogan of Charl over his shoulder.

"All right, thanks," Charl flashed an eager, grateful smile. Yes, he was with the battalion, a part of it now.

On their left loomed a large shape, angular at the top, and with big rents in its metal sides. The over-

turned gasometer. The ditch and sparse hedge on their
right gave way to the walls of houses. Often there were
only the remains of the walls, and the standing brick-
work carried old scars. As they went on, they saw
that still fewer of these walls carried any roof, and
inside them glimpses through gaps and holes showed
glissades of rubble, heaps of old timber, and broken
tiles and other rubbish. Once they slipped over a
mass which had pitched as far as the roadway, but
even so soon some members of a Labour Battalion were
busy cleaning up the mess. What did they think of
the war, these small, shambling, oldest men, who lived
like moles somewhere in the debris? They stood by
stolidly while the battalion writhed past the obstacle,
and answered the grinning "Ah, 'ow goes it,
choom?" with solemn "Ah, not so bad, Aussie." It
seemed their point of honour to keep the way not
only clear, but clean, these old men, become like
decent old women meticulous in their task, inspired
only by an occasional glass of their weak canteen beer.
Indeed, the road was quite remarkably neat, preserving an appearance of respectability, while, behind,
and only to be seen through the gaps and holes, was
a welter of disorder. And as it were out of shame
that disrespectability should be perceived at all,
attempts had often been made to conceal it by filling
up the spaces with sandbags and odd bits of iron. But
when the battalion entered the city, not even a labour
man was to be seen. They had come into a city of
the dead. Only now and then they passed an entrance
shooting down from the street line into a deep cellar,
tucked around or sandbagged ever so neatly, from
which a face might look up strangely contemplative

C

and wistful with a sort of instinctive homage, like that
of the drivers on the lorries and limbers who, on the
main road, had looked down sideways from their comfortable perches on the infantry tramping up to the
Line.

The grey atmosphere seemed suddenly to deepen as
the head of the thin, crawling line, hugging still the
right hand walls, turned into a large rectangular open
place. Each man debouching into it cast his eyes
inevitably down the long, ruined facade on the
opposite side—blank window spaces, scarred and torn,
fire-bitten wall in places down or half down, but which,
owing to the pervading neatness of the Labour men,
seemed to have fallen with no single exception
inwards. A long, tortured wall with a shattered tower
against the mournful weeping sky—the Cloth Hall of
Ypres.

"It's a damned strange feeling," Jim Blount muttered to himself.

Who were these intruders? Ghosts of the present
come to haunt the past?

There was a sudden crash beyond the wall in the
ruins near the cathedral. The spell was shattered.
Someone's excited staccato exclaimed, "A rubber
gun!"

They were alone there but for one upright figure
at the far end, standing dead still so that he seemed
in that sepulchral place like a statue set down off its
pedestal. As the line drew up, and edged past, the
figure performed jerky, mechanical movements,
salutes, reacting automatically to the magnetic stimu-
lus of the proximity in turn of each company commander.

"Ah, the bastard!" exclaimed Sucker, and spat.

It was a Tommy M.P.

The battalion, still further elongating itself in a movement which passed down it from head to tail by allowing three paces now between each man, pushed forward out of the square along another silent street much more ruinous than that hitherto threaded, and, after some further progress, passed a rampart which bore great gashes in its ancient face, and had here and there slid down into the dark, sedgy water of the moat.

The suddenness of the change from the ghostly gloom of the ruins to the open scene which started around before Charl's eyes came like a shock which awakes a sleeper from the bemusement of a dream. All the long journey from Havre, as far as this very spot, he had been projected through a narrow tunnel of countryside and sky. What lay beyond the immediate line of his path he had not been able to see, and had been unable to investigate. It was the terra incognita. Now, in the next hundred yards, he realised, for the first time, as he cast his eyes over the wide, bare terrain of the old battlefield, spreading greyly before him on both sides of the road, and stretching far into the mist, the immense sweep of the war. He gasped, as a man might, carried down through darkness along the channel of a river into the vastness of the ocean. This new landscape had been blasted into an awful desolation, deserted, its ravaged expanse without buildings, trees or hedges to catch the eye, with no cultivation, but rank with straggling grasses and muddy, stagnant pools. Across all this, the road on which he stood, spectral with the fragmentary skele-

tons of trees from which flapped the rags and tatters
of broken and rotting camouflage, went straight onwards. Swaying friezes of the discoloured hessian
hung every fifty yards between opposite tree trunks.
They suggested a sort of cynical contemptuous
decoration, and Albie Chomley, waving his hand aloft,
called back, "Crikey, I feel like the Governor-
General."

On the right, just beyond the walls, was a cemetery
with its gaping vaults half filled with stinking slime,
and its head-stones, a few still standing awry, but
nearly all of them broken and pitched about as if by
giants.

"Cheerful, ain't it, bringing the troops to a ——
graveyard." Albie was superstitious. Ted Marshall
grinned back at him.

"You remind me of old Whitcombe, the undertaker,
boy. 'Bloody respect,' he uster say when he was
shicker, 'Bloody respect for the bloody dead, that's
my motter in business, boy.'"

Immediately opposite the last corner of the cemetery
was a gigantic howitzer, heavily camouflaged. It was
the appearance of the men fiddling around the gun,
and some low huts and cupolas near it, and a stack
of shells on end covered with a tarpaulin, which opened
Charl's eyes to a clearer discernment that this wide
stretch of country was not so deserted as it had first
appeared. Further along the road, where a light railway broke off, there was a scattered dump and a
number of low humpies. Not far off, on the other side,
were some horse lines, and a sprinkling of tents and
scattered shelters almost hidden in an old trench line.
Around these a few men also were moving. All over

the place the eye, now keener, could pick up signs of
this low-lying life and activity. A good way further
down, a sausage balloon was up. Approaching out
of the mist, along the road, came a line of donks, from
which, as they passed, the weary drivers of an
ammunition column looked down at the straggling
line of infantry. It was slowly dawning on the troops
that they were on the Menin Road.

A heavy cloud, spreading over the leaden sky,
brought with it more rain; this time, much steadier
and heavier than the previous showers. Those towards
the rear saw the head of the battalion turning from
the road into the open country on the right, towards
a low embankment running almost parallel with the
road half a mile away or more. Out of the belly of
the black cloud the night seemed to have fallen in a
sort of premature birth. From beyond the embankment, which concealed a railway track, there came a
tremendous roar and stab, and fan of flame. The
balloon was almost down. As if the long railway gun
had given the signal, other guns began to thud, and
beyond their sound in the east, the strange pallor
grew, and began to wax and wane as if there were
about to take place, while the last red glamour of the
sun stained the west, a new abortive dawn. But now,
as Charl perceived, that light in the east was more
livid and distinct than when he had watched it from
the hill near Poperinghe. Even before the tail of the
battalion had left the road, the night's traffic had
begun to appear upon it.

The head of the battalion had come to a halt, and
drew its long tail up to it in the centre of a field—
if that waste of ground stretching unbroken between

the road and the embankment could be so described.
The other sole boundary was a few scattered low
thickets, the remains of what had once been a high
hedge. The place was blank of all shelter except a
small malthoid hut.

"Three hearty British cheers for our generals,"
called Hurry Mullane. The colonel, hurrying around
from group to group with words of cheer, overheard
it and laughed.

"I'm sorry, boys; there were to have been some
tents for some at any rate, but they seem to have
forgotten us."

The platoon had gathered in a bunch together. For
a while they were morosely silent, except for brief,
earnest curses; but in the end, the sight of each other,
like half drowned rats, was too much for them, and
they began to exchange lugubrious grins, which burst
into sporadic cacklings. But the point of the joke was
soon blunted. If there had only been a bare trench
it would not have seemed so bad. They were used to
that. But this naked, rain-swept, muddy space con-
founded them. When Captain Gilderoy appeared with
a dim hurricane lamp, they straggled around him with
the rest of the company.

"Well, boys," he said wryly, "make yourselves at
home."

"A damned fine home. They've given you the wrong
place on the map," a voice came from the gloom.

"I was always a oner for the open life," moaned
another.

Gilderoy shrugged his shoulders. "This is the place
they gave us."

They, the remote they; they were cursed again for

the umpteenth time, but it didn't do any good. The platoon shuffled apart again with its new lieutenant.

"They say a meal will be along soon, so don't go away," he said.

"I've never been to such a nice picnic since I went to Sunday school."

"O now, serg., for God's sake don't start telling us now you ever went to Sunday school," came from Ikey.

"Well, I don't suppose you ever did, Ikey," replied someone. It was Skinny, who deciphered himself by a demand for a fag.

The groups began to break up. A night standing in the rain! Shelter for 600 men! Out of nothing! It was clearly a job for the individual.

Bill and Charl stuck closely to Jim Blount, and, under his guidance, pinched, in a series of raids, as many ammunition boxes as they could carry each time from some Tommy artillery lines on the other side of the road. Most of the battalion scattered out on similar expeditions. Ted Marshall and Albie Chomley had a brain-wave. They scraped out a hole like a grave about two feet deep with their entrenching tools. In this they sat, backs against each end, facing each other, with their waterproofs stretched over the top. Their heads, sticking out above, gibed at the shadows forlornly passing them of more ambitious spirits. Frank Jeffreys wandered off alone. After awhile he came back with nothing, enviously anxious to see what others had done. Charl and Bill were at work on the walls of their shelter, while Jim Blount was away hunting for something to complete the roof.

Others of the robuster, more energetic, sort, had somehow improvised little huts and mia mias. He passed
Fred Rogan sitting hunched up under his cape in the
stolid, phlegmatic posture in which he had determined
to see the night through. Fred would not steal like
the others. Frank could not help a wry smile at Ted
and Albie, when he found them standing lamenting by
the side of their hole, which the seeping water had
filled to a depth already of about six inches. The sight
of what so many had done sent him hurrying off into
the darkness again. He cursed his own wretched
solitariness of mood which had prevented him joining
Jim Blount. It was too late now. He could not bot
in on them. It was impossible to keep on tramping and
blundering in the muddy dark. The need of finding
some place to spend the night sent him hither and
thither in a sort of dementia. He stopped, suddenly
aghast at his condition of mind, and tried to make his
search more methodical. Wet and miserable, cursing
the fools who had planked them there, he poked about
among the scattered thickets of the old hedge. His
hand encountered a piece of tin. It was roughly tri-
angular, the longest side about two feet, and it had
a jagged hole two inches wide in it. For some time he
carried it about with him. At last he hit on a bush a
little larger than the others. Careless of the thorns,
he dragged and scraped a hole in it, and fixed the bit
of tin in the twigs. Squatting huddled in his cape
under this almost negligible shelter, he summoned his
harassed nerves to endurance. All night long, in a
cold which struck to the bone, he gazed out half uncon-
sciously towards the lights along the line, and listened
to the dull thudding of the nearer guns, which

punctuated the steady accompaniment of the drum fire
to the south.

CHAPTER VIII.

A MORNING without rain, after such a night, was
as jocund as early summer. After an ample breakfast, the troops joked and skylarked about, cleaned
and dried themselves, and began to explore the
country a bit, and to perfect their primeval dwellings.
An old fallen-in trench, discovered a mile away,
yielded a fair supply of timber and fragments of iron
from its decaying revetments. Jim Blount, hearing
with some tribulation of conscience from Frank
Jeffreys how he had passed the night, set Bill and
Charl to extend their hut to hold another. Though it
was quite open at one end, it had been almost warm,
for its roof was only two feet from the ground, and,
at any rate, it had kept off the rain.

After dinner, which was mainly a good issue of bully
beef stew, Captain Gilderoy called the company
together. The bayonet men of each platoon drew an
additional cloth bandolier, making two, and four
Mills bombs a piece; the Lewis gunners, four bombs
and four extra magazines for the gun; the rifle
grenadiers, an extra bandolier and six grenades, and
the bombers, eight bombs. In addition, there were
five short shovels to each section, and a packet of Gold
Flakes for each man from the Comforts Fund. Bill
Potter and Charl Bentley both got shovels.

Towards the close of the afternoon, the men took
their ease quietly, as if to drain from those few tranquil hours the strength to be drawn upon in the stress

and storm to come. Backs against their hut, and pipes in mouths, Frank Jeffreys and Jim Blount, and the two reinforcements, squatted idly regarding the sausage balloon beginning to bob and duck as the tension came on the cable for its withdrawal. Jim alone was not entirely idle, for he was engaged, in between times, in fitting a couple of sandbags over his putties. Beyond the balloon a heavy cloud was approaching. A plane shot out of the cloud into the open.

"A Fritz."

The four men sprang to their feet.

"A Fritz."

The balloon jumped violently about as the sudden tautening made itself felt along the cable.

"Too late, he's got him."

The plane swooped down and flattened out. A distinct rattle and red darting points came from it. A thin trail of smoke began to ascend from the balloon as the incendiary bullets tore through its envelope. The airman swerved and looped upwards, and then, turning above his prey, beat it straight back for the shelter of the oncoming cloud. There was time only for a few white puffs and smacking explosions from the Archies, and he was engulfed in it. The observer stood forlornly a moment on the basket edge, and then, with a glance upwards at the first licks of flame, leaped into space to fall like a plummet till his parachute opened—not too soon either. The tension of the watchers dissolved in laughter.

"Good for Fritz."

The sausage melted in fire and smoke, and the basket dropped earthwards.

At tea the troops were served with an issue of rum, which was so meagre as to make, according to Artie Fethers, only a dirty mark on the bottom of the dixie. Charl followed Jim's example and bound a bit of sandbag over his lower legs. The cloud, which had carried the plane in its bosom, brought also a renewal of the rain. When night closed in, the men began to make their preparations, doing one little job, and, then, after a while, another. The hours passed by slowly. Officers began to move about, and commands were shouted. Action, which put an end to suspense, was almost welcome, and, when Gilderoy's voice was heard, "Fall in, D Company," followed by that of the sergeant-major, "D Company, fall in," the men quickly got into their harness and hurried towards them. They collected in little knots of platoons around the platoon commanders.

"Gawd, just when a man's got a decent possy, he has to leave it!"

Gilderoy came up to the new lieutenant and spoke to him in a voice loud enough for the men to get the benefit.

"See they don't lose touch, Mr. Burney. They'd better fill their magazines now—two clips, please. And see they don't unintentionally on purpose forget those shovels."

"—— the shovels."

The shovels were awkward to carry, but those on whom they had been thrust got their neighbours to push them down between the haversacks and backbones so that the blade stuck into the belt.

"I feel like a bloody camel," moaned Willy Wallace.

"Well, write to Billy Hughes about it, Weary."

Mr. Burney ventured to ask Skipton a few low questions. He had been, since he joined up, uneasy in the present of the sergeant. He rightly suspected that his arrival had deprived the other, for some time, of his chance of a commission, and he was relieved now by the camaraderie in Skipton's quiet voice.

"You and I'll lead, sir. Corporal Jeffreys will bring up the rear. He'll be all right, and he'll have Jim Blount and Marshall with him."

Soon A Company, and then B, had shambled off in long line into the darkness after the guides, and C was moving. Each platoon was drawn up in single file. They were off. Corporal Jeffreys, the last man in No. 4 platoon, was the last man of the battalion, and trudged on blindly over the soft earth after the others. Soon Captain Gilderoy came back to him.

"See they don't straggle, Corporal, won't you?"

"Righto, sir."

"How are you, Frank?"

"All right, Gilda, thanks."

"I'm glad you got your leave. You were looking a bit seedy. Good luck, old chap." He hastened on ahead with a joking word here and there. Slowly they stumbled forwards over country which became muddier and rougher. The fragment of the moon was impenetrably veiled in that black sky which dissolved inexhaustibly in soft rain upon them. There was a stoppage ahead while the guides adjusted their bearings. Heedless of the new lieutenant's mild protest, the men at once squatted down for a rest. They knew more about it than he did. There was only a moderate amount of gun fire. They were off again. Gilderoy, hurrying along his command, fell into a shell hole and swore vehemently.

"Mind yer step, sir, mind yer step," piped Tug Wilson's cockney. He stretched out a hand.

"Ark at Gilda; naughty, naughty."

There was another halt. "The bastards have lost their way."

Albie Chomley was in the middle of one of his richly imaginative stories of an amatory exploit with a girl at Bailleul when he discovered that Ted Marshall had disappeared.

"Catch up to them, quick!" came Frank Jeffrey's anxious voice. Grabbing up his rifle, Albie stumbled on at a run, with the others after him.

"Christ, I thought I'd lost yer," he gasped when he butted into Ted's backside and caught a retaliatory kick on the shin.

The texture of the earth was rapidly changing. It became raw and bare, and was pitted with a number of shell holes. The rain had fined to a sort of mist, but it was just as wet. The lights of the line could now be seen occasionally flaring where the salient swept round to the south. They ploughed upwards through the mud of a long ridge. There was a low whine and a bang to the left. Charl jumped. That was his first shell, and he was entitled to.

"The mud's some ——— use."

Another bang, and then another. A shudder passed down the wrigging line, and there was a slight pause. It moved on again. A black figure came towards them. Ted recognised it.

"Luck's in, Roly."

"Jack Martin's got his issue."

"Ah."

The figure went by holding its arm. Charl's eyes, scouting about, saw a dark thing with a white blob at the end of it stretched out on the ground. He had only time for a glance at Jack Martin, one of the old originals. Gilderoy, stepping aside for a few moments, saw, one by one, his men appear and vanish onwards again. They had been going a good long time now, and another dark ridge appeared fitfully ahead of them. When the flares beyond it hovered every now and then, the darkness lifted a little with the lights to disclose dark shapes scrambling and slipping through the mud. The earth now was all shell holes. The sounds were distinct and near, and the lights seemed to have spread around them. All at once Frank looked up. There was a perceptible increase in the volume of sound. A shell banged past behind. A few seconds afterwards another, and then another, shook the jellying earth just on the left. There was a momentary hesitation and slackening of the line, and then the pace quickened as some shells went over their heads. It was not long before shells were commencing to fall everywhere. The noise grew into a din—grew and grew beyond description. A man crawled by on hands and knees. The mud belched in a geyser near Frank and he was flung to the left. Somehow he kept his feet. He panted for air to his bursting lungs as he hurried on. Caught in a barrage! The flashes and a dull, livid light showed figures ahead trying to run. He fell over two bodies. The line was broken. He was in a group with a few others. He saw Fatty Gray holding his head. He recognised Jim Blount, too, near him in the weird dark light which illumined them. A sort of numbness descended on his senses. They floundered in the network of holes, in a stubborn, deliberate fashion, as if this environment of belching earth, the howling and crashing of projectiles, and roar of guns, was part of the ordinary human lot; as if they had known no day but this livid night. Charl and Bill clung together. Springs of mud bubbled and burst about them. They saw Tug Wilson on his face, recognising him by the scarf around his neck. Shattered air. Earth in a state of flux darkly heaving. Frank found himself alongside Fatty Gray. He saw Jim Blount again near enough to touch; Jim Blount, with his head up, his lips drawn back tight over his teeth, his calmness crying defiance, as if he were the last man in the ultimate chaos of a world. On the left, someone alone—My God, out there twenty yards alone. A shell burst under their feet, knocking the wind out of them. They got up and grabbed at each other while the earth rocked. Frank fell down the next moment. He crawled some yards before he got to his feet. The others had left him. He charged madly after, and bumped into them. A lightning flash for the fragment of a second illumined the lone figure on the left. It disappeared into nothingness. The three stood dead still. Fatty turned to Jim, the words plain on his lips, "Skinny sniped by a five point nine."

The corporal began to cackle like an idiot. The next second he was on knees fighting for consciousness. He got up and went blindly on. He must get out of it. He kept on trying to walk through the mud. Until at last he noticed a change. The air was calmer, though still full of sound. The earth was still. Just thick mud. He looked up and saw before him the sergeant-

major—Paddy Mahon—the man's face in that awful
shimmering ghost of light, radiant. Like Christ's.

"Good man, Frank—you'll be the last that's coming.
Just over there on your left."

The corporal followed the arm and slipped down on
his behind into a big shell hole large enough to give
ample space around its sides for the new lieutenant
and nine or ten of the platoon. Jim Blount was there,
the two new reinforcements, Ted Marshall, Albie
Chomley, Sucker Sykes, Fatty Gray, Fred Rogan and
Johnny Wright.

Sucker turned his head from one to another. "Poor
old Tug, the poor little bastard."

Mr. Burney, with his mouth in the corporal's ear,
said that the rest of the platoon was in two holes
adjoining.

"We thought we'd lost yer, corp," said Ted Marshall jovially, his voice lowered beneath the noise of
the shells screaming overhead back on to the ridge.

Fatty Gray had a shallow gash along his cheek
which Johnny Wright had bound up with a piece of
dressing.

"Like a gippo woman," yelled Albie.

Half an hour passed before Frank recovered sufficiently to follow Rogan's example and clean the mud
off his rifle. It was too hard to talk, and they kept
silent. The dim flickering light was sufficient only to
enable identities to be revealed by tricks of form and
attitude. Some of them set to scraping the mud off
their clothes with their bayonets. Charl Bentley was
shaking with excitement. That he should have come
through the barrage unharmed was so wonderful that
he felt ready for anything. Such an escape was an

assurance of continued good luck. Soon he would be going over the top. He wondered and wondered, and looking affectionately at Bill, pressed his arm. Half an hour, an hour, they dozed.

Time must soon be up. Mr. Burney and the corporal bent their heads over the illuminated dial on the former's wrist. They, all of them, knew what was to be done. They had been told, and had discussed it the night before they had left Poperinghe. The Mth were to go to the green line, and then they would go through them to the black, and the Oth through them both to the red. On the right of the three Australian was a British division, and, on the left, the New Zealanders, and then some more Tommies. All of them would be out there now in the shell holes dwelling on zero.

All at once, without warning, there was a change. The men looked up with one accord into the air. There had been a sudden increase in the shimmering light, so that they saw each other clearly—figures in paroxysms of St. Vitus' dance. The next moment a tornado of sound dropped upon them, beating their senses flat, so that a few minutes passed before they realised that this was not Fritz's, but their own, barrage. The flickering light was like continuous sheet lightning. The lips of the men moved as they looked in each other's faces. Never had they imagined a barrage like this. Awestruck, they heard the shells in one continuous stream overhead, lashing down on the German lines. By Christ, poor old Fritz. There came a new note piercing the sound. Swelling to a crescendo, there came the vibration of a thousand machine guns.

Gilderoy knelt on the edge above them. "You there, Mr. Burney?" "Yes, sir." "I've seen Skipton." His lips gave the sense. The new lieutenant felt the blood flush in his face. Should he have seen the sergeant? His conscience cried accusingly that he had so weakly gone on sitting there just as if he were one of the men. But he was so strange; he felt they looked at him askance as an outsider. "Get ready, boys. Only half an hour to go," yelled the captain. Off he went. The men fixed bayonets quietly, removed the breach and muzzle cloths from their rifles, and adjusted their equipment. The noise was beating them almost deaf. The corporal looked up at the black, shrieking sky. He must do his duty. Duty! all the time; day and night he was harassed by it, by doing it and by his conscientious efforts to see to others doing it. He screwed his nerves up—screwed and screwed until his whole body shook with their fraying tension. He and Burney looked at their watches. The Mth were off ten minutes now. Twenty minutes to go. It seemed, however, less than five when they saw the captain standing above them. He waved his hand to the lieutenant and ran to the left. The men in the shell hole got up and clambered out, holding their rifles up out of the mud. Ted Marshall stopped behind a moment to light a fag and give Albie a light. The platoon adjusted itself into sections as it moved forward. Bombers on the left flank, bayonet men, rifle grenadiers and Lewis gunners. They were part of an irregular line of dim, uncertain, flickering figures. They of the second wave advanced slowly. Sucker Sykes sank to his knees and was left behind. Charl Bentley noticed that the others who saw Sucker fall glanced aside at him with only a casual sort of curiosity. The new lieutenant, however, who was next to Sucker, shook so much that he nearly jerked off his revolver. He quickened his pace as if to get clear of that moment of horrible fear. If he had not felt so inexperienced, so much alone, so much alone. Jack Smith halted a moment, and, pressing his finger to his nose, cleared his right nostril. Frank Jeffreys, alongside him, with set face, looked straight ahead, a cry silent on his lips, "O Christ, protect me, protect me!" Men with cavernous helmets and big boots were coming out of the eddies of dark mist and smoke, gaunt and bemused, with hands up, white eyes, and lips twisting on their teeth. There were hundreds of them. One of the Mth, seated on the ground, cried to Charl, "Give us a smoke, for Gawd's sake, dig." Charl fished out his packet of comfort fags and box of matches and threw them in the man's lap. Ted Marshall yelled to him, "What you give all those to that lucky cow for?"

How could Charl explain the rush of his sentimental sympathy? Ted's rebuke was a lesson that to be wounded was not necessarily a misfortune. There were bodies lying here and there—many Fritzes—some of them half buried in the mud, and a few Australians. Mingling with the prisoners were Australian walking cases, Germans and Diggers possessed with the like anxiety that their luck might hold until they were out of it. A good deal of shrapnel was bursting near the line. Isolated coal-black clouds puffed out of nothing.

It was perceptibly lighter when the platoon, and the long string of men of which it was part, reached the

Mth, digging themselves in on the first objective. The barrage hung fifty to a hundred yards in front, while the second wave got its wind. It lifted, and the Nth followed. It was their show now. A shell flung stinging mud into Jim Blount's face. Whining whispers sometimes lingered in the ears. The cloth of Bill's tunic, under the arm, ripped, and he staggered, holding his hand to his side, believing himself knocked. When he discovered himself unharmed, his shame made him wild, and he fired on two Germans getting up out of a hole. One fell back and the other put his hands up high and started to run. More and more prisoners were coming forward. So apprehensive! Ludicrous; grinning weirdly at any grin. Some obsequious. Half dead with shock. On the right, someone was throwing bombs, and then, straight in front of the platoon, untouched by the barrage, which lifted, a machine gun splayed. But its first burst was too high. The attackers dropped on their stomachs and slid into holes, edging their heads up to see the heads and shoulders of the gun crew above a hole ahead. The new lieutenant dropped down, too. What was he to do? What were the men doing? Things whipped stingingly into the mud. This man, Blount, beside him, with his cold, deliberate air. No, he could not bring himself to depend on him. He was their leader. Then, before Jim Blount could put a hand to stop him, he got up and made only two steps before he sank on his knees. He pitched forward on his face. Jim Blount pulled him back by his feet. Blood gushed from the back of the tunic where the bullets had come out. Poor little cove. Clean through the heart and lungs. Jack Skipton'd have his com-

mission now if his luck held. Jim got his head up
and slipped like a seal over into the next shell hole,
where he found Charl Bentley and Bill Potter. "Come
on," he said. They started to run, crouching from
one hole to another. A glance by Charl to the right
showed Blue McIntosh had got his head up and was
letting the Lewis gun loose—a burst broken off short.
On the left of the machine gun nest, almost out-
flanking it, two figures were running—Artie Fethers
and Willy Wallace. They were throwing bombs.
Willy fell. Two of the Germans were trying to
straighten the gun up. Jim Blount, with a quick snap,
got one of them. The lieutenant in charge of the post
fired at Artie with his heavy automatic, but Artie
ducked, and his lunge took the officer through the
chest. For a moment he was at the mercy of the
remaining three, for his bayonet was stuck somehow.
With a tremendous thrill, Charl, on his knee, pressed
the trigger, and the Fritz facing Artie bent up in the
middle. Half a dozen men, led by Jack Skipton, were
jumping over the holes, and one of the two surviving
machine gunners threw up his hands. The other did
not, but stood up, his face contorted with bitterness
and despairing defiance. Someone shot him—Jack
Smith probably—and the life of the other hung in the
balance a moment before, with a guttural cry, he ran
forward, and they let him go. Artie Fethers bent
down and souvenired the officer's pistol, and Mick
Flynn quickly ratted his pockets. The sergeant broke
the group up into line, with himself in the centre, and
they went on. After the episode with the machine
gun nest, they risked the shorts, and kept closer up
to the barrage.

The daring German airman, sweeping down low, saw a long, irregular string of men walking slowly and heavily tramping forward with heads bent in the face of a fresh rain squall sweeping over the universal brown-black pitted mud and pools of water. Ahead of the men, a little distance, moved a long swathe of swirling grey cloud faintly pink in spots, through which he could see the earth belching out in one spot after another in close and quick succession. Behind the wave were little groups of carriers and stretcher-bearers. Here and there the line was bent back, and at these points the figures were sporadically still, and then moving with little spurts of feverish activity. Some of them fell. It was at one of these points that A company was held ten minutes before it took the big pill box. Out of the barrage more and more of the airman's own people were coming, with hands up, to meet the advancing enemy. His heart, as he zoomed up near the platoon where the attack was deepest, was panting with the bitterness of the defeat, but now that his job was done, his tight-lipped courage weakened, and a terrible fear possessed him that, before he got up above again, his plane might be struck by the unseen shells that were plunging past. Rather face five fighters than that unseen death in the air. Up, up, above it. Jack Smith fired a clip at him.

Gilderoy came along from the left.

"This is a cakewalk. Where's Mr. Burney, sergeant?"

"Knocked."

The leading figures in the line were stopping and dropping into the shell holes, while the others still dragged through.

"Bad luck — a cakewalk," reiterated the captain. "They can dig in just up there. Do you know what's happened. We caught him just as he was going to hop over himself. That's what his barrage was for."

Frank Jeffreys saw a deep helmeted figure kneeling and firing, but, before he could draw his sight on it, it had disappeared. He fired the shot—the only one he was to fire that day—into the air.

"Helping the barrage, corp," cried Ted Marshall joyfully.

They began to dig while Gilderoy and Sergeant Skipton stood on top, just above Bill Potter, Charl Bentley and Jim Blount, directing the men to form the trench in irregular form by linking up the bigger holes. It was easy to burrow into the soft earth.

To Charl's amazement, the captain began to curse vigorously, even wringing his hands with a sort of angry despair.

"The bloody fools, sergeant; Passchendale is ours for a bag of nuts. And we have to stop."

The Oth were going through them grimly. Now it was their show. Plunging through the brown, rotten swamp which had once been a small, green, willow-lined becke, they went to their objective with few casualties, and looked with amazement at the German gunners trying to pull their guns behind the long, high ridge crowned on the left by the ruins of the village.

Gilderoy hurried off to find the colonel to see whether something further couldn't be done. His eager eyes saw the opportunity being lost. They had the enemy on the run, and the great ridge would be theirs for the taking. He came back with his runner at his heels, furious.

"Orders! Orders! —— the bloody —— orders!" Fritz caught just as he was going to attack. That was remarkable. Each going to make a big attack that morning, and waiting opposite each other. He saw the future clearly. Now the golden chance gone! The weather broken! The months of bitter struggle in the mud! The tremendous cost! Oh, the dear ridge from which it was said one could look far, far away over Belgium. He had other news too. The sergeant-major was dead.

Frank Jeffreys sat down, the strength all at once gone out of his legs. "Paddy Mahon!" He saw, vividly, in front of him, again Mahon's face as it had appeared to him, radiant in the ghastly, shimmering light as he had stumbled out of the Fritz barrage. Jim Blount, perched up on a mound, could see the Oth digging in, openly and safely exposing themselves. Fritz was done that day. The British barrage had finished, and spread out into fitful fire over the ridge and on the lines of communication beyond it. Jim Blount, too, knew what it all meant. Surely this had been the greatest victory in the salient ever. And yet a greater had been missed. What was at fault— the method of modern war itself, when those in command were perhaps, of necessity, too far away to develop the opportunities unfolded by the battle? That was what they would say, but they couldn't excuse themselves by that. What did those "they" lack — the comprehensive and flashing mind, the initiative and the will to develop the opportunity in actual battle themselves? A man like Gilderoy could handle it with his vision, his energy, and his instinct for war. He understood what the captain felt about it, the deeper pain which arose from the consciousness of his own instinctive power for war helpless, and the dull, irritating prospect of a slow progress to the command he desired; the summit of his ambition. So poor Paddy was dead.

The rain had come on again steadily after the first squall. Luck again, for it would protect them from observation. Sufficient unto the day was the luck thereof.

It was an indication of the demoralisation caused in the enemy by the tremendous bombardment to which he had been subjected, that all that day, and the next, the British and Australian divisions had hardly any molestation from hostile fire. Only the rain and cold discomforted them. Gradually, into the grey mist of the second day there filtrated the darkness of the night. The relief was late, and the platoon cursed it. It was in the dark bleakness before dawn, indeed, before figures appeared and scattered in group along the line of sodden holes, and gazed down at the dim, long faces of the Australians looking upwards malevolently. The raw youths of the Manchesters sent up through the mud with—what idiocy!—full packs and heavy rolls of blankets, as if they were going into billets or some home from home, like the trenches at Armentieres! They were dead beat; uneasy, too, before that almost silent malevolence of the Australians, angered at being kept waiting six hours for them. A youthful voice, its shrillness almost screamingly petulant, commanded the men to keep standing. His ——— orders. The men, breaking for once that military and social discipline with which they had been enchained, dropped down and loosened their packs. The Aussies' bad temper

evaporated, and they began to chaff and even invite
the Chums into the holes. Like half of the Tommy
company officers, the boy was fitter for the nursery
than to command men—as if to be a boy just out of a
good school were the best criterion of fitness for this
job. Frank Jeffreys saw a few feet away the livid face
and trembling hands of the boy officer, in the light of
a match lighting a cigarette; saw him as he tried to
ease the numbing pressure of the straps on his
shoulders, and understood his fear as he heard the
voices of his men insolently loud, as if urged on by the
mere presence of the Australians. How he hated them,
that young officer fresh out of Rugby O.T.C., these
colonial bounders. He tried to keep standing, but it
was too much for him, and he sank down with a weak
cry.

"Could you gurgle a bit, sir?" Jack Skipton's huge
form loomed heavily over the slight, lax figure, and,
almost like a nurse, got a good swig of rum and water
from his water bottle down the boy's spluttering
throat.

"No, sir, we ain't got an officer. No, sir, there's
nothing to hand over. When we get out, you slip in."

The lieutenant heard an Australian voice. "What
the hell's the matter with the sergeant?"

The men were getting impatient. Desultory shelling had commenced. Fritz was getting his wind back.
In single file, the platoon splashed off into the mud,
and in a few seconds the last of it, Corporal Frank
Jeffreys, had disappeared.

They arrived at the camp, near Ypres, late in the
morning without any further casualty, and slept until
they were roused for the march back to the Nissen

huts, near Poperinghe, where they slept until tea time the following night. Just before they went off with their dixies to the cookers, the sergeant reckoned their losses. Lieutenant Burney, killed—they hardly counted him, though, he was so new, and they'd only seen him a few times; Skinny Paul, killed; Tug Wilson, killed; Sucker Sykes, wounded only they thought; Willy Wallace with a Blighty—one of the carrying party had seen the stretcher-bearers pick him up. Harry Mullane and Fatty Gray with light wounds. They all felt that they had done very well in the way of casualties. They were bucked, too, by their success—the ground covered and the big toll of prisoners, and praise in Orders from the heads.

When they came back to the hut with their tucker, the empty space in the far left corner caused Ted Marshall to ask, "Where's the bloody sigs?"

"Napoo," said Blue McIntosh. "They were blown up together."

"So Con Johnson says."

Les Henderson burst into song, in which he was joined by Norman Lampard, an old hand joined up again, whom they had found sitting on his blankets waiting their return.

"There's a long, long trail awinding
Into the land of my dreams . . ."

CHAPTER IX.

IN the orderly room, Sergeant McGill, with one green envelope in his hand, picked up another, and, transferring it to the same finger and thumb, tapped on the table with them. The same girl, Mary Hatton. What had Paddy Mahon said—one writing was Frank Jeffreys. He looked at the name and grinned. He did not like Corporal Jeffreys, who treated him contemptuously, and thus had shown his concurrence with Ted Marshall, who, in face of quite a number, had called him a sucker, and informed him he was lower than a snake's belly.

"It would be amusing if they were both in tow with the same girl."

He threw the letters down. There was a little difference in their contents. Charl and Frank had each hastened to write a letter which would let her know he was safe, who had not known his danger. The letters were, perhaps, rather ebullitions of their own relief and satisfaction.

After a week passed in idling and cleaning clothes and equipment, the battalion moved up—this time with no religious service beforehand—into its former camping ground on the other side of Ypres. It had been raining steadily for two days, and it was therefore with relief that, switching off the Menin Road, they saw that a number of bell tents had been set up. These, however, when crowded to the absolute limit, did not hold everyone by a long way, and Jim Blount, Frank Jeffreys and Bill and Charl preferred to occupy again the hut they had constructed before the last stunt. They brought their blankets with them this time, and were quite comfortable by themselves, thank you, sergeant. The men were under no illusions as to the immediate future, and cursed with great gusto the "They" who were to be responsible for the folly. Colonel Bedford felt the bitter atmosphere which hung over the camp like an accusation to which he was forbidden to plead Not Guilty. After all, the men would know well enough it was not his fault, but he was to them the representative of the higher powers, and they'd like him to feel it. He spoke plainly at the meeting at brigade, but what was the use? It was not brigade's fault, nor division's either, for that matter. It was the Tommy command. When he came back and saw the cynical looks of the men, he was glad that he had discouraged the visit from the remote serene which had been hinted at.

That night, the balloon went up in smoke again. Fritz was doing what he liked in the air, and shooting balloons down each night. The next, the battalion moved off, its objective the Passchendale ridge to the right of the village which some other battalion was to take; accent on the "take." It was very dark and very wet, and progress became the veriest crawl when the mud was properly entered. Occasionally, the going was what might be termed ordinary, but all the low-lying ground between the low rises had become swamps. Sometimes the soup reached as high as the thighs, and they had to pull each other along. The shelling was frequent over the whole area, but only in three places, so far, was the thin line wounded. Frank Jeffreys, trying to walk on the edge between one hole and another, once plunged, head down, into a stinking pool—stinking and cold. The bloody rain kept beating mercifully down. No daisy cutters in this mud. At last they came up out of the worst of the swamps. Guessing their condition from his own, the colonel gave them five minutes' spell. When they got up, he tried to hurry the pace, but it was impos-

sible. It was better to be late, and, keeping the
battalion in touch, stick to their direction. A man
might get lost in twenty yards. A straggled line of
hump-backed men plodding and staggering on in the
night. On the right they could see occasional enemy
flares where the line swung round. Fritz could be
depended on for a few lights. Gilderoy came back,
encouraging the men. He was afraid that they would
be so late that they'd have to go over after dawn
was well up, which would be worse and worse.

Now they came to a road recognised as such only
by hard patches between the shell holes, and a little
less depth in the mud. The colonel gave a grunt of
relief, for their direction was right. They toiled up a
long, low slope, towards the top of which uneven banks
of mud rose on each side of them. And then along
the sunken road came the shells. They smote the
battalion down its whole length. For a minute the
men tried to run through it, and then, following those
in front, broke, and scrambled up the left bank. The
bottom of the road and the banks belched dull red
flashes of mud and iron. There was a sharp smell of
gas. This was the third time that night the road had
been shelled, but no warning had reached the battalion
which was to move up along it, for none had been
sent. The ooze slipped down with them. Frank, striking a firmer patch, got up and stretched down his
rifle to Jim Blount, who gave his hand to Charl. Charl
looked back. Where was Bill? Bill! Bill! But
Blount's strong pull hauled him up and away. Bill
was left behind dead, or wounded and waiting death
in the explosions, with about seventy others. A hundred yards away, the colonel and the three company

commanders out of the original four gathered the battalion together in groups of companies. They pushed on while the first lights of morning began to tinge the east a dirty, sulphurous yellow, and in another half an hour they passed Tommies in holes who were keeping the front line. A hundred yards ahead they stopped and lay down. After a time, Gilderoy came along, sorting out his company. Jack Skipton joined him.

"It's past zero a good bit, and there's been no barrage," said the sergeant grimly.

"Stonkered in the mud. The colonel's been in touch with the Mth. They're going on. Everyone's late, and some won't start."

"Lovely, ain't it—like ——— bloody hell, and in this light; the bastards up there must just be waiting for us with their thumbs on the buttons."

"Never mind, sergeant. Get your platoon ready; you'll see me lead off."

All of a sudden, men began to run forward up toward the low spars of the trees in the copse before the high ridge. Frank Jeffreys and Charl Bentley were running one on each side of Jim Blount. They covered about fifty yards of the slope, and then, with a shrill, vibrating cackle, the machine guns met them. They dropped flat. Because he could not drop straight down into a hole, Jim Blount had his dixie riddled on his back. Catching their breath, they began to slide forward from shell hole to shell hole, and then, jumping up, ran forwards and dropped again. This was murder. Ahead of them, a hundred yards, they had perceived at the front of the sparse copse of lopped and shattered tree trunks a pill box, low and very big. But the machine gun fire was not only coming from it, but from the whole line of the ridge beyond, and from the left flank almost behind them. Something had happened further away there, but on the right the —— Brigade was advancing. C company, under Lieutenant Meadows, and D, under Captain Gilderoy, converged on the pill box, and now they were to some extent sheltered by it from the fire from the ridge. There was a good deal of wire still about the fortress, although it had been much cut up by the bombardments of the 4th and 9th, and the holes about the place seemed to be full of men. But these the Lewis gunners to some extent kept down as the attackers crawled forward, working all the time to the flanks. Every occasion they showed, however, the fire from the concrete roof bit into them. Charl watched Jim Blount and Jack Skipton. The sergeant found it difficult to compress his size, and kept grunting. As they moved in, the grenadiers discharged their grenades. Suddenly the noise of the rat-tat-tating became more virulent. C company was charging. D company, too, bent low down, ran forward. By ill luck, C, which had drawn the first fire, struck the strongest wire and were caught on it, the hands of some frantically tearing at the barbs before they fell. But D company was in through it, Gilderoy and Skipton like a bull, and Tom Boyle the first through. Tom Boyle, just beyond the wire, flung bomb after bomb before he was shot from one of the holes. And now the remnants of C company came in on the other side. As the men scrambled forward, they, too, began to fling their Mills bombs. The Fritzes began to put up their hands—too late for most them. No "beg pardons." For the first time, Frank Jeffreys killed a man, stabbing him in the stomach. A number of the enemy in the holes got away, but not those at the pill box. There, the C company men especially, mad to avenge their dead on the wire, slaughtered the enemy clinging against the concrete, and those who ran out shouting from the exit. Into the interior of the blockhouse a dozen bombs were thrown, and, when at each momentary respite between each explosion, a survivor ran out yelling, he perished on the bayonets; until, when it was over, all about the entrance you had to walk on their corpses, and corpses, too, were littered about the holes.

It took under ten minutes to mop up the whole of the copse. Captain Gilderoy gathered his company together. There were not enough now of them, and there was no time to split them into platoons, but the men sorted themselves out, more or less. The place about the pill box was becoming too hot. Guessing what had happened by the sight of their own men running from the position, the machine gunners on the ridge had commenced to rake it. Scattering into wide extended order, the company moved out, circumventing the gunners above by crawling fifty yards before they were discovered. The members of the platoon gained the shelter of a fold of ground, gasping, without another casualty. Gilderoy, with his runner at his heels, wormed his way ahead to reconnoitre. He could see that the attack of the Mth had come to a halt for the time being, but that they were gradually collecting for another spurt forward. On his right, where the low hill crest on which he lay ran up to the main ridge, some figures were moving. What calm-

ness compared with only a few minutes ago. All quiet
except an occasional tat-tat-tat in front, and only on
the right was there any concentration of fire. Beyond
the Mth there was a little movement over about a mile.
That would be the —— Brigade, and, perhaps, the N.Z.
division, and thence, nothing. The big wood—the
Tommies must have caught it from there, and left
the flank of the New Zealanders exposed, or why
should there be the constant fire from that direction
almost catching them in the back. Guesswork, as
much as sight, helped him to his conclusions. He sent
word, by his runner, to the colonel where his company
was, and what he thought of the position, and that
he would move when he saw the other companies
going. He suggested in quarter of an hour. Mercifully, it was raining again, and the enemy's visibility
was very obscured. Looking around at what remained
of the company, he almost laughed, so hopeless and
idiotic was the task they were to essay. The Fritzies
up there knew it too. He had seen them moving
about. They must have brought up quite a number
of fresh divisions. They would have had need of them
to replace those almost wiped out a week ago. Good
troops they were, too; those men at the pill box had
been Jagers—Jagers and Prussians probably—their
best to defend that ridge. If they only knew how
many were attacking them, why, they could retake
all they'd lost a week ago. They must be 100 to 1.
"You there," he said aloud savagely, "don't you
think you'd spend your time better trying to clean
that rifle."

A heavier squall thickened the rain and darkened
the atmosphere. He looked to the left beyond the pill

box expectantly. Bedford was moving. He rose and aroused the stiff, recumbent men, and went along to the left, where he could see better. They commenced to run, but the curve at the crest came full under the fire from the ridge. There were no enemy immediately in front—only swathes of machine gun and rifle bullets screaming down the low slope and into the slight face and crest where D company was advancing. To an onlooker it seemed as if these scattered small lines were struggling with some force which was invisible, but palpable, and which kept pressing and pushing against them. This low fold could not have been more than a few feet, and it merged into the long slope up to the village. There, others were trying to run toward it—so thinly. It was really laughable. Enough to make Gods laugh! Enough to make Tommy brass hats laugh! Whitehall ought to laugh. Gilderoy led his company a bit to the right. Now it was to be the really open going. On they stumbled, scattered well out, and then a concentrated burst cut down a third of the survivors. They could see the Germans walking about, calm and scathless. The company lost all cohesion. Some crawled to the left, and others, including the corporal, Jim Blount and Charl Bentley, to the right, just as the cover suited. Nevertheless, those on the right still worked forward along the top of the little low offshoot of the main ridge, and half way there met some of the ——— Brigade. Together they got up a bit further, but it was hopeless, and for a considerable time they lurked there in shell holes before, somewhere about noon, they commenced to dig in. One thing now was in their favour. The sky had darkened over its whole expanse, and the line of the main ridge itself became indistinct. Meanwhile, the other three companies had gone forward over the swamp past the big pill box and up the hill on the right of the Mth battalian. They got half way up, but the Mth, in greater numbers, went on, individuals and isolated groups of two or three getting thinner and thinner as they crept up from shell hole to shell hole. Men of another battalion, under a captain, reached the village itself, and entered as far as the church, a dozen or so alone. They left some of their number there, and, as the Germans, in hundreds, gathered in on them, the diminishing dozen fought and dodged through the cordon back into the shell holes.

CHAPTER X.

IT was over. The machine gun fire ceased almost suddenly, and only an occasional whizz bang came over. The quietude of exhaustion descended on both sides as the day darkened. Jack Skipton, creeping forward, looked over the chaos of rotten, turbulent earth and the dreary sky. Nothing seemed to move. As his eyes became keener, he could see some movement in the mud where the rest of the battalion was digging in on the line, to which it had been withdrawn a hundred yards or so in front of the big pill box. From there to where his few men nestled with the left of the adjoining Brigade, was a vacant space in the line of about two or three hundred yards. The platoon of the Nth, and the company of the other brigade, occupied a point of a sort of triangle on the

little col, and then, further to the right, the line fell
away down its side into the dip before the main ridge.
He realised that they were horribly advanced and
exposed, but there was nothing to be done for the
present but stick there. Something, at any rate, had
been achieved. Whoever should attack in the future
had only the two to three hundred yards of the slope
to traverse before they were on the top, the very top.
He crawled back to his little command and counted
them. Himself, Corporal Jeffreys, Jim Blount, the
new chap Bentley, Fred Rogan, Ted Marshall, Jack
Smith, Blue McIntosh and Micky Flynn. He started
them digging more earnestly, and went off to find an
officer of the next company.

Frank Jeffreys fell into a heavy doze. When he
awoke, it was almost dark. He saw Jim Blount's
figure leaning back against the shallow trench with
an arm around someone's shoulder. Yes, it was
Bentley.

"Had a sleep, Frank?" said Blount, and then
remarked on the hoarseness of his voice. "Damn it,
I've caught a cold, or got a bit of gas."

"What about eating, serg?" cried Ted Marshall.

What, had they forgotten their stomachs till now!
All at once they felt faint for food, and squatted down
to a meal of bully beef. The biscuits had been reduced
to pulp by the water. A little way beyond them a
man of the —— Brigade, stretched out in the shallow
trench, kept groaning. "Go on, say grace, Fred."
Blue grinned towards Rogan's silent angularity, and
was startled when the other took him at his word.
"O Lord, for what we are about to receive, make us
truly thankful, for Christ's sake. Amen."

"You'd better said, 'For bein' 'ere to receive our victuals, Lord make us truly thankful, Fred,' " said Mick.

Charl Bentley laughed. He was beginning to feel better.

After they had eaten, the two Lewis gunners began to clean their gun, and the others their rifles. The gun, they were relieved, was in working order, but the rifles of the corporal, Bentley and Marshall were choked and clogged with mud, and it was impossible to push their bolts home. Those of the others went in grittily and with difficulty.

Just before the last sickly lights faded out of the sky, they heard someone scuffling on the left, and, half in alarm, called out. It was a corporal and some men of B company. As part of the battalion carrying party, they had not taken part in the actual attack, but, later in the afternoon, had been collected by an officer and sent up to reinforce the front line, and then sent on to fill the gap of two hundred yards or so; nine men. There had been fifteen originally, but the officer and the others had been lost on the way, and it had been all the corporal could do to get the eight there, worn and tired as they were by tramping backwards and forwards with heavy loads, through the swamps, all day under the shell fire.

Without a word, the corporal, a slightly-built boy, sank down in the trench, completely exhausted. It was fully half an hour before Jack Skipton succeeded in getting him to take any notice. With the new arrivals, they were now too thick in their little piece of trench, and the sergeant made them connect up a few shell holes on the left, which would act as a small flank overlooking the slightly lower ground in front of the main position of the battalion.

Apropos of nothing, the new corporal demanded of the sergeant, "Did you know Peter Baring?" and continued without waiting for an answer. "I think it was him, but I didn't make sure. You see, I couldn't. We were coming round a heap out of one shell hole into another, just like round a wall, with boxes of ammunition. I slipped and dropped the box, and nearly put my hand on him to steady myself. There were four others lying in the hole, but he was stuck there kneeling. He must have heard it coming. His head was cut off clean as a whistle, and I nearly put my hand where it had been. Just missed it, where it was bubbling. I couldn't bring myself, sergeant, to make certain it was him."

And Skipton remarked to Jim Blount a minute later, "I think that corporal who came up's getting the dingbats. Cobber's head blown off, or something. He says the big pill box away back's full of hoboes."

"Once you get in, it takes a hell of an effort to break out."

Some time after midnight, the enemy shelling recommenced.

"I think we're going to cop it," said someone.

He was right, for soon the closeness of the explosions indicated that the enemy's observation had been fairly accurate. A shell lobbed on the line to the right. A little while after, there was a hit on the trench there again, and then another amongst the men of B company, who had come up with the corporal. Frank Jeffreys could hear groans. The men of the platoon extended a little and stood waiting for each shell to come over. It was no use going backwards or forwards, for there were shells there and no trench. There was a swift sound in the air, and a shell buried itself in the mud just behind them. When the sound and shock of the explosion were gone, Frank Jeffreys found himself suspended by his heels, head downwards. Something heavy was pressing on him. All around him. He tried to move, and could not. He could not move his head or his legs. He could not open his eyes. He was buried. He was beginning to suffocate; to drown in the spew. He was about to die; he was about to die. He tried to live without breathing. Then he lost consciousness.

Charl Bentley gave Jim Blount, who was only partly covered, a hand, and they both, when Jim had shaken himself, pulled the corporal out by his heels. When they had wiped him a bit, they could see no blood upon him. The heart still seemed to be beating. So they cleaned the mud out of the nostrils and Jim held the mouth open.

When the corporal recovered consciousness, the shelling seemed to have ceased, but just about dawn it recommenced. Luckily, at no time during the night did there appear to have been any gas, and Fritz seemed to have drifted off the spot to about two hundred yards behind.

The corporal heard Ted Marshall call out, "Something's up out there, serg."

The men stood up and looked out into the semidarkness.

Figures were moving out there. Machine gun bullets commenced to whine past as the rat-tating increased from the ridge. Firing had commenced from the Aus-

tralian line on the left. The counter-attack had come.
The corporal roused himself and stood up, just as Jack
Smith reeled back holding his jaw. Frank took up
Jack's rifle and started to fire towards the figures,
now quite visible, coming towards them.

Someone screamed. "When they come near to us,
let's walk out to meet the bastards."

Blue now had the Lewis gun in action. The Australian line, a curve of fragments, viciously waited
the impact. And then the figures in front began to
fade out. Fritz, floundering in the mud, had lost his
heart for it. The counter-attack was a washout. Only
on the far right did it reach close quarters. With its
failure, the shelling ceased.

It was well on in the morning when Frank woke to
find Jack Skipton shaking him. "Wake up, corporal,
we're to go across and join our own crowd." The
platoon and the carrying party started to straggle back
boldly across the open, but Fritz paid them no attention.
The wind was cold, and pleated and flapped the corporal's waterproof sheet about his legs. Half way
there, Jim Blount missed him, and, looking back, saw
him crawling. Charl and he returned and lifted the
corporal up between them. Charl was suddenly feeling fine again, and his saying so brought a laugh
through the stubble on Jim's gaunt, dirty face.

The battalion's line was a series of holes inhabited
here and there by one man, but usually by two or
three. The companies were all messed up. They
stopped at the first hole, occupied by a man alone, a
fellow out of A company, who was peacefully smoking.
He looked up with a welcoming grin on his ugly
chivvy.

"Got room for one?" asked Jim. "It's Corporal Jeffreys; he's about ———; been buried."

"All aboard. Chuck him in!" agreed the other.

"You're Dick Walton, aren't you?"

"Yer; still."

They lowered the corporal down and went off to dig a funk hole for themselves. Frank sat back against the side, his nerve broken and the tears dropping slowly down his cheeks. His companion, rough diamond—usually no diamond, either—looked at those tears with distress and a sort of shame; shame not of the corporal, but almost of himself for being squatted there to see them. He tried to wile them away with uncouth blandishments. After a time, Captain Gilderoy came along with the sergeant, who, in a few brief words, explained the case.

"Hullo; feeling better, Frank?" asked Gilderoy.

The corporal nodded wearily. As the day wore on, he became haunted by a terrible fear. He tried to keep his reason by focusing his memory on other scenes. Home—now would be night time at home. He could see his father walking in the quiet back garden where the young leaves of the fig tree were like tongues of pale green flame springing upward out of nothing into the sharp night air. Something of the calmness of that memory soothed him. Occasionally, Jim Blount looked in on him.

Towards one o'clock, the following morning, word came round that they were relieved. The men in the hole hauled Frank vigorously up on top. They could see nothing of the relief, but they followed black forms turning back into the dark. The sound of gun fire was dull and intermittent, but they had not gone far

when Fritz started to shell at random the support areas.
Heaven knows whether there were any supports in it.
Frank stuck close to the heels of the A company man,
who, seized now by the common panic to get out, and,
with little thought of the corporal, followed hard on a
Lewis gunner and his mate who were carrying the
gun. The gun had become as heavy as an 18-pounder,
and they carried it turn and turn about. They had no
track or objective except to get away from the line.
A mist-encrusted half moon thinned the dark a trifle.
As they drew further off, the yellowish horizon lights
turned to the old waxing and waning. Around them
was a mysterious sea, as barren as a dark, glutinous
sea, the waves of which seemed to catch their only
motion, a ponderous, slow motion, from the movements
of the occasional dark figures who trod it, unsinking,
like Christ, the Galilean. Frank Jeffreys, like the
others, when he fell down into the thick stinking ooze,
was afraid that he would fall one time or another into
one of the black, putrid pools where the water was
deep enough to drown a man. Not a few, wounded and
exhausted, had drowned. The A company man waded
through the mud with stubborn automatism. Desperately, Frank staggered on, haunted, too, by another
fear that he might he left alone. Pitching forward
on to his knees, there came a stinking sigh from
beneath him, and a deep-helmeted, ghost face rose
slowly in front of him. He pushed it away with his
bare hand. The A company man, who now had
emerged from his first panic, gave him a lift up, and
they went on. They had followed behind the Lewis
gunner and his mate, for Frank saw them now just
a few paces off ahead. There was another man with

them. A big shell spurted near, and by its red
lightning, which lingered on the air, he saw, as in
a dream, guns all awry half sunk in the mud, and,
sticking up stark, the four legs of a mule. That one
vision revealed the fate of the artillery, and why there
had been no barrage. They went on and on, dripping
with the rotten wet—bemused like idiots. "How's
she going, corp?" the A company man asked once, but
didn't trouble to get an answer. Another shell
spurted only a dozen yards away, bespattering their
filthiness with more filth. When he picked himself up,
Frank couldn't see the others. He went on alone.
Surely he had seen those half-sunken guns and stiff
animal legs before! The terror possessed him of a man
who, lost in the bush, and seeing still the eternal same-
ness of the green trees, but, in particular, one oddity
distorted to a shape like one he had seen before,
believes that he has at last completed the dreadful
circle. Never so dreadful a circle as this. Never was
such a ghastly, dark desolation ever imagined. Only
the elemental instinct for life kept his legs moving.
At last he felt under his feet a harder foothold beneath
the layer of mud. It was the broken surface of a
road, to which he stuck with dim hope, careless of the
more frequent shells about it. This, in time, brought
him to a low structure and a dull light, an overturned
motor lorry and odd masses of debris with bandaged
men squatting and reclining thickly about or lying,
some in the mud, and some on stretchers, and in the
road a couple of waggons with their donks. From
this place arose, now and then, groans, punctuated by
sharp cries, but, on the whole, it was remarkably quiet
there. A few men moved about with dim hurricane

lamps. The dressing station. Though he had no wound to show, he sat down there with the others, his head fallen forward on his arms.

How long had he sat there! He must get on. Ah, if he could only have climbed into that waggon moving off with its load. He was out on the road again, treading like one who walks in his sleep. He got off the side of the road a little, right alongside a series of camouflaged humps. He was quite unconscious of them. They were just humps. He could almost have touched one. A tremendous shattering roar and flare burst from the two 9.2 howitzers. He was knocked down by the concussion. He got up and screamed in a shrill squealing scream, and ran. He went on now like a drunken man. Every few seconds the mental flash of those guns seared his eyeballs, and their crash split his head in twain.

Some time later, one of the battalion drivers found him wandering on the road, and took him to a tent in the horse-lines. These drivers, their souls wrought to the highest and purest agony by the few words dropped by those who first had wandered back, concerning the fate of their battalion, and by the gaunt, blank, far-away look on the rough, mud-streaked faces, gently and tenderly wrapped him in their blankets. While one propped him up, another poured a mug of rum down his throat. The other two patted him, saying, "It's all right now, corporal. It's all right now. There, there, it's all right now, corp." He fell back into unconsciousness. All that day he lay there, and the following night, before he woke. In the afternoon they took him across to the main camp and handed him over to Jim Blount and Charl Bentley, whom they found smoking quietly in their old shelter. Jim was cleaning his leg with a little water from his water bottle. He had got a long deep scratch from a piece of wire. They both, while they welcomed him, made a mental alteration of their tally, for they had been reckoning their losses.

The following had not come back out of the stunt, and were killed or wounded or missing: Jack Smith, Albie Chomley, Bill Potter, Tom Boyle, Les Henderson, Norman Lampard, Billy Carter and Dopey Kendall. Of these they knew that at least Tom Boyle and Les Henderson were dead. This left the platoon which, including its new officer, had been 28 before the first stunt, at a strength of 14. It seemed to have fared better than most, for of 600 odd fighting men in the battalion, there were left about 200. When the company fell in, it looked like a collection of ragged deadbeats.

SCENES DE LA VIE DE CAMPAGNE

CHAPTER XI.

JIM BLOUNT awoke fairly early after the arrival, late the evening before, at the village of Bousousarbre, near Desvres. Leaning on his elbow, he first buttoned his cardigan over his grey flannel shirt, and, having lit a cigarette, propped himself on his elbow and gazed about the space of the timber and daub barn. Through the open doorway, which was about a foot above the level of the earthen floor, the soft light of the morning was spreading across the floor, losing itself in the corners and leaving the lofty vault of the roof still impenetrably dark. The others seemed all heavily asleep. Blue McIntosh was grinding his teeth and convulsively twisting in the grip of nightmare. They would be allowed to lie there, unmolested, as long as they liked that day. The whole battalion would lie in, from the colonel downwards, preferring the blankets to breakfast; that is, if the cooks should get any. The idea of going out alone, the first into the unknown village, occurred to him. He would have it absolutely to himself for the only time, and, walking solitarily through it, could capture it in its virginity, and absorb its scene into himself for ever. When his cigarette was finished, he got up, therefore, and, as silently as he could, pulled on his clothes, which were stiff with the ingrained mud of Ypres. He only had one puttee, and his tunic had a big tear in the back. If his movements woke any of them, they gave no sign. He tiptoed to the door and stepped over the ledge out into the road.

The mist, which had descended in the still night, had held off the intenser cold in the upper air. The world was all soft grey and softly diffused green. Everything exuded and dripped moisture, which increased under the trees to a visible shower, like light, steady rain, except that the drops fell, not in thin shafts, but integrally and roundly, like pearls. On the other side of the road, beyond the narrow strip of grass where the elm trees grew, was a hawthorn hedge, above which the boughs of the elms leaned over a field that swept upwards, just as they arched and stretched upon the road half the distance to the barn.

When he had walked slowly a couple of chains to the left, he stopped just before he came to a cottage, of which the roof and a chimney were visible set back a little way behind the hedge, in which there was a narrow gate. Half concealing the front of this deserted looking dwelling some old fruit trees, so old that their gnarled limbs were marked with long patches of silver lichen, were shedding their leaves with the moisture. Yet it was in those fruit trees—crab apples and plums —because they were so perceptibly aged, rather than in the big, sturdy elms along the road, that the double tempo of tree life, the shorter seasonal growth, decay and rebirth of leaf, flower and fruit, and the slow life growth and decline of the tree itself, beat more clearly. The peace which lay on everything touched the soldier's heart to a sharp momentary pang of pain.

An old man in a blue blouse appeared through the grey light, leading a horse silently on the muddy carpet of the road. Jim gave him a "Bon jour, M'sieur,"

and received a grin which cracked the weather-beaten
face into a thousand wrinkles, and a "Bon jour,"
M'sieur," in return. The old man's sabots trudged on
to the point where the road forked, and took that
which mounted towards the left. After a few minutes,
Jim followed as far as the shallow, muddy edge of
the pool. The old man and his horse had disappeared,
probably into the farmyard yonder, the white walls
of which were visible in places beneath the foliage.
Because he had some view of what lay in that direction, Jim took the other branch, and came shortly to
a wide gate which was open to a yard. The house was
ramshackle and poor looking, and, contrary to custom,
the barn was at the back of the yard instead of
abutting on to the road itself. There was no one about,
but on the broad, brown side of the hill beyond he
could see the dark shapes, magnified in the mist
through which the sun was now shooting, of two
women and a man working. They were taking some
root crop from the earth and placing it in heaps, their
stooping and straightening and slow walking, with
arms full, over the heavy soil, regular and unceasing.
For some time he watched their rhythmical labour,
before he returned to the pond and took the road to
the left. This brought him a little further past the
barns and, on the opposite side to them, to another
house with whitewashed and clean walls on the road
itself. Its being on the road was like the house on
the other fork, a contradiction of custom at first sight,
but not in truth, for the latter had originally been
probably only a labourer's hut, and this before which
Jim now stood was different also. It was no ordinary
farm, as he was to see when he peered through the

open door into the interior. The room into which
the door opened was furnished with a long bare table,
a big enamelled stove, some forms, and a sort of
buffet on which was a collection of gaily-labelled
bottles. A noteworthy and pleasant discovery, for this
was a village auberge or estaminet.

There was no one there at this hour, and he retraced
his steps to the billets. He heard no one moving and,
without looking in, went on under the trees. Inter-
spaced by hedges were dull white barns beyond which
he could see, through gateways and gaps in the hawthorn, the whiter walls of the farm houses on the other
side of their courtyards. These dwellings were so
scattered along the road—the hedge lines between
were so long—that it seemed hardly worth while to
have dignified the place with a name at all. The large
trees which hung over the bottom of the vale seemed
to keep everything there in a perpetual condition of
damp which might hardly dry out even in mid summer,
so thick, then, would be the leafy screen overhead.

In time he came to a larger building, a long, two-
storied edifice of old worn brick facing the road, which
widened so that it made there a considerable open
space in front. There were two doors, a large one
in the centre, and a smaller at the far end of the
facade; and a dozen windows, the frames and sashes
of which had one time been painted bright blue.
Such a village as Bousousarbre, Jim thought, was un-
likely to boast a chateau, and this, the principal edifice
of the place, would belong to some family native to
the countryside which had risen to superiority in land
and coin through the exercise over fifty or a hundred

or two hundred years of a more intense rural economy. In front of the smaller door he saw the colonel's and adjutant's batmen talking to a big French woman. They were the first of the battalion he had seen abroad. Headquarters would be near by, and in a minute he passed what he guessed was it, for he caught sight of the orderly room sergeant in his greatcoat walking across the yard, and the horse and transport lines in the flatter field at the back. From here the road began to mount, and the trees to thin out, until, at last, the road showed itself nakedly crossing over the ridge on which the barrage of slanting sunbeams was striking. He went on until he found a comfortable place overlooking the dark, umbrageous roof of the valley which, still dark green below, was seen from above to be autumn-tinged and thinning. When he had smoked a pipe, his stomach began to feel empty, and he set off back towards the billet at a smarter pace. The troops had begun to show themselves in various stages of undress. When he approached his own quarters again, his steps became slower, as if he were reluctant, notwithstanding the increasing discordances of the men, that it should be by any aid of his own volition that the harmony of quiet calm and beauty should be shattered for him. When he got back, at last, he found Charl Bentley and Fred Rogan outside, half dressed, and quizzing about them. Within, some of the others were climbing into their pants.

Charl Bentley and Fred Rogan had been deputed to go and find the cookhouse, though Ted Marshall's voice, muffled in a comforter, had been sceptical, "You can save yourself the ——— trouble. I bet the babblers aren't up yet."

Dingo William's voice groaned. "I'll 'ave ter get up. I can't stay 'ere no longer."

"What about the corporal's boot?" Micky Flynn picked it up and gammoned to throw it.

Frank Jeffreys lay flat on his back snoring. Sleep seemed only to have increased the haggard anxiety of his thin face.

"Don't wake him, Mick," Jim interposed.

He collected his hold-all and towel to go and look for the pump in the yard.

CHAPTER XII.

TED MARSHALL and Jack Costello knocked with a deprecating apologetic sort of knock on the door of the farm in one of the barns of which they were billeted. Costello was one of four men who had arrived the day before, and were added to the strength of the platoon. He and Sydney Barton were old members of it. Just before the stunts they had had the good luck to be sent, with eight others from the company, to form a working party for the engineers, and so had missed the slaughter. The other two were Steve Wilberforce and Mervyn Hill, who had both belonged to the reinforcements before the last, and had just been sent across with a raked-up draft, the first from the N.C.O.'s of the instructional cadre and the other from the officers' mess at Larkhill.

The barn on the other side of the gate also faced the road. Along the two sides of the courtyard were stables, fowl runs, duck houses, rabbit hutches and such like. The front of the farmhouse itself and the

waggon shed faced the barns across the space of about
thirty yards, in the centre of which the manure heap,
like a miniature volcano, was reeking upwards in a
thin, bluish spiral of steam which the sun both aug-
mented and made visible. In the corner near the
waggon sheds, not far from the manure heap, was the
well, taboo for drinking, under the pump of which
the platoon performed each morning its ablutions, the
men waiting, in grey flannel shirt and pants, their
turn with dirty bit of towel, soap, and usually tooth-
brush, out of reach of the splashing. On the right side,
facing the house, there was a gate which led into a
vegetable and flower garden, which merged into a
small orchard. The house was two storied and had
white walls and a roof of dull red, mossy tiles. The
windows were hung with white curtains, dazzling stiff
and clean, and the big brass hinges and door handle
were shining.

Ted Marshall's knuckles smote the wood more
loudly. He and Jack were in a way ambassadors, or,
rather, commercial envoys, from one nation to another.
That morning's breakfast had been a lean one, and
talk had turned on the occupants of the farm. All
that had been seen were an old woman, who scarcely
ever seemed to leave her chair, and another of about
thirty-five, and of these only glimpses, the old woman
in the doorway, and the younger one hastening with
a big jug to the pump or feeding the poultry. Her
pale olive face was always immobile, and her eyes,
though she must have been conscious enough, a little
fearfully conscious of the enquiring eyes of the men,
were always turned down. Usually she was dressed
in some dark stuff with a snowy white collar. At

times she wore, also, a sort of white coif, but more often her head, with its heavy black hair parted rigidly in the centre and carried to a knot at the back, was bare. Sometimes, too, they would catch sight of her in the garden, which she must have entered from the unknown further side of the house. Indeed, to avoid the soldiers, they must have, if they left their own place at all, been going in and out that way.

It had been suggested that, as rations were low, eggs and chips would go well. The Madame might sell some. They preferred to buy rather than plunder. Ted Marshall, whose brick face could conceal the hottest blush, claimed to have a way with Madames, and to be able, in some mysterious manner of his own, to surmount the difficulties of language, or love would be dumb as well as blind. He claimed the job, though it was suggested Corporal Jeffreys or Jim Blount might do better.

Jack Costello, who was always earnest and prepared to take any amount of trouble about food, had volunteered as offsider. Ted, now that he had arrived, almost repented his rashness, for the quietness and reserve of the inhabitants had become disconcerting and almost alarming.

"Here, I'll give 'em a rouse," exclaimed Jack, who, not only inspired by more material hopes, was bolder also because he would not have to talk. He gave the door half a dozen sharp cracks with his hairy fist.

It opened. They both slipped back hastily. The younger woman it was who stood before them. They had a glimpse, before they managed to look at her directly, of a stone-flagged floor, still blue damp with scrubbing, and old, yellow, rush-bottomed chairs. The woman's face, a healthy olive complexion and dark eyes, was flattish rather, but with a deep inward beauty of its own. Her gaze was controlled and calm, and, they perceived, with relief, not hostilely enquiring. Only her breast's more rapid rise and fall showed sign of any perturbation. Almost startled by it, they noticed that she was nothing near thirty-five, as they had imagined. She was not more than twenty-five.

"M'sieurs?"

Ted shuffled from one foot to another.

"Bon jour, mademoiselle."

"Bon jour, m'sieur."

She waited. Ted felt it was up to him, but how. Jack gave him a kick with his knee. "Get it off your chest."

"Compree, mademoiselle, compree."

"Qu'est ce que vous voudrez, m'sieur?"

Ted drew breath. "Compree, madame, uffs?"

"Non, m'sieur."

Ted looked surprised. "Non compree uffs, madame?"

"Non."

Impasse. She waited patiently. Ted could feel Jack's traitorous grin in his back. The mouth of the young woman twitched.

"Compree erves, mademoiselle?"

"Non, m'sieur, pardon. Je ne comprends pas."

The old woman shuffled into place behind the younger, who made room for her.

"Ah, les pauvres soldats," exclaimed the old one, and exchanged a few quick words with the other.

Ted brightened a little. "Ah oui, madame, soldats Australiang, bon soldats."

"Oui, les soldats Australiens."

"Talk to 'em, boy," urged Jack, encouraged at this exchange. "That's the stuff to give 'em."

Ted tried the old woman. "Compree uffs, madame?" She shook her head blandly.

Ted had an inspiration. "Compree pulley, madame?"

He looked hopefully from one to another, but, after pondering earnestly a moment, they both shook their heads.

"Non compree pulley?" It was too much.

The two women babbled apologies, but the fact was undoubted; they did not compree.

"Wait till Jeffreys and Jim Blount come back," suggested Jack disgustedly. Ted, however, stood his ground, but, as though anxious to see that a way of retreat lay open, he glanced behind him. Then his face broadened.

"Non compree pulley, madame?" he exclaimed reproachfully; non compree pulley, la—la—la." He pointed triumphantly to the fowls pecking in the yard.

"Ah, oui, m'sieurs, les poulets, les poulets, oui."

The four of them were now all excitement. Ted pressed on with elan.

"Ah, non compree huff, madame—no compree? Derriere the pulley—bon pour mongey—derriere, comme ca," his hands cupped, "derriere the pulleys."

The women started to laugh. "Ah, des oeufs, des oeufs, oui, m'sieur, oui."

"Combieng?" Triumphantly he fished some franc notes out of his pocket.

Still laughing, they waved his money aside.

"Rien, pour les soldats, pour les soldats Australiens."

The young woman went inside, and in a minute came out with a china bowl half full of eggs, which she puts in Ted's hands.

"Merci, middemoiselle, merci. Tres bon for the troops. San-fairy-an."

The two women exchanged a few words. The younger, to Ted's delight, addressed a few to him, and he responded sapiently, "Bon! Bon!" She disappeared inside again.

"Wonder what she's up to?" said Jack, and then, ecstatically, "Perhaps she's gone to get some ham."

She reappeared, however, with a small basket, and those who were at the barn door saw the four of them go into the garden, through which they went to the fruit trees.

"Des pommes," muttered the old dame.

"Oui, des pommes," echoed the young one.

The four of them gazed up at the ripe fruit on a crab apple tree. It did not take Ted and Jack long to fill the basket.

Ted felt it behoved him to maintain the conversation when they stood together again. "Vous marry?" he asked the young woman brightly.

She looked at him a moment almost alarmed, and then, with a slight gesture, so sadly proud, so heavy with fate, she answered, "Mon frere et mon fiance, ils sont a la guerre!"

He understood—the fiance was at the guerre.

"Bon chance, then, mademoiselle, bon chance," he said earnestly.

She smiled gently. "Oui, m'sieur, bonne chance!"

"The guerre no bon." Poor cows, he thought.

"Merci, madame, merci," he turned to each, indicating his basket of fruit and Jack's bowl of eggs.

"Yes, merci, bon eh?" declared Jack, and they walked away leaving the two women in the garden.

The next day the platoon made its return. Ted and Jack were at the door. Again it was the younger woman, but she came more quickly this time.

Ted handed her a tin of Swallow and Ariell's pudding (there had been a few parcels in the mail), two slabs of chocolate and four tins of bully, contributed from iron rations.

"Bon," he said, "bon for mangey."

Once she said "Ah non," and then, looking from face to face, turned to her as she stood on the steps, her eyes suddenly shone, and very quietly as she took their gifts in her arms, she said, "Merci, messieurs de la section, merci, et la bonne chance."

CHAPTER XIII.

LIFE was easy that first week. The troops paraded by platoons in the morning, and were supposed to do platoon drill and musketry for three hours, but only a pretence was made at it. They would march out of billets well enough, but when they were lost in some by-path, and had done about an hour's drill, they loafed away the other two. The afternoons they had almost to themselves, except for sundry odd company inspections, at which Colonel Bedford might sometimes be present, and attendance at the Q.M. store to make up losses in equipment. There were changes, too, in personnel. There was a new company

commander in place of Captain Gilderoy, for whom
Bedford had wangled a staff course with the idea
that if a successor of himself should be needed,
Gilderoy would best fill the bill. The new man was a
Captain Slade, about forty years old, and reputed to
have an unpleasant disposition. The platoon had, too,
a new commander, Lieutenant Skipton, D.C.M., who
made up for the new captain. It also had a new sergeant. Tom Burke, M.M., a big man without much
sense, a bit of a bounce sometimes when his mood was
bad, but a good soldier. He went on the bender too
often, that was his main trouble. It was all so quiet
in the village that Charl Bentley, who, after the stunts
at Ypres, felt he was entitled to an opinion, could
remark, "Here, you'd never know a war was on." On
the third day, a big Aussie mail was distributed,
letters and parcels. Charl got three letters—two from
home, and half a page of acknowledgment from Mary
Hatton of his own letters. He also got a parcel, but,
when he ripped off the linen cover and opened the
box, it was plain something had happened. A pair
of socks and a scarf were thick and stiff. There were
a few bits of paper and some rusty tins, the contents
of which were in a peculiar mess. Something stamped
on the wrapper caught his eye and he read, "Salved
from torpedoed ship." He put it in his pack so that
he might show it to his father and mother when he
went home. Frank Jeffreys had two letters—one from
his father and one, addressed in a feminine handwrit-
ing, which, almost afraid, he held unopened for some
time. At last he got it out—two pages from Mary
Hatton. He could not read it coherently with all the
others about, and he put it in his pocket after the

first glance at it. He intended to sneak off by himself
later to a quiet spot along the road.

Something attracted their attention to Fred Rogan.
He was staring in front of him in a strange, fixed
fashion with a black bordered letter in his hand.
While they thought, "Someone dead," he got up and
walked to the door and bumped into the post before
he found it. He had not come in when they went to
bed, but in the morning they saw him lying down,
fully clothed, in his usual place. He was still lying
there motionless when they returned from parade.
They regarded him silently and uneasily. At last
Johnny Wright, who knew him best perhaps, got the
man outside. They walked into the country some distance together before Johnny knew. Fred's little girl
had died of diphtheria in the Warragul Hospital.

CHAPTER XIV.

From Charl Bentley to Mary Hatton

Dear Mary,

I was very glad to get your letter and to hear that
you are well. I have just had a letter from Bill
Potter. I thought he was killed in the sunken road,
but he's in hospital at Rouen. He only got hit in the
bottom part of the back. We are having a rest now;
are pretty comfortable in a barn. Of course, I can't
tell you where I am. I hope Bill's uncle and aunt
and cousins are well. I wish I could get leave, but, of
course, I can't for about seven months. That was a
great week we spent going about together. I had some
letters from Australia, too, and a parcel which had on

it, "Salved from torpedoed ship." All the chocolate
and biscuits had melted. I'd love to see you again.
How much you can't tell, and it's hard to write, isn't
it?

With best love from

Charl Bentley.

Charl was truly glad that she was well. The thought
that there might be consequences of that last night in
the dining-room had occasionally made him uneasy.

From Corporal Frank Jeffreys to Mary Hatton.

Dear Miss Hatton,

If I could only tell you what pleasure your letter
gave me. When I had first glanced through it I went
out of our billets and walked out of the village, where
we are, up on to the top of a hill where I could read
it slowly at leisure. That you should have written to
me such a letter was beautiful of you. From the hilltop the village in the valley was green, turning brown,
spotted with white walls, and the dull red of the roofs,
and the hills are round, and the people in them remind
me of the pictures I have seen sometimes. How
peaceful it is after the time we have had. I have not
been too well, and my nerves are bad. I was buried
by a shell. A man named Jim Blount, and Bentley,
whom you will remember, were near, however, and got
me out. I look at some of them sometimes and wish
I were a chap like Bentley. Nothing seems to trouble
them. They seem to have no nerves. Like everyone
else, they must be afraid often enough, but the next
moment they seem to forget it. I suppose good health
helps them, and I am not well. Jim Blount you would

like, though he is a strange fellow. I think he is by far the best soldier of us, because he is always the same—without any heroics, but calm and efficient. He won't take any promotion, though he could have got it often enough. He is not a man one can be very friendly with—I mean, not really friendly. He always seems to keep himself, his real self, to himself. Another one of us is like him outwardly, but not really. A man named Rogan; but his quietness is of a different sort—gentle and simple. He had bad news the other day. His little girl in Australia has died.

On the whole, our platoon has been a happy family, and the men a pretty decent lot. There is only one I dislike much—a man who has just come back named Barton. He is one of those with an easy, jovial way with him which goes down with most of the others, and makes it worse, for he is an irritating, low, foul-minded bounder.

I have got another job. They have started an educational stunt. Each afternoon the officer in charge of the platoon is supposed to give a lecture on some educational subject. Ours, who was formerly our sergeant, is like a large number of our officers—not very well educated; not well enough to teach; and as I was once a teacher, he comes along to the billet and I give the talk. The men don't mind, because they don't have to work, and some are interested, especially in history. They have issued us with a few text books, which one needs I can tell you. I am quite interested in the job, and it gives me a chance to think of something apart from war, and shells and mud and explosions.

Sometimes I go out with Jim Blount and the young

chap Bentley. I am more friendly with Jim than any of the others, and I like Bentley. He's one of those eager fellows without many brains, but full of animal spirits. They seem to do things right—I was going to say by instinct—but rather, things seem to come out all right for them—by Fate. And then he is strong and healthy, which means so much out here. You can't help liking him. His friend, Bill Potter, I forgot to tell you, has been slightly wounded.

Please write to me. My mind seems to want something to look forward to. How can you tell how much it wants it? I have had a bad time, but I can never tell anyone how bad. It is perhaps mean to write to you like this, as if I was crawling for pity. Would you think so? I suppose it will end some day. Perhaps I shall see you again, and perhaps not. I am ashamed of the end of this letter and despise myself, but I can't help writing it. I meant to tell you something about the place where we are, but I don't seem to be able to now, and I will finish this.

> Yours very sincerely,
> Frank Jeffreys.

CHAPTER XV.

IN the afternoon, you might, if you liked, walk for five kilos westward to the little town of Courtrelles, which, in its little square, boasted two estaminets where one could get not only plenty of fried eggs and chips, but steak. Steak it was, true enough, though most people declared, owing to its coarse fibre, that it had come off a horse. All you saw of the town, as you came along the road, was the top of a grey spire peeping through the tops of green trees, until, approaching up the rise of the road with trees in a sort of park on the right and fields behind a stone wall on the left, you saw, when you came to the corner where the road turned a chain before it started to descend, the whole village at your feet. Men of other Australian battalions went there, too, and in the village were billeted some Tommy artillery—the Hon. Horse Artillery, as the diggers called it. In deliberate, sarcastic tones, they kept asking uneasy gunners and drivers how it was that they came to have been in these cushy billets for getting on six months. Solemnly they inquired whether the lives of the Hon. Horse Artillery were too precious to risk, or whether it was a sheer case of forgetfulness which they had tactfully not waked up. The time of these Chums had been mostly put in polishing their buttons and whitening their lanyards. They protested it was not their fault. They were in reserve waiting for the time when it should be open warfare again, and the cavalry would ride through. After all, they were not to know, all the while they polished, that the whippet tank and the armoured car were already on the way to usurp their place on that day. In the meantime, their spickness and spanness was a sight for sore eyes. They only grinned good-humouredly at the Aussies' envy, for it was devoid of malice.

"The next war?" asked Charl, half drunk, in spite of Frank Jeffreys, and so much more the old-timer, "is the one they're interested in."

"No, the one before the last!" said a man of the Oth dryly.

Courtrelles was free to all, but to go to Desvres, the bigger town, with the railway on its outskirts, you needed a pass. At least, you were supposed to have one, for Desvres was quite a considerable little place. The Heads, the men alleged in their complaint that the issue of passes was small, were trying to keep it for themselves.

But life, even in Bousousarbre itself, was not without its amenities. Mostly in the evenings after tea, Blount, Jeffreys, Johnny Wright and Charl Bentley would be found in the estaminet, on the left fork of the road, drinking vin blanc and vin rouge with other Diggers and old Froggies. Because it was at the end of the village, away from the main body of the battalion, they usually had it pretty quiet there. When they left—Johnny, mildly drunk; the corporal, who was a teetotaller, worried, as usual, over something or other; Charl Bentley, his feet and his brain dancing, and Jim Blount, sombrely magnificent—they went to Madame Lantier's house. Madame Lantier's was the place on the right road at which Jim had stopped during his explorations of the village the morning after their arrival. A decrepit shack, with one fairly large room with a stove, a bedroom opening off it on the left side for madame, and another smaller one for the children, and, similarly on the right, two other rooms which were pent against what had been the original structure. The troops did not mind. It was just what they wanted—a place where they could sit down before the red bowl of the stove with unbuttoned tunics and legs stretched out, while they sipped small hot cups of coffee and exercised their French on madame and the old man, her father. Madame, about

B

forty, with the vigorous frame of a labourer, commencing, at last, in spite of work in the fields, to run to fat, and the old man, thin and long, half dotty with senility. Madame, working off her few words of English, her broad, grinning face with cunning, covetous peasant eyes, quick to sparkle at the interchange of bawdy humour; the old man blinking and uttering never a word in reply.

Madame's niece had come to help her, a girl of about seventeen, with big firm body, and fresh stolid countenance. But, usually, when the men came, madame had sent her off to bed in the nearest of the small lean-to rooms. The niece was named Germaine.

CHAPTER XVI.

BECAUSE Desvres was forbidden without a pass, Artie Fethers had a strong inclination to go there. Why should the officers go there when they liked and not he? Besides, on the first time, when legitimately he went, he had found something to entice him back. He had decided to buy a watch. Continuing down the main road, he had turned, after some preliminary exploration, into the cobbles of a narrow side street, and there found a jeweller's shop. His knocking had brought out, not the jeweller, but the jeweller's daughter, a pretty sort of girl, well dressed, of the more comfortable class of a provincial town. What remained of the French he had learned at Geelong Grammar School had immediately become appallingly inadequate. Still, he had done his best, and believed the coquettish glances of the girl were sufficient warrant for another visit. But this time his knocking had brought out only the jeweller, and, to add to his chagrin, he had been pounced on by two M.P.'s and his name and number taken. By good luck his pay book had been handed in, and they did not see that. They had let him go, but the next day he was placed under open arrest and warned for the company orderly room the day following. The platoon felt that they could not trust the case to their new captain, especially as Artie affirmed that that officer had reason to dislike him. They resented a decent coot like Artie being crimed. No one in the battalion could throw a bomb so far or so accurately as he. And they remembered what he had done at the machine gun nest in the first stunt a few weeks back, and averred that he would have been in the list for the issue of M.M.'s if their lieutenant had not gone and got knocked. Johnny Wright's professional advice was sought, but he could suggest only an alibi, supported by the allegation that someone must have wrongly given Artie's name.

The orderly room was a room in Captain Slade's billet in the farm next down the road. In addition to the O.C. there were Lieutenants Matthews, of No. 1 Platoon, and Skipton, and the orderly sergeant. Johnny Wright marched the whole platoon except Fred Rogan up outside. Each man in turn, Blue McIntosh first, went in and swore that on the night in question Lance-Corporal Fethers, now in custody, had been in the billet at 10.15 p.m. The prisoner's friend suggested that someone must have given Fether's name, and ridiculed the notion that one could swear to identity when the night had been so black. An unfortunate mistake.

Three children of the house exchanged impudences with the soldiers, and kept peeking in the door; the youngest, after some attempts, managing to get in unseen, and ensconce itself, finger in mouth, in a corner. Skipton could not tell whether it was a boy or girl. He ruffled its head and called it a little polisson.

Frank Jeffreys went in. He was there unwillingly, but he felt that he could not stand out and let the others bear any blame that might come.

"Swear him, at any rate," ordered Slade, his heavy, pallid face mottled with rage.

"I suppose you haven't come to back up the others, corporal?"

"I don't know, sir."

The corporal, forgetting his former shame at his impending perjury, returned the captain's gaze angrily.

"When did you last see Lance-Corporal Fethers?"

"About 12 o'clock to-day."

"Are you an N.C.O.? Say sir, damn you."

"Sir."

A growl came from Skipton.

"Well, he knows what I mean. He's impudent. I won't have any more of this farce. A pretty sort of company and a pretty platoon."

He glared at the corporal as he bit his penholder.

"Well, either the military police are liars or all your platoon are, Skipton."

"Perhaps there has been a mistake," suggested Jack Skipton.

"Mistake be damned. I'll dismiss the charge."

He looked around vindictively. But he was afraid really. He did not dare to isolate himself from his company, just after taking over, by provoking the hostility of a whole platoon.

The corporal saluted and beat it with his news to the others. They did not conceal their derisive delight when Artie Fethers, grinning broadly, came out to join them. The whole platoon followed Artie to the estaminet.

The next morning the company commenced an intensive program of company drill which lasted all that day, and so continued from then on, with the exception, during the afternoons, on four of the last five days, of Lewis gun, grenade and bombing practice at the range which had been set up.

CHAPTER XVII.

"THEY" were only going to give them a fortnight's rest instead of three weeks, the swine, and the divisional commander was going to review the brigade. The battalion was drawn up with the rest of the infantry, in columns of companies, on a slightly undulating plain to which the battalion had marched about eight or nine kilos. On the right were the artillery and on the left the engineers and a pioneer battalion. In front, a hundred yards, the massed bands were playing. The horse of one of the engineer officers was playing up for the amusement of the waiting troops. The officer's section called out sarcastic encouragements just loud enough to reach his red ears. "Ride him, Joker, ride him, boy."

The bands blared out with renewed vehemence as the divisional staff arrived at the gallop, the general in front like a jockey on a racehorse. The others, handicapped by weight, good living, bad riding, and less expensive mounts, trailed behind him in some confusion. The men were at attention. Soon the artillery were off. From the quick step of the bands, but more deeply and mightily from this mass of common fighting men, there arose in Corporal Jeffrey's breast a sort of exaltation. His throat for a minute constricted painfully and his eyes glinted. The Australians—the Australians. Ah, if the five divisions had been there, company on company. But they were scattered into different corps. They should all be one —one corps, one and indivisible in body as they were in spirit. Were the Tommies afraid of the new nations? Standing to attention, dreaming to drums and trumpets.

Now the company was moving to the right in fours. They reached the end of the paddock and left-wheeled, and then, when they reached the marker, left-turned and formed two deep. Forward. The line was pretty straggled, for the ground was uneven. Coming up the rise they caught the full beat of the band. The corporal was at the end of the line furthest from the saluting flank. They were only thirty yards off, and would the centre never straighten up. His anxiety made him incredibly vicious towards the centre platoons. If he could have only implanted a spike in the backsides of the laggards. The line straightened. What relief! They were moving along together. What pride! What relief! Heads up, while the bands blared Tara—tara— They were the Aussies—the Diggers, the Diggers— tara—tara—the Diggers—the Diggers—tara—tara.

"Eyes right!"

They were there—they were past the Heads. The generals and brass-hats.

"Eyes front!"

They were the Diggers—the Aussies—the Diggers—tara—tara—. The battalion moved back to its position.

CHAPTER XVIII.

"ENTREZ, m'sieurs, entrez, entrez."

"Merci, madame."

The four soldiers entered.

"Fermez la porte, Phillipe, et va coucher—"

"Asseyez vous, m'sieurs."

"Merci, madame, il fait froid ce soir," said Johnny.

"Oui, oui, tres froid. Ah, merci, messieurs, le pudding ploom. I know heem, eh, tres bon—et le bullee bif, heem aussi." Madame placed her hands on her stomach and rolled her eyes.

"Regardez la, Germaine."

The young girl regarded the viands with a smile of some anticipated pleasure also, for there was little variation in the menu at the farm. Her youth made her attractive, and her face was almost beautiful in the soft light cast upwards from the bowl of the stove, so warmly that the light of the lamp, which hung from a black beam in the ceiling, seemed to be shadow, to be like a moon above the setting sun.

"Oo la, la, du vin, du champagne." Madame raised adoring eyes to the bottle Charl held aloft. She launched a Rabelaisain wink at the corporal and Jim Blount. "Tres bon pour les soldats, hein, du vin et les mademoiselles."

"Couches, Phillipe, cochon, couches," she launched a blow at the head of her eldest, an awkward boy of sixteen who had lingered, entranced by the vision of victuals. He side-stepped adeptly and disappeared through madame's room into his own den, where his brother, Pierre, and his little sister of five were already asleep.

"Partons demain, madame," said Jim Blount, taking off his scarf and opening his tunic, for the room was heavy with heat.

"Ah, m'sieur, non, non."

"Too true."

She wrung her hands. "La guerre, c'est pas bon—bloody bon. C'est toujours la meme chose—toujours. Vous venez, vous partez et vous ne retournerez jamais."

"No bloody bon, you're right, madame," agreed Charl.

"Pauvre enfant," she nodded at Charl to the others.

"Sanfairean, madame."

Soon Charl had edged his knees further across to press against that of Germaine. She did not move, and he pressed harder. His face was tremendously hot, and he found it difficult to pay attention to the conversation. He made a pretence of sipping his coffee —coffee made most of it out of dried beetroot.

"Ah, O!" cried madame all of a sudden.

Charl was too late in withdrawing his knee.

"Regardez, regardez."

The others roared with laugher. Only Germaine herself did not smile, but continued knitting stolidly.

They opened the champagne then, and all of them laughed when old grandpa, who sat as usual in a dark corner clamping his toothless jaws vacuously, shambled up for his issue. Jim Blount was waiting for Germaine to raise her eyes again. When she did, she looked into his own burning, lingering ones.

"Bonne chance," was their toast. "Bonne chance."

Jim Blount's eyes travelled thoughtfully, every now and then, over Germaine. They spun the wine out, and then madame produced some cognac to flavour the final cup of coffee. At last the time came to go. Charl was loath, but felt it was no use, just waiting—waiting for nothing. They shook hands and cried out their adieus.

Outside under the dark trees the four men drew the thin pale mist into their hot lungs with deep breaths. They had not gone fifty yards when Jim stopped.

"Take Johnny along with you, Frank," he said imperatively, and whispered to Charl, "Come with me, Charley."

Charl turned back with him, trembling with a sort of excitement, though he had no idea what was in the other's mind. When they entered the yard again, Jim slipped to the window. Madame was alone, still sitting sprawled in her big chair before the dull red glow of the stove. A faint light came through the half-open door of the girl's crib. Screened by the night, he stood there a few minutes peering in, and then, with a cynical flicker of his mouth's corner, made up his mind and went back to Charl.

He pointed across the yard to the big barn half full of oats for winter feed, and said to Charl, "Go in there and wait, Charl."

"What's doing, Jim?" the boy whispered.

"Go in there and you'll find out."

He saw Charl disappear into the barn, and went and gently opened the door. The woman stood up.

"Qu'est ce que vous avez oublié?"

He smiled.

"L'amour peutetre, madame. J'ai mene le jeune—Il vous attend dans le grand grenier."

"Et vous?"

He shrugged his shoulders, watching her. He saw her hesitate a few moments before her breath quickened, and she looked at him, her eyes glowing like coals, and her body seeming to swell with cupidity, the cupidity of her flesh. Softly she went out, and he watched her into the barn. He waited a few minutes. There was no sound, and he shut the door and turned his eyes to the girl Germaine's room. She must have heard him already, and heard all that passed. He slipped across and pushed the door of the little, low, candle-lit chamber wide open. Germaine was seated on the blankets of the dilapidated iron bed. She had taken off her dress, and now, clad in a grey flannel-shirt and dirty black petticoat, had paused in the act of pulling off her other stocking. Her eyes hung on his heavily and she made no sound—neither sound nor movement—when he shut the door softly on the two of them.

PALPITATIONS UP THE LINE

CHAPTER XIX.

THE farm of La Platte was in the front line between Wytschaete and Messines, not quite between, for the Messines ridge had been captured early in the year and La Platte was on the downward slope, about at its bottom, where the country flattened down to the river Lys, almost submerged in its mud. A few miles north, and the line began to curve outward into the Ypres Salient, and south it meandered five or six miles through La Basseville and across the front of Armentieres. About three miles from the craters which had engulfed Messines, a little south of east, Warneton lay on the bend of the river, a legendary place, for did not it possess a concrete tower off which 9.2 shells bounced like Mills bombs. The tower often engaged the thoughts of the occupants of La Platte, who believed it contained eyes perpetually spying upon them like the eyes of God. La Platte had once been a substantial place, a big house and three or four dependent dwellings, barns and stables, etc., strung together. It now consisted of scattered debris, broken brick, powdered mortar, bits of slate and iron, shattered beams and spars. Now, also, it seemed that even this debris was being absorbed slowly into the uniformity of the earth's desolation. La Platte was cunningly approached by a well-tended, deep, communication trench, and sundry secret ways. The trench crossed the Messines ridge at right angles to the road, which had once upon a time run from Ypres to Armentieres, that is, at right angles to something which was invisible because it had ceased to exist. The Wytschaete-Messines ridge was an off-shoot of that main string of Flanders hills which included Kemmel, and at the other end of which was the Mont des Cats. This offshoot terminated at Ploeg-stoert (Plug Street) Wood, and was, otherwise, remark-able, because it contained in its bowels the long-tun-nelled shelters known as the Catacombs.

"Ikey," demanded Charl Bentley, apropos of noth-ing, "Do you remember that chap, the officer, I pointed out to you on the way up?"

"What officer?" asked Ikey.

"The one sitting down by the road in the — Division."

"Well, what's biting you? The chap who looked as if he'd been on the bust?"

"Yes. That was Lal Wilton."

Ikey said nothing. What Charl Bentley had on his mind had no relevance to him and he dismissed it, and Charl was left to ponder it by himself. He had had a shock. The sight of Lal Wilton there like that, beaten, exhausted, haggard with too much drinking, afraid, had seemed all wrong. It had occurred on the second day of their route march, when they had passed out of the country of white barns and green valleys to a harsher scene, where the very air seemed to have become darker, and the houses, instead of standing back, were naked and hard up against the ditches which bounded the cobbles. They had halted for five minutes stand easy alongside another battalion which was squatting for a spell along the other side of the road. Lal Wilton, the great man of the school, to be seen like that! It seemed, somehow, unnatural to Charl. He was glad he had repressed the impulse to call a greet-ing. Nevertheless, with first instinctive loyalty, the

aura of schoolboy glory floating around Charl's mental picture of his hero strove to attach itself to that
emaciated figure with the pale face, the staring eyes,
and sagging mouth. It was so impossible that the very
attempt made the man appear more pitiable. Perhaps,
like Corporal Jeffreys, he had been blown up some time
or another.

His gaze, seeking to pierce the night, caught the
smudge of the first of the wire about ten yards in front,
black against the thin, whitish blotches of the last snow.
All out there was No Man's Land, and beyond it was
Fritz. The boy shivered in his sheep's skin jacket,
which he wore like the others contrary to regulations,
but in conformity with good sense, the hide outside and
the wool inside. The wool, if you wore the jacket the
regulation way, became heavy with dags of stinking
mud. Ikey Harris was fiddling with the tape over his
shoulders, which joined his gloves together.

"They waste this tape by making it six inches too
long," he said.

The platoon was holding three posts on the right of
La Platte, with which it was by this time well acquainted. The centre post, No. 1, was in a cellar, which was
covered overhead by a tangled mass of ceiling which
had fallen on the big joists of the floor. It was protected immediately in front by a mass of rubble and
other debris which had been heaped up five feet high
where the wall had once stood. This was Lieutenant
Skipton's headquarters, who had with him there Sergeant Burke, Llew Jones, Johnny Wright and Dingo
Williams. Dingo, as usual, combined the duties of the
officer's batman and platoon runner.

About two chains away, in the open, was the second

post in charge of Corporal Jeffreys. This consisted of two large shell holes which had been cleaned out and improved and connected by a shallow passage six or seven yards along. The improvements were some holes about two feet deep under the bank, which had been strengthened by sandbags and an uneven fire step tramped into the earth. In the first of these holes were Fred Rogan, Jack Costello, Merv Hill and Pete Hansen, and in the other, beyond which some fifty yards was the flank post of the next brigade, were Frank Jeffreys, Jim Blount, Charl Bentley and Ted Marshall. In the daytime No. 2 post would be vacant. Just at daybreak its garrison would slink back one by one to the cellar, in which a slight amount of additional room for them was made by the departure of Mr. Skipton and Dingo Williams to company-headquarters in a deep dug-out further on. The inhabitants of No. 3 post, however, Artie Fethers, McIntosh, Flynn, Barton, and Wilberforce, with the Lewis gun, lived like troglodytes day and night in their hole. It was just a hole that somehow had got formed in a bank of debris during a bombardment. It was barely large enough to hold them. It was really like a cave, the interior of which sloped slightly downwards from the entrance. The entrance, itself, was set half way up the bank, but even this little height was sufficient to permit the Lewis gunners to command an excellent field of fire towards the German lines. No one looking from there would be likely to imagine the existence of the chamber beyond this entrance, even should he pick the entrance out for any special attention, unless he should notice a movement, or some other sign of life. The place was desolate by day; there, as everywhere, nothing moved about the line—only at night was there life—and death.   And life, too, in this shallow cavern presented, therefore, a problem quite unique, which may be guessed. A bully beef tin was a very small and inadequate receptacle for the purpose, and, besides, there was always the chance that some concealed watcher or sniper out yonder might note an increasing semi-circle of tins. The earnest request that the other two posts should save up any tins had received a malicious, mocking refusal. It had, therefore, been a happy thought of Blue's to souvenir that old saucepan. It had a handle, too.

A sort of dull pop and then another.   Some time each night this popping would start, the first somewhere in front on the right, and the second somewhere in front on the left, for usually they were in pairs. It was hard, though the inhabitants of No. 2 Post became quite expert at it, to watch the two sparks in the air, one first describing the apex of its parabola, and then the other, but both falling towards somewhere about the same spot on the map. Bang, bang; the heavy detonation of the minnies; minenwerfer, name of a special kind of trench mortar now usually applied by the platoon indiscriminately to all.   The men in No. 2 Post were tense, like runners at the start, for the simple reason that they expected to run, to run for a prize, which was life. Out on the right somewhere, the first two went, so there was no start. After awhile, pop, pop. And then again, pop, pop. This time, those in the corporal's bay, started for the other, and those in the other, ran out on top and ducked into shell holes. ''Christ, you're standin' on me hand!'' ''Let me go———you.'' The explosion took place about ten yards to the side of the further bay. A false start. Back to the starting place again.

Rat-tat-tat, and a machine gun splattered around La Platte. Somewhere a mile away some 60 pounders were firing at Fritz's supports. The moon came out and two rats fought for a moment in silhouette upon it, like black, moving pictures on a white circular screen. The men in No. 3 Post, looking across to the river, which was caught up out of its muddy obscurity by the moon like a silver snake, were trying to pick out where Fritz could have those submerged bridges they reckoned he must have to link his front line to the shelters in Warneton.

There were no more minnies coming over to disturb the night. The hour before dawn. It was now they were supposed to stand to, but they did not observe this formality because they knew that any attack would be preceded by artillery fire, and a silent raid could not be made just then. And yet their senses quickened, though not according to orders, but by the eternal mystery which hangs upon the dawn of another day; yes, even so, though perhaps more by the desire to vacate that place of suspense for sleep and rest in the cellar.

"The Tommies told us this was a quiet sector, but it's lively enough now, what with the Stokes chucking their muck and running, and leaving us to collect the crabs."

"And that raid of the Mth."

"And this bloody idea of educating Fritz that there's to be no more two-way traffic in No Man's Land."

"And the 18-pounders stirring up the bloody minnies."

"I reckon it's about time, corp."

"Another ten minutes." He knew that once he started letting themselves off at their own call, they would be slipping off earlier and earlier each morning.

In five minutes, he said, "Right." They slunk off two by two, bending down low and taking advantage of the cover, for the light was now growing quickly. Though it was still reasonably dark, the beginning of the dawn made them windy.

In the cellar, each went to his own position, and soon all were wrapped in their blankets, comforters round their heads, sometimes two sleeping together, for it was damned cold. Only the sentry, Llew Jones, was on top, concealed in a little alcove in the trench, which ran out about a dozen yards further on. It was 2 o'clock by the time most of them were awake again. Some still lay in their blankets. Others, with their puttees off and their boots undone, busied themselves at a dry toilet, cleaning rifles, half melting cubes of soup on Tommy cookers, chewing a remnant of bread while they yarned and wondered whether the hot ration due about 7 o'clock would be stinking with petrol like the last, enough to set the breath alight, because the new tins hadn't been properly cleaned out by the babblers.

Sergeant Burke produced a parcel which he had concealed until they had had their sleep out, and two letters —one for Merv Hill and the other for Corporal Jeffreys.

The parcel contained Comforts Fund stuff, said the sergeant, and slit it open with a bayonet. Socks, knitted socks, from Aussie. The sergeant tossed them a pair apiece and kept the three over for himself. The chaps in No. 3 Post would be unlucky. Socks were as useful as anything they could imagine.

It was old Pete Hansen who made the first discovery. "My oath!" He bent over the paper flattened on his knee, and read slowly, "Dear soldier boy," "What she say, eh Charl?'' ''Dear soldier boy. I hope you well and will soon be back.'' ''What she say now, Charley?'' ''A big kiss from Minnie Martin. Sale.''

''Minnie! Christ, what a name! We've had enough of minnies.''

''Mine's from Sale, too.''

''Sale, who comes from Sale? You told me you did, Hilly.''

Hilly was only too anxious to appear in the role of a provincial Don Juan.

''Aw, Mary Clements, she's pretty—pretty hot, too. Her old man keeps a boot shop.''

''She'll do me, then,'' cried Ted Marshall, ''Damn me if I don't drop her a brief.''

''What about this,'' demanded Dingo. '''Dear Mr. ———, I hope you'll find the socks comfortable and the right size, and that you'll soon be back with us after fighting so bravely. Constantia Gilbert.' ''

''Haw, haw, Constantia, some la de da.''

''Constantia! Cripes!''

''She lived in the next street. She's a pretty old tart. Sang in the Methodist choir.''

''———her, then. Old! She don't get no letter from me, then,'' said Dingo.

''Here listen t'this. 'Dear digger, here's a pair of socks. May they keep your feet as warm as my heart. Miriam Schwartz.' ''

''Gawd struth, she's a yid. You'll have to write to her, Ikey.''

''Go on, give it to Ikey.''

''Chuck it here, then,'' demanded Ikey. He would, too, he thought. That was a damned good note.

He whispered to Hill, ''What is her father? Eh!''

"Fish and chips."

The chatter went on. Frank Jeffreys paid no heed to it. He wanted deliberately to take his time to taste to the full the delight of having her letter there in his hand—paper her fingers had touched. He sat hunched up in a corner alongside the big dud, which stuck out of the floor. On this side the cellar was half caved in, and squatting there, he could touch the roof with his hand just above his head. Next to him, Jim Blount was reading as usual one of his two legacies from Horrie Calverley—The Renaissance by a man named Pater. Frank turned secretly to his letter.

Dear Mr. Jeffreys.—You should not be ashamed of what you wrote to me. You must have suffered awfully. If it has done you good to tell me I am glad. I am glad for my own sake, too. Your letter gave me a chance to feel what so many others are feeling who have brothers in the Army. One longs and longs to know what one can do to help the men out there in France. I know I do, and I was glad when I got your letter. It is something to know things might have been worse. I looked back in the papers to see if there had been any battle just before you wrote, but there did not seem to have been anything important. Some day you might tell me about it."

He let the letter fall from his eyes. Yes, he'd tell her. He'd like to tell the world the liars the heads were. He read on: "I have not seen my cousin recently. Indeed, I don't see them very often. I don't go out much, and am really quite a stay-at-home. We are not busy at the office, either. There is no news here. What does it matter what happens here? All we think of is news from France. That's one reason why I'm glad you wrote to me, and I will look forward to hearing from you again if you should find the time to write. In the meantime, believe me,

> Yours sincerely,
> > Mary Hatton.

A swift, tearing sound in the air just above, and a detonation somewhere behind. Like a full stop. Another. Whizz-bangs. Another and another in quick succession. Fritz for the last few days seemed to be sending them over just above where they were. What a lot of ammunition was wasted!

CHAPTER XX.

THIS time it was the battalion's turn to go into reserve. The routine was reserve, supports, line, reserve, and so on, and this had been repeated twice. It was the third time they went to the little village of X, where they inhabited some rows of rather dilapidated malthoid huts. The village comprised a straggling line of houses, with three or four shops of sorts, and an estaminet on the main corner, and a few houses close to the main road on the side streets. All were of a dark, worn, red brick. The small windows of the shops, hardly distinguishable from the ordinary dwellings, contained nothing, except in one case some postcard souvenirs of Joffre and French, and some awful green and yellow scarves and handkerchiefs, on which were gaudily painted pictures of Ypres in flames. The houses and the shops alike had to be entered from the road by culverts or little narrow, wooden bridges over the ditches, which bordered it on each side.

In supports, as well as the ordinary trench fatigues and working parties, there had been for each platoon in turn the job of carrying the hot rations up to the line each evening. Now in reserve, they were free of that, and the working parties did not usually go so far forward.

The very day after they entered into occupation of the huts, there was a working party. The whole company was marched some kilos to a siding on the railway and set to unloading trucks of coal into a fleet of motor lorries.   They resented this labour, not only because soon their uniforms were covered with black dust along which the rain trickled streakily, but because they felt its unfairness.   They grumbled loudly.   It was more than an indignity; it was an insult put upon them, according to their conjectures, by the machinations of Tommy brass-hats.   They were first-class troops, storm troops, and they guessed the Tommies did not give their own first-class troops such menial fatigues as that. Labour battalions' work.   The grumbling was intentionally made loud enough for the supply officers to hear it, and there was talk of a protest.   That night the company sergeant-major mentioned to the captain that the men were feeling sore.   Shells they would not mind handling, but they were swearing that they were not going to lump any more coal.

Jim Blount put in most of the following morning, cleaning as well as he could the coal black off his uniform, for he was by nature a tidy man.   And then, because there was little to do in that miserable village but spend the time in the estaminet, he set off to walk out of it—anywhere.   After he had tramped along the road awhile, he swung himself up behind on a passing motor lorry, which carried him to the outskirts of a larger

village, where it pulled up at some ordnance stores.
This place was different to the other villages in that network. The trees were tall along the side of the road, and
the buildings were large, a few of them of two storeys.
They were built of the predominant dark brick, all except one which, larger than the others, he could see up
the hill from the main crossroads was brighter in colour,
a light, red brick against the pregnant belly of the grey
sky. This was the convent of Neuve Eglise, large enough
to hold a battalion. It, like most of the other buildings,
had suffered slightly from shell fire some time or
another, but it was still quite habitable even on the
upper floor.

The first thing he did was to seek out an eggs and
chips joint, which he discovered in a house in a street off
the main road, where two girls, still fairly young, were
making money hand over fist while the sun of the war
kept shining. They had a sharp, merry repartee, and
they needed it, not only to counter the jocosity of their
patrons, but the whispers that hissed up slyly to them
as they planked down the dishes. Did they ever succumb
to any of those chance whispers, Jim wondered, as he
settled down to his four fried, or were they couchéing
with some steady lover, or were they, after all, as perhaps they might be, good girls. He did not try to find
out, not that the girls weren't good-looking and well
enough made, but he was instinctively too fastidious to
join the mob of those who, as soon as they came into
the yellow-papered room, spent their time either openly
or secretly eyeing the girls off, and, in the end, ventur-
ing those ridiculous whispers.

When he went out to go down to the village again a
light layer of snow covered everything. It was still

snowing. Now he saw the place again, saw it actually as it really was, the blue, grey mistiness of the trees through the flecked air, the walls of the houses and other buildings sombre and almost black under the whitening roofs, the black marks of the traffic of waggons and horses and lorries in the thin snow, the heavy, downward sweep of the grey sky. He wondered why there was all that space on the right, and why all the village itself was collected on the other side of the road. His eyes followed the curve of the road round by the Brasserie, where a sentry stood guard at some battalion headquarters. The road continued past the few shops and the sparse trees beyond where the ground fell away to a lower level, and on the other side lay the open space where the troops sometimes played football, now covered with a litter of bluish-white smudged here and there by the dark shadow of some old shell hole.

Last time he had been here it had been with Horace Calverley when they had come up north out of the Somme. He looked back over the old life before he had known him—before the war. An adventurer in the world at fourteen, station lad in the west, tram conductor, runner of ponies, picking up a bit where he could and careful of it. The coup they had made at Warwick Farm after he had settled in Sydney for awhile with Bully Squires and Morry Abrahams. It wouldn't bear looking into. He had pulled out of it then feeling a bit dirty, but he had over four thousand pounds. He could wash his hands afterwards. He had always had that idea, and he had bought the McManus' stud place near Kyneton when McManus went broke, and early in 1915 he had enlisted. He had put his brother, who was married

and had four kids, into the place, and the occasional letter from home told him things were going all right. Then
Horace Calverley had joined them with some early reinforcements.

The spirit of the dead man was never far away from him,
and now it seemed to be walking there alongside saying,
as it had so often said in the flesh after that first time
he remembered so well when they were marching to
Fleurbaix, "Open your eyes, you poor, blind bastard,
and see the colour of the world."

He stopped at one of the small shop windows, in
which some debris of foodstuffs and a few wrinkled
apples were displayed, and saw, exotically among the
litter, a small box of preserved figs. He went inside
and bought half a pound from the quiet, plumpish Flam-
ande, who came in answer to his sharp rapping on the
counter. Continuing on his way, he came to a low,
brick building which had suffered more than the other
places in the village, and was now patched up as a
Y.M.C.A. It had been, perhaps, a pottery, but he could
not say for certain even when he went inside the long,
main chamber with its earthen floor, so completely had
it been gutted and its appearance so changed that only
a former acquaintance might know it for what it was.

He sat down to rest on one of the wooden forms with
which the place was furnished, and smoked his pipe
almost out before his attention lit upon a packing case
of illustrated papers half under a trestle table. His
gaze passed naturally from this case to another, from
which one board had been prised half off. He was not
sufficiently interested to disturb the last, sweet draws
of his pipe, but when he got up to go out, he went across

idly, and pulling aside the broken board, saw that the case was half full of books.

His interest flared into excitement; so much had Horace Calverley done for him. To Horace, he knew, this would have been an adventure, and so now it became to him in a more modest degree. This odd collection of old books had been gathered in England from the offerings which had been made in response to some appeal to patriots to provide reading for the troops. He set aside Hereward the Wake, and one volume of Macaulay's History, and Dr. Barrow's Sermons, and another which made him chuckle, Little Women, and came upon a volume of Byron's poems in the Everyman's Library edition. He set this on the table, and, rummaging around, found five others of the same sort, which he placed there beside the first, glancing at the titles as he laid them down evenly and tidily. He had out of this lot to make exactly the right choice, for choice was demanded by the obvious limitation that the small space of a pack already stuffed with oddments of clothes, etc., imposed, especially when that pack contained two books already. Choice, also, was necessary, or rather the discrimination which must be applied to it, because this had become as much the adventure of the spirit of Horace Calverley as his own. He was as it were put upon his mettle. Two only could he allow himself. Which? Byron's poems, Vol. III, Demosthenes' Select Orations, Voyage of the Beagle by Darwin, Past and Present of Carlyle, Peveril of the Peak by Sir Walter Scott, and Cellini's Autobiography. He deliberated, turning over pages a quarter of an hour before deciding on the first and the last, the Byron and the Autobiography. Perhaps when he next got a chance to come to Neuve Eglise, he might be able to get two more. He put the others at the bottom of the case, and pushed it with his foot under some refuse in a corner.

"What do you want for these?" he asked the fellow at the counter.

"A franc apiece, dig."

Jim looked at him, "I suppose that's two francs profit for someone, or perhaps, one for the Y. Emma and one for you. I'll give you a franc for the two."

He put down the note and, careless whether the Young Christian wanted to argue or not, stalked out with the two books. He squeezed one into each side pocket of his tunic and started off home to his village.

When he entered the hut again, he nearly tripped over a couple of packs with rolled blankets over their tops, and a tangle of Webb equipment. Fatty Gray and Harry Mullane, recovered from their very slight wounds, had come in only ten minutes before him.

"A cove," complained Fatty," ought to have got to Blighty out of that while he was about it."

The door banged again, this time after Blue McIntosh, lit up from the estaminet. He made a kick at the heap.

"Cripes," he exclaimed, looking Fatty up and down, "the little malingerer's fatter than ever. I believe he's come back in the family way."

Jim went across to Harry Mullane, who was warming his hands over the brazier. "Hullo, Harry."

"Why, hullo, Jim."

They shook hands and grinned at each other.

Bang went the door again. This time it was the sergeant, messenger of ill omen. "Corporal Jeffreys in?"

Frank stood up.

"Platoon's to fall in at 10.0, corporal—fatigue dress and rifles."

"What the ——— hell!"

"Garn, yer kiddin', serj."

"What, another working party, sergeant?"

He grinned at their consternation.

"My oath."

"Well, why the hell weren't we warned this afternoon?" demanded Llew Jones, hotly.

"Not my fault, d'yer think?"

The sergeant barged out.

"That's the bastard Slade again."

"Gawd damn him."

A few minutes later the corporal caught sight of Syd Barton quietly turning the door. "You'd better be back at 10.0," he warned him. He knew what Barton's excuse would be, that he was not told there was to be a working party.

Barton turned around viciously, "What the bloody blazes has it got to do with you?"

"I'm just telling you."

Frank tried to quell the sudden spasm of anger which shook him, but knew only too well how the shrillness of his voice betrayed his weakness.

"You, —— you, you bastard!"

Frank's face was white and twitching. "I'm just telling you, that's all."

Barton tried to cover himself by an impudent, jeering laugh as he came back into the hut. Letting it pass, Frank went out to seek Artie Fethers and Pete Hansen at the estaminet. His nerves, his nerves, his nerves, they were all in pieces, he thought. Damn that fellow,

Barton, damn him. Why had he let him speak to him
like that? If he could only get away for a time. He
was ill, just as ill as if he had been wounded. The
cur knew he wouldn't crime him—the foul-mouthed
blackguard, damn him. He must find the other two
now or there would be trouble. That's what Slade was
expecting, that there would be some missing. He'd have
to find them. What a relief it was to discover them
large as life in a steamy, smoky room, and not quite
drunk yet! They played cruelly upon his too evident
anxiety by making believe that they would not go. He
was, as Artie Fethers said, like an old wet hen. He
tried to cajole them when he felt like screaming. At
last they condescended to go outside with him. And
now a fresh anxiety was riding him that some of the
others in the hut might, out of resentment of the captain's unfairness, have gone off somewhere with a "Be
damned to him." Yes, they were all there, even Barton. When he got into the hut he counted them over
furtively from time to time as he lay propped up on his
elbow on his pile of blankets.

The platoon had a rotten night of it carrying cupola
iron to the new dug-outs at the back of the line. Each
man had a sheet. It was heavy and nearly broke the
hearts of the weaker. It was so awkward and its curve,
unless you carried it inverted on your head, prevented
you seeing more than two steps ahead, so that when
there was a gap in the duckboard or an end of one
was loose, you usually slipped into the pit of the trench,
which was half full of icy water. Sometimes the end of the
duckboard sprang up or shot down under you, and
the result in each event was that you fell down with
the weight of the iron on top of you or pinning you

to the side of the trench. The damned iron, too, stuck at the corners, and when the man ahead stopped, your own sheet clanged against his with a jar which shook your whole body. Progress became a series of wrestles and tussles with the brutes. One piece of luck they had to be thankful for. Fritz was not sending anything over on the communication trench. Probably he was reserving himself until the time the ration parties would be going up.

Like all things, the fatigue came to an end, and early in the morning Frank pitched under the blankets, his muscles in a state of uncontrollable tremor.

The next day he reported sick. He had the excuse that he was suffering what he thought might be an attack of dysentery. Barton, also, went sick. While they stood waiting for the quack in the little hut where he was quartered in a space at the back, curtained off by a couple of blankets, Barton grinned knowingly at the corporal, as if to say, "You are here just for the same reason as me."

"After all," thought Frank, "have I any reason to resent it?" He knew that he wildly hoped that something might be found really wrong with him. But when the sergeant dug the quack out of his bed, the latter said it was only a slight attack of diarrhoea, and ordered medicine and duty, while Barton was relieved of duties. The corporal turned his eyes away from the other's derision.

CHAPTER XXI.

BUT Barton did not escape the next turn in the line, either, and the two of them went up with the rest of the platoon into the old position at La Platte. The garrison of No. 1 Post was now increased by Barton and Harry Mullane, and Fatty went with the Lewis Gun to No. 3.   It was the custom in No. 1, because it had to provide sentries during the day time, to divide the hours of night into two reliefs. Barton and Harry now did the first five hours until 1 a.m., when they were relieved by Johnny Wright and Llew Jones, who went on until daybreak. Dingo Williams was not required to perform this duty, because he had to accompany either the officer or the sergeant, who took it in turns to visit the other two posts.

Leaning back against the wall of the trench, Johnny Wright looked up over the jagged edge of the debris to the fainting stars. A little further along, Llew Jones was seated immobile on the top of the trench. Just past him was the alcove of the new latrine, a great improvement on the old, which had been put in by some pioneers when the last company had been there. La Platte was unnaturally quiet. On the left a couple of machine guns were exchanging a few gibberings of hate, and there, too, Fritz was sending up an occasional light. Where the two men were they could see only the faint flush on the ruins about them, as each flare burst and fell. What a still night it was, not a breath in the air, and fairly clear for that time of the year! Johnny, however, drew his coat about him, for he had begun to feel the first light tendrils of the ground mist which was creeping up from the marshes along the river. It would trouble his rheumatics. He was, he felt, a damn fool at his age to be a soldier, and worse, to be in the infantry. It was time there was another mail. Little Bill had had a cold, and he was anxious to hear how the kid was. About two months ago. He might be better. He might be dead—like Fred Rogan's kid. No, little Billy wasn't the dying sort . From somewhere away behind them came a series of harsh thuds, which were followed in succession by smacking explosions out beyond in Fritz's territory. The sounds came sharply through the stillness.

"Why can't they leave us in peace," he was moved to complain to Llew, who shifted only his head to indicate he had heard.

The slight shelling seemed to have annoyed Fritz—not unreasonably on such a night, Johnny thought—and his machine guns opposite began to crackle. Llew got down into the trench, for when the crackling became more distinct, he had heard certain waspish whines overhead. Skipton came up out of cellar with Dingo at his heels.

"Quiet!" he said.

"It was quieter," said Johnny.

"I'm going round the posts."

He clambered out of the trench and gave his hand to his batman. "Upsadaisy!"

After a time they came back.

"Yesterday, when I got down, I nearly spiked myself on that chap Barton's bayonet," said the lieutenant; "I'm damned if I know who got the biggest shock, him or me. If things get lively, give me a call. I didn't get much sleep to-day. The captain wanted to play bridge all the time, and we didn't finish till we'd finished Mr. Johnson's whisky.''

"Right O.''

About an hour later, Johnny, after a short consultation with his mate, went to the entrance to the cellar, and called in a low, troubled voice, "Mr. Skipton."

Burke answered, "He's asleep."

"Wake him up. You'd better come up too, serg."

In a minute or two the lieutenant and the sergeant joined the two sentries in the trench.

"Things are getting pretty lively. I thought you'd better take a look," said Johnny, his voice shaking slightly, partly with nervous excitement and partly with the cold.

Skipton nodded. Things were decidedly livelier. Any awake in the cellar must have noticed it, but fatalistically would not shift till they had to. Fritz seemed to have got the wind up about something, for he was shooting up his flares fairly often, and quite a few of his machine guns were loose. Guns were barking, and the line working itself up into a ferment.

"It's the minnies," said Llew, breaking his taciturnity.

The eyes of all four caught the twinkle at the same time. Instinctively, they retreated a few paces to get into a position where they'd have a clear run. Bang. The detonation was terrific, and dust and fragments fell on them. It had fallen twenty yards in front of the heap of muck.

"That's the second there, sir. He's put half a dozen over there towards No. 2 Post."

"Bang, bang!" over on the right.

"My Gawd!" stammered Dingo, "that must a been near them."

"Bang, bang!"

"Christ, listen to that."

The lieutenant gathered himself together. "I'm going over, sergeant. Get the others out into the little trench at the back of the cellar. You two can stay here and slip round if necessary. Keep an eye on the end of the sap. He may be going to come across."

He went off with Dingo, who buckled himself up so low that the sergeant said, "He'll take the skin off his nose with his toes if he don't look out."

"Bang, bang!"

"Christ, listen to that."

They waited anxiously, almost three-quarters of an hour by Johnny's watch. There were no more explosions. Everything seemed to have become suddenly quieter. Fritz must have concluded that he had been agitating himself needlessly. A sound put the three men on the alert. They backed a few paces with their rifles half up.

"It's me."

The lieutenant and his dingbat slid down into the trench.

"What's up, sir?" asked the sergeant.

"They've blown in No. 2."

The next question did not find words.

"Three of them. Williams, go along to company headquarters and tell them to send three stretchers. I think that's the end for to-night," he said, as if out of an intense weariness.

"Not three of them?" cried Johnny, aghast.

"You go and have a look at the other post, sergeant.

F

Three of them—yes. Rogan, Costello and Pete Hansen. Came right on top of them before they could clear out. The others are in some holes out in front.''

"Three of them, and all three at once," the others muttered, their minds boggling at the thought of it.

Towards dawn, the survivors came in, quietly dropping into the trench and waiting there without any words for the others. It was glimmering light as the stretcher bearers came along. Fred Rogan came first. They held his legs to prevent him slipping off when the bearers tilted the stretcher as the first two got down into the trench. Then came Jack Costello, and then Pete Hansen.   How calm their faces were.   Only Pete's mouth and chin were stained darkly.   Heavy drops still dripped from Jack's stretcher.   They went past, and as they went, the soul of Johnny Wright was magnified in him.   Hail to thee, Fred Rogan, serene in Christ in death as in life.   Dost not thou see thy little child clapping her hands for joy.   Hail to thee, Jack Costello, old soldier and generous-hearted one, merry lifelover, borne up now in the quietude of death.   Hail to thee, Pete Hansen, Norwegian sea wanderer, bound not now to thy Antwerp, terrestrial paradise of sailors, but like a warrior of Odin to the halls of Valhalla.

CHAPTER XXII.

IN advanced supports half the platoon was in one dugout and half in another. They were not really dugouts, but only shelters supposed to be thick enough on the top to keep out a small shell. Because the trench was a deep one, the men could move about freely in the day time. They were disturbed very little. One day, Fritz decided that the latrine, which was connected with the main trench by a narrow sap, was a machine gun post. A salvo of whizz-bangs caught Ikey Harris in medias res. He shot out of his rumination with a terrified yelp, and, though hobbled by his pants, he beat it down the sap in time which was truly remarkable. However, because it was quite a good latrine, they continued to use it rather than put themselves to the labour of constructing a new one. Fritz might shell that, too, and one could not spend one's time making latrines. Fritz's mistake was, after all, quite a natural one, and was not without precedent in the memory of the old hands. All the same, Nature's business was henceforth conducted with a despatch entirely antipathetic to its proper aesthetics. When one went there one was far too anxious. But forewarned was forelegged and, though two or three others were actually interrupted, their successful flight was even more rapid than Ike's had been, for they took the precaution of keeping a firm hold on the tops of their breeches.

Living in these shelters, the troops had not very far beneath their consciousness the hope that Fritz would drop nothing on top of them heavier than a small howitzer shell. There was always a doubt whether the roof would withstand that, let alone one of heavier calibre. Inside were wooden bunks in two tiers. The lower ones were preferred on account of the doubts about the shell-resisting qualities of the roof, though those in the top ones always declared you got more chats in the lower.

Food for some reason had become extremely light. But when Wilberforce and Mick Flynn, the mess orderlies, came in one afternoon with only five tins of pork and beans, two of Maconochies and two loaves; God, there was room, the platoon felt, for another miracle.

Frank put the small loaf for his dug-out on a blanket, and cut it as nearly as possible into nine pieces. It required all the care he could exercise to make the division as precisely equal as would satisfy the others who, standing or squatting hungrily around, offered suggestions with profound seriousness as his jack-knife hovered.

"That's as near as I can make it," he announced.

"By gum," ejaculated Blue, as Frank handed the little, rectangular pieces to them, "It's like being at 'oly communion."

There were still three hours before they were due for the night's fatigue, of which they had been warned. What it was to be they did not know yet, and therefore, didn't worry about it. It had been snowing again, but it was warm in their confined quarters, and they had plenty of blankets. It was not only the blankets themselves which kept them warm, but the carnivorous inhabitants that kept the troops constantly at the scratch.

In his bottom bunk near the door, with a candle stuck in its grease on the edge, Jim Blount was reading Don Juan.

Charl Bentley poked his head over the bunk above with, "What are you cackling about, Jim?"

"Did you ever teach your kids Byron in school, Frank?"

The corporal had a recollection of "Roll on thou deep and dark-blue ocean, roll"; what was the next line, something, and then—
"Man marks the earth with ruin, his control
Stops at the shore."

What came after that.   Surely he couldn't have forgotten?

Charl, too, remembered something, "I see before me the gladiator die." Nothing more. He had an idea that that was by Byron. How far away it all seemed. He remembered old Mugger booming it out. Old Mugger used to like to hear his voice declaiming. The chaps used to kid him on and doze peacefully once he was set going.

"Well, I reckon none of you read Don Juan. I'll read you some now so you can't say your education was neglected in the army.

> "The sun set and up rose the yellow moon.
> The devil's in the moon for mischief: they
> Who called her chaste, methinks began too soon
> Their nomenclature; there is not a day
> The longest, not the twenty-first of June,
> Sees half the business in a wicked way
> On which three single hours of moonshine smile—
> And then she looks so modest all the while."

After a few stanzas, those who had drawn up out of curiosity came closer, and settled themselves comfortably. They had reached the 199th, when the sergeant interrupted.

"Fall in in half an hour," he said, "we're going to carry some duckboards cross country up to the line."

Artie Fethers, who had come in at his heels, gasped, "What about the moon?"

They went out into the trench. The yellow moon was up full and big, with only a few wisps of cloud about, too slight even to dim it, and the snow, as the sergeant saw when he climbed up to look at the effect on the landscape, was chill and blank and clearer than the day with a bluish and yellowish whiteness.

"They're mad, sergeant," said Frank Jeffreys.

"Of course they are, they're bloody lunatics."

"They've forgotten about the moon and the snow, the bastards."

"It means nothing to them, the bloody swine."

"It's stinkin' murder."

Harry Mullane touched Jim on the shoulder and chuckled.

"The sun was set, and up rose the yellow moon;
    The devil's in the moon for mischief!"

"I'll go an' see Mr. Skipton," Burke undertook. When their officer arrived, they put it to him bluntly.

"Well, what about it, sir. Fritz'll see us for miles."

"Fair dinkum, sir, it's murder," and so on, and so on.

Skipton, at the sight of that moon, had been no less perturbed than they. It was a hundred to one they'd be slaughtered if they went over the open at the line on a night like this. He went off to see his company commander. Skipton told Slade if he didn't go to the colonel he'd go himself. Ultimately, the colonel rang brigade about it. "It's no good," he said, "they want the duckboards there. I don't know why. Perhaps they don't themselves. I suppose they think you've got the wind up for nothing. I felt like suggesting that the G.S.O. come along and lead the party."

"It's no good, she's on," said Skipton, phlegmatically, when he got back.

"Well, —— 'em."

It was no use crying about it. Their men climbed into their gum boots, hitched on their skeleton equipment over their sheepskins, and lifted their rifles down off the nails, where they were suspended. They had to wait now for an engineer subaltern, who arrived twenty minutes late. He came along at last, apologising to Skipton, who grunted. The men shuffled out into the trench.

"It's a fine night for it," commented the infantry officer ironically.

"Too damn fine, by far. It's quite got the wind up me."

"Me, too."

"Quite."

Off they went along the communication trench called Mug's Alley, the engineer leading with his two attendant sappers. There must have been some shelling along it last night after the ration party had passed. In three or four spots the A frames and wire revetting had been blown out. The engineer officer who led was, of course, the first to discover the damage. Tramping along moodily under a waterproof cape which he wore for no apparent reason, the night being so clear, but because, perhaps, it made his shadow so melodramatically swashbucklerish, he was thinking of many things in addition to his shadow, and now, in particular, was attempting a mental reconstruction more satisfactory than the event had been of his brush with that rotten beast Rodwell. Rodwell was screwed, of course, but you could tell best when a man was drunk whether he was a gentleman or not. When his foot plunged down off the broken duckboard, the other followed, so that he was altogether removed to another and lower plane. "Damn," he gasped, when his bottom jarred, and then as the water ran into the tops of his gum boots. "—— it, I say, —— it." "What the devil are you standing there for?"

The two sappers, concealing the mirth which in the infantry openly cackled, hauled him up.

"I've got a bad cold, too, already."

A mimicking voice was heard back along the trench.

"Yes, the dear boy's got a bad cold already. I'm sure it'll be his death, Mrs. Gallagher."

"Yes, Mrs. Sheehan—by rights, he shouldn't be out at nights at all."

The engineer circumvented the hole and went hastily on. In his perturbation he did not perceive what the others saw. Sticking out of the earth where the frames had been blown off was a forearm and a hand, an arm on which hung some dirty shreds, and the skeleton of a hand, thin, white bones stuck together by withered sinews and mud. Neither Fritz, nor Tommy, nor Poilu, nor Digger, nothing but a string of bones. The men edged round on the other side of it. It was uncanny, that stiff, white framework of a hand, and they feared bad luck. Sergeant Burke, the last of the party, had just shied past it like a brumby colt, when there was a stoppage ahead. Ted Marshall squeezed his way back past the others.

"Wish us luck, mate," he said, and he laughed as he gave the thing a hearty grip. It came to pieces in his fist, and, putting the thumb into his pocket for a souvenir, he squeezed back again to his position in the queue.

After another hundred yards they left the trench for the open, and immediately they all had the wind well up. Behind them arose the long, pale crest of the ridge, and before them the country sloped downwards in a series of small undulations to the flats. The scene was pale-bluish, spectral white, pitted with small shadows and grey blotches and crossed behind by the zig-zagging shadow of the communication trench. To their front right lay the longer smudge of La Platte. As yet, they were screened from observation by the low, upward fold on which stood the ruins of the big farm.   The moon swung tauntingly in the sky like a buckler of burnished steel. Not only did each man realise that he was outlined distinctly against the snow, but he felt that the moon had cast a spell over his body, so that it assumed gigantic proportions. It was all right, as yet, but wait until they got on the skyline and down the other side of the curve in the ground.

Still keeping in their shelter, they came upon a dark splash on the pallor, which disclosed itself as a scattered dump of duckboards.

"Here we are," announced the engineer subaltern.

"Cleverer and cleverer," muttered a voice in the darkness.

They had a short spell before they went off with a duckboard apiece.   The timber was wet and heavy. Skipton lifted up two with greater ease than most of the others lifted one. Frank Jeffreys, who staggered as he settled his piece on his shoulder, cast a look of envy at the officer's strength. Soon, a long, straggling line was jigging up the slight slope. As each man reached the skyline, he could not help it if his heart did give a jump. They were no better off over it, worse even, for now, in the full view of Fritz, they were silhouetted against the pale screen of the snow. They went forward in a tremendous hurry. Nothing happened as yet—quicker— still nothing. They reached, one by one, the dark, lower spot on the line where they were to dump their burdens, and as each pitched his down, he scurried back up the betraying slope again, over the crest at last, there to get breath in gasps of thankfulness. How lightly they trod once they were free of the weight.

Again they made the trip and once again, going slowly at first to conserve their energy, and then tearing along like mad—stumbling, falling, cursing. The windiest working party he'd ever been on, someone said. Still nothing happened. True, a machine gun on the right started to chatter, but not at them—as yet. Again they made the journey. This time, even on the dangerous side, they were slower, for their perturbation as well as their frantic haste had robbed them of their strength; and they plunged along with a sort of weary desperation—spurred on by terror, but incapable of a gallop—sweating in their sheepskins in spite of the brittle, freezing air. Still nothing happened. The first of them were back and shouldering the boards for the next trip. There would be still a few left over, and the engineer said brightly, "One more trip does it." "Go to hell." Such luck, they felt, should not be imposed upon. The leaders were well up the slope when the tail pitched their boards down.

Rat-at-rat-tat-tat, swish, swish. They were copped at last. Bending low, they ran, slipping, sliding, up again while the rat-tatting grew to a frenzy and the snow splashed about them. Yet no one was hit. Each man gasped to himself, "I'm not hit—not hit." Just towards the top of the incline, Frank Jeffreys fell down. It was as if a hammer had hit him. For a few moments he lay there before the spurts in the snow about him made him try to get up. He had lost any feeling in his left arm, and his side was all pins and needles, but the pins and needles were extra large and red hot. He heard a faint voice. Sergeant Burke was bending over him. "Christ, get up. I can't stick here no longer." He was hauled to his feet, and half supported and half dragged onwards through the whipping bullets. They got over the line and out of view. The sergeant could see the others ahead making for home like hares.

Frank, sitting in the ground, had recovered from the first shock. With his right hand he could feel the blood running at his other shoulder.

"He'll start shelling soon," said the sergeant. "It's last home lousy. Can you walk, corp?"

He helped the corporal to his feet, and with one arm around his waist, they started off in the track of the others.   Two men clinging together, moving slowly across the spectral desolation of the snow. When they came at last to the trench, he was carrying the corporal, whose legs had become shakier and shakier and then buckled up. The sergeant laid the body on the duck-boards, and took the field-dressing out of the pocket of his tunic. He poured the iodine into the wound where the bullet had come out towards the front, and bound the pad over it with the bandage. Then he turned the body over and applied his own dressing to the wound in the back. The sharp stinging of the iodine brought Frank round a little, and he tried to smile, but when he opened his dry, hard lips, only a moan came out. He tried to say, "Thanks, sergeant," but there was only another moan.

"Christ, you've got a blighty this time, corporal," said the sergeant, with a mirthless grin. "What the devil," he wondered, "was the best way to carry him?"

Some shells were commencing to smash along the trench further on where he would have to go. No, he'd go round on top, he thought. "If the poor cow weren't so heavy," he muttered, as he got his arm under and took the weight. Someone was coming along the duckboards. It was Mr. Skipton and Jim Blount.

"We missed you," said Skipton.

"Corporal Jeffreys knocked, sir," he said.

"We'll have to go round on top a bit, sergeant. We just got through before he started putting them over." As he spoke a shell screamed and exploded just beyond them.

"Quick, we'll get one here in a minute," Jim urged.

They yanked the corporal up out of it. His agony burst into a low, gurgling cry. Skipton swept the body up into his arms, staggered a few steps, and then strode on with the others behind him.

"Thank Heavens," gasped the lieutenant, "there's a moon and a man can see where he's going."

AMATORY ATOMS

CHAPTER XXIII.

UNDOUBTEDLY the rest to his nerves, the complete
rest in the London Central Hospital, helped Frank
to an earlier recovery. Oh, the peace in that quiet
ward! His wound was a severe one, but at the same
time a lucky one, as the bullet, which had penetrated
obliquely, had after touching his shoulder-blade passed
out beneath it without injury to any vital parts. But
the real aid to the healing, both of mind and flesh, lay
in that same feeling of profound satisfaction and joy,
which reached its climax when propped up in bed with
pad and lead pencil, he made a start with the words:—

Central Hospital,
London,
2nd March, 1918.

Dear Miss Hatton,
    I am in London . . . .

When he concluded his letter he looked around for
the sister in charge of the ward. His eyes ran down
the two lines of beds, in which a few were propped up
like himself, a few men reclined on their elbows, but
most lay back on their pillows, still pale faces and
shaggy hair showing above the white sheets. Nearly
at the far end of the opposite row was a screen around
one of the beds, and at last she came from behind it
and, after exchanging a few words with the doctor and
one of the nurses, tripped silently up the aisle towards
him. Sister Emily. She was a slight, young woman,
worn to an almost transparent fineness by the con-

stancy of her devotion. Her eyes were large in her sharp, eager face, her mouth quick with a smile which cheered you, but nevertheless, as if in spite of itself, left behind in the heart a feeling of indescribable pain.

"Sister," he called.

She stopped, and came to the end of the bed, where she automatically straightened the blankets.

"Yes, corporal," she said, twinkling.

"Will you post it?"

"Yes, corporal."

"You, yourself," he demanded, anxiously.

She laughed at him softly. "I hope she's very nice. O, you're blushing, you're blushing."

"Yes," he thought, "she'll see she's nice if she comes."

Would she come? He had hardly dared to ask her. It was one thing to write when it meant only writing.

As the days drew on he fretted himself into a sort of fever, and brought about him Sister Em's flare of anger. He had met her only once, and yet, how was it life held out now only one objective, to see her again! Was it only that he had worked himself up into a longing for this one thing for some reason which was existent, but undiscoverable, deep in his own self; clothed this unknown girl with all the figments of his imagination until she was herself only an imaginary person; so that when she came, if ever she did come, the creature he had created would vanish and his dreams fall away into nothingness. He became afraid at times, almost dreading her arrival through that far door, and yet in spite of his fears he kept waiting and watching.

When on Saturday his gaze had continually lingered about the door, leaping towards each of the few women visitors and falling back each time in chagrin, and when at five o'clock he saw the last go out, he sank back on his pillow with at first the bitter relief of a coward. This feeling changed soon into an agony of shame and despair. "And all this," he told himself, "all this I feel over a girl I haven't seen more than once. What's the matter with me that I should get into such a state?"

"And so, corporal, she didn't come."

He opened his eyes to see the sister at the end of the bed. She went on, "I really didn't think she would to-day." He looked quickly at her. "If she's going to come I should say it'd be to-morrow, so don't worry now."

"Why?" he asked.

"Oh, just women's ways."

He smiled wryly at her. It was uncomfortable that she should read him so easily. He went to sleep, and noticing it as she passed half an hour afterwards, she smiled.

He saw Mary the instant she stood in the door sixty feet down the shining strip of linoleum. She hesitated a little timorously as the two long lines of cots spread out before her, and the strong hospital smell assailed her nostrils. Then, as she came on, she saw him. Self consciousness seized them both. His doubts had fled at the first sight of her, her neat figure about the middle height, in a warm, brown coat over her blue dress, the black hat, with a wisp of brown hair above her pale, fragile face, to which emotion had added two faint pink patches, making her quite pretty just then.

"I didn't know whether you'd come, Miss Hatton," he stammered.

"I didn't quite know whether I ought to," she said

nervously, "but after corresponding with you while you were in France, it was the least I could do."

"It's very good of you."

"It's not at all, really."

"Isn't there a chair?" He looked around wildly for a nurse or orderly, and seeing none near, reached for the bell.

"O, please, don't—I'll sit on the end of the bed if you don't mind."

"No, no. I mean I don't mind. Do sit down there if you'll be comfortable."

What was he going to say to her now? What the devil was he going to say? She, too, seemed stuck for words, and then it occurred to her she hadn't asked him how he was. Ought she to ask him about his wound?

"I haven't even asked you how you are. What must you think of me?"

"O, I'm all right. They say I'm healing pretty well, though I can't use my arm yet and my back's strapped up."

It sounded very bad to her. Perhaps he was injured for life. Why didn't he tell her?

"Well, corporal, aren't I always right?" The sister's voice startled him. He had fallen dreaming while she, whom he had been waiting for, was sitting there before him wondering why he didn't talk to her. Mary got up and turned around.

"O—er sister, this is Miss Hatton. Sister Thorpe."

To Mary's prim, "How d'you do," the sister smiled in her usual quick way, "How do you do! I'm glad this boy's got a visitor. He mopes too much. You must cheer him up."

"He hasn't even told me how he was wounded."

"Oh, they're mostly like that. Just say they got a knock. Why don't you tell Miss Hatton about your wound. I've only got three wild Australians now. One of them needs me very much just at present and I must go. I've got a soft spot for them."

"She's bonza," he said.

"Who's the one who needs her?"

"An artillery chap down behind the screen. He's about done in."

"You were going to tell me how you got your wound?" He looked at her and exclaimed hastily, "No, don't. I can't talk about the war now."

"Well then, don't, please," she hastened to pacify him.

"You see, I've been wondering what you really looked like, and whether you'd be really like what I remembered of you."

"And am I?"

On the sister, secretly observing them, the young woman's assumption of coquetry had the same effect as a miserable man trying to be funny, or, rather, a timid man trying to bluff.

"Yes, in a way," Frank answered, "and yet in a way you're different and yet the same."

"That's rather mixed, isn't it?"

He admitted it. How could he tell her directly how beautiful she was!

Sister Thorpe was, however, glad for the man's sake the girl was what she was when she might have been so much worse. She had seen some amazing females in that ward at times. "No, you couldn't call her a girl," she thought. "Nearing thirty, one of the thousands and thousands of office girls who just about that age usually can stand out no longer and marry one of the men clerks. A neat thing, though—too thin; with the remnants of a decent ancestral constitution, which had gradually become weakened and anaemic from lack of exercise, and from work in some stuffy office. She was certainly decent, for her face reflected the repressed abominated sex hunger which at that age has begun to terrify a certain type of woman when she has begun to fear she will never marry—a woman, who, more than others, has need of marriage. The sister had experienced in a different fashion a certain bitterness about the marriage question herself.

"Hey, Yorkshire!"

It was the long, rusty-headed, third Australian, Montgomery.

"Yes, Monty."

"How's the artillery joker?"

"Not too well, Monty."

"Hey, don't go away now. When're you going to get some new nurses, some like that yaller haired one in No. 3?"

"O, I saw you getting eye strain yesterday morning, and I haven't any time to waste on you."

"Ere, don't go. Cripes! I ain't said nothink yet. I say," he yelled vindictively after her, "Oo told you Yorkshire could play cricket?"

Monty waited. That's all he did most of the day, lay in wait to engage her a moment as she sped by. She distressed Monty. It wasn't fair a little thing like her should work like a nigger. She did ten times as much as the others. He had told her so and, when she laughed, sworn at her. "She must be in her little cubby," he thought, and waited patiently another chance, while he amused himself in the meantime observing the coot out of the Nth with his girl.

"Hey, sister"; he raised himself up on his elbow.

"Quick, Monty, I haven't a second."

"Take a captain cook at love's young dream. Cuckoo, cuckoo." He winked wickedly.

"Well, I suppose I'd better go now," Mary was saying.

"Stay awhile yet."

"I'll have to go. They won't know where I've got to."

"You'll come again next Sunday?"

"I don't know whether I can. I'll try. Would you like me to bring you something?"

No, he didn't want anything, only that she'd come. But if he asked her to bring something, she'd have to come.

"If you've got anything to read?"

"Would some magazines do?"

"Yes, anything."

They said good-bye and shook hands. She was walking away from him. At the door she half turned.

CHAPTER XXIV.

SHE came again next Sunday, and also the following Sunday, the sixth after his entry into the hospital, when, elated, he was waiting for her, sitting up in a suit of blueys. His shoulder was still heavily bandaged, so that the left sleeve of his jacket flopped empty at his side. He had been allowed to make his first few steps, he told her, on Tuesday, and was now getting quite steady on his feet. He took her to a sort of sitting room,

where he made a retreat for them from the other convalescents in a corner by a window which overlooked
the park in its wintry, drab green and mist.   Next
Sunday, he continued triumphantly, he would be allowed three hours' leave.   Would she wait for him in
the hall?   She agreed, and when he wanted to know
where they would go, suggested they should go out to
her home in Cricklewood.

When the day came, and at last they were in the bus
together, she experienced for the first time in her life
the possessory feeling for a man, in which some women
like so much to indulge themselves.   She could not help
the thought, when she saw the eyes of the other passengers glancing first to herself and then to Frank, "Yes,
he belongs to me.   I know what you think, and it doesn't
matter if he is an Australian."   Yet, she could not still
the fear that one of her parents might let out some word
of that other.   Hitherto what had happened that night
had seemed like some external catastrophe, just something which had happened.   But now her fear of it
became a heavy dread, even though she guessed she
might rely on a mother's caution not to mention her
former acquaintance with Charl Bentley, and to keep
her father's tongue still also.

They had gone into the little back garden, enticed
by a freakish glimmer of winter sunshine, and they
lingered even after Mrs. Hatton had called them to
afternoon tea.   It had become urgent in Mary's mind
to discover for her soul's ease how close was the friendship between Frank and the other.

She said, "My cousins have had a letter from Mr.
Potter.   He's out of hospital and in camp now,   I
suppose you saw a good deal of him and his friend."

Frank laughed. ''Well, we were in the same platoon, more than that, in the same section, but I don't suppose I'm very friendly with anyone. Jim Blount, more than any one else, perhaps.''

How pleasing he found it to make a confession of his essential loneliness over there when, now that he had her to himself, it lost its old pain and became even a deeper joy. He was loath to leave the quietude of that tiny, suburban garden, with its few shrubs, its meagre greens—as she called the few vegetables Mr. Hatton grew—and its stunted elm against the brick wall. There he had her alone in the dear quietness. She, too, was quiet and peaceful in her manner; like a nun.

Tea was laid in the front parlour. Frank shook hands with Mr. Hatton, a thin, nondescript man in a blue twill suit which, though not new, was obviously his Sunday best. Mr. Hatton was nervous in the presence of this stranger, who not only came from a country he had only heard of, but who might possibly be, according to his wife, Mary's young man. Mrs. Hatton had discovered from Mary that Frank was a school teacher, and had a steady job in the Government service to go back to. While he was a soldier, it would, of course, be better if there were nothing definite, but if he went back to Australia and Mary wanted to go with him she would not hinder it. Better that than deprive her of her chance. Mary was twenty-eight and could not hope reasonably to have any more when this was the most substantial, the only substantial one Mrs. Hatton was forced in her heart to admit, she had had so far. You had only to look at the corporal to know he was a chance. If it had been any other than this man she might have opposed the whole affair, but he was, in spite of the

tremendous drawback of his foreignness, just such a
sensible, quite fellow as she would otherwise have wished.
As for Mary, all her hope clung now to him. It was
enough that out of all the world he had come to her for
her to love him.

Fortunately for their case, there was one line of conversation upon which, like any other suburban Englishman, Mr. Hatton could embark with safety.

"I've heard a friend of mine speak about Australia,
Mr. Jeffreys. He's got a brother out there in the dairy
produce business?"

Frank confessed he had not met Mr. Green.

"And what sort of a place is it where you live?"
asked Mrs. Hatton.

Frank found himself soon engaged, as he warmed his
hands to the fire, on a description of his little school in
Gippsland, the long, rutty road winding alongside the
creek through hills scarred with settlements and farms,
the bridge across the river, from which the road swept
upwards in a quarter circle and passed the stores, the
bank, the pub, the blacksmith's shop, and on the left,
the school of yellow weatherboard on a little knoll in its
gum-sheltered paddock.

"Would your school be near Mr. Potter's place?"

"Perhaps two hundred miles."

"Ah." Mr. Hatton nodded with a thin satisfaction.
The Colonies, they belonged to England and he was an
Englishman, so that "two hundred miles" was almost
like a tribute to the extent of domains in which he had
a personal proprietary interest.

Every now and then Frank turned to look at Mary.
The room about her, her father trying to look wise to
an immense empire, her mother rigged up in dull black,

edged with yellowish lace, genteel, with a constant little grimace, and her cup at the end of two fingers, became unsubstantial and remote. But she! He saw her all the time vividly, distinctly. Even her mother, who had always been a little disappointed in her daughter's looks, remarked to herself that Mary did look nice. Mary, too, knew it, and the knowledge itself helped her, and added to her charm. None of them, least of all Frank, saw any quaintness in the formal performance, the stiff, polite gestures, the conversation sustained by question after question. He had been brought up in just such an atmosphere himself, even though the conventions and formalities may have differed slightly in some small particulars. Such formality was to each of them inseparable from the occasion. That this was an occasion, they were all the time aware, though it was first openly recognised when, later, Mary raised her face, like a pale flower, to say good-bye to him. Hitherto when they had said goodbye, he had had to demand of her, "Will you come and see me again?" or "When shall I see you again?" and on the answer, it was required of her to deliberate "Yes" or "No." But now, when he said, "When shall I see you again," it was an understood thing that she would be seeing him at the earliest, and the question demanded only the logical answer—the time. The relationship had subtly changed, and this change became stamped and definite when, on the following Sunday, sitting together in a secluded alcove in the National Gallery, he took and held her hand until the arrival of some more thorough sight-seer compelled him to withdraw. That Sunday, too, though they were not aware of it, was to be his last in the General Hospital. He wrote on Wednesday that he was being transferred to a V.A.D. convalescent hospital at Chetley, a village about thirty miles away from London.

CHAPTER XXV.

THE party of twenty, which included five Australians, was taken to the V.A.D. Hospital by car. In the common, blue uniform, the Australians were distinguished only by their hats, which had been sent from the stores at Horseferry Road. They regarded these hats with some disgust, for they knew them. They were made not of the thin, stiff, Australian felt, but of thick stuff like carpet felt. "Seven day leave" hats they were called, because by the end of that period they would change their colour to a bilious, purply shade. Still, they were better than nothing to men who were anxious when they went abroad to show some sign of their distinctive nationality.

The cars, having entered through iron gates set in a six foot brick wall, proceeded slowly along the gravel drive, which led through a small park and then around a lawn to a large house of late Georgian construction. They were met at the door by the village doctor, who was in his major's uniform, the matron in charge, who was called the commandante, and her offsider, a freckled, pleasant-faced woman of thirty or so, and taken by the latter, after the roll had been called, to No. 2 ward. This ward had once been the ballroom. The severity of the beds, black enamelled, and white counterpanes was in striking contrast with the rich gilt of the room's decorations. At each bedside there was a white painted cupboard for the few clothes and personal belongings of the convalescents.

Frank had hardly finished putting his gear away
when the second in command, her healthy flesh all the
redder in comparison with the starched white uniform
and her blue cape, returned, and asked the Australians
to follow her. She led them, when she had the five in
the hall together, along the polished, wooden floor of a
long passage. Frank, as the senior in rank, followed
first after the sister. Then came a man whose build
reminded Frank in some way of Jim Blount. He was
fuller in the features than Jim. Next came Montgomery, tall, hawk-nosed and rusty-headed. These
three, who were infantry, were followed by a squarely
built A.M.C. chap and a little sapper.

The sister stopped and knocked at a door, and in response to a command to come in, ushered the file into a
room, which was at once boudoir and office. Now, however, it had quite evidently to be treated as office, for
the commandante was seated in a swivel chair at a roller
top desk, around the side of which she eyed them through
her pince-nez in quite an orderly room manner. She
was a thinnish sort of woman of fifty or so. At present,
her lips were pursed up, and her eyes behind the glasses
went along the line so militantly that the men wondered
what was up now.

"Ah—hem"; she commenced taking off her glasses
and tapping on the blotting pad with them. "I have, ah
—asked you men to see me, ah—because, ah—you are
possibly unaccustomed to our ways. We, ah—have
nevah had any Australians heah befoar. I, ah—want
to put you on your honah not to do anything which
will, ah—reflect upon the reputation of the, ah— hospital. What I mean is, I want you to, ah—understand,
we are all ladies heah, even the young ladies who ah—

work in the kitchen.'' She glanced around even more severely, and pursed her lips up tighter than ever. ''As I said, we ah—are all ladies heah, and I, of course, expect you to ah—and I know now that I ah—have mentioned it to you, you will, ah—realise that and ah—treat us as such.'' She smiled sort of confidentially at them. ''Won't you? Ah—that's right. You will ah—each find a set of the ah—rules of the hospital, the ah—orders I mean, hospital orders, in a frame above each of your ah—beds. Yes, I think that will do for the present.''

The audience was evidently at an end, and the men shuffled out, all rather dumfounded except the man who reminded Frank of Jim Blount. When they were outside in the passage, this man stopped the others with ''Ah—men, befoar you ah—break off, ah—I feel I must be more explicit. Ah—you must understand that we ah—all ladies here, from commandante to scullery-wench. There must be no ah—lustfulness heah, and certainly no ah—raping. That may be very well for common people, but you ah—understand we ah—are all ladies heah. Yes, ah—I think that will do for the present.''

They laughed, and sauntered back to the ward. In a few minutes Frank and his neighbour, the man who had delivered the supplementary address in the passage, escaped through the big doors at the end of the room out on to the terrace. Disturbed by their advent, a group of four nurses fluttered away, not without, however, some curious glances at the Australians. The manner of their flight made it obvious to both that the commandante had very recently delivered a short, sharp talk on the habits and characteristics of the male Antipodean. They descended together from the terrace to

the lawn feeling lordly. You could not help it as you
went down the wide, shallow steps of stone with the
grandeur of the house mounting behind.

"Your name's Jeffreys, corporal?"

"Yes, Frank Jeffreys."

"Mine's Gil Marshbanks."

Still a little transported by their surroundings, they
continued to the small park of beeches and elms, and
from its edge looked back with common accord at the
house.   Its soft grey, formal architecture above the
terraced lawn satisfied them both. They mentally approved it.

"It's not so far from London, either," said the corporal. They went on under the trees until they came
to the wall.

"That's the limit," said Marshbanks.   "I've been
reading the rules. Interesting. They're like the dame;
put you on your honour."

"Not to go outside?"

"It's the unfair advantage women take or try."

"They couldn't post the nurses as sentries."

"No-o. Still, they're much too emphatic about it. I
refuse to have honour thrust upon me."

They walked along to the left, where the park opened
into small plow-land and grazing paddocks, and then
back to the house.

Two young women, one rather buxom and heavy, and
the other neat and pert, English country girls of the
better class, as fine and vigorous a type as there exists
in this world, were waiting portentously.

"You know," commenced the bricky buxom one,
"you were told not to go away."

"Yes," explained the other, "the commandante's just been through, and she's annoyed, very annoyed.

"She'll recover," replied Marshbanks easily.

"It was very wrong of you. You've read the rules and you mustn't break them."

"In the future," he said, "I'd as soon think of breaking one of the ten commandments. Even that which the commandante thought in danger."

As the youngest daughter of the village parson, the smaller girl knew the commandments, and giggled.

"Please don't let it occur again. You, corporal, ought to have known better at any rate."

Frank smiled, and, when he could get away, went off to the common room, of which they had been told in the orders, and commenced his letter to Mary. One thing of interest had also been revealed in the rules. On Wednesdays and Sundays he was free to go outside, within certain bounds, which included the village. Half a mile or a mile away on the other side of the village, he had also discovered, was a railway station on the London-Brighton line.

CHAPTER XXVI.

TO go out of London thirty miles and back again in one day appeared to Mary a remarkably courageous feat on her part, for in those days before the advent, hardly to be called holy, of the cheap motor car, London people did not often venture into the country proper. The suggestion to her, almost alarming, that she should come to Chetley had been to Frank, used to travelling as a matter of course over greater distances, nothing out of the ordinary. But even he was influenced now to some extent by the magnificence of distance, almost inevitable, in a small country, so that waiting on the station on Sunday afternoon for Mary's train, he was eager to applaud her on her readiness to journey so far to see him.

Anxiously, he glanced backwards and forwards along the length of the train. He could not see her. His heart dropped. She had not come. And then he heard her voice. She was descending from a second-class carriage just at his elbow. He took her hands, laughing with delight, and held them until she exclaimed that she must look for her ticket, and he became aware of the porter waiting a few feet away stolidly, but with a benignant look about him just the same. The air was sharp but, as they congratulated themselves, there was no rain. Mary was wearing her coat with its imitation Astrakhan collar open over a dark brown dress, and a small, brown hat. Her pale face, flaunting its two gay bannerets of excitement, was wistfully charming, moving Frank not to admiration so much as a deep tenderness for its fragility. His lean figure was plumped out by his thick British warmer, and she declared her conviction that he was getting fat.

With his hand tucked through her arm, they set off to walk to the village along the hedge-lined road which curved through the small, rolling hills of green and brown-patched earth. The entrance to the village led beneath an avenue of oaks, the buds of which were already plumping and giving an air of new solidity to the branches after the misty thinness of winter. Out of the trees you came right into the village, which was all an English village should be, a line of narrow, old

houses on the street, a few thatched cottages with gardens, two or three more substantial houses, one the doctor's, a few shops hardly distinguishable from the
dwellings, an inn, with big stables at the back of its
yard and an almost indistinguishable sign of a boar's
head on the board hanging from the iron brackets over
the main door, some more old cottages in their gardens
on the side lanes, and, further along the main road, an
old stone church with a squat tower, separated from the
little stream by a graveyard, and over the stream a low,
parapeted bridge.   Immemorial peace and quiet were
there. How different, though Frank, those shell-torn,
desolated and blasted villages of France.   Yet there
were villages in the zone of war which, a few years ago,
had been as tranquil, and in their own French way as
beautiful as this.

They had tea in a little shop behind a small window
with diamond panes. Tea in cups of painted china and
one plate of biscuits, and another of warm scones with
thin pats of dainty butter. An old, apple-faced woman
served them. For a few moments when they had finished, she stood munching her gums softly, as if eager
for a crack, but finally, with a reluctant acceptance of
the futility of her desires, left them alone together. If
she had spoken, it is doubtful if they would have heard
her.

They stayed half an hour, and then went down the
street to look at the church which, twice re-built in the
course of history, was, even as it stood now, the oldest
thing in the countryside, seeming even as old as the hills
themselves—a hackneyed comparison, but inescapable.
The door was open and they walked, hand in hand,
down the aisle to the transept where, set in the floor,

were the dull brasses of the ancient sepulchres of
manorial lords, while, beyond them, the decorated
cross above the altar caught on its edges the rosy light
streaming down, as if re-created and manifolded, from
the stained glass window of the Magdalen at the feet
of Jesus.

He wanted to show her the hospital, and she was
ready enough to see, with her own eyes, the place
where he lived. They slipped in past the gate, she,
fearful of the commission of that most heinous English
sin, trespass, into the cover of the trees until they
reached a spot where she could catch glimpses of the
house. She would only stay a moment. It was just
as well, for, when they were outside again, he looked
at his watch and gasped. How time had fled! She
must catch the train which went through at 4.56.
They hurried back. She was tired and leaned on his
arm as they tramped the stretch from the village to
the station. She was afraid his watch might be slow,
and they were panting and almost exhausted when
they reached the platform.

"The train won't be in for six minutes yet, lady,"
the porter replied to Frank's question. It had grown
bleak as the afternoon closed in, and they took shelter
from the thin, penetrating wind in the little waiting-
room. When they sank on to the seat, she shivered,
and he put his arm around her shoulders and drew
her close to him. She nestled against the coarse fabric
of his coat. They were all alone—alone, as if they
were the only human life, nourishing between them
the last vital spark, in a dead and dreary world.

A long whistle along the line startled them like the
clap of doom. The time had come. She threw back

her head to look at him. He bent over her and she
stifled her sob on his mouth, while the brakes of the
train grated along the platform. Quickly they ran
out and along the carriages for a second-class com-
partment. She was in. The whistle blew and the
engine snorted. She was going; her white face,
pressed like a ghost's against the glass, was slipping
away from him, away and away.

Just before he got back to the gates, Gil Marshbanks
turned out of a lane and they went in together.

Sister Bleasby, at the big doors into the ward,
regarded them severely.

"You're twenty minutes late."

"Is that all?" Gil smiled at her. "You wouldn't
report us."

She couldn't help smiling. "Well, I'll allow you a
little grace this time."

"Grace before meat. I feel like tea," he answered
her.

She felt she was justified. Contrary to the commandante's gloomy forebodings, the Australians, even
though they were rather scornful of the rules, were
quite well behaved so far. Even a man like Montgomery, who had been discovered smoking a stinking
pipe in bed last night, and had other odd habits.
They had this in their favour, too, the five Australians
—they kept mostly to themselves, and did not try to
contaminate the Tommies. But, fortunately, the sister
did not know what was in store for them all.

CHAPTER XXVII.

IT was indeed a terrible time. The commandante summoned both the major and the captain. How little a soldier the poor major looked with his long hair; useless, just the sort of man her wretched fate would give her. Indeed, the moment she saw that sly flash of laughter in the major's eyes, she determined that he must go, and she would speak tactfully to the Duchess herself about it. There was only one thing to do in the end, and that was to write to the D.M.S. at the War Office about it. But for that she would have to whet her courage a bit or have sheer desperation whet it for her.

The V.A.D.'s tripped about with masks of breathless awe, which they took off when they were by themselves to indulge in secret, shameless giggles. Even the Tommies displayed a cumbersome restlessness. How could the few there remain unaffected when the discipline of the whole British Army had been shattered! The disaster of the Fifth army was nothing to this. The Duchess of Stexe, patroness of the hospital, had graciously intimated that on Wednesday she would be glad to receive some of the inmates at the Castle; not more than twenty, and they were to include the Colonial troops. And the Australians had refused to go.

In vain had the commandante dealt with them in her most acidly military style, and in vain had the major and the captain, after the first use of sweet reason, attempted a weak show of military authority. The Australians seemed quite unmoved by it. They went about their ordinary daily routine of loafing, when and how they could, as if nothing was the matter. They still intimated that they did not desire to visit the Duchess. Though neither commandante, the major, nor captain, but only a few of the slyer nurses, were aware of it, the trouble had arisen because the commandante, believing that the men would be edified by hearing real ducal words read from the crested notepaper, had read the letter to the assemblage of the chosen twenty with what Gil Marshbank described as such holy unction. It was he who started it when he said: "I am afraid that I can't do myself the pleasure of accepting Her Grace's invitation."

The four others — Montie, Joe Woods, Mucker Murphy and the corporal—felt that this was a matter which ought to be left in Gil's hands, and they left it. Frank did not feel like paying visits, for on last Saturday morning he had received a telegram, "Can't come. Mother unwell. M."

The major found it difficult to answer Frank's quotation of Gil; "Yes, sir, if it was a proper, lawful command, but I've yet to hear that an officer has the right to order anyone to pay a social call. Not in our army, anyway," and conveyed his difficulty to the commandante when she hinted at his incompetence for military command. One of the worst features about the whole affair was the fact that the men did not seem to realise how hideous, sacrilegious, blasphemous, anarchical and perverted their conduct was. Yes, perverted; the commandante found the word the most expressive of all.

Tuesday came. She had sent to Her Grace, by special messenger, a letter expressing her appreciation of Her Grace's excessive kindness, and saying that they would arrive punctually at 3.30 as desired, and that she would herself lead the party, and how happy she was, etc. She could not admit, as yet, that it might not be so. Now something had to be done— something desperate, urgent. So she sent off the following telegram: "D.M.S., War Office, London. Australian troops Chetley convalescent Hospital in state of mutiny. Have refused obey command visit Duchess of Stexe. Wire orders, Commandante."

The five Australians were together in the common room when there came in Sister Bleasby and Misses Joan Meredith, the parson's daughter, Celia Warton and Barbara Dunne.

"We're a deputation," commenced the sister.

"Are you?" cried Mucker. "You don't look like it. We know all about deputations. In Australia we average two thousand a day."

"O, don't be silly," exclaimed Miss Meredith, and the deputationists then, in spite of Mucker's appeal to them to speak only one at a time, started off all at once, "we want you to go to the Duchess's."

Barbara looked at Gil Marshbanks. "You will, won't you?"

"Ask me again?" he roared.

"You will, won't you, Private Marshbanks?"

"Once more."

"You will, won't you, General?"

"That'll do. It's nice to be asked. Do you really want us to go? Waste one of our Wednesday afternoons?"

"It would make everything so much pleasanter."

"Oh, we don't mind going to see the old geezer," said Monty. "Me, I don't."

"Oh, well, your request is granted," said Mucker. Sister Bleasby bore the good news to the commandante. Soon the the commandante began rather to regret that telegram. But it was too late; the wheels of Whitehall were in motion and would not easily be stopped. Already there were hurried consultations at the office of the D.D.D.M.S., and telephonings to Australian Headquarters at Horseferry Road, and to the Provost Office for the home division. These first manifestations soon, however, died down into a monthly correspondence which lasted till within one month of the end of the war.

The commandante's uneasiness was now, however, forgotten in her momentary satisfaction. When the time came, the Australians and the carefully-selected Tommies were ready, all dressed up at the front door, prodding each other up into the cars. The commandante was in charge in front in the car the Duchess had sent. It was only fifteen minutes' run before they were approaching the place, seen for a long way off over a vista of pools and fountains and arabesques of various colours—grand—magnificent. On the right was the round keep of the old fortress and the old wing, and in face of those approaching there stretched between the keep and the new tower, on the left, the wonderful ornate facade three stories high.

"Some joint," said Joe Woods tersely.

Marshbanks admitted it. Even he felt it. The place imposed itself on you, overwhelmed you. He felt like an outer barbarian in the face of this monument to the haughty English greatness. It made him swear. Was there ever an age worthy of it? Yes, some joint.

They were met at the main door to the old wing by an old gentleman in black, with silver facings and white sideboards. Trailing with elastic necks and sprouting eyes at the furniture, the armour, the weapons and at the tapestries, the head of the line poked itself at the heels of the commandante into a sort of reception room, while the tail spread across the hall. Here nothing more alarming met the eyes of Frank Jeffreys peering over the commandante's shoulders than a young man in glasses and semi-clerical attire, who advanced with both hands out and an Oxford drawl, "Ah, my deah commandante, here you are with your little flock. Ah think they would be more comfortable in the hall a few moments while we arrange, ah—arrange."

Beaming gently, he shoved them out like a flock, indeed, of sheep or geese.

"I don't like it," Joe expostulated peevishly; "she's our commandante. It's wrong for us to leave her alone in there with that brute. Perhaps she's gorn an' lorst herself already."

"O, she's safe."

Nobody else took any notice of them, and they sat or stood about stolidly, except two or three, who walked about and poked the armour. Monty took a two-handed battle-axe off the wall and balanced it in his hands.

"Something like a broad axe," he said. "'Ow'd you like a knock with that, chum?"

"Wot abaht yerself, digger?"

In about ten minutes the door opened and the commandante emerged trumpeting gently, and followed

by the semi-clerical young man smiling and rubbing
his hands.

"T'seems domned pleased wit' himself," whispered
a Tommy to Joe. "Must ha' been more in t'laad 'an
your choom thot, digger."

The digger and the chum nudged each other and
cackled. The chap was going to address them. He
said, "Well, men, Her Grace has asked me, who have
ah— the honour to ah—serve somewhat in the capacity
of chaplain, to show you over the castle, ah—one of
the oldest keeps, ah—and finest homes in England.
One thing I ah—ask you not to do—not to touch.
But before we go on, I think you ought to find it
interesting if I should ah—tell you briefly something
of the history of the castle and its noble House. Will
you ah—just stand easy for a few moments?
Now—," and he went on for fifteen minutes of
genaeological history. It might have been longer, for
he had only reached the period of the elevation of
the line to ducal rank, and was pointing to the change
made in the ducal arms which appeared over the door,
when Gil Marshbanks, in a loud voice, interrupted,
"Do you mind me asking a question, sir?"

"Not at all, man."

"Is that black band sloping down there what you'd
call a bar sinister?"

At the sudden pause, the eyes of everyone turned
profoundly on the young fellow. He glanced hastily
towards the commandante, who, occupying a rather
high carved chair, glanced stonily in front of her.
"Ah—ah think we might proceed now ah—dear commandante."

The voice came remorselessly, "You haven't

answered my question, sir, and I have another. What does a bar sinister mean?"

"No, no, a bar dexter."

"That's all right. It's a bar dexter. What does a bar sinister mean?"

"Well," drawled Monty, "I know what sinister is —sly and dirty work at the crossroads."

The commandante, by a decisive movement, came to his relief, "I think you had better take the men with you now, Mr. Willoughby."

"Ah, yes, yes, Commandante, certainly."

So away they went from room to room and hall to room and room to hall. It was Gil Marshbanks again who interrupted when they were in the picture gallery by asking their guide whether he had ever read Mark Twain. The young man raised his eyebrows in an expression of annoyance, almost exasperation, at the entire irrelevance of this remark when he was actually explaining to one of these poor, simple men, the one who was called Monty, what an ancestor was.

"And d'yer mean ter tell me my old Dad's an ancestor?" demanded Monty.

"Yes; that is, if he is, unfortunately, ah — not alive."

"Good Gawd, there's nothink unfortunate about it, padre. The old woman always used to say it was the best thing ever 'appened to us kids the time he fell down the shaft comin' 'ome shicker from Wombat Flat."

"No damn good callin' an ole man like that a nancestor, Monty."

"Would you call your ole man, sir, an nancestor if

he fell down a shaft coming home shicker from the
village one night?''

"What'd you call your old man, choom?''

"Ah, Aussie, he ain't ever had no old man.''

"Jove, a dinkum bastard!''

The young semi-clerical led them on, but Joe Woods
stepped after him and prodded him. "Here, sir, half
a mo. What's that cove got the big yard-wide collar
round his neck for?''

"That's a ruff.''

"A ruff? Then how . . .'' the rest was lost in a
gurgle with Murphy. "Rough on him.''

Their guide pointed hastily to another picture of a
florid, pig-eyed, dirty man in a rich blue velvet robe.
"That is Sir John Croke, who suffered for his treason
in the reign of Henry VIII. Of course, you will ah—
remember the family was not raised to the dukedom
until the reign of the second Charles, son of the
Martyr.''

"What do you mean—suffered for his treason?''

"His head was ah—removed.''

"Well, he's got it on in the picture, sir?''

"Yes, yes, of course. He had it on while he was
alive.''

An argument had developed between Joe and
Mucker. "Aw, I know all about King Charles.''

"You! Gawd, you've got him mixed up with King
George.''

"No I ain't. I once went to a play all about him.
Nellie Stewart was in it. It was called 'Sweet Nell
of Old Drury,' after her.''

"He wouldn't marry her, would he, sir?''

"Ah, who?''

"King Charles and Sweet Nell."

"Had he er—betrayed her, do you mean, Joe?" asked Gil.

"Aw, betrayed her—something awful."

The bland voice of the old gentleman who had met them at the door saved Mr. Willoughby from further embarrassment. "Her Grace is able to see the soldiers now. You will find her in the blue room."

They strung out after him and following the commandante, who now reappeared and put herself at their head, were ushered at last into the presence of the Duchess of Stexe. They saw a long-faced dame with a complexion a little raddled, but which was clearly the decline of a product of infinite care; pale, almost silly, eyes, and a figure tall and floppy, and clad in a mist of pale colours. The commandante hurried forward and bubbled over the flaccid white hand, "So kind, so considerate of Your Grace. These poor wounded men." The young man beamed around, conscious of good works, for it had been his idea that Her Grace should have some more soldiers over from the hospital.

"Yes, yes, Gertrude," said the Duchess, and turned to the men standing with flopped shoulders and heavy red hands in front of her. "Well, I hope you have had a pleasant time, and that Mr. Willoughby has shown you all there is to see, haven't you, Willoughby?" Willoughby made a general motion of his whole body to express the thoroughness of his duty, and she went on, "And soon you will be better and will be going back to fight for us again, won't you?"

She touched a bell which promptly brought the old gentleman. "Albert, take the men away and see they have some suitable refreshment and have tea sent here.'' Leaving the commandante and their guide sinking with expressions of heartfelt thanks into two gilt-embroidered chairs, the men followed Albert along passages and down stairs into what was called the Lower Servants' Hall. There they were regaled with sandwiches, seed cake and a sort of home brew ginger beer. Regaled, as Gil explained, after a short burst of oratory from Murphy, who had once been a Union organiser, was the precise term. It was inevitable. He made a pretence of reading. ''Our Chetley correspondent reports that on Wednesday Her Grace the Duchess of Stexe, entertained a number of wounded soldiers, including some Colonials, at Chetley Castle. After the men had been shown over the magnificent, historic structure, they were presented to Her Grace, who, in her usual kindly way, spoke a few words of encouragement to them. They were then regaled in the Lower Servants' Hall with sandwiches and ginger beer. The men, even the Colonials, expressed themselves as overcome by Her Grace's condescension and liberality, and declared that the afternoon had not only been instructive, but not without amusement.''

Frank Jeffreys exclaimed bitterly, ''Damn them! I'd like to wring their necks.''

Gil only laughed. ''Don't you like being in the servants' hall, corp. You're a true socialist.''

CHAPTER XXVIII.

THE next Sunday it rained and rained, but she came. The station was like an island in the steady flow of water. O, he was wet, she exclaimed, when she put her hands on his shoulders as if for a moment she expected him to kiss her. Into the waiting-room, where they stayed half an hour, the damp penetrated into a sort of fog of fine spray. It seemed that they would have to spend the afternoon there; but, just as they were resigning themselves to it, the porter, after a discreet knock, appeared to inform them that if they wanted to go to the village, old Tom Chugg had his cab outside.

Simultaneously it occurred to each that they might go to the little tea shop and spend the afternoon there. Neither of them thought for a moment of going to the warm comfort of the inn. They ran from the shelter of the station, through the rain, and clambered up into the ramshackle square cab, and the old horse put his head down and jogged off. In front, under a dirty cap, the red nose of the cabby hooked on the top of his oil skin. Inside, the two passengers, a white girl in a navy blue coat with black imitation astrakhan collar about her ears and hands in woollen gloves grasping an umbrella, and, opposite her, a soldier, in a dewy, wet British warmer over a blue uniform too small for him, so that his socks and fractions of hairy legs were visible above his boots, and with a wide hat which had gone limp and run into shades of brown and bilious purple.

In between their attenuated smiles at one another, they gazed out of the door at the muddy road slowly slipping away beneath them, and the dirty curtain of the rain over the dull hedges and fields. Under the trees, at the entrance to the village, the big drips off the twigs struck heavily on the roof. Down the street they creaked and rattled, and were carried a little way past the shop before Frank succeeded in arousing the dormant cabby's attention. When he took them back so that they would have only the width of the footpath to cross, Frank added sixpence to the shilling fare. They darted inside and he tapped on the counter.

The woman came sidling in, a creature whose eyes belied the warmth of her apple cheeks and her comfortable plumpness. She could give them some tea and biscuits and bread and butter, but no scones. Who should she bake scones for on a day like this? She did not know whether she could put a fire in the grate. She had no intention to do it until his abrupt order startled her. He'd pay for it. To make sure of getting it quickly, and a decent blaze, while she was about it, he gave her a hand, leaving her aghast at his lavishness with her none-too-large stock of fuel. She kept thinking, while she padded about getting the tea, reckoning it up this way and that way, and wondering whether she might venture to demand a shilling for the fire.

Frank soon had the coals spurting little geysers of gaseous flame. The fireplace was in the wall at the back of the shop itself, from which it was cut off by a tier of shelves. Mary he had settled in a low horsehair chair from which the stuffing bubbled out in patches, and now he got from the shop a hard one for himself, and another from behind the counter, on which he set their coats to dry. They laughed softly at each other as they stretched out their hands to the heat.

"This is a bit of all right, as you Tommies say," he barracked her. They were keen set for the afternoon tea when it arrived. After they had finished the last of the bread and butter and biscuits, he followed the old woman with the tray and shut the door after her with almost a bang.

"No one's likely to come into the shop to-day," he said in reply to Mary's "O, Frank." The bang of the door after her had indeed prevented any interruption from the rear, for it had, as the woman afterwards described it, "Set her all in a tremor," and it was doubtful if she could have dared, even in answer to a summons from the door bell, to enter and go past the man and the girl by her fire. "One of those Orstralians and the girl like from Lunnon."

For a while they sat there, their heavy consciousness of each other almost creating an invisible barrier between them, until it was almost with an effort of desperation that Mary cast a look of supplication to him. He moved awkwardly across to her and, kneeling by her side, laid his cheek against hers. For the first time they confessed their love in words. When it was all said for about the fifth time, he moved back a little. "And when the war is over, you'll come back to Australia with me?"

"Yes." She said "Yes," but the look of dread in her eyes was so plain he had to answer it and he half misunderstood her.

"I know," he said; "I might get knocked for good next time. How long is it going to last, Mary?" he whispered. I've been thinking and thinking about it. I can't ask you to tie yourself to me straight out. It wouldn't be fair."

"Some . . ." she commenced, but could not find words to frame her suggestion, and he did not understand, so engrossed was he with his own soul searchings. "Do

you think I could do a thing like that—leave you perhaps unprovided for and perhaps ruin all the future
for you?'' It was as if he were talking to himself, but
he turned to her now. "I'll come back to you. I
swear it. Will you wait for me?''

She nodded, hardly able to speak. "Yes, Frank
dear, I will.''

They clung together as if the death out there in
France had sent its whisper about the shadowy
corners of the shop to chill their flesh with terror.
The war, like a grisly shadow, had slipped in to make
a third to gibber over the irony of it. He would not
dare to marry her before he went back, because he
was afraid if he did, and was killed, he might have
harmed her chance of some other marriage, while she
herself knew in her heart, with a sort of added dread,
that he was her first and last chance. Yet how—for
her own face and pitiful fragment of feminine pride—
dare she formulate her fear and confess it to him—to
him least of all, in whose eyes she was so beautiful
and desirable that he could not think anything else
but that other men should find her so. Poor puling
cries of the insignificant human souls in the general
human cataclysm.

But they were still young enough, young in love, to
escape a little from their fears, and the grisly shadow
became less distinct as they gradually surrendered
themselves to their immediate happiness. Out of their
fears there bloomed in their love-making a deeper
tenderness. He was even more shy than she about
their now-acknowledged love, and, when the old
woman at last whipped up her curiosity in feminine
fashion into a trembling courage and opened the door

and went and fumbled at a shelf, there was very little material for the latter half of the highly imaginative story she afterwards spun for her neighbours. Poor Frank and Mary were to suffer in that story, when it came to be told, an amazing transformation.

It was the cabby's knock which summoned them."

"Time to go for the train if ya wants t'ketch it, sojer."

There was no diminution in the rain. Sitting side by side, they looked out of the back of the cab at the mud slipping slowly away underneath, and the fog, darker now, of the rain covering the heavy blurs of the hedges, the fields, the trees.

When they were again in the now familiar waiting-room, she took hold of his coat, saying, "Frank, it is true we are really engaged, even though we keep it quiet?"

"Why, of course," he cherished her.

"I would like to tell my mother." She wanted not so much the candour itself, but the evidence it would give of the substantiality of his promise.

He agreed readily and went on, "It was the others I was thinking about. You can't tell what may happen."

"Oh, Frank, don't talk about it again."

He kissed her. "I am just talking. My luck's set in."

They drew apart when a middle-aged, jovial, farm-ing sort of man entered with his wife. The man winked a humorous eye. "Can't go outside nohows," and then, after a minute, "You'll be one of them Orstralians from the 'ospital, eh?"

"That's right."

"My boy's been wounded too."

"Praise God," said his wife, "our lad's coming home soon."

"There," whispered Frank, "what was I telling you? It's good luck for us."

They heard the whistle of the train. One last embrace and in a few minutes she was being borne away from him once more.

CHAPTER XXIX.

THAT week was Frank's last at Chetley, for, with the rest of the Australians, he was sent to Park House, near Salisbury, that being the depot from which the convalescents were ultimately dispersed to the training areas. He had eighteen days at the depot before he went to Lark Hill. He had, during all the time he was at the hospitals, deliberately shut the war out of his mind as far as he could. Until now it had counted little with him that the affairs of the Allies had again reached a crisis during the successive German attacks towards Amiens and Calais. But, back at Lark Hill, he could no longer overlook the fact that there was a war on. There were not very many troops in the training battalions because, during the preceding months, all that were available had been sent across the Channel. In the hut into which he was put, the other eight occupants warned him that they could not hope to stay there long, however hard they might swing the lead.

One relief they had. The bull ring drill was not so prominent in their training. One other, too, they

could congratulate themselves on. Winter was over
and spring was in the air, with summer to follow.
The more you thought about it, that became the sweet-
est consolation. You could understand, then, the welcoming of the spring in England, much more heartfelt than in Australia, even Melbourne, after you had
passed a winter there. Frank felt much stronger.
Succoured by the long rest and the happiness of his
love for Mary, he knew with deep thankfulness that
his nerves were steadier. What it meant to him to
feel so well he alone can tell who has been sick and
had to carry on as a soldier, one of those suffering
from general debility just on the medicine and duty
line, especially he whose nerves have been frayed to
the breaking point. After the first week he received
three letters from Mary in a bunch. They wrote, by
arrangement to each other, twice a week.

Each evening, when the company had been dismissed, he would take a sharp walk, after which he
would drink a glass of malted milk at the Y.M.C.A.
He went to bed each evening at 9 o'clock, or, if it was
letter day, at half past.

They had news, too, of the battalion—that it was
back on the Somme now; how, when Fifth army was
in retreat, the five Australian divisions had been sent
down to stem the enemy's advance; how one had been
recalled on the way when the Germans had broken
through in the north, while the other four, disembark-
ing from lorries, buses and railway trucks, had
marched eastwards and held the Germans along the
Ancre and in front of Corbie and Villers Brettoneux
down to the French at Hangard; that how, along the
established line, they were constantly nibbling at

Fritz and seizing from here and there some point of vantage. Though the Allied command may have been worried enough, the Australians were full of spirit, the fervour of which had percolated even into the camps in England. And then, while Frank was still in hospital, the news had come to the camp of the great coup d'armes at Villers Brettoneux, when, after Fritz had driven out the English garrison and broken through, two Australian brigades, marshalling into position in the night, had recaptured the village, saved Amiens again and re-established the line on the far side once more.

Too right they were; those who had lugubriously foretold only a short stay in England. After a fortnight at Lark Hill, Frank, with a number of others, got his seven days' leave. They would be on the next draft. But that hardly counted in the deep joy with which he entered the train at Amesbury which was to take him on the first stage to London and Mary. They had been packed off at such short notice that he would be in London perhaps before she got his letter. He would give her a surprise. As soon as they were dismissed at Horseferry Road, after the usual rigmarole and invitation to use the Blue Light joint, he beat it to the city proper and, after a snack at an A.B.C., went down past the bank into Throgmorton Street in search of the building where she worked. When he found it, he had twenty minutes to wait, for she knocked off at half past five usually. He took up a position about forty feet from the door, where he observed the people coming out—or, rather, only the girls—first one and then another metamorphosising from bookkeepers, stenographers and typists into girls and young men—feminine creatures seeming different even to the men who bossed them once they were outside. He began to look anxiously at his watch. She was five minutes overdue. Eleven minutes. And then he saw her. For a few moments she stood talking with another girl. They separated and she was approaching—alone, thank heaven. He strode to meet her, with her name on his lips. She stopped and put her hands to her breast before she stretched them to him.

"I've got leave."

"O, Frank; O, dear; what a surprise!" she exclaimed with a thrill of wonder and delight in her voice.

"I knew you'd get a shock."

He must come home to tea. Before they got on the bus she bought some ham and cakes, which enabled Mrs. Hatton, when they arrived home, to compliment Mary's foresight with "Though she does work in an office, Mr. Jeffreys, Mary's a born housekeeper." Of which he, on his part, had no doubts.

He left early that night because he had to find an hotel. The next day he and Mary had tea in town and afterwards went to Chu Chin Chow, which had a special claim on Australians because the producer and principal actor, Oscar Asche, was an Australian. They enjoyed it tremendously, even though they were seated at an immense distance from the stage. The distance rather helped their enjoyment, for this was the first of the big spectacular pieces, and its prodigality of colour could better be appreciated from the back of the theatre than the front. It was his final leave and he determined that she must have a good

time—something to remember—a climax to their happiness before separation. During the remainder of
his time they went also to the Colosseum, where a
Russian ballet, Mark Hambourg and Vesta Tilley were
on the bill, and to The Boy, at the Adelphi. On Saturday they went to Madame Tussaud's, and on Sunday
to the Zoo, where Mary wanted, more than anything
else, to see the kangaroos. There was in this plan of
enjoyment also a feeling of the necessity to keep themselves from thinking of the shortness of the days
before he went to France, and, yet, what they did only
made the time pass the quicker. Monday night came
—their last together. He bought stalls for the Maid
of the Mountains, at Daly's. The audience was like
the others. In the theatres you had a perception of
the repressed hysteria—the mob expression of the
emotion in the individual—which laughed and cried,
spume on the mouth as their hearts danced to the dull
thudding of the Dance Macabre, the monotonous
drumming of the deathly guns not far away. To Frank
and Mary the light, pleasant music was indescribably
beautiful. Their hands clung together with a sort of
frenzied tenacity; their souls were caught up in a
rapture of almost unbearable agony and pleasure,
listening to that dancing, melodious music like the
treble above the sinister, monotonous base of the unheard guns.

They were a long time going home—stringing out
the seconds by the smallness and the slowness of their
steps, and, on the last stretch from the light at the
corner, stopping every few paces to clasp each other.
There was still a light downstairs, and it provided an
excuse for him to go in. Mrs. Hatton stood behind

a candle at the foot of the stairs. She had a grey flannel wrapper over her nightdress and her hair was tied at the back with white tape.

"Hullo, Ma!" exclaimed Mary, her voice sharpened by her parent's lack of consideration.

"It's very late. I've made some coffee for you and put some biscuits out."

"I'm sorry, Mrs. Hatton," Frank apologised. He looked at his watch. "By jove, it's twenty past one."

"Half past one I make it. Seeing as you were going to be so late, I thought Mr. Jeffreys might stay the night. The bed in the spare room only wants the sheets to be ready. That is, if Mr. Jeffreys cares."

Mary looked at Frank. "Would you?" "How decent of mother," she thought.

"I'd be a trouble."

"We keep the room generally pretty ready for my Uncle Sam when he comes down from Wolverhampton. He has to come to London once a month on business."

The dreadful minute had been shifted back by hours.

"All right. It'll be bonzer," he agreed.

"I'll tend to the room while you have supper. I'll catch my death in this passage."

While she flat-footed up the stairs, the other two went into the dining-room, where Mary blew the fire up a little and prepared the supper of coffee and cake. Sitting there, when they had finished, before the dying fragments of the fire, she saw herself clearly and plainly like a different person as if a door were opened, in spite of her own hands trying to hold it shut, into a room in her consciousness; sitting bent back in Charley Bentley's arms. Frank, startled by her low cry of entreaty, sprang across to her, cherishing and petting her.

"I almost fell, dreaming," she said, endeavouring to laugh it away.

"Then let's go to bed."

Her parents' room was on their right when they stood, tip-toe, upon the landing. Mary's was the further of the two small rooms whose windows overlooked the kitchen roof and little garden beneath like a dark pool at the bottom of steep, hard banks, in places perpendicular. On the landing they kissed silently and turned away. Frank did not completely undress, but sat on the bed for some time in his shirt and pants. To know her so near him, to hear her movements, just like the rustling of a mouse, as she got ready for bed, aroused in him all the gentleness and tenderness of which he was capable. And then there came a silence. He listened. There was no sound. He was waiting for the creak of her bed as she slipped into it. And then, at the bidding of some instinct, he went and opened his door and found her there, her face white, without will and with a strange appeal, in the mass of her hair which hung down like a cloak over her thin blue dressing gown.

"Frank" was all that came to her lips from the unreasoning, irresistible impulse which had carried her silently to his door. He was quite without the slightest intuition of the deeper cause of her emotion. His innocence was greater than hers. Alone in her room, immersed in her hateful but persistent recollections of her physical submission to Charl Bentley in the room downstairs, and her dread that the war would rob her of her only lover and the marriage he promised, she had fallen into a state in which there was no thought, no fear—only the surge of long-betrayed instinct.

In her arms he felt the abandon of her body through the thin calico of her nightdress, and saw her eyes white and misty, and felt her mouth moist and open beneath his, and did not dream—such was his own chastity and his reverent exaltation of her—that her passion was uncontrolled and that she offered herself to him absolutely and completely. At that moment, when he might have taken her, not only resistless but willingly, into his room, he believed her desire to be only to take a last farewell alone by themselves which to-morrow would be denied them. Slowly her passion ebbed, leaving her shivering and exhausted, and she suffered him to lead her to her room. The door shut and she was alone.

SCENES DE LA VIE DE GUERRE

CHAPTER XXX.

EVERY now and then, in your goings to and fro, you might see, trudging along the road, a little group of men, a straggling lot usually, nominally in charge of some corporal or sergeant. Their pace would be slow—slower than ever any schoolboy's creeping, like snail, unwillingly to school—and they would be labouring along, bent forward at the shoulders under the weight of their packs and blanket rolls. In the winter their faces were blue with the cold, and now, in the summer, sweat ran freely down their red cheeks and necks, for their skins had not yet become hardened and tanned by exposure, and they were not in the best condition. These little groups did not consider themselves confined to five minutes' spell in each hour of their marching, but you would, as often as you saw them on the road, see them lolling alongside it. Nor were they possessed of any great cheeriness or heartiness of spirit, but rather of a sort of stolid fatalism as if it were no will of theirs, but a mechanism beyond their control, as indeed it was, which sent them journeying. Often they would address to some passer-by some such words as "Good-day, dig; where are the Nth now?" Those who composed these little parties were drafts of men who had been wounded or on leave, and were returning to their battalions. A passing car of brass hats, which might either cover them with dust or splash them with mud, would provoke perhaps an ironic comment or two. Only very occasionally would you notice a bigger draft of new reinforcements, and these it was easy enough to distinguish from the old hands.

In one of these first-mentioned drafts, Frank Jeffreys had set off along the hot, dusty Amiens-Albert Road, through Querrieu to Franvillers, where, after enquiry, they had turned aside to Heilly and down its steep street of cobbles, between barns a little shell-worn, across the Ancre. Thus he had come through battalion and company headquarters back to the old platoon which just then wanted another full corporal now that Llew Jones had been gassed with mustard three weeks ago. He found the battalion in supports on the higher ground above the marshy flats along the river towards Sailley Le Sec, on the Somme. In front of the line on the left was the village of Morlancourt.

It had been good, all the same, to see friends like Jim Blount, Harry Mullane and Johnny Wright again. Yet there was a change, natural enough in an infantry platoon after so long an absence. Faces were there which had almost been forgotten, or which he had never seen before. Because of the lack of reinforcements, the strength of the platoon had been increased by two men from the Light Horse and two from the Engineers, who had suffered the sad fate with which members of other arms had been threatened some months ago—of being sent to the infantry. This liberty, which had been afforded to engineer and artillery company officers, etc., of getting rid to the infantry of men who were unsuitable for the technical and other units, was in some instances misused by the unscrupulous, who, under

cover of it, removed men to whom, for some reason
or other, they had a personal dislike.

Other things there were which, at times, made the
corporal feel almost a stranger in the little unit of
which he was a member, particularly the occasional
chance references to scenes in which he had had no
part—the pianos in the trenches at Fouilloy, the bombing near Blangy Tronville, the soft beds at Villers-
Brettoneux, the wounding of Colonel Bedford and
Gilderoy's appointment to command of the battalion,
the episode of the raid on the 7th May, the stuffed
birds at David's in Corbie, and the wine in the cellars
there. O, the wines there, the ripe and the unripe
vintages; they often remember them, and how they
rigged themselves in female undergarments in the
house on the corner near the Abbey. They were
cocky, too. Their good luck had set in after the misfortune which had dogged them in the north. Since
they had come down they had had only two killed
and four wounded. It was almost inconceivable.
Dingo Williams had been shot the first day they had
gone out towards Fritz to hold the line, and Tich
Carson was the batman runner now. Billy Carter had
been killed by a stick bomb during the raid on the 7th
May. Mick Flynn had got the M.M. and had had
his arm taken off, it was reported. Merv Hill and
George Summers and Llew Jones were casualties and
gone to Blighty also. Half the platoon had had
dog's disease. Steve Wilberforce, who had been
wounded a week after Frank, had only got to Rouen
and had returned three weeks ago. Ikey Harris had
been sick in hospital at Etaples, but was back a week
before Frank, and Sergeant Burke was boozing and

often no better than a cot case. The platoon was now composed as follows:—

Lieut. Jack Skipton, D.C.M.
Sergeant Tom Burke, M.M.

Riflemen :

Corporal Frank Jeffreys, Jim Blount, M.M., Ted Marshall, Artie Chomley, Bill Potter, Charl Bentley, Cock Walker.

Lewis Gunners :

Lance-Corporal Blue McIntosh, Fatty Gray, Sucker Sykes, Syd Barton, Bob Allison, Steve Wilberforce.

Rifle Grenadiers :

Harry Mullane, Johnny Wright, Tich Carson, Darky Lansdowne, Scratcher Nunn.

Bombers :

Lance-Corporal Willy Wallace, Artie Fethers (reduced for impudence to Captain Slade), Ikey Harris, Eddie Hecht, Dopey Kendall, Lorry Swift.

The Somme in summer was to Frank, too, a different country. In Flanders he had never succeeded in getting his bearings. Cassel, Mont des Cats, Bailleul, Wytschaete, Ypres, Neuve Eglise, Poperinghe, Locre, Romarin, Steenwerk, Armentieres — they seemed all jumbled up together, set at the corners of triangles of all shapes and sizes, and then the hills were short and quick, the fields were small and lined high with impenetrable hedges, and it was always raining and the visibility was obscure. True, in winter it rained enough and was cold enough on the Somme, but the north was a darker country. But now, in summer, on the Somme, you did get something of a view over low, rolling country, the rippling grass of which in June had quite a yellow tinge that reminded him of the summer grass at home. From so many points one had the tree line of the Somme and the Canal to guide, the roads were long and straight, and away behind one might catch a glimpse, when the sky was clear, of Amiens Cathedral, with hump-back high over the houses like a hen crouched over her chickens to protect them from the peril in the air. And, too soon, Frank knew that when you went up that hill in front, the grass of which was spotted with holes ringed by whitish, chalky earth, particularly frequent along the line of the communication trench, you came to the trenches and posts of the line. A couple of hundred yards beyond there was Fritz, the old fellow himself, building his line as usual into a state of more than comfort—luxury—as if he intended to stay there forever, whereas we, on our side, scratched our dwellings out like the gypsies of the Troglodytean race as if we were ashamed to admit that they might acquire a permanence which would warrant greater depth and comfort. Fritz seemed, after the effort of March, anxious now to spend the halcyon days of summer in quiescence and the statu quo, but the Australians kept harrying, nibbling a bit off the line here and there, and raiding. "Only waking the old bastard up," as the men complained of their own activity.

But in the heat of clear summer days there was an omen of storm which the more intelligent sensed afar. Autumn would soon be with them, and, after autumn, winter. Another winter on the Somme; good God, like the one before last! They knew and they feared it, and they feared, also, the caution and stupidity of generals who would attack, as they had done in the past before the winter, depending on winter itself to save them from the consequences of failure, always fearful and chary of the issue of combat. There was, therefore, a feeling of unrest disturbing the ease of the summer days. To that clearer vision of the men there contributed restlessly, through a hundred slight manifestations, the sense of oneness, the awareness and insistence of distinct nationality, the deep pride of the soldier in an army which is conscious, even before the struggle, of its shattering, terrible vitality and invincibility. The physical eye, too, contributed, for the Australian soldier could, wherever he looked, describe a sector manned solely by his comrades. Now it only wanted the arrival of the division from the north, where it had been engaged in encountering, like the others, the head of a German offensive, for the whole five divisions to constitute together the army corps which already they were in name.

There was thus ready for the former civilian, Monash, and Rawlinson, his leader, and Foch Generalissimo, a weapon of magnificent cold temper, hammered through the fires of many an engagement and battle, experienced and skilled in warfare more than any others, dangerous so that some of those who were to use it were almost afraid of it themselves. Frank Jeffreys, returned from Blighty and become a particle of it, knew, in his own personal thrill, the spirit and morale of the whole. The question was—Would it be used? For what ultimate stroke? He who had the right to use it for that, now whetted it in a series of small engagements. Nor

should it be overlooked that the weapon itself, as has
been hinted, was not without prescience of its high
purpose. It was confident of its mettle and was cyni-
cally aware, like someone to whom the Fates have
mouthed a prophecy without doubt because it arises
logically out of the past and conforms with the
present, that whatever the end might be, defeat or
victory or stalemate, its destiny would be to make the
essay. It foresaw that, even should defeat come, turning the world into a chaos in which alone and far
from its native shores it might forever be lost, returning thither only in wretched, scanty remnants, its
flash and clang in the crisis of the war would be like
a thunderbolt and forked lightning through the storm.

CHAPTER XXXI.

SQUATTING on a bag in the front line trench, Frank
could hear the rumbling of a waggon on a road
beyond Fritz's supports, so clear the night was and
sensitive to sound. The front line was a replica of
the support trench, except that the shelters were
merely holes in the compact, chalky earth, with the
entrances covered by little porches of old blankets
and bits of iron. Bill Potter sat beside him while,
on the fire step, Jim Blount and Charl Bentley stood
peering out over the parapet. A working party was
strengthening the wire on the left, making, thought
Charl, a hell of a row, as if, as he said to Jim, they
were playing the xylophone on the pickets.

Jim smiled. There was a certain live and let live
about these trenches. Fritz, clinging to a little out-

ward buckle of his line, here insinuated by his own quiet a wish not to be disturbed. The Australian scouts and patrols had driven him out of No Man's Land and, anxious about the buckle, he would be content if his delicate position there should remain undisturbed until he should perhaps have the chance some time to take advantage of it. This was probably the reason why the wiring party, having completed what it thought was a fair night's work, was left unmolested. On the right a few shells were coming over from the vicinity of Morlancourt, and, in the dip towards the Somme, a machine gun distantly displayed a spasmodic irritation.

A cool breeze shivered the grass. Quiet—all was quiet now that the wiring party had vamoosed. Amen, so let it be.

There was a movement in the trench on the right. Someone was coming. The corporal and Bill Potter stood up to let Lieutenant Skipton pass. In a few minutes he came back accompanied by Lieut.-Colonel Gilderoy and Captain Slade.

"Mr. Skipton," said the colonel softly.

"Yes, sir."

"I want to have a look at Fritz. I'll take two men. Hullo, corporal, you ought to be fresh. You'll do, and you, Blount."

Charl and Bill, who had felt his eyes waver on them, breathed a sigh of relief.

"See you warn those on each side of you we're out, Skipton."

Frank and Jim Blount felt the bombs in their pockets and picked up their rifles. The battalion commander exchanged some low words with the captain.

He did not like Slade. He would have liked to have
taken him just to shake him up. The man spent
too much time in his dug-out. However, he did
not entertain the idea, for it would have been silly
risking another officer. The others along the trench
were wondering what Gilda was up to now. While
admitting that he was the best colonel they knew, they
rather deplored his activity.

"You all right, you two. Come along. Let them
know the word along the trench. What'll it be?
'Dingbat.' That's not a bad 'un, eh?" He undid the
button of his holster.

He got up out of the trench and, the two he had
chosen following, they wormed their way through the
wire. When he cast a quick glance back, Frank could
see only a grey, blurred line where the trench was.
They were out in No Man's Land, and, after going
a short distance in a semi-upright position, followed
the example of their leader, and began to crawl forward almost on their bellies. The grass lapped their
faces. As they moved slowly forward, Frank and Jim
cast quick glances about them. You couldn't reckon that
Fritz might not unexpectedly have a patrol out or a
listening post in some shell hole. A heavy stink made
them draw away to the left a little. Every now and
then some slight sound froze them, and they stopped,
with ears intent and furtive glances here and there.
After a while they saw a dark shadow ahead—the
enemy wire.

"You wait here," whispered the colonel.

There was a shell hole a few yards away, and Jim
Blount slid into it so that he could sit up and watch
all round, while the corporal lay down where he was

with his rifle stuck out in front of him and a bomb in
his right hand. That they were closer to the wire
than they had thought, they were apprised by a low,
merry laugh and someone commencing to hammer with
a muffled mallet. Every now and then they would
hear the sound of voices and that low, merry laugh.
It was young, and it had no bitterness nor malice nor
fear. Coming from the unseen out of the ground in
front of them, it had something of faery in its
musicality. The corporal thought, "If I gave a bomb
two seconds, they'd have no chance to get away."

Only five minutes had gone, but he now thought
Gilda's been a long time. And after a few more
moments he repressed the inclination to crawl over
to Jim and ask him "How ———— long were they going
to be out there bloody well waiting?" The violence
of his thought's expression, and its bitter anger, unexpected even to himself, made him tremble. He was
suddenly and fearfully aware how thin was the veneer
of sanity which his convalescence in England had
spread over his old nervous disorder. He was afraid.
"Mary, Mary." His thoughts clung to her name. She,
in her quiet goodness, could be his salvation. After
the war, what? If there were to be any such time
for him. Security for himself and Mary. What better
assurance of it would he have than his job in the
Education Department? Security—that's why a man,
specially a man outside the Government, wanted pro-
perty; security for wife and children. When he
thought of it, he, a sort of socialist, could imagine
the Family of more importance than the State. He
shook himself out of the trance into which he was
falling, and looked to Jim Blount, whose head stuck

H

up immobile like the stump of a sapling lopped close
to the ground. Jim, too, while he kept his eyes and
ears automatically alert, was thinking. So tranquil
was the dark that you could not help but think. He
was about due for leave. He would have liked to go
to Paris, but he had to collect some money in London.
There was a rumour that the banks, at any rate the
Commonwealth Bank, was limiting the amount you
could draw. What damned impudence! He wanted
his leave badly. The war seemed to be closing upon
life just when he was tasting its richness. And yet
but for the war he would never have met Horace
Calverley. Would he be killed ultimately? They said,
jokingly, the first seven years were always the worst.
His last leave had not been too happy. But he knew
himself changed since them—become securer in himself, able to maintain his own individuality which then
he had only first been finding.

"Hiss."

The corporal jumped in his skin at Jim's warning.
The colonel wriggled up between them. "Swish."
Fifty yards away on their right a flare went up. As
it slowly fell, they lay quite still. By its glare, Frank
could see a small insect climbing laboriously up the
slope of a grass blade just in front of his nose. When
the light faded, the night was pitch black until their
eyes had recovered from the shock.

"Ther're some Fritzes in the trench just in front.
I'd like to sling them a bomb," whispered Jim.

The colonel deliberated. "I don't want to wake
them up."

They started to move back, Jim in the rear, remov-
ing, as well as he could, the marks where they had

lain and the tracks of their bodies through the grass.

Another flare froze them. "I say, sir," whispered Jim, "it's about time I got my leave."

"Then you'll get it in time."

"Not much to our platoon if Captain Slade has any say."

"I'll remember."

They were at the wire. From the trench came a hoarse "Who's there?"

"Dinkum," replied the colonel, standing up.

"Dingbat, you —— fool." It was Ted Marshall. He was chuckling.

"All right, Marshall, I'll remember you for that." They slid down into the trench.

"Where's Mr. Skipton? O, there you are, Skipton." He went off with the subaltern along the trench.

"What's up, Jim?" asked Harry Mullane.

"A raid I suppose."

"No, really?"

Seated on the fire step, the corporal laid his chin on his hand. Some memory when he was out there had bubbled from the depths of his memory and kept his mind uneasy and perturbed. Now that he had at last tracked it, it appeared to have no significance. The event he recalled was the mistake about the letter. Young Bentley had picked up a letter out of the bundle with "That's for me," and handed it to him with "I thought I knew the writing."

It was nothing, of course. Bentley had met her, but that she should write to him was absurd. He laughed.

CHAPTER XXXII.

COLONEL GILDEROY had a reason for his noctural reconnoitre. By the seizure of the buckle in Fritz's front trench, he would make his line untenable for two or three hundred yards, and force him back to the more disadvantageous position of his support line. He reckoned he would need only one company for the action itself, and that the two others, one on each side of it, could be used to extend and protect the new flanks while he held the other in reserve. There had been some talk at brigade of making another raid, and apropos of this he now made his suggestion to the brigadier and the staff major. His little show, he pointed out, would have all the effects of a raid, but would, in addition, not only mean the capture of some ground, but leave the enemy in a yet more awkward position. His argument was too forceful to be withstood, and, in due course, his plan was approved at divisional headquarters at St. Gratien and Corps, wherever that was. The colonel's idea was that the affair should be a surprise. Artillery would only be needed to stifle any counter-attacks and cut the enemy communication trenches. He could provide a barrage in miniature himself. He would want a few engineers to drive a trench out to the new position. The quiet on the line thereabouts led him to believe they would catch Fritz unawares. A night stunt. It would take place just before the divisional relief, so that, as soon as the new position was consolidated, the attackers might be relieved by the troops coming into the line.

By the time it was determined, D Company was

in supports again. He would use it for the attack.
It had had a lucky spin lately; indeed, ever since they
had come down to the Somme. It was left to the
platoon commanders to instruct the men, which was
done two nights before that which had been fixed on.
They were given not only their own allotted tasks,
but as much information as Gilderoy himself possessed,
except the actual hour. Each platoon had a helio print
of the plan to study, and talked it over with its commander. What was to happen was this. D Company
was to sneak up to the German wire, which was to
be cut by two amatol torpedoes and the wire cutters
with which the N.C.O.'s and a number of the men were
supplied. The operation of D Company itself was to
be composed as follows, without regard to the
platoons. Because it would be too dangerous, if the
night were clear, to attempt to gather about a hundred
men close up to the enemy wire, Gilderoy determined
to cover the advance of the main body over the fifty
yards which would be between where they lay out
and the enemy trench. He therefore detailed a Lewis
gun, with a crew of three, to approach close to the
wire on each flank, and a party of three of the best
bombers in the company, who would carry twelve
bombs apiece. Counting the two men who were to fire
the torpedoes, there would thus be only fourteen men
against the wire itself. The Lewis gunners and the
bombers, at the sound of the detonations, would open
a miniature barrage, the gunners keeping the enemy
in the trench into which the bombers would pitch their
bombs. Under cover of this, the others would make
their way through the wire. While the entire section of
trench was being mopped up, the other two Lewis

gunners, assisted by three more bombers, would clear the trench out where it bent back on both sides and make barricades in it. The two flanking companies would establish the connections to the new line by developing shell holes into a series of posts, and the engineers, assisted by some of the reserve company, would drive a slanting sap to the centre of the position.

The following afternoon the troops knew that the show was to be staged that night. They waited stolidly in their dug-outs for the dark, and then for the appointed hour. Though there was only the whiff of a rising moon, the sky was clear and the stars were amazingly bright, so that the air had a certain luminosity which, once you got used to it, enabled you to see what you were about quite easily. At half past three the company moved off down the communication trench, and in half an hour had taken over the front line. The other companies were already in their position. Twenty minutes were allowed, for those they had relieved, to get back, which they did well in time, congratulating themselves it was not they who were going over, as they fervently whispered to the men of the in-coming platoons, "Good luck, Dig."

"And when you get to Blighty, along'll come Birdie's daughter and say, 'Daddy wants you over there.'"

"O hell, we've done with Birdie."

They could feel the rum curdling in their insides and mounting up their spines to their heads. It couldn't make you drunk just then though. Blessed rum, blessed rum.

"For God's sake, serg, see that Fatty don't fall over himself."

"Shut up, ——— you."

Sergeant Burke was not enamoured of his job of setting off one of the torpedoes. Who would be? He was taking Bob Allison with him.

Soon they were wriggling forward in No Man's Land. The line halted, and only the flanking Lewis gunners and bombers and the four men with their torpedoes went forward on to the wire. The men waited, their lips tight and their hearts thumping. A light went up fizzing into the night. It was out and no sound, thank God. The night borrowed a greater profundity from the expectation of the racket to come. Surely the time was up. Another minute, another. Bang, bang. Two big explosions, succeeded immediately by the sharper sounds of the bombs and the rattling of the Lewis guns. They were running forward towards the spot where one of the torpedoes had exploded. They were into the wire, cutting at it, tugging it and scrambling through its barbs. The first of them were through. Skipton nearly fell on a man whose face, white with the fear of death, like the reflection of a full moon, he dashed aside with his knobkerry. Another, trying to climb the opposite wall of the trench, was stabbed by the sergeant and Bill Potter simultaneously. Albie Chomley shot another at the muzzle of his rifle. Charl Bentley and Frank Jeffreys pitched some bombs into a dug-out. Everything was now a welter. Lights began to shoot up all along the line, and machine guns to rattle into a mad crescendo of terror. The rest of the Germans in the trench were being despatched. One, as he died,

shot Bob Allison in the thigh. There were more dug-
outs, deep. Fritz did himself well in the line.

"Share that among you," yelled George Hecht, who,
with Ikey with his bayonet ready alongside, held the
bomb two seconds after the lever had sprung off before
he pitched it down.

Where the trench curved back, Willy Wallace and
Artie Fethers lobbed bombs into the bays ahead, clear-
ing it of the enemy for 50 yards at least, while those
beyond range retreated. Some Fritzes came up out of
the dug-outs, ten or eleven of them, with their hands
up, preferring the danger above to further bombs
inside. They were sent back to the face of the trench,
against the side of which they huddled together. The
guns now were in action, adding a deeper note to
the fury of sound. A shell, probably a short, pitched
just behind those who were at work on the barricade.
No one was hit, and the men there laboured frantically with their entrenching tools and shovels.

The German shells were bursting along the old line
now quicker than ever, not yet on the new position
because the gunners yet had no word of who held it
now. The Australians, with the trench firmly in their
possession, began to look around and take stock.
Someone found some coils of concertina wire, and Jim
Blount and Charl Bentley unrolled it on the other side.

Only fifteen minutes had passed since the commencement of the attack. So far it had been easy. The
noise had diminished with the cessation of the Lewis
gun fire, and the hostile machine fire, too, had died
down. The change had been perceptible, but it
brought a thrill of greater apprehension. The new
quiet was the presage of the counter attack. The

worst, they knew, was to come. The colonel came
along with Captain Slade to organise the defence. He
took a dozen men and a Lewis gun out beyond the
trench on the German side, where they established
themselves in shell holes, spoke to the men on the
right barricade, and then hurried back with his two
runners to the old line where his headquarters were
now established, and where the men of the reserve
company, who had already lost about a dozen men,
shrunk back into the holes in the trench. Everything
was well. The flanks were caught up, and the engineers and the working party were pushing forward
the head of the sap deep enough for the present if
a man could crawl in shelter along it. Almost half
an hour had passed. Fritz was slow about it. The
colonel lit a cigarette and took a swig from the
adjutant's flask. The enemy barrage remained a
quarter of an hour on the captured position before
it lifted to the former No Man's Land and the old
Australian line. In the deep enemy trench the company suffered surprisingly few casualties. At the
height of the storm some of the troops knelt, making
themselves as small as possible in the bottom of the
trench, while others sheltered in the passages down
into the dug-out. Frank Jeffreys was one of those
who stayed in the trench. That was his form of
courage, if it could be so called. Rather, it was his
effort to do his duty which kept him there in the
more dangerous place. It was a form of desperate
pretence by which he sought absolution for the fear
which had rendered him so ineffective in the attack.
Like one who would first burn the hand which had
recanted, he was one of the few who stood up and,

from time to time, observed for a second or two the
hostile position. Some instinct made him shrink back.
At that moment a howitzer shell burst in the low
parados and flung him down. As he lay there he saw,
in the reverberating whiteness of the flash, like a
murderer's remorseless vision, the stark, belching
mouths of the 9.2's on the Menin Road.

The barrage lifted. The men, waiting in their
retreats for that signal, ran out and mounted the
footholds they had made. Fritz was coming up the
trench on each side and over the top. Again the
scream and roar of battle rose to its height—the indescribable noise of modern battle, even of such a
miniature as this. And Fritz copped it. Only on the
right did he get any way on. There, gallantly led,
the wave almost reached the trench. Like a small
heavy cloud, it rolled forward over the ground, only
to be scattered and absorbed by the flame which met
it.

When the Australians looked up, they saw the dawn
streaking the sky, and hailed it. The counter-attack
was broken. The enemy would not have time to
launch another before the light of morning, when it
would be impossible. The noise began to die away,
and the enemy's effort sank to mere shelling of no
great intensity. Some gas, however, came over, and
the men had to put on their masks for a while. It
was morning, herald of the day, and the soundless
blast of its bugle was the cease fire. The stunt was
finished, and the more acquisitive in the platoon commenced to gather souvenirs. Ted Marshall was the
most fortunate, for from the body of an officer he got
a Lubin automatic and a pair of field glasses and a

gold ring. The total losses of the platoon were only three wounded—Bob Allison, Scratcher Nunn (one of the fellows from the Light Horse) and Willy Wallace.

At the mention of Weary Willy, Artie Fethers exclaimed to the sergeant, "Why, the cow's no sooner back than he's off to Blighty again."

It was a fairly quiet day. Fritz contented himself with throwing over a fair amount of gas on the rear positions from his further batteries. Only occasionally did he trouble the line. The relief took place that night before he had really started to show his vindictiveness, and the battalion's speed along the trenches left nothing to chance. There was no desire to linger until Fritz showed his temper on account of last night. Soon the line was only a glimmer on the horizon, a little more lurid than usual, for Fritz, badly shaken, was sending up a multitude of flares, repopulating the sky, from which the wind had shaken the natural inhabitants. The whole division was going out. What a change! Last night there, and now, this night, tramping peacefully along the road, and not too much tramping either, for, on the other side of Heilly, the battalion which had made the attack was picked up by motor lorries which carried it to Querrieu.

CHAPTER XXXIII.

AS a favour for the success of its little stunt, room was made for the battalion in the billets in the village. Charl Bentley and Bill Potter sat side by side on a litter of dirty straw with their backs against the wall of a shed, one end of which was open to a dirty yard where the fowls were scratching in the refuse. Charl was smoking a cigarette, while Bill Potter read two letters from his cousin, Myrtle. Though he knew that, when they came to France, Charl had been enamoured of Mary Hatton, that was so long ago that it did not trouble Bill's mind when he remarked to Charl, "Do you know what she says? When he was in Blighty, Frank Jeffreys used to go about with Mary Hatton a lot. Cripes, you wouldn't think he was one for the tarts!"

Charl, though he heard the words plainly enough, made no reply, but bent his head in case his face might betray him. In spite of the fact that his correspondence with Mary had long ceased, and it was only when he thought what he might do when he got his leave, that he recalled her to his memory these days, his face flared up. He instantly remembered the occasion when he had handed over the letter to the corporal. It must have been her writing. It was the shock to his vanity which hurt. She had chucked him for the corporal. She had made a fool of him. He thought with chagrin of the letters he had written her. He had wanted to marry her and asked her.

"O, her!" was all he said to Bill.

But all the afternoon it rankled. He saw plainly that he had made himself a fool about her. It was only a slight satisfaction that he might have been a bigger one. Viciously he thought to himself, "Well, at any rate, I gave her what she was looking for." That was some consolation. He knew now how many men made fools of themselves about girls in England. He had almost been one of them. Just a kid. He hated even those cousins of Bill's knowing anything

about it, let alone Frank Jeffreys. To be laughed at
by that dopey coot!

However, when Bill and he left the two-up school,
where, following Jim Blount's betting, he had won
twenty-five francs, he felt more reasonable. He
wondered whether the corporal had got his oats or
whether she had made a fool of him too, and because
he knew the corporal, he guessed perhaps she had.
Why else should she be writing to him if she wasn't
stringing him on? His own part, because of his
escape, became less unpleasant to him. He rather
liked this new picture of himself, which now presented
itself to him, as a doggish fellow. That was clearly
the line to take if the subject of Mary Hatton ever
came up. The memory of that night, embellished by
time, gave it reality. In the expectation of what
would happen on his leave, he began to feel almost
pleased with what had taken place. Because he had
so long since ceased to think much about her, and
then only with vague discomfort that he had been an
ass to write to her about marriage, he assured himself that when he saw her again it would be a different story. She would see, then, that he was no fool,
and take a full wake-up to it.

In the evening the whole platoon went off, with the
exception of the lieutenant and the sergeant, who was
already drunk, to the former Lion d'Or to celebrate
not so much their success in the stunt as their
removal from the line for a spell. Even the stunt did
little to dispel the monotony of war, its constant
arduous routine, and the despondency when you knew
too well your chance in the course of the never-ending
succession of months. That was why even the few

teetotallers were tempted and fell from grace so often.

After they consumed a plate of eggs apiece, most of them started to wallop into the wine—vins blanc et rouge. They had appropriated one of the rooms to themselves and turned away all others. They sang songs—all the old silly songs—but they had to sing something, and they banged on the tables, making the glasses and bottles dance. A young woman named Gabrielle waited on them, passing uncontaminated through the desires which enveloped her, like the lady amidst the riot of Comus' crew. Preserved by holy thoughts, maybe. The three teetotallers, too, were swept up into a sort of intoxication. The scene acquired a sort of orgiastic rhythm to which old Johnny Wright, seated with a Silenus face on the floor, at first beat time on a dish, and which, after a time, he seemed to control like a heathen priest beating his people to a frenzy with the tom-tom. The men swayed where they sat, or danced about to his drumming— tom-tom—tom-tom to-to-tom. Occasionally someone would lurch to the door. Gradually the orgy passed its climax. Still the tom-tom beat, not so insistently now, but softly.

Frank Jeffreys sat on a form with his back against the wall. The explosion of that accursed shell in the parados had set his nerves loose again. The side of his face kept twitching, and he could not keep it still. The whole of the evening he had sat there trying to keep it still, massaging it with his fingers and exerting tremendous efforts of will. It was all of no avail. It would keep twitching. If he shut his eyes he could see in the flare of flame the big muzzles of those flaring 9.2's poking up.

Bill Potter lay back against his chair with his long legs poked out. One of his puttees had come undone and was trailing in the dirt on the floor. Charl Bentley leaned forward on the table on which Sidder Barton reclined. Further along on the form were Harry Mullane and Jim Blount.

Bill and Charl and Barton had been talking of women. Now that he was drunk, Charl pondered over what had befallen his love for Mary Hatton with growing resentment.

He was angry, too, at Barton's sneer at his inexperienced youth. It was a lie.

"Damn you, Barton," he said.

Barton's bloated face sneered his disbelief.

"I got the address of one now.

He sorted a dirty, stiff piece of a paper out of his wallet.

"There y'are."

He could read it only with difficulty. "26 Goldsmith Street, Elwood. No, that isn't it. That's Aussie. 154 Milton Crescent, Cricklewood. That's the place."

Frank Jeffreys heard the words plainly and pressed back against the wall as if to escape through its solidity what the boy would say next.

"Friend of my cousins," agreed Bill, owlishly.

"I had a good time with her, I tell you. Didn't I, Bill?"

"You bet."

Charl looked defiantly across at the corporal, who shrank away from him. Reassured by the movement that there was no need to take it all so seriously, the boy winked and grinned at him. "She's pretty hot, isn't she, corporal? You know her, don't you, corp?

Wen' on leave with her, didnya, corp? He knows,
Sidder, ask 'im.''

He became involved in sentimental dreams, through
which sounded Johnny's faint tom-toming.

He felt like crying. He had his head down on his
arm. A soldier; yes, he was a soldier. Alone, quite
alone, so far away from dear old Dad and Mum for
the duration. The war was all about him. He felt
surrounded, shut off forever from what he had been,
from all that dear love of him at home. Mary
Hatton!—her. What did he want with her, with them
all. Gentle Jesus, pity me. He was alone, all by himself, and all this had just happened. A feeling possessed him, growing almost to a conviction, that it
was not he himself here at all, but someone else. And
yet it was he after all. He was sick on the table.

The others were all silent, bemused with drink and
sleep. Jim Blount was helping Harry to the door.
Their movement touched some spring in the corporal,
and he staggered out after them. Johnny Wright's
tom-tom beat no more, for Johnny had bitten the dust
and his false teeth had fallen out. Frank followed
Jim's slow progress to the billet, as one, who is careless of his direction, will follow another by instinct.

Jim Blount helped Harry along easily enough. Harry
was fairly steady on his pins, but his mind was in a
deep trance. It was the first time Jim had seen Harry
so drunk, and it startled him. Underneath his usual
quiet gaiety, poor Harry, too, must be feeling it.
They all were. The interminable war. He knew
Harry was finding it difficult to keep going. It was
like another world to which the troops were adapt-
ing themselves, becoming beings of a different nature

to the inhabitants of that natural one in which they had formerly existed. Slowly, too, because the replacements were of poorer quality, the common physique was being worn away. He remembered the men he had known—the platoon as it had first existed. No, it was not now what it had been then. It was like a man who had passed middle age, whose muscles perform the job perhaps as well as those of younger men, long custom and use equalling in effectiveness the strength of youth which wastes itself through its very exuberance.

Before he entered the gate of the billet, he looked up at the moon. It had become a firm, polished crescent cleaving into the clouds like a curved dagger. In a week, Fritz would be over bombing. Instinctively he listened as if to catch already the distinctive pulse of his engine. He put Harry to bed and undressed himself; that is, he took off his tunic, his boots and his pants, put on his cardigan and pushed his feet into the top of his pants and wrapped himself in his blankets. Sleep; forgetfulness. What a sad night it had been!

Corporal Jeffreys came into the shed. He seemed already asleep on his feet. He did not bother to undress, but only wrenched open the top of his tunic and covered himself with the blankets.

Jim was just falling asleep when Harry sat up.

"What was I tellin' you in th'estaminet, eh? I know. Y'there, Jim. I was talkin' to fella named Armand las' week. Artillery joker. I'm sick of the war, Jim. I've had enough. Yer, I've 'ad 'nough. I'm no 'ero. No nero. He said he was an internashlist. No more wars. I said 'ave to be good Aussie

first. Eh, Jim? Good nashlist and good internashlist
at same time, eh, Jim?"

"That's right, Harry. Go t'sleep, damn yer," said
Jim, and gave Harry a push in the chest which sent
him on his back. This time Harry went to sleep.

CHAPTER XXXIV.

HOWEVER horrible and blasting verification of his
fearful suspicions would be, the corporal desired
it as a man desires the absolute, for its own sake,
come what may. During the next few days he put
together each word Charl Bentley had uttered in its
proper sequence, and then was afraid he had got the
sentences wrong. The boy had said after he had read
out the address, "I had a good time with her." And
then he had winked as he said, "She's pretty hot,
isn't she, corporal?" That was enough—that he had
said she was hot. Mary!

He tried to reassure himself that, after all, it had
been merely a youth's brag, the commonest sort—the
brag of being a hard-doer with the girls. And yet
it had not been entirely that. In the boy's look there
had been something hurt and resentful. One conclusion he could not escape. Mary had hid from him that
she had ever seen Bentley again after that night
they had met at Bill Potter's cousins. He resurrected
Myrtle and Hilda, who now seemed to have been
pretty free sort of girls. Mary was their friend. One
of them had got to know of his own acquaintance
and going about with Mary, and had written of it.
Why? Because they guessed Charlie Bentley was con-

cerned. One thing he tried to avoid, but he could not. If Mary was hot! That night when she had come in her night dress to the door of his room. If she were, that scene had another significance. Was she just like so many other girls of whom he had been told—hot, desirous of physical excitement and satisfaction? In the war, girls were letting themselves go in a way they never had before. There occurred to him one of the many stories he had heard, a ghastly story of a dopey fellow who had married a girl on his leave. Another, in the same platoon, when his turn had come to go, had visited the wife, at the request of the dopey chap, to give her some souvenirs, and had ended up with sleeping with her. The dopey chap had been killed, and the other had thought, therefore, that he was free to relate the derisive story of his adventure.

One thing was plain to him—that Mary had concealed something from him. How little it was or how bad, she had, at any rate, concealed it. It must be something worth hiding. He must know; he must find out somehow or another. Charl Bentley's presence filled him with a sickening aversion, and yet, at the very same time, exercised upon him an irresistible attraction. He could not help looking at him, observing him, with his pleasant face and the curly head which held the intolerable secret of that short span of Mary's life before he himself had met her. And yet some sort of justice forbade him blaming the boy when he himself had deliberately written to her and asked her to correspond. So when he heard that Jim Blount, Harry Mullane, Johnny Wright, Darky Lansdowne, Potter and Bentley proposed to go to a sports meeting near Allonville, he, too, decided to accompany them. They did not know exactly where the place was, but the day was beautiful and warm, and they set out with alacrity, after dinner, along the road to that village.

Half way, when they had passed the lip of Querrieu Wood, they sat down on the side of the road. A big car went by full of brass hats, but, seemingly engrossed in their own conversation, the men took no notice of it.

"That was Monash and his mob," said old Johnny.

"Well, he had the good sense not to stop. I hate these cows who pull up to speak a few cheering words to the troops," said Harry.

"He must like himself now he's a corps commander," Darkey said, and removed his pipe to shoot his spit out into the dust which still eddied above the road.

"Ah, I suppose the cow'll want to do something flash just to show 'em," added Harry.

"The better he is, the worse for us," agreed Jim.

When they drew near Allonville, they were led by the sound of a band, and the direction of a number of other diggers, to a large hedge-lined field which was sheltered by a bend of Gorgue Wood. There must have been about 2000 men collected about the circular track, which had been marked out by white tape held down by pegs. Inside the arena, tapes had been strung on sticks for the sprints, and a patch dug up for the long jump.

Like everyone else, those in the party did not consider themselves necessarily confined to the space outside the circular track, but wandered across the arena to inspect the little groups of competitors. The pro-

gramme had already been commenced some time when
they arrived. Though there was a considerable assort-
ment of costume, the meeting was evidently being held
in some style, for quite a number of the participants
wore white or coloured trunks and singlets, and carried spiked shoes purchased out of unit funds. Some
of them, however, had been able only to improvise
on their military wardrobes. It was one of these
whose appearance particularly provoked the undis-
guised amusement of the onlookers. He had on a grey
flannel shirt, and, tied up at the waist with a piece of
string, a pair of tight army underpants cut off just
above the knees, and a pair of grey issue socks.
Rivalry between the various arms and the battalions
was keen and the barracking vigorous. The race,
which was finishing when the party arrived, was the
440 yards. It was won by a speedy youth out of the
artillery, who, before the war, had been a light in one
of the Melbourne amateur clubs.

The 100 yards Allonville Gift was the next event
after the tedious long jump, and the six new arrivals
mooched across to the start where the competitors
were collected, some rubbing their calves and a few
practising starts. A twinkle came into Darky's eye
as he cocked it down at one of these, a strong, sinewy
cove with a face like an axe. Approaching the man
cautiously from behind, just as he was set, Darky
put his foot against the protuberant backside and gave
a vigorous shove.

"Nothing like a flying start, Chick," he said with a
grin in the angry face which whirled around when
the runner recovered himself.

The anger died in a corresponding grin, and the two shook hands.

"Darky," exclaimed the sprinter, "the last I heard of you you was a bloody corpse."

"Well, I ain't, I'm glad to say."

"So'm I. D'yer remember Peter Rose? 'Twas him told me."

"Peter?"

"You know."

"Of course I know. 'Ow is he? Still alive and kicking?"

"Gone back to Aussie."

He always was a lucky bastard. Who's going to win?"

"I am."

"You?"

"Yes, dinkum. I'm on seven yards. Take a wink from a blind man, Darky. I've got seven yards. You'd better lay a bit on."

"Jake?"

"I'm telling you. It's all serene. I'm letting you in on it."

As the party went back across the field to the other spectators, Darky excitedly gave the others his information. It was all fixed for his cobber to win. He surprised the others with his own enthusiasm, and they sought out the men making the books, finally deciding that an artillery chap with a beautiful tailor-made tunic, just like an officer's, except that it buttoned up at the neck, looked least like a welsher. They got 2 to 1 against Chick, and put their cash on him as lavishly as they could. They congratulated

Darky as he led them back to a spot opposite the finishing tapes.

The long jump was finished at last, and the six starters in the final of the Allonville Gift were getting on their marks. The little group in the know kept their eyes on the Chick. Yes, they told each other, he looks a certainty anyhow. What did amuse them was that the chap in the underpants was a starter too. It was amusing and yet perturbing. Darky questioned a sapper near by. He's on 12 yards; he just came second in the first heat because the handicapper gave it to him. Darky was reassured. Besides, it was all fixed.

The men were set. They broke and capered and went back. This time the pistol sent them off. Half way, Chick was in line with the other two in front. And then he seemed to fade back a little. Looking at the finish, they lost sight of their man. From the middle distance the cove in the pants shot out like a streak and left the others standing.

"By Gawd," said Darky softly, "thirty-two good francs I've done."

He was conscious of the eyes of the others.

"He's a damn fine runner, that chap Chick," said Jim Blount.

"The bastard's sold us a pup," cried Darky, and, with the others tracking after him, he strode out toward the group at the finish. Quickly he cut his man away from some others who were bitterly arguing together, and collared him.

"Hullo, Donaldson," he cried grimly, "I thought you was a good thing."

"So I was."

"Run, you welsher; you can only run at the nose. What about our dough?"

Chick became eloquent. He worked his lantern jaws furiously and waved his arms. "Dough? What about mine? The push's broke. That bastard McCann turned dog on us."

"Garn. You only came third."

"Well, ain't I telling you about if ye'rd give me a chance. McCann turned dog on us. He ought to be crippled for life, the bastard. And it didn't do him no good. He only came second. The fella in the underpants diddled the lot of us. He used to be sprint champion of Sydney University—came out in his socks, but by hell he ran in spikes."

Those who had gathered around Darky and his cobber turned to look at the winner, who, with a tunic now over his flannel shirt, was being escorted off by his demurely gleeful backers.

"Now, you look at his legs instead of his pants; he looks as if he could run like blue lightning," nodded Harry.

"J——, the books must have got a plaster."

"They might have been in on it."

"So they might."

The group from the platoon, now that it had done its cash, went off to take a more impartial view of the subsequent events, becoming enthusiastic only when Skeeter Johnson, out of their own battalion, whom they never thought could run, went out 50 yards from the tape to win the mile.

That night Fritz dropped five eggs on Querrieu, and the company of American Engineers, who for a few days had been the wonder of the village, suddenly

knew there was a war on. He got seventeen of them.
The next day the infantry of the —— Division started
to practise with the tanks for the Battle of Hamel.
They didn't know, of course, their objective. Apart
from anything else, the feeling of the platoon was that
it was glad that some other division than its own
was to try out the tanks again, for it was not doubted
that those manoeuvres had such a definite object even
though it was not yet disclosed. One thing would be
in favour of the new arm. This time it would not
be expected of the heavy, unwieldy monsters that they
could swim through mud or thrust through it like
bluff-bowed steel ships.

CHAPTER XXXV.

IT was a poor, wretched sort of place in the barn
and stables in which the platoon was billeted. Leaning against a daub wall on the side of the courtyard,
Tich Carson, Ted Marshall, Albie and big Dopey
Kendall looked across the filth of the yard to the
dwelling opposite where M'sieur himself was seated
on a chair in front of the door, moaning as usual. He
and his wife were of the few who would not, like the
others, pack up their traps and get out—become
refugees, homeless, with their household goods in cart.
They stuck it out in the place which belonged to them,
and to which they belonged, and this might be counted
to Madame, if not to M'sieur, as something worthier
than avarice. They regarded the man with a certain
deliberate appraisal, as wolves might regard an old
goat, and wonder, before they leaped on it, at the

difficulty of sucking any juice out of such toughness.
A dirty sort of cove this M'sieur, with a stiff, grey
growth of about a week old on his face. He was crying like a baby and holding his jaw. An affront to
decency. They knew all about it. He had toothache.
His wife worked the place while he loafed and had
the toothache.

Tich had explained to her that he could fix it all
right. To his cobbers he backed his boast by the
assertion that he had once been the assistant to a
travelling dentist, and, for a time, even a mechanic of
parts. Not that he succeeded in convincing them of
his alleged professional ability until now, when he produced a pair of forceps which, somehow or other, he
had wangled from the batman of the dental officer
established in the village. Armed with these, he and
the others contemplated their prey.

They were all short of cash owing to their losses at
two-up and the sports, and they wanted some more
badly.

"I'll stick the fangs in him all right," Tich averred.
He had already, he explained, worded the Madame to
some order. She was quite favourable to the operation.
She was sick of her man's moaning and weeping.

They mooched across and surrounded their victim.

Albie pointed to Tich when M'sieur Vanet squinted
up out of his hand. "Bon jour, M'sieur, camerade him
tres bon docteur, tres bon dentist, oui."

"Compree," Ted shoved himself forward, and, bending down, went through the motions of drawing a
tooth. "Pour the soldats, him, tres bon."

The woman came out.

"Eh, Madame, M'sieur mal, eh? Comme ca?" Ted

repeated it and then danced about to show the joy which would accompany the removal. "Toots sweet."

"Sank franc." Tich held up his five fingers.

Into the man's visible eye there had shot a wild gleam of hope, but when he caught sight, first of the forceps, and then of the five fingers, he shrank back with "Non, non," and moaned.

"Damned blubberer, ain't 'e?"

Madame shrieked at him. She did not mind the five francs.

He was an old miser. It was not as if she was ever going to get her fist on it. Her eye was malignant.

The prospect of relief was too sweet for the sufferer to hold out. They barracked up his courage. He gave a half consent and they hauled him into the kitchen. He took only a passive part, and was plomped, moaning, into a chair. Tich yanked his head back and got the mouth open—a cavern of slimy, yellow teeth.

"Righto, I see it," cried Tich.

He got his forceps in while the others bent forward to see the operation.

"Get a good grip, Tich," urged Albie.

"Yow."

The whirling arms and legs of the patient sent them all scattering except Tich, who clung on grimly.

"Grab him," he gasped.

The other three hurled themselves on the patient.

Ted grabbed the legs and Albie and Dopey an arm each, and Tich sat on the stomach.

"It's like murdering a pig," said Ted when the screams subsided into a choking gurgle.

"Got him," gasped Tich, and held up the bloody tooth.

"Five francs a piece," he grinned. "What O!"

"We'll have a few more at that."

"Trois, Madame."

She nodded wickedly.

Again Tich yanked and twisted and pulled.

"Number two."

He forced the mouth open and got a hold somewhere or other, and, in due course, out it came.

"Fifteen francs," cried Dopey unctuously.

The Froggie lay back moaning. Tich held his hand up three times. "Francs, Madame."

The woman shouted something in her husband's ear. It revived him.

"Non, non."

He looked around the ruthless faces.

"Grab him," cried Tich.

"Non, non. Ah, oui, oui. Non, non."

His struggles were overcome. Oui, oui, merci, merci" Those terrible forceps.

"Another for luck."

There was no kick in the patient. They let him go, but remained on the alert. Fingers up for twenty francs and threat of more torture. He'd had enough. A single motion by Tich put an end to his wavering. They wanted payment on the spot. Somewhere out of his clothes he produced some notes, and counted out four fives to tally with Tich's upheld fingers. Tich grabbed it and M. Vanet sank back in his chair.

"At any rate," said Tich, when they were slipping through the muck back to the barn, "the extra three'd soon have gone bad on him. He's much better without them. Any dentist'd tell you that."

Monsieur Vanet walked about next day with his jaw swollen out as big as an orange, and muttered maledictions when his tormentors asked him, "How's the gnashers to-day, m'sieur, bon, eh?"

And then the swelling went down a good deal. He felt his jaw. He opened it and prodded his gums with his fingers and then he essayed a grin. They caught him at at.

"Hullo, m'sieur, how's it to-day, pas de mal, eh?"
He grinned again.

They gathered around and smote him on the back till he wilted. "Eh, soldat, bon dentist come ca, eh?"

"Ai, bon, bon."

"Cripes," said Tich, "we let him off too light."

Jim Blount, who had heard the story, did not see the recovery of the patient. He had been at the two-up school. This trait of the old days he retained. He liked a gamble, but it was not so much that which took him to the schools. It interested him to be there, breathing the lean, hungry passion which hung about them. It was the day after the operation that he was summoned to the company orderly room, and told his leave had come through. The others accused him, good-humouredly, of having worked the oracle somehow. Only Frank Jeffreys really envied him in any serious way. No, not that, but he thought how much it would mean to him to get leave now. The solution of fearful doubt was over there in London. Mary herself. And from her lips he could and must have the truth once he was face to face with her.

Jim Blount was two days departed when Monsieur

Vanet came along with "Ai, bon, bon." His swollen jaw had subsided to normal. His sorrows were not at end, for during the afternoon Fritz put a fair number of shells into the village. An order came around requiring the immediate evacuation of all civilians. They might crawl back later if they liked. Some of them might even circumvent it by lying low, but a shell in the empty house next door convinced Vanet. The members of the platoon helped him and his Madame to pack his beds and mattresses, chairs, etc., into the waggon. It was done in haste, for shells were still coming over every now and then, and two or three of the civilians had been wounded. The poor old madame, who lived by herself down the street, was dragged out of the ruins by the troops, badly knocked.

When Ted Marshall hoisted Madame Vanet aloft on the load, she was weeping. The soldiers formed a little escort and accompanied the waggon beyond the outskirts of the village. They shook hands all round. "Bon chance, bon chance."

Old Vanet, after giving the horse a roost in the stomach, took its head and led it off in the direction of Amiens. It was a wonder it could shift the load, but it did it, for it knew M. Vanet.

THE PATH OF THE THUNDERBOLT

CHAPTER XXXVI.

WHEN Jim Blount returned some days overdue from his leave, he found the battalion, with most of the Brigade, in supports to the left of Villers Brettoneux, where the higher ground commences its first slope down towards the Somme at Corbie and Aubigny. Down there, too, the front had been extended by the capture, while he was on leave, of the little village of Hamel. It was a sector with which the battalion was already well acquainted, for it had occupied it at different periods since the time it had come down from the north.

Harry Mullane, in expectation of Jim's return, had kept a place next to him in his dugout. Frank Jeffreys joined them after tea that night, and the three men lounged on their bunks and smoked their pipes out in almost silence before Harry, knocking out his ash, enquired, this time seriously, "You had a good time, Jim?"

"Not so bad. Yes, a good time this leave. Not like the last."

"Do anything special?" Harry asked after another silence.

"I met a girl in a paddock. Had afternoon tea in what they call a manor house like a poor, lonely soldier. There was a garden with roses, red and paling in the centre like the flesh of a wound. Afterwards, I walked across the fields with her and went for a walk with her early next morning. Country they call downs or dales or something. Fine and fresh, with racing clouds. Then I just shook hands and we said good-bye. I added that for your benefit."

Harry looked up slyly, but said nothing when he saw Jim still ruminating.

"I went to the theatre."

"See The Boy?"

"Yes. I went to the opera, too, at the Garrick. Yes, I think that's the place. Ever been to the opera?"

"Aw, a bit," Harry admitted.

"I'd seen one before—Lucia di Lammermoor—but I didn't like the dagoes in kilts. The first night I saw The Boy and then Traviata—that's the opera—and when I came back from the country I went to Boris Goudounov—I think that's the name. Ever hear it? Russian. There was a cove with big bass voice singing. The second night before I got on the train I was in an air raid."

"I was in one, too, on my last leave," Harry interrupted. "Strange sort of feeling it was. Different from being bombed here."

"I'll guess where you were. You needn't tell me about it," said Jim.

"I'd never tell a lie."

"Yes, it's different. It's being in the city makes it different. I'd come back to London feeling pretty miserable. I remember—I had tea at the first joint I came to—a cheap place where the food was bad. I wouldn't like to be going there every day to eat. Most of the coves were reading the papers which had some big headlines. I hadn't ever bothered to buy one outside, but I did inside—to keep my mind off the tucker. Big black lies as usual. I suppose the coves who print them know most people have taken a wake-up to them by now, but I suppose people like to be told everything in the garden's lovely, even though they know it's only rotten rubbish. I was a fool to go there because I had plenty of money. Hadn't spent much at all. I didn't feel like going to the theatre."

"He must have been badly hit by that girl in the country," said Harry to Frank.

Jim, however, continued. "So I just wandered about until finally I crossed the Strand and came to the railings along—I don't know whether you ever turned in there—Adelphi Terrace. There's a drop down from it where I was, into a yard with a lot of barrels, and then the embankment and the river. Couldn't see the river where I sat. I sat a good while there before I went back to the Strand and into some small streets at the back of its other side. I came, in a little while, to a bigger street in which there was a good number of people. I don't know what it was, but it seemed to be a short cut from somewhere to somewhere. It was a pretty calm night and fairly clear. Standing there on the kerb, feeling alone, I heard a noise which was a damned large noise and a continuous one which I hadn't heard before. It was just the sound of the city. And, while I was thinking of noises, I heard some more. Some sirens started hooting, and soon there was quite a lot. For the moment it didn't strike me what was doing. The lights were going out—all the lights. The lamps of the cars were being turned off. A lot of people were running or pretending they weren't. You could hear windows being pulled down and doors banging. Hardly a glim of a light could you see anywhere. It was a pretty quick change. The searchlights had

I

had started to flicker on the sky. They had a lot of them. I tried to catch the sound of any Fritz engines, but could only hear our own planes getting up."

Harry and Frank listened patiently to the disjointed narrative. There were considerable pauses between the sentences while Jim marshalled his memories. It was almost as if he were recapitulating it all for himself rather than them, and it was the wonder as to the reason which mainly held their attention so far.

"It wasn't long," he went on, "before I heard the noise of the first bomb. It was a good distance away. A few people still hung about looking along the beams of the lights. They had caught nothing except one or two had a bit of cloud. Stars, too, they must have caught; but, of course, you couldn't see them in the light. They vanished like phosphorescence in a bucket. The bombs were coming my way."

"A kid at my feet I hadn't noticed, asked me, 'Where are they, Aussie?' He was a little ragged, bare-legged fellow of about ten holding an even smaller kid by the hand. Funny, sharp little kid—the bigger one. I said I didn't know. An old woman came along the street with a tray of matches and bootlaces and bits of flowers hung around her neck. She didn't seem to know where to go, and I supposed the sight of a soldier standing there seemed to reassure her a little. It turned out afterwards that she wasn't very much troubled. Anyhow, she hooked on alongside. So there were four of us then. Just then, too, we saw the Zepp. Up there in the lights, it was just like a silver cigar. There was another bomb. A whole lot of the lights caught it."

"And caught the Sultan's turret in a noose of light," Harry chanted.

"The anties started going hell for leather. But they were lower and it kept going up. Tricked 'em all the time. I heard someone say, 'Ah, the good old Zepp.' It was a Tommy officer, captain—a bit shick. 'God,' he said, 'the fools have lost her,' and somehow or other they had."

"I said there must be quite a few—four or five I reckoned. The lights were concentrating on that number of spots. The Tommy agreed and stuck with us. The next bomb was not far off and rattled the doors and windows. When I cocked an eye down at the two kids, 'I'm not frightened,' the bigger one yelled in his shrill kid's voice; 'I've seen 'em before, I 'ave.' He had the wind up, but he was game. It did put the wind up you a bit, the bombs on that quiet city— quiet, as if it was lying doggo. When I looked up I found that someone else had cottoned on to us—a woman, fairly young. She must have crept out of some doorway. She came up to me with her hands up and looked in my face. 'Where shall we go?' she says. The last bomb had been as close as the other. I reckoned it was time to beat it. The others tailed on after the Tommy and myself, and we went into a little alley, like a deep trench, six or seven feet wide and fifty feet or more high. I told them we'd do all right there. It'd been better if it had only been six feet instead of sixty if a wall fell—but what were the odds! We found an old codger there before us. He said, 'Aye, stop 'ere. The toobes'll all be filled up, I'm thinkin'. The peoples run there like so many rebbits. Yus, like so many blame rebbits.'"

"The Tommy captain lit a cigarette and I lit my pipe. The young wench reckoned we would draw the crabs. She was annoyed and the Tommy had to tell her a few times that a match light couldn't be seen from right up there. He suggested we might as well make ourselves comfortable, so we sat down on the bricks close to one another for company." Jim ticked them off on his fingers. "There was the Tommy, the old woman, the old man, the wench, the two kids and myself. The little kid was sleepy, so I took him on my knee and he tucked his head under and went off. The old woman gave us one to go on with, or the Tommy rather. We could just see our figures, for it was pretty black in there. He leaned over and patted her on the shoulder. 'Cheer up, mother; don't be afraid,' he says. 'Now I have my wits,' she says, 'I'm not frightened. I am saved and with the Lord Jesus Christ.' "

"The Tommy looked at her and then turned to me and said, 'Fancy that. There's an enigma for you, Aussie.' "

"I said it was a mystery."

"He seemed to like the word, for he said, 'That's it, Aussie; you've hit in one—a mystery.' "

"A funny thing about that Tommy was that he didn't try to come the officer stuff over me."

"I was thinking that," said Frank.

"Well, he went on about the old lady being out on the kerb all day and night with the tray, and being with the Lord Jesus Christ being a mystery. He reckoned it was a pretty hard thing for an old dame selling matches at hapenny for a box to be with the Lord Jesus Christ. I thought it was too. She told

him it was two boxes. He said if it was him he'd
think it was the Devil. I thought he was grinning at
me. For a moment I thought of giving him one in
the chops, but I was glad I didn't, after.''

"The shooting had stopped a few minutes. The girl
wouldn't have it that Fritz had gone off, because there
was no All Clear. They knew more about it than me.
Then the old cove chipped in. 'I wish I was a sojer
again. I was a sojer once. In the Boer War I was.
I'd give them 'Uns 'ell, droppin' bombs on Lunnon.
They didn't use to do such things when I was a sojer.
I fought the Boers, I did. I got wounded when I was
with Roberts, I did. 'E was a sojer. 'Aig, bah!'
You'd have thought he won the Boer War—he and
Roberts—between them. And so the kid says, hearing him, 'I wish I was a sojer.' He was leaning against
me and scratching his legs. I asked where he lived.
He said he lived with the old woman, and he just
finished his papers when the Zepps came. He'd seen
all the Zepps. He'd seen every Zepp that had come
over London. 'I 'ave; strike me dead if I 'aven't.
Blimy.' The old woman had told him to take Albert
out, as it was time he earned his living. Poor Albert.''

"I asked the kid how old he was. He was twelve
he said, and Albert was seven. He said they never
went 'ome on Fridays or the old woman 'd knock
their heads off.''

"The bombs started again. First there was one,
and then another close by. In between we heard the
old chap say, 'Ah, the Boers, they had plenty of shells,
but they didn't 'ave no airyplanes, they didn't.' ''

"There was another bomb, also pretty close.''

"They sound closer than they are," Harry interrupted.

"When the concussion finished, the girl started to grizzle, and the old chap says very distinctly in the quiet, 'Now Roberts, 'e was a general.'"

"It was that set the Tommy going. I'll tell you what he said as near as I can remember. He was a clever devil, that Tommy. 'I don't know anything about Roberts,' he says, 'but I should say your generals were as good as ours. Would you say, digger, we are blessed in our generals? Do you know what I'd like. I'd like the good old Hun up there to drop fifty of his very biggest eggs all at once along Whitehall, and then we might win the war—what?' I said that would be a good idea, and he goes on, 'I'm glad I'm not one of the exalted ones, Aussie; but the trouble is they didn't know. But do you think they don't know, Aussie?' I shrugged, and he reckoned I was right, and that they had become so exalted it didn't matter to them. He'd come to the conclusion he was a bit of Jonah. He reckoned he'd been in every rotten stunt—except Mesopotamia—there had been. He mentioned 'em all. I forget them. He was on Gallipoli, at Loos, at Thiepval and other places on the Somme—Arras, Ypres. He had a great idea; if he went to one of the heads and showed them that every stunt he went into had turned out a washout, they'd give him his discharge."

"They'd let out most of the armies on that idea," grinned Harry.

"Didn't I tell you. You see, he hadn't been wounded or killed."

"Ah, well, there wouldn't be so many get out after all."

"Shut up and let him finish," said Frank.

"He wanted to know whether, if they didn't know, they couldn't feel. 'But perhaps they have their moments, Aussie, do you think?' he says, 'when they have some idea of the ghosts stalking about in the dark outside their headquarters messes—thousands of ghosts—and take an extra bit in the glass to keep off the cold shivers. Aussie,' he says, 'do they ever feel humble and abashed before the sublime patience of the troops with them?' I told him I thought they didn't, and so he asks me another. 'Don't you think it a strange thing, Aussie, old chappie, that while England has generally managed to rake up a decent general in the past after a while, it hasn't been able to in this war, which is the biggest?' He reckoned there wasn't a damned one."

"I won't call him a liar," said Harry.

"No more did I. He said there must be a reason for it and it'd have to be found out. 'So it all sits on the shoulders of poor Tommy,' he says. Then he went off about ghosts again. He had ghosts on the brain. He wanted to know whether, after some stunt like Loos or a big show like the Somme, the coves in Whitehall mightn't see the ghosts come back, thousand upon thousand, marching down past headquarters. But he reckoned they didn't see 'em. He had a plan about generals. He reckoned in the next war. 'What I mean is,' he says, 'war's too big a thing these days —too many get killed in a short time—to monkey about finding out that this lord general's a dud and the next senior's a dud, and so on.' What he suggested was a committee of three civies appointed by the cabinet, and these three to have power to pick the big generals—everyone to have a chance, from a colonel up.''

"If he made it majors, I'd agree," said Harry.

"God knows how long he'd have gone on on this idea, but a bomb dropped close. Glass and bricks were cracking and falling, and the ground rocked to some order. We all stood up—me still carrying the little cove—and looked up, wondering whether the next would be misguided enough to come in the six feet of our little alley. But the next went further away, though a splinter of shell tore down half a chimney and a lot of slates, and set them sliding down and over the edge near the street.''

"The Tommy says something about being bombed at St. Omer, and the old woman said 'Jesus is with us.' ''

"We wished He was, and the young woman wanted to know why wasn't He up the street where the bomb fell?''

"The old un didn't like that, and yelled at her, 'The wages of sin is death,' which made the Tommy say something about the Magdalen being beloved of Jesus.''

"He told me he'd once thought of being a parson, but had become a fellow—that's what he said, a fellow—and did economics and history. I thought that's be about the last bomb—it was quieter up on top—and asked the young 'un, barracking him and calling him an old hand, so he ought to know.''

"He reckoned I was right, and so I bucked him up by telling him he had more spunk than all of us.''

"The Tommy was feeling talkative again. 'Were you ever on Gallipoli, Aussie?' he asks. He'd already asked me once. I told him again 'for a bit.' He reckoned that was a fine mess. 'It'll take some years to get clear of the lies so that we could see it in its beautiful proportions,' he says. According to him, it was on his conscience. He reckoned England—that is, the heads—had let us in for it. He said he knew what he was talking about. After the war there'll be debt. After all wars there have been. He reckoned Australia would owe England money, but that England would owe money to the Yanks. All the world would owe them money. What he thought was that, for the losses the heads in England had let Australia in for through their messing at the Peninsula and all the other places like the Somme and early 1917, and Ypres, England ought to let Australia off the debt to make up. He said that'd be fair. When I said that the Tommies had copped it about as much as the diggers, he said, 'But the Tommies have Tommies for heads and haven't had someone else pushed on 'em.' "

"I told him to write to Billy Hughes about it, and he said he would. I wonder if he will!"

"It had been quiet for about half an hour before the sirens and things started to give the All Clear."

Jim put a match to his pipe and, after that, his yarn was continued between draws. "It was rather funny—the little mob of us standing there making up our minds to do a bunk. The Tommy broke the ice. 'All safe and sound, sir. Well, I must toddle; good-bye, good-bye.' He gave the old woman a ten bob note, and when she said 'God bless you,' he said he had more need of it than anyone ever. We shook hands. 'So glad to have met you, Aussie,' he says. 'Soldiers' farewell, Aussie, eh? Well, so long,' and off he went. The old woman followed, and then the old sojer cove and then the young wench. The little chap I had been nursing was crying now that I had put him on his feet. The bigger one took him by the hand and they followed along after me. Poor little kids they were. I wasn't to be beaten by any Tommy captain, so I gave the elder a quid. 'Cripes, digger,' he says when he grips it, 'it's a Brad.' I told him to stand Albert a ride home and a feed of fish and chips, and he said he would, and he wished me luck.''

Jim stooped and continued, so thoughtful, that the other two waited some time before Harry said, "Cough it up.''

"Well, I wasn't going to tell you, but I will, a bit. I had just turned round from the kids and moved off, when I saw the girl waiting for me in a doorway.''

"I was expecting that,'' said Harry. "Go on.''

"Were you? I half expected her there, too. I thought she'd take me before the Tommy.'' Harry made a derisive noise. "'Are you going my way, honey?' she says. I shook my head. She says, 'I'm all right, digger; honest I am. I'd do you no harm.'''

"That ought to have been enough.''

"I think she was jake. You see, she dropped her professional style. It's hard to tell with them—I mean their age. She was anything between twenty-five and thirty-five. Pretty — not so bad; but a bit anxious looking. When I was thinking how to get away, because I didn't want anyone just then, she started. She said she was lonely and afraid. She lived by herself and was all alone. Her trouble was, she didn't

want to be left alone. She told me I needn't worry
about the money if I was broke or near it. She was
trying to read what I thought of her, but I didn't
let on. 'Aye,' she says, 'here's another mystery for
that officer—that a girl on the game would want a
man to go with her and not want money for it, and
him not her fancy. There's a mystery for him. It's
true enough,' she says, 'I don't want to be alone.'
She asked me whether I noticed how still everything
had been during the raid in between the shells.
London in the early hours, she said, is never so still.
As if everything was dead. She said she was one of
the particular sort and had a little flat of two rooms.
The night of the last raid she was alone out in the
street, and she came back alone, without any luck,
when it was over, and went to bed and dreamed. Her
dream—I'm telling what I remember of it—was, she
was out in the street again and the city was still and
quiet—all still and quiet as it was between the shell
bursts during the raid—but there was no air raid. It
was stiller and quieter even, and she saw no one. There
were no buses nor cars, and there were no people. So
she walked about, wondering. They'd shut up the
promenade at the Empire and the Alhambra.''

"Have they?" interrupted Harry. "Turned 'em out
on the streets. Never mind me; go on.''

She couldn't go there, so there was nothing to do
but hang about the streets. She remembered stopping
to look at some hats in a shop. Still she saw no people.
She started, for the first time, to get the wind up.
She didn't know why—she hadn't before. The streets
were absolutely deserted. There was nothing. And
then she got the wind up properly because she knew

she was alone in London. A drunken sailor off the docks would have done her. That was a nightmare for you. She said she's been frightened ever since, and, now that there'd been the raid, and, hearing the city so quiet and still, and no one in the streets, and no one moving anywhere, she was afraid she would go back alone, and, if she did, she would dream that dream again. She wanted me to go with her to her little joint. 'Tis too true,' she said; 'I am alone for, for all I am, the rest of the town might be bloody well dead.'"

"Well, what did you do?" asked Harry as he looked strangely at his friend.

"What do you think? It's hard to believe there's such loneliness as that. Only when you're dead, perhaps. What do you think I did?"

"I suppose you went with her," replied Frank.

"Of course, that wasn't the only thing. I didn't want her, and, if I went with her, she'd want to be grateful."

"Well?" demanded Harry

"You see, all she had to be grateful with was what she'd give anybody—or, because she was particular, anyone with a white collar and tie and a quid or ten bob in his pocket. But to me, as she would be grateful, she would be giving all she had to give. The only thing. What was I to do if I didn't want her —not at any price? Go with her and refuse it. That might hurt her."

Harry looked up. "Yes, it's possible that might be a ghastly insult."

"What did you do? You went with her?" said Frank.

Jim got up. "Well, I'm damned if I'll tell you what I did." He went outside.

"He's got it on his mind — on his conscience," Frank turned to Harry.

"On his mind, perhaps. Something on his mind. I don't know what. Not on his conscience. It'd be hard to find where he keeps his conscience. I bet he told her to go to hell. He might even reckon that kindness."

Jim put his head back. "One thing I forgot to tell you I noticed coming back—things are going to move and become lively soon.

CHAPTER XXXVII.

A FORTNIGHT after Jim Blount's return, the war entered the month of August. The troops were uneasy in their minds, for they had their own secret communications—reports by this man and that, leakage from the officers by means of the batman, the stealthy movements of battalions, the gradual concentration of artillery, the intensity and purposiveness of the training of those out of the line and the manoeuvres with the tanks, the formation of dumps here and there, the thickening traffic by night on the roads. Jim Blount's prophecy only forestalled the general foreboding. All this could portend only one thing. Each day lent truth to the furphies. And all this while Fritz remained quiet and passive, cursing, no doubt, the bombing planes which visited him so frequently.

Behind the Australian lines the first stealthy movements acquired now a determined urgency, and the mass gathered at once in size and intensity. The platoon had to depend on its senses rather than anything else for its knowledge. One piece of direct evidence it did have, however. The whole of the brigade by the fifth was thickly gathered into their support trenches. It was therefore with a feeling of anticipation that, in the shelter of the little quarry where it had taken up its quarters, they sat around the following day to listen to Slade, who came into their retreat with Lieutenant Skipton.

Slade hawked and spat nervously before he commenced.

"No man is to leave here on any account. There is going to be an attack—a big thing. To-day you will get your equipment in order, and each platoon in turn will draw," he looked at a piece of paper, "extra iron rations, four extra bombs and an extra bandolier of small arms ammunition and eight shovels. The tanks will co-operate, and the colonel depends on you to see that you work together. There's to be no nonsense about the tanks. They did all right at Hamel. Mr. Skipton will be able to explain things to you to-morrow. That's all for the present."

"Good-bye, you ———," said Ted Marshall in a voice just sufficiently low for the words themselves to escape Slade's ears, though he guessed an insult in the tone.

After tea that evening, which was particularly lavish—and it had grown dark—Frank Jeffreys pulled out of his breast pocket Mary's last letters. A glance at Jim Blount showed him safely reading. Each had a stump of candle alight. The corporal slowly

read the letters through once again as if fanatically
he compelled himself to endure an agony which he
might have avoided. Reading her letters, it became
almost impossible to believe that she was what he had
grounds for suspecting. He folded them up at last
and put them away again. Ever since that drunken
night he had been seeking for some means to make
Bentley disclose the truth. He had formed the plan
of endeavouring to cultivate a friendly goodfellowship
with the boy, but he shrank himself from his own
tentative overtures. How was he to get the boy to
tell plainly what he had hinted at—more than hinted
at! It meant that he must get him into a mood of
salacious braggadocio, and to do that he would have
to seem like Barton—absorbed by nastiness. In his
unnatural attempts he had hitherto been successful
only in making Bentley look at him even more dis-
trustfully.

Those unanswered letters; her letters unanswered.
They were going into another stunt and he could not
leave them unanswered now. This time he would
write to her—this once—as if nothing had happened;
just as if she were as he had believed her. When sur-
rendering himself completely to this impulse which
he had no power to control, he did not worry about
his duplicity in suggesting that he had been writing
to her as usual, leaving it to her to imagine that his
letters had gone astray. He even warned her that,
owing to imminent events, she might not get a letter
for some time. Paradoxically, he discovered that this
pretence that he had no reason to doubt her only
made his doubts seem more like the truth. The
wretched effort finished at last, he enclosed it in its

green envelope and slowly addressed it and then took it to the company dugout.

When he came back, he at once got under the blankets and tried to sleep. Perhaps this stunt would be the end, but he knew he did not want to die. He had not even the strength of will for that. He was afraid. His nerves could not stand it. They were worse than they had ever been, and he knew that the men in the platoon were of the opinion that he was going to pieces. The few bad or stupid ones slyly tormented him, and, if it had not been for the tolerance and gentler understanding of the others — the protection of Jim and Harry Mullane and of Ted Marshall, the latter's being perhaps most effective, for it came from the roughest of the crew — God knows what might have happened. From the next hole came the thin, quivering sounds of Darky Lansdowne's mouth organ playing "There's a long, long trail."

The next morning, Lieutenant Skipton, who had the sergeant at his elbow, gathered his platoon about him in a semi-circle. The men were feeling lively. Skipton had a large map, a few other papers and some aerial photographs.

"Plenty of bumpf this time, sir," said Burke.

"Yes, isn't there? Hold these, sergeant." He retained a printed slip of paper.

"Well, boys," he said. "You'll know all about it in a moment. Corps orders." He went on to read.

"Corps Headquarters, August 7, 1918,

To the soldiers of the Australian Army Corps. For the first time in the history of this corps, all five divisions will to-morrow engage in the largest and most important operation ever undertaken by the corps.

They will be supported by an exceptionally powerful artillery and by tanks (bloody tanks, said someone) and aeroplanes on a scale never previously attempted. The full resources of our sister Dominion, the Canadian Corps, will also operate on one right, while two British divisions will guard our left flank.

The many successful offensives which the brigades and battalions of this corps have so brilliantly executed during the past four months have been but the prelude to, and the preparation for, this greatest culminating effort.

Because of the completeness of our plans and dispositions, of the magnitude of our operations, of the numbers of troops employed, and of the depth to which we intend to overrun the enemy's positions, this battle will be one of the most memorable of the whole war; and there can be no doubt that, by capturing our objectives, we shall inflict blows upon the enemy which will make him stagger and bring the end appreciably nearer.

I entertain no sort of doubt that every Australian soldier will worthily rise to so great an occasion, and that every man, imbued with the spirit of victory, will, in spite of every difficulty that may confront, be animated by no other resolve than grim determination to see through to a finish whatever his task may be.''

Skipton drew a long breath and wet his lips.

''The work to be done to-morrow will perhaps make heavy demands upon the endurance and staying powers of many of you; but I am confident that, in spite of excitement, fatigue and physical strain,

every man will carry on to the utmost of his powers
until the goal is won; for the sake of Australia, the
Empire and our cause. I earnestly wish every soldier
of the corps the best of good fortune and a glorious
and decisive victory, the story of which will re-echo
throughout the world, and live for ever in the history
of our homeland. John Monash, Lieutenant-General,
Commanding Australian Corps."

For a moment there was silence, and then Ted
Marshall ejaculated slowly, "Christ."

Someone else said, "You know what to do with it,
sir."

In a minute or so, however, their spirits brightened.

"Anyone'd think from that that no one was going
to be stonkered."

"I suppose," remarked Dopey Kendall, "it's what
you must expect in any ――― war."

"Good heavens, was that just sheer profundity or
mere irony, Dopey?" said Harry Mullane, turning to
look at old Dopey, who was scratching himself.

"――― if I know," replied Dopey.

"Brigade's orders are that all troops are to get as
good an idea of the show as they can," recommenced
the officer. The sergeant's got a plan of the country
and so've I, and there're the photos to look at. We're
in the second wave."

They gathered around the maps and photos, discus-
sing the country, marking out the present front line
and the jumping-off tape, the objective of the first
wave, and their own objective beyond Bayonvillers
and Harbonnieres, and the country even beyond that,
where other units would operate. A British division
would be north of the Somme, and during the advance

the railway from Villers and its embankment would divide the Australians from the Canadians and beyond the Canadians would be some French divisions.

Skipton left them in order to attend a meeting of the company officers with Colonel Gilderoy in the deep dugout where company headquarters were situated. The O.C. explained what he wanted of them. Each officer must, when possible, use his own initiative, but keep constant touch with the units, however small, on his flanks. He intended to use the battalion as if it had been a division, improvising for it a battle plan at each obstacle as the occasion required. He had, in fact, been longing for such a chance. The action of the battalion, by its various platoons and companies, would be co-ordinated as if their own engagement were an open battle, and companies were brigades, and platoons battalions.

When night fell, the last movement forward to the forward zone took place, and the array assumed its battle position—infantry, artillery with their shells, and those which were to move with their limbers and teams drawn up near the guns; engineers and tanks, the aeroplanes waiting in the dromes behind the lines, supply and ammunition columns, and all the rest, gathering like a storm in the night to the sulphurous, bursting point. A tremendous intensity of force.

The deep current of excitement had seized the members of the platoon, and the men fiddled about cleaning their rifles and adjusting their equipment. They discussed with considerable earnestness what might seem to have been a mere question of fashion. Amongst some units, entrenching tools, instead of being worn on the back in accordance with the prescribed mode, were being worn in front. Would the platoon do likewise? There was, however, a practical view of it. The blade of the entrenching tool might easily stop a small splinter or piece of shrapnel.

Ted Marshall was all for the change. He knew one man on Gallipoli who had been ruined for life. He could not imagine life being worth while as a eunuch.

It was he who carried the day against the conservatives, who would have stuck to the old rule merely because they would not do what others did. Word came through by Lieutenant Skipton, who now came and stayed with them, that zero hour was 4.20. The men did not need the corps orders to tell them that this was no small stunt on which they were to embark, even though they themselves had only the furphies to inform them of the magnitude of the preparations. A few of them snatched a bit of sleep, but most of them could not. It was to be all in. Some of them —and not only the most intelligent—dallied with consequences. Failure might mean perhaps almost annihilation. They asked themselves the question, unanswerable as yet, whether Fritz was awake to what was about to occur. There had been a burst of shelling in some place on their side and to the rear of Villers Brettoneux, and some gas had gone over on the artillery. It was this shelling which destroyed a number of tanks which were to carry engineer and other stores. In the deep current of the men's excitement was mingled now even some sort of relief that an issue might be forced, as promised by the orders. The sharpness of the night air and the hazy heavens, through which odd stars floated wanly, gave a promise of decent weather, and at the battalion headquarters of the front waves they were hoping for a morning mist. The platoon sprawled about. smoking or talking softly, occasionally bursting into laughter which had a nervous tang in it. The night wore away to midnight. They recalled old times. Some—the three or four who were able—harked back to the days which seemed centuries ago, of the Gallipoli Peninsula. They recalled men who had been in the platoon in the past. Ghosts sat about with them. From time to time they heard the plaintive notes of Darky Lansdowne solacing himself with his mouth organ. The hours trickled away minute by minute. Ten past two. Quarter past three.

"Hell, I thought time was up." Four, ah—four! It was all set now, and the night looked like any other night on the line. So you would think. The men gathered into little knots of sections. Out there on the tape the infantry were waiting, and the air seemed lighter now. Perhaps that was only imagination. The crews were in the tanks; the artillery were standing to their guns all around for miles behind. The officers kept looking at their synchronised watches. Those of the men who had watches, adjusted theirs by the officers'. Would it never come? Skipton told the minutes.

The earth heaved up with a roar and a flash of flame. At one instant a thousand guns shattered the night.

CHAPTER XXXVIII.

AFTER the due period of time, the platoon followed their officer up out of the quarry and got into a sort of artillery formation close together.

Fritz was copping it this time.

They were waiting for the word. Now they were moving forward under the weird flickering light they knew of old, and the storm of steel which was ripping the air above them.

Everywhere about them the dark figures, looming up, magnified by the darkness, of men in little groups, were tramping forward with their bayoneted rifles slung on their shoulders. The second wave. Occasionally someone spoke as if to banish that strange, terrible feeling of loneliness, to convince the imaginative lonely individuality which was himself that there were others in the world with him, comrades moving towards that doubtful issue in which life or death for each would be determined.

Soon they were crossing the main road which ran straight through from Villers Bretonneux. Turning beyond the little town, and then turning more directly eastward with the road on their left, a mile tramping brought them to the first jumping-off point, and, in the half light, to the beginning of the battlefield. There were scattered bunches of prisoners and walking cases coming to meet them, and, in the broken front trench system of the enemy, they noticed German dead, and occasionally Australian bodies, and a few wounded, whom stretcher-bearers were picking up. The first line system had been taken—that was clear; and men coming back, wounded, and runners, reported the attack making fast progress. Hardly a shell was coming over as yet.

The mist was rising a shade and, with the growth of daylight, the country was expanding before their eyes, so that they could see on the left the low ruins

and few shattered tree trunks about Warfusee
Abancourt. It was at some time after six that they
came upon the first wave ensconcing itself on its
objective—the green line beyond Warfusee. A little
over a mile away they could see Bayonvillers—a
shadowy blotch. While they were waiting, the platoon
saw a sight most of them had never seen before during the war—a battery of field guns gallop into
position, and the guns unhitched, swung around and
trained and commenced firing. The episode aroused a
transitory enthusiasm in the infantry looking on. The
brigades of the second wave collected and set themselves in order for the attack, watching the shells of
their artillery plonking on to the terrain ahead. They
were off, spreading out into more open order. The
tanks went a little ahead at their peculiar elephantine
amble. Only once before they approached the village
did the battalion strike trouble. It came from a group
of machine gun nests and soon faltered away. The
resistance, however, both from field guns and hostile
infantry increased as they drew nearer the village.
It extended towards them in two lines of ruins, making two angles, one facing, roughly, north-west, and
the other south-west. The platoon, after it had got
on a bit, was inclined to give any tank a fair amount
of room. The one which had been nearest them had
too frequently drawn the crabs. The shells were coming over, particularly from the direction of Marcel-
cave, beyond the railway. Gilderoy, keeping the battalian well together, moved it under what cover the
ground afforded around the lower or southern arm.
It was now some time after nine.

His casualties hitherto had been hardly noticeable,

but now began to increase. Flinging C company forward to outflank, almost from the rear, the lower projecting arm, he sent the A and B forward north towards the centre of the town. D company was on the extreme right, and its movement was rather a threat at the communications of the garrison, while the centre companies and two tanks went in. It was then that Albie Chomley was wounded. They left him there, happy enough, with a wound in upper part of the leg, grinning and smoking a fag in a shell hole. The capitulation of the Bayonvillers was announced by the stream of Fritzes that began to come out with their hands up. The platoon, which had hardly done anything but walk forward, found itself in the eastern quarter, from which it shot down some of the enemy who were endeavouring to retreat. The battalion, in the shelter afforded by the captured position, at once reorganised itself and then set off again. Leaving the road to the large village of Harbonnieres on the right, it continued still parallel to the main road. It began to be fired on now from the left, where the country dipped towards some narrow bits of tattered wood, which ran down from there, in a series of copses, to the bend in the Somme. Coming over a little rise, the platoon saw another sight — two Fritz whizz-bangs firing point blank in front of them. The men on the guns did not see the little group appear on their right, and Blue McIntosh turned the Lewis gun on them. He got two. The others turned and ran, doubling behind the protection of a bank of earth.

Blue cursed with disgust when some of C company, coming up from the other side, quite evidently preened themselves on the capture of the guns. Turning slightly to the left, the brigade deployed along the frontage of the wood and stifled the points of resistance with fire and the use of a tank or two. Gilderoy's battalion again carried out a flanking movement, while D company, elongating its front, maintained the continuity of advance. The men of No. 1 section were bent low over the grass and somewhat scattered. Bill Potter and Charl Bentley saw the shell lob about ten yards away, right under Cock Walker, and heard the splinters whizz. Swathes were cut through the grass. They ran towards the body which had been tossed on its back, and hopelessly looked down at it. Cock was unconscious. His trunk was cut about and there was blood all over him. He gave a faint movement with his right hand and that was all.

"Poor old Cock," stammered Charl.

With a glance behind, they left him when Sergeant Burke called. They were now beyond the line of the wood through which patrols had already worked forward, cleaning it up and sending back a dose of prisoners. Their objective was on the rising ground, and they commenced to dig a few holes, and had only just got comfortably down when the company was ordered to fall back while some of the Oth moved across from the right. In a short time they rejoined their battalion in reserve at the rear of the wood. There, in some gun pits in which two captured howitzers stuck their noses up futilely, they commenced to make themselves comfortable. They dragged a few Fritzes away out of sight, who first were ratted for what they had, which was little. It was, Frank saw by a glance at his watch, about a quarter to ten. They were hungry, and most of them gnawed their biscuits, wondering when they would get a decent feed. There was no shelling worth speaking of to trouble them, and, wearying of lying about and playing cards, a few of them—Jim Blount, Harry Mullane, Artie Fethers and Johnny Wright—crept up to a higher spot from which they could see the troops of other brigades and some cavalry and tanks moving about in a line beyond Harbonnieres. Three aeroplanes went across, flying low. A few stray shells, however, sent the men back quickly enough. Early in the afternoon it was known that the division had taken all its objectives. Those who bet on a hot feed at some odds were right, because Sucker Sykes and Syd Barton, at about seven o'clock, returned from company headquarters with two tins of bully beef stew. An argument arose as to whether it was hot. It was tepid, and there was no doubt that it had been hot. There was a consensus of opinion that those who had maligned the cooks, chiefly Ted Marshall and Harry Mullane, ought to pay up. But both Ted and Harry were unable to meet their obligations, and Jack Skipton, called in as arbiter, finally decided that they should settle the next time any pay was drawn.

"Cripes," said Darky Lansdowne, "I mightn't be 'ere."

"Your executors will collect it," said Johnny.

"You be ——— for an old shyster."

Johnny unwound his puttee. He always had trouble with his puttees. When they were on they bulged, and they were always coming down.

"I suppose old Cock was stonkered," said Charl to Bill. "I was thinking . . ."

"Of course he was," interrupted Bill reassuringly.

They commenced to make themselves comfortable for the night in the pits, which showed signs of being newly dug, for not only was the earth fresh, but there were no dugouts—only two or three shelters.

They slept that night in spite of the cold, and got an issue of bread and jam, four men to the loaf and five to a tin—strawberry it was—for breakfast.

Blue McIntosh had an objection to strawberry.

"It brings the ——— wasps," he complained.

The others near grinned maliciously.

"It was when you were on leave. Blue got a wasp in his mouth," Fatty Gray explained to Jim Blount. "Cripes, even that lousy tart he had in Salisbury wouldn't have kissed him."

They wanted to know what was going to be done that day. Nothing, they hoped. Skipton said the ——— Division was going to hop over. It was not long, however, before they were made to get up and go to their original objective, where they occupied, slightly to the northern side of Harbonnieres, an old trench system, which had been dug there in the time before the retreat of the Fifth Army or heaven knows when. By noon there was no sign of the other division, and the brigade headquarters was beginning to feel anxious. It came on towards one o'clock and still no sign of the ———. It was about then that Gilderoy called his company commanders together. They were to take Vauvillers and the country about it. They could see the village just beyond them to the right. Brigade had decided some advance had to be made, so that the day's action would commence all along the front.

The platoon guessed they were to do a job which

had originally been someone else's, and were annoyed. Gilderoy led the the battalion, with a front of three companies in columns of companies, in which the platoons kept a decent interval between each other, through the outskirts of Harbonnieres, keeping A company in reserve to follow.

Emerging, after a rest of a quarter of an hour, from their position, the battalion proceeded towards the small hamlet, a good deal of which had been razed to heaps of rubble.

"No damned barrage," complained Harry, as the platoon moved forward under what cover it could get.

Their objectives were about three-quarters of a mile away. They conjectured that, because it was opposite the newly-captured Harbonnieres, the village would be strongly held, but there was no strong opposition as yet. The platoon advanced to within a few hundred yards of the place before it was fired on. It scurried under cover, and then started to crawl for a bit through a field filled with weeds and rank grass. Skipton led them at a run, over the last hundred yards, to the shelter of the first bits of houses. They ran hard, for some shots whined about them. Charl Bentley flopped down so suddenly that he grabbed his knee.

"What's up?" demanded Bill.

"I've nearly broken my knee."

Bill, whose heart had jumped at his cobber's cry, said scornfully, "——, is that all?"

As they moved forward along the road, under cover of the fragments of walls, some of which supported the skeletons of roofs, on the bones of which hung, in places, a broken tegument of tiles. They caught

sight of some Fritzes and fired at them. And then
a machine gun turned towards them and splattered
about while they kept their heads down. When they
got going again, the Fritzes, where the fire came from,
suddenly started to run out with their hands up.

"That's no game," said Eddie Hecht, and he
fired at them. They took the gun, and, continuing
along the outskirts, ran right into about twenty
Fritzes who were gathered in a protected space
between two walls. Lorry Swift threw a bomb which
exploded so near that it was almost as dangerous to
himself as the enemy. Two or three tried to run
away and were shot, and Jim Blount stabbed another
who came at him. The others cried "Merci, camerade." While this was going on, C company, which
has gone straight ahead in spite of the opposition, had
occupied most of the village, and A and B were digging themselves in in the open to the left. The village
itself yielded about 150 prisoners and 18 machine guns.
The garrison, feeling perhaps rather isolated and
lonely, were on the whole pleased, if the faces of its
individuals were any indication, that the affair was
over. The only casualty the platoon had suffered was
Sucker Sykes, who got a black eyes from a piece of
brick chipped off by a bullet.

When the battalion had reorganised after its successful advance, the troops at once commenced to make
themselves comfortable, ever hopeful, in spite of
repeated disappointments, of a decent rest. The
platoon ensconced itself in a cellar which first they
explored gingerly for mines. Fritz had left a fair
amount of gear and blankets about, but the place was
dirty and had to be swept out. Not that the platoon

blamed him much for that, for it recognised that he had had other things to think of.

When you went outside and perched up to peer over the ruins, you could perceive ahead the low but commanding hills on which stood the village of Lihons, with a bit of wood on its northern end. At last the advanced guards of the —— Division began to appear, and the platoon mustered on top to see them go through.

"What the hell happened to you? You're late." said Burke to the sergeant in charge of the 1st patrol of the new division who came along.

"What do you think we are, —— racehorses? We've been going for hours."

"Well, you'll have a worse time up there, so it's your funeral."

"Touch wood!"

"Touch your bloody head," said Sucker.

The platoon settled down to the enjoyment of its comfort. Early in the morning, Frank Jeffreys and two guards saw the first of the wounded and a batch of prisoners coming through from Lihons. Nearby a battery of howitzers was firing, and other guns round about which had come up in the evening. Lihons was spattered here and there by flares of flame, and, beyond it, a dump of some sort was burning. The walking wounded reported that the engagement in operation was a severe one. Fritz was holding on. It was some time before these reports became hopeful. Lihons was taken.

A few 5.9's now commenced to create a mental discomfort in the troops in spite of the material advantages of their position. Frank Jeffreys, Jim

Blount, Harry Mullane, Charl Bentley and Bill walked back two or three hundred yards to look at a tank out of action. Charl was first there, and put his head in a hole in its steel side. He stepped back and motioned to the others.

"Have a look in there."

One by one they looked and saw the shambles, the splattered red mincemeat which the direct hit had caused.

"Not much fun being knocked in a tank," said Bill.

"God, no."

When they returned to the village they met Slade.

"Who said you could leave the lines?"

"No one, sir," answered Frank Jeffreys.

"You're a non-commissioned officer and ought to have known better. I'll attend to you afterwards, corporal. You can consider yourself under open arrest."

Frank saluted and said nothing.

"The bastard's half sozzled," said Harry with disgust when Slade had gone. "Never mind him, corp."

It was eight o'clock in the evening and Frank commenced to look about for an easier bed than the damp bunk on the cellar floor in which he had lain the previous night. Skipton came down the steps.

"Where's the sergeant, corporal?" he demanded.

"Outside somewhere, sir."

"Gone for a bog," said someone.

"Get him, then. We're to fall in at once."

"Wher're we going now, sir?"

"Don't know yet."

In a quarter of an hour they were stumbling along

the broken streets while members of a reserve brigade headquarters of the fresh division watched them into the darkness. The battalion, in double file, marched in a northerly direction, veering round a good deal to the west. In the dark they then had no idea of where they were going. They were going somewhere—that was all; and with the stolidity of the marching soldier they accepted it as sufficient. The way led over the open paddocks which were not divided by hedges, as in the north, each field here being marked only by the faint remaining signs of a different stage of cultivation. The thick grass was wet with dew.

Once only they got an idea of their whereabouts. They were crossing a straight, tree-lined road.

"That's the main road to St. Quentin," said Jim to Frank Jeffreys.

"I don't know."

He did not care if it was the main road to hell. A stupendous weariness possessed him, and he planted his feet heavily at each step. There were few lights about the front, but here and there they caught the flash and heard the sounds of the guns firing. A flight of bombing planes whined overhead. Fritz seemed to have been driven out of the sky also. How different it was in '16 and '17! Every now and then they halted, sometimes for quite considerable periods, which did not rest them, for they dropped asleep only to be aroused, in a few moments, dazed and rotten. It was this bloody marching here and there that was the killer.

At last it began to grow light—a cold, chill dawn— which was welcomed. They came, as the day grew, to the trench line near a fair-sized village, and here they halted, squatting and lying around while the positions were allotted to them. They were now a fair way behind the line. Jim Blount found a chalk pit just handy to the side road, and Frank, Bill Potter, Charl Bentley and Ted Marshall followed him to it. Their luck was in. A bit of tarpaulin had been rigged into a sort of roof, and under it they all nestled in together and went to sleep—a disturbed slumber, grunting and starting, one hope penetrating through their dreams that they would not be kicked up for a while at any rate to go tramping somewhere else. During the night there was rain. Some shells fell in the village.

CHAPTER XXXIX.

THEY were now not far from the Somme, towards which the new line curved back to a defensive flank because north of the river the Tommies had not been able to get so far forward, being hindered by the difficult task in the valley and their own left flank, for there had been as yet no advance by the —th Corps next to them. All that next day the platoon had an easy time. The little expenditure of ammunition was replenished. It had good meals, for Gilderoy was more definite now than ever that the cooks should understand they also were in the war and the supply columns were commencing to function. In a paddock behind them there were lines of Tommy cavalry.

There was a chance to write letters. Frank Jeffreys wrote again to Mary Hatton. He could not help himself. After writing that first letter, before the attack, he found this one easier. It had made this further difference to him. While, before, he had been tormented by the necessity to find the truth, now that he had written, he began to implore God to allow him to remain ignorant of it. He even comforted himself on his own weakness. He did not want to know, but to forget.

Charl Bentley saw him writing and guessed to whom. It was real disgust which made him him say to Bill, "There's that swine Jeffreys writing to Mary Hatton, the tart I used to knock round with on leave. He sneaked about her when he was in Blighty. Bill, I used to think she was dinkum. She seemed so, really. But when he goes there she takes up with him. I bet they reckon I'm a silly, poor fool. I ought to have known better, considering. I was a fool."

"Damn her, never mind about her; she ain't the only girl in England," Bill solaced him, for he understood the feelings which Charl's tone, rather than his words, expressed.

"It was a dirty trick. He knew about me and her."

"Dirty! Lower than a snake's belly."

In the interval, the enemy resistance, taking advantage of the favourable ground, was strengthening. They heard that one of their divisions was being transferred north of the river. It was night time, somewhere about the 14th, before they moved forward to the line which was held in posts by the platoons. Morning showed across the valley the village and woods about Fontaine les Cappy. The ground was more broken than that through which they had passed, but was more suitable for the gradual encroachments they were ordered to make.

Tich Carson brought news. "Slade was sick."

"I bet he'd get sick," remarked Artie Fethers significantly. "What's the matter with the cow?"

"Dysentery."

"Too much whisky and excitement. Who've we got?"

"Lairey Ridley."

They laughed. Frank, when conscientiously he reminded Lieutenant Skipton that he was still under arrest, was told by that officer not to be a damn fool, and that was the end of that.

In the morning they were glad to get a sight of the new captain when he came along with the sergeant-major, Dave Grant. Captain Ridley had been a recognised hard-doer. His helmet was tilted rakishly over his left ear and his tunic and light coat were of the ultra fashionable style, and his strides would not have disgraced an officer in the Guards. A fag was stuck on his lower lip. He gave them a knowing grin and said to Jim Blount, "Hullo, Jim!"

"Hullo, sir; glad to see you're back."

"Damn it, I wish it was my back."

When Captain Ridley joined up, he had brought with him a batch of reinforcements dug out of all sorts of places. Of these the platoon got three—Sibthorpe, who had been a batman on divisional headquarters; Scratcher Nunn, whose wound had been slight; and a man named Thomson, who was silent as to where he had been; but it was rumoured that he had come back in company with Ridley from a prolonged stay at Bulford. He had previously been in A company. As a matter of fact, the man had spent a year in the clink for sand-bagging when overstaying leave. The platoon hailed the advent of Wally Sibthorpe with laughter.

The next morning, in the early hours, the brigade edged itself forward. Skipton divided his little command into two patrols, one under himself and the other under the sergeant. The wind was flurrying the clouds in the sky, while the pallor of the day was spreading out of the dirty yellow of the east. The platoon advanced carefully and avoided the traverse of a machine gun from the woods. Finding some holes about two hundred yards out, they connected them into a little post by a shallow trench. With due respect to the machine gun, they stayed there all day, and, nibble by nibble, ate their new biscuits until the evening, when the ration party from C company brought forward some bread and a couple of dixies of stew and cold tea. Some shells came over in the night, but in the morning the machine gun was gone, and they set out again. This time their objective was a small road from which two machine guns engaged them. Slowly the two patrols converged towards them.

"They've got us bluffed," said Blue McIntosh, but Skipton took him and his carriers forward to the right. Blue got his head up. "Ah, Blue's got his head up," they said. We started to fire, and Skipton led the others forward in little rushes. A man, when he dropped down, would fire at the post, which helped those who were up and running. Fritz put his head down, and the platoon, Skipton and Artie Fethers in advance, got close. They thought Fritz had chucked it, as usual, and crawled away, so ran forward without cover. Suddenly one of the guns cut loose on them. Ted Marshall fell, and then Sucker Sykes, and the others, aware of some down, lost their fear in their furious anguish. The Germans, about fifty yards away—seven or eight of them—jumped up and put their hands over their heads. Two still fumbled at the gun. Johnny Wright had been alongside Ted, and his mouth was working. He ran right up to an officer and shot him, and then the man beside him. The remaining Fritzs cried out. Jack Skipton shot one of the men at the gun with his pistol. The Australians crowded around the group of prisoners, and Dopey Kendall punched one, who seemed to say something nasty, in the mouth. For a few moments the Germans knew themselves in danger of death, and looked it; all but one, an N.C.O., who had been the other of the two who had stayed at the gun, and who had now folded his arms and faced the Australians with a firm and intrepid gaze. With the exception of the man who knelt, shaking and nursing his face, the survivors, inspired by the behaviour of their corporal, stood closely together and endeavoured to imitate his coolness. The participants in this scene forgot for a moment the occasional whine of the bullets.

"Let them go, sir," stammered Charl, who found it hard to swallow.

The lieutenant nodded.

"You're prisoners," he said to the corporal.

The German expostulated, in English, "We're soldiers."

"You can't expect to turn a machine gun on us and then throw up your hands."

"I didn't."

His men looked from one speaker to the other, anxiously trying to discover hope in their demeanour.

"No, you didn't. The others did," Skipton acknowledged.

"It's no use standing here."

At this they all descended in a hurry, under the shelter of the bank—Australians and Germans alike—where the man Skipton had shot was groaning. The German corporal gave him a drink and Frank Jeffreys helped him to put a dressing on the wound.

Skipton, with Tich, Kendall, and Johnny Wright, shooed them, two supporting their wounded comrade, up on top and towards the spot where Ted Marshall and Sucker had fallen. Sucker was sitting up. He was hit above the knee and was rocking gently with the pain. At the sight of Ted Marshall sprawled out, face downwards on the grass, a spasm of fear drew the Germans together. There was no need. All the fight seemed to have gone out of old Johnny. From where they stood the little hill went down leisurely to the former line.

When they had done what they could for Sucker, Skipton turned to the N.C.O.

"You'll carry him."

"Yes, certainly."

"Where'd you learn English?"

"In England," the man replied. "I was in Australia once for my firm."

"You two," Skipton ordered Johnny Wright and Kendall, "stop here and keep an eye on them till they get back there."

Ted Marshall's death had stirred the imagination of the platoon deeply. They felt they had done enough. Ted Marshall—he had always been reckoned the luckiest of them all. The roughest and the most genuine diamond.

Sitting under cover of the narrow road, they brooded on Ted's death, and then over their lot, to which it had opened their eyes in the clearest visibility. All were aware of the marvellous luck which had hitherto blessed them. Looking into the future, they foresaw themselves, one by one, dropping away. If this series of stunts was to continue, how many in the end would be left of them? Made the spearhead of the main attack, anxiety and ambition would not suffer their withdrawal. They perceived themselves sacrificed to the new hope and dedicated to victory. So as they sat about on the side of the road or stood up on guard overlooking the smaller valley running down to the winding tree line and banks of the Somme, or gazing across at the broken villages which hid the shame of their violation in their sparse cloaks of trees, they ruminated frankly on their chances, so that, from then on, they accepted the long-drawn-out battle with a deep, steady fatalism which, replacing the first excited ardour, was of even more service to their commanders. Their fatalism now had a baleful quality. It was ferocious.

That night they brought Ted's body in and buried it by the side of the road. Skipton, as he looked down on the corpse, marked the fall of yet one more of the old soldiers. The sight of that great rakish frame of bone and flesh, consigned to shallow earth, reminded him more rudely of the gradual decline in the general physique of the troops which the war was making. There were few now left like old Ted. They buried him and stuck his rifle in at the head of the grave, and hung his tin hat on its butt. It was the first time Charl had taken part in the burial of one of their own, and for some time after he had the wind well up.

CHAPTER XL.

THE front became quiet for a few days and the brigade lay in reserve. On the 22nd, however, the attack of the —— Division toward Fontaine les Cappy, Chuignolles and Chuignes provoked heavy artillery retaliation from which the platoon had the good fortune not to suffer. This bombardment was the heaviest the battalion had experienced since the 8th August. At the crash of each shell, Frank's nerves broke, and then tightened again in expectation of the next burst, which, when it came, would flash like a lantern slide into his brain the black muzzles and the flame, accompanied by the appalling detonation, of the 9.2's at Ypres. He was almost glad when the brigade was in action again. The division marched in a general direction east by south-east, taking Assevillers and Fay, and establishing itself along an old trench system through the narrow woods east of that village, and west of Estrees, through which the patrols percolated, to be checked at Belloy-en-Santerre. On the night of the 28th, the enemy retreated, as usual, after his guns had used up their ammunition in a burst of hate, and the villages of Belloy-en-Santerre, Villers Carbonnel and Barleux were occupied with little opposition. The battalions, entering into a network of old trenches, came under fire from the high ground beyond Peronne and the Canal du Nord, where the

Somme flowed south to north. The advance patrols began to clear up the country right through to the Somme.

On the other side of the river to their left, and along it, the Australians pushed forward, taking Clery. During the whole of the 30th the battalion remained under the cover of a sparse wood. Along the river the heavy increase in the shelling indicated the intention of the enemy to resist here, where he had the natural defence of the river, the fortified town, Mont St. Quentin, and the higher ground beyond the eastern bank. The town, with its ramparts, a fortress since ever battles were fought on France, formed a knob on the elbow, where the stream flowing north turned west towards Corbie and Amiens.

The platoon lay about under a tree which spread its branches widely, contrary to the custom of French trees in general. Darky Lansdowne was playing his mouth organ and six or seven of the others raised their voices in song, so that any stray general or staff officer, coming through the woods, might well have supposed the troops were in high spirits and noted it up in his diary later on, though there was nothing very gay in . . .

"Wrap me up with my stockwhip and blanket,
   And bury me deep down below, below,
Where the dingoes and dogs won't molest me,
   Down where the coolibahs grow."

Possibly "If you were the only girl in the world and I were the only boy," or "Take me back to dear old Blighty," sounded sprightlier. No doubt the unexpected rum issue was responsible.

Johnny Wright sat some yards apart from the others with his knees up near his chin, and just when the last quaverings of Darky's organ had finished the long drawn-out "Madelon, Madelon, Madelon," he commenced to sing. It was the startling character of that song which stopped the protest which the prospect of a solo from Johnny's roughened larynx might have provoked.

"Little Bo-peep has lost her sheep,
    And doesn't know where to find 'em;
Leave 'em alone and they'll come home,
    Wagging their tails behind them."

They smiled and listened. He continued, unaware of their derisive silence.

"Little Bo-peep was fast asleep,
    And dreamed she heard them bleating,
But when she awoke she found it a joke,
    For they were still a-fleeting."

He paused a minute before he continued, in the stillness of the distant thudding of the guns. The others were no longer derisive, but ill at ease.

"She took up her crook, intending to look,
    Determined still to find 'em;
She found them indeed, but it made her heart
    bleed,
    For they'd left their tails behind 'em."

They would have liked to stop him, but they dared not. Something held them still — a feeling akin to horror, a fear of the innocent, unseen—by all but old Johnny. He went on . . .

> "She heaved a sigh and wiped her eye,
> And ran over hill and dale-O—"

The others got up and walked about, taking care not to notice the squatting figure with its bent head. Wouldn't someone make a noise, say something— swear blue, bloody blazes.

It was Jim Blount who, in a voice he attempted to make casual, called out, after a while, "What about a pipe of your baccy, Johnny?"

Old Johnny looked up and, taking out his pouch, tossed it over with a deprecating grin. What a relief it was, that response. It made their apprehension, that Johnny had suddenly gone off his nut, absurd. They could imagine that whimsical grin. There he was, just the same old dag.

At nine they were aroused and went marching northwards into the black waste in the valley of the river. The next day they did nothing, but each company, one by one, learned from Gilderoy's mouth the first suggestions of what was in store. One Australian Division on the other side of the river, supported on its left by another, was to attack Mont St. Quentin, and they themselves were to take Peronne, advancing to it parallel with the river. The magnitude of the task which was set them itself had a rousing effect on them. Their morale, as usual, gradually became stiffer to it, the worse it was.

It was thus given to the Australians to attempt one of the greatest feats of arms of the whole war. Into the troops in the line at Mont St. Quentin, Luden-

dorff sent the finest division he had at his disposal—
the 2nd Prussian Guards Division—with instructions
to hold the hill at all costs. Against this position there
was advancing one weak Australian Division, supported on the left by another, which had an objective
of its own in the Bouchavesnes Ridge to the north.
On the right was the platoon's division, which also
had been fighting since the 8th August, to which
was allotted the task, almost as difficult, of storming
the fortress of Peronne, garrisoned by volunteers and
picked men from many regiments, armed with many
machine guns.

The position against which the weakened and weary
battalions had soon to move was one of the strongest
on the Western Front—almost impregnable if held by
determined troops—protected by a carefully-devised
trench system with good communications and thick
wire, a commanding hill and ruined village from which
fire could sweep the attackers, belts of wood and
points of vantage, and the town itself.

From Clery, on the north bank, the course of the
river twisted south a little, and then, bending back
past the village or suburb of St. Radegonde, divided,
the northern water filling the moat below the ramparts of the town, which was divided into two by low
ground with a small lake in it, and the smaller further
part being known by the name of the Faubourg de
Bretagne. Before you came near the town there was
a trench system called Florina Trench, and then a
wood, Anvil Wood, covered by thick belts of
wire. North of this, a mile away, was Mont St.
Quentin itself, protected on its slopes by trenches and
wire. Straight ahead, past the cemetery, on a line

between Peronne and Mont St. Quentin, were the sugar works and brick yards and the hamlet and wood of St. Denis. In the corner of the bend, where the river turned almost at right angles, impassible in the swamps and the depth of its stream, was the suburb, unprotected by the ramparts, of Flamincourt. Peronne would have to be taken from the north side.

On the nights of the 30th and 31st, the platoon, moving in single file, crossed the swamp and the river at Buscourt, with the rest of the brigade, by a foot bridge supported on cork floats, which had been made by the Engineers, a number of whom watched the infantry test their handiwork.

Colonel Gilderoy sat down on a knob of earth while his men stepped by him down to the bridge. His heart was heavy, for he, at any rate, was aware that if the enemy resisted to the utmost the weak battalions who were to attack him would be almost annihilated. His own strength was about 300 fighting men. The venture was desperate almost to madness. Against the blackness of the trees in the valley the figures of the men passing a few steps away were hardly discernible. Overhead the few stars went dipping through the clouds like the lights of ships dipping through dark seas, the tops of which were broken into pale foam.

The battalion clustered, safe from the shelling, under the high northern bank. The platoon spent the day lounging about, smoking and yarning. Some of the time a few of them played euchre and nap for a while, but mostly they lay about.

Further along, a youthful voice started, "To-morrow is my daughter's wedding day, ten thousand pounds

I'll give away." A few responded, "Good old dad."
The voice continued, "On second thoughts I think it
best, to stick it in the old oak chest." Two or three
voices, "You miserable old bastard." It was not
repeated. It had been a mistake. A man might play
cards for a few moments, for that did not prevent
him thinking the dark thoughts of his particular and
personal fear. Some feared bullets and some shells,
and some feared everything. Those who had the wind
well up sat moodily alone, and so did some who were
impervious to fear.

Later in the night they assembled, company by company, and set out. They skirted along the ruins of
Halle. In the darkness they had no knowledge of
where they were going, but each man followed blindly
the figure in front of him. They halted for considerable periods every now and then in the folds of the
ground in the cover of some line of trees. Shells
plumped spasmodically about them. The company
came up to a spot where the colonel stood directing,
and, at his orders, D company switched off to the left.
Their own guns now were firing briskly and the roar
grew steadily.

It was somewhere near six in the morning when
Skipton led the last platoon in the battalion through
the wire into the Florina trench system. This long
trench, leading from the outer slopes of Mont St.
Quentin down to the river, had previously been evacu-
ated by the enemy, but his advance patrols, finding it
empty, he had commenced to occupy it again. On the
left the few Fritzes there retreated, but on the right
the trench was only taken after some fighting, which
delayed the advance.

"Keep your heads down," Burke warned the men;
needlessly, for the spurts of the bullets from the direction of Mont St. Quentin striking the parapet and
parados of the wide trench were effective enough.
Those machine gunners, however, soon had something
else to occupy them, and when the men followed
Skipton over the top that fire had ceased. The battalion advanced in the neighbourhood of a road lined
by trees that looked ill-treated. Soon it became engaged by fire on the front from what had been an
aerodrome, and from a small brickworks beyond.
Just south of the kilns there was a wood stretching
towards Peronne, which it shrouded from view. This
wood, called Anvil Wood, was protected by thick
belts of wire. Brigade, anticipating the trouble, had
some artillery concentrated on both the brickworks
and the wood.

The platoon halted in the cover of a thick group of
shell holes. As yet it had suffered no casualties, but
further progress was held up owing to the fire, nerves
requiring to be screwed up to a higher pitch to face
it. The direction of the company was around the
end of the wood. The companies on the right
attacking the wood directly lost severely at the wire,
and, in the wood itself, mopping up was difficult. The
movement of D company was a threat at the rear of
garrison. Lairey Ridley led his men now at a shallow
flanking trench, approaching it pretty closely before
the occupants, who were more concerned with the
struggle at the wood, discovered their proximity. The
Germans turned at bay too late, for the Australians
were running towards them and, indeed, were upon
them, throwing a few bombs. A brief combat took

place. Tich Carson received a bayonet wound in the side and Bill Potter went sprawling and did not move. The surviving enemy surrendered. It was only when the platoon had emerged from the trench, and were commencing to move forward in the open again, that Charl noticed Bill's absence. They told him he was wounded in the trench, and he grinned as he said to Frank Jeffreys, "Good old Bill; I hope it's a Blighty this time. Where'd you think I'd go if I got a Blighty, corp? You know."

The corporal turned away without giving an answer.

Colonel Gilderoy, standing with his adjutant, sergeant-major and runner, and perfectly aware of the rather striking picture he made for a moment there, stood on a knoll, from which he tried to discern something of the general situation. But the battle now had reached the commencement of the crisis, which involved a series of confused local actions by battalions, companies and platoons. The troops to the right seemed to have passed St. Radegonde, and to be drawing near the ramparts, while, on the north, things seemed, at any rate, to be going not badly. One assurance of that he had in the absence of any fire from Mont St. Quentin on objects such as themselves. The scattered machine gun fire was coming from the sugar factory and large brickworks ahead, towards which the battalion which had been originally on his left was advancing, and from Peronne, whence it was intermingled with rifle fire. Of course, the troops on the left might not have reached the main lines of resistance, as he himself had not. He should have, for Fritz should have met the attackers in the Anvil

Wood position and used the defences of the town only in the last resort. Against Mont St. Quentin and Peronne of what use would have been the valour of troops who were only a handful—one to every fifteen yards or so—unless—and this was the sole justification of the risk—the spirit of the enemy was weak and he were bluffed into believing that only a preponderating force would be sent against such a position? So the vigour and dash of the few Australians would have to be magnificently intrepid and determined to convince him. In that, also, the Heads were no doubt justified in believing.

The fire from the ramparts made Gilda descend in a hurry, so that the platoon hard by, having grinned at Harry's sarcasm, "Look at Gilda being Napoleonic," now laughed.

They admitted, though, there were few flies on him. He was now in a position from which his attack on the town must be launched. He called together the commanders of his companies. Captain Reed was dead and Captain Stockfield wounded, and their places had been taken by the still existing senior lieutenants, their places in turn being taken by the sergeants. Their entrance would be over the northern causeway, across which first B and then C company would advance, covered, as much as possible, by the fire of the flanking companies. It was somewhere near eight o'clock when the battalion commenced its attack, each small unit manoeuvring through the lank grass, in the grey atmosphere, for cover from the fire. A driving squall of rain beat into their faces. Shells were crashing into the town and along the ramparts in greater numbers now as the artillery, operated to schedule,

adapted to the actual situation by the order of
brigade headquarters, to which Gilderoy had sent a
runner after the capture of the wood. The platoon
occupied portion of a wide shallow trench which,
meant for defence, was equally suitable for the
attackers. It was a relief to drop into it. It should
have been held by the enemy, but it was not. Pushing forward a little, they lay flat in the grass or in
the shell holes and opened fire on the enemy posts.
The causeway was blown up by a mine. Blue McIntosh
noticed Syd Barton cough and kick and, after a
minute or so, begin to drag himself backwards towards
the trench. Progress was held up for a while in spite
of some magnificent examples of individual daring.
Charl saw one man run forward to the approach and
engage a whole enemy post single-handed before he
fell. The atmosphere was very dull, and the open
grass, the trees, the rise to Mont St. Quentin and the
ramparts and the town were overlaid with a dead grey
colour.

The leading company commenced to run forward,
men falling, and then the others were running and working through on the eastern side of the entrance to the
town. Their cunning, aided by the covering fire, out-
witted the trained machine guns. The next company
followed, and then the next. And now the platoon
was running. Frank Jeffreys' heart was bursting.
"O Lord, protect me." He was untouched. Bent
almost double, he ran on the far side where the ground
had been thrown down to the moat. He noticed, as
he ran, bodies half in the water where they had slipped
or rolled down the declivity. They were in the town,
Skipton gathered his men together, to get their wind,

under the ruins of a house, the whole front of which had been torn down and precipitated into the narrow thoroughfare. They were in the town. They didn't know how the devil they got there, but still they were in. In the last dash they had lost only one man, the quiet fellow, Steve Wilberforce. They walked along the edge of the street, halting at the signs of habitable cellars, into some of which a bomb was thrown. At the entrance to one a few Germans were killed. Somehow or other they got too far to the right and found themselves in what had been the main street. Here they halted for a moment, protected by a heap of rubble from the fire which came down it.

In the few moments' grace, Artie Fethers, who had picked up a piece of white plaster, printed carefully on a brick wall in large letters, "Roo de Kanga," and called to the others to admire his wit, which they did jocosely.

They went back now towards the ramparts and came across other units of the battalion who were dislodging the posts there from the rear. Bit by bit the mopping-up went on with the explosions of bombs and splutter of infantry fire and the crash of some ruin collapsing, until, in the course of time, the whole town was in the possession of the Australians, with the exception of the outlying portion known as the Faubourg de Bretagne, to which the Germans clung desperately, and Flamicourt. To their dislodgment from the first, the platoon, mingled with other units, advanced some considerable time later. Skipton took them across the lower ground. Near the ramparts, Wally Sibthorpe collected a fragment of a bomb. Frank Jeffreys and Sergeant Burke carried him about ten yards and propped him up against a wall, where they left him, happy enough, with his leg tied up. Frank lit a fag for him, for, notwithstanding his grin, the man's two hands trembled too much to strike the match. Under cover of the ruins, they shot down some Fritzes on the mound who were commencing to creep away. Peronne was now almost completely occupied. It was the morning of September the 2nd. The fire from St. Denis had slackened, so that Gilderoy, who had scaled a rickety wall which gave him some sort of view, believed that the battle must have about ended there, and that Mont St. Quentin had fallen. Troops of the right brigade were in the town also, and the position on that flank became clear. The suburb of Flamicourt was being mopped up.

The platoon lay that night in two cellars. Haggard with exhaustion and begrimed with dirt and dust, they sprawled where they had tossed off their equipment. A single candle spluttered in its grease on Jim Blount's tin hat, and threw wavering, grotesque shadows on the faces and dropped mouths of those nearest it, before it guttered out. The sleep of Frank Jeffreys and some of the others was not like sleep, but the unconsciousness of a person tossing in a delirium. Others—the majority—lay like corpses.

With the capture of Mont St. Quentin and the fortress of Peronne, the line of the Somme was turned.

The issue was determined, though the last of spasms of the struggle occupied most of the following day. The hazard had succeeded. The rattling of the machine guns had died almost away, and the big guns were firing only fitfully on the enemy communications and the positions to which he had retreated.

CHAPTER XLI.

WHEN they awoke, the next day, the platoon, to its joy, found that the battalion was in reserve, and those who had the inclination had a chance to do some souveniring. Field glasses, pistols, watches, rings, money were the articles most valued. The subject recalled memories of poor old Ted Marshall, who had been a master hand, and who would exercise his craft no more. "But I draw the line at gold teeth," Ted used to say, they remembered. Johnny Wright, however, looked for one thing only—something to drink; and at about noon he came back with four bottles of wine. One he gave to the sergeant to divide with Jack Skipton, and the other three he took with him into a room in a house, from which half the ceiling had fallen, giving a view of the open sky through the bare rafters of the roof. Frank Jeffreys, Harry Mullane, Jim Blount and Charl Bentley squatted down in the litter on the floor with him. The corporal had not touched a drink since he had left Australia, and then he was a teetotaller, but he stretched out a trembling dixie for his portion. Even now he did not have as much as the others. The wine produced in him a sort of stupor indescribably pleasant and restful. Wonderfully—almost, it seemed, miraculously—it gave him the only thing he desired—rest and stupor.

Excited by the success, Charl Bentley was inclined to crow a bit. Jim Blount smiled wryly to Harry at such youthful enthusiasm as he said, "I'll tell you what I think, son. Great victory is what the Heads'll call it. But if Fritz had stuck it out there wouldn't have been many of us left, and those wouldn't have

been here. We got here because he had his bellyful
of it and ran away. He's not the Fritz he was.''

Charl lapsed into an abashed silence.

''All the same,'' remarked Harry, ''because we did
it, doesn't mean that anyone else could.''

It was a bit of skite, but they were inclined to
believe it true.

Some of the others came in.

''Sidder Barton seemed to get a good knock,'' said
Blue.

''Poor old Sidder.''

They shook their heads. They seemed to have forgotten what sort of chap Barton had been. How he
had been always dodging work; how, when you were
carrying anything with him, he let you bear the
weight; his malingering and his dirty yarns. Even
when he was with them, all that had not counted for
much. Their life together, and the common dangers
of the war, bred in them a certain strange toleration.
It imposed a sort of code of conduct to which they
all generally conformed—a necessitous cameraderie to
which the individual was subject, so that even ''Poor
old Sidder'' found a general endorsement of regret
for him.

Old Johnny became a bit garrulous.

''You know, Jim, if it were not for getting drunk
now and then I couldn't stand it. I usen't to drink
much when I enlisted— hadn't been drunk for years
and years, Jim. I've got a wife and two kids—two
boys. I don't know why I did it now. Yes I do.
Thought I ought to do my bit. Partner older than me,
and good practice. He's keeping it going till I come
home. Sounds funny now.''

"Never mind, Johnny. It can't last much longer."

"Perhaps they'll take us out for a spell."

But the hopes of the troops, so sweetly indulged in, that now they would be withdrawn, were soon dispelled. Early in the afternoon the battalion was drawn up and put in order. The platoon was now only sixteen all told—Skipton, Burke, Jeffreys, Blount, Bentley, McIntosh, Gray, Thomson, Mullane, Wright, Lansdowne, Fethers, Harris, Hecht, Kendall and Swift. They had, as Harry said, been lucky. For instance, No. 1 platoon had been reduced to eight men.

The men passed the next few hours cleaning themselves, and most of them boiled dixies of water over fires in the cellars and had a shave.

In the evening, in two columns of companies in file, the battalion left Peronne and moved slowly forward, while the patrols of the advance battalions, under cover of a smoke screen, occupied the villages of Doignt and Bussu. During the next few days the troops plodded on after Fritz. They encountered little opposition. Field artillery followed just behind them, and the planes overhead dropped smoke bombs and live ones, and sometimes gunned the enemy, swooping down on him when he showed himself in sufficient numbers to afford a target.

Only once was the platoon in the front of the advance. Standing on a low, grassy hilltop, with their waterproofs flapping in the rain, they watched the smoke screen twisting in the valley and the bursting of shells. They were in single file, Skipton in front.

As Fatty Gray pointed out to Blue McIntosh, "It's all right old Jack is so big. How'd you feel walking behind a little skinny coot like that fella who was killed at Ypres? What was his name? I've clean forgotten. If Jack gets knocked, we'll make Dopey go in front."

"No good to you, Fatty. You stick out too much at the sides.

THE LAST FIGHT OF THE PLATOON

CHAPTER XLII.

IT did not require much ground to hold the battalion in its reduced condition of just about 200 men. After the first day, when it rained, the arrival of a few bell tents helped out the dwellings the men had made for themselves in the ruins of the hamlet. Frank Jeffreys made a hole for himself alone. This impulse towards isolation, when the others continued to make possies to hold at least two, was only one sign of that moodiness and irritability which the others had noticed in him for some time past. They thought he was becoming a bit queer. He was becoming what they called dopey. They had known other cases—a good number—of men whom the war had turned queer. Poor little Lorry Swift was likely to be another. His nerve had broken and his ill-concealed terror was obvious. They knew that in Peronne he had got away in a cellar by himself and come out only when the place was mopped up. Frank found their pity as hard as anything else to bear. His cave was in the debris of a wall, and barely contained his lanky body. It was his own place—his alone—and it was to its retreat that he took Mary's letters, with the furtiveness of one jealous of observation, when he received them on their second day of rest. He read them again and again, the last in date in particular.

Dearest Frank,

I have got your letter of the 7th August, in which you say you are going into battle again. And then,

during the next few days, the papers had it all in
about the wonderful victory, and how the Allies are
pushing the Germans back, and the British and the
Australians and Canadians are going on, and you are
out there in it. That's all I can think about. I wish
you were not in it. When the papers came out I could
hardly do my work. All the time I kept thinking
and thinking. O, dearest Frank, be careful of yourself. Do not go unto unnecessary danger. It seemed,
in the end, I could not even think any more. I could
not sleep, and the next day I did not eat my lunch.
I couldn't — but went out into the street. Perhaps now it will soon be over and you will be coming
back to England again. When I went out, I did not
know what to do, but I kept praying for you, and
I thought I will go to some place to pray. At first
I could not think where to go. I thought, then, that
I would go to some holy place, the holiest place in
London—some place where God must hear me. I
found myself outside Westminster Abbey. I don't
know how I came there. Perhaps God guided me. I
thought that, and I went into the quiet and walked
down to the Chapel, with the stars in the roof and the
beautiful altar. I knelt down and prayed. Surely
God will hear me. He must, Frank, dear, if there is
a God; I believe He did. O, I want to believe it. It
was all so quiet and still—He must have heard me.
I was selfish, too, Frank. I prayed for myself too.
I had to. I was late back to the office, and Mr. Coates
was annoyed, but I could not worry about that. It
didn't matter.

How happy we were when you were in England!
Do you remember that time when I went down to

Chetley and it rained and rained, and we met the farmer and his wife on the station, and how you said it was good luck, and that you were sure to come back? I remember every minute of it.

My uncle has been staying with us. He's in London again. He comes every month. He's always been fond of me, and I couldn't help telling him about you. He was very pleased. I know you won't mind me telling him. He's anxious to meet you. He made fun of me going out all the way to Australia. I loved him for it, but it hurt so, because I could not help thinking would I ever go. I can't help thinking it. I try to force myself not to, and tell myself you will come back to me. If you only knew how much it means to me. I even envy those poor girls—the W.A.A.C.'s—and wish I could go to France somewhere just to be nearer, even though you tell me women never go within miles of the Line.

Perhaps you will be able to get leave, but I can't bear to think of that, because it sounds so impossible now that all those battles are being fought. Sometimes it all seems so strange that there should be a war and men being killed—so many of them. You can find out about our own men, but the only way for me is to wait for your letters. O, Frank, can you dream what it means to get your letters? So write and write whenever you can. They seem to be the only real thing that makes you a real person. If I did not get them I would begin to think you were only a dream—as if you were not real. And then comes a letter and I know you are. They tell me that you love me. I love you, and am waiting and waiting. If this terrible war would only stop now. But some-

thing may have happened before I've got your letter
—after you've posted it. If it had only stopped that
very moment you wrote to me, you would soon be
coming back.

I have sent a pair of socks and am knitting a comforter because it will soon be getting colder, and I
know you don't like the cold. Do be careful and keep
yourself warm, and God keep you from harm. How
terrible it is to finish each letter. Do you feel like
that? But it has to be finished or you would never
get it.

Your waiting and loving
Mary.

At first he thought, with bitter irony, that Westminster Abbey was the last place she might have gone
to, but, later, when he read it again, he had to gulp
down his emotion. Kneeling there for him—she! And
Bentley was promising himself to go to her if he had
the luck to get a Blighty. What a mysterious mess
was his life, the lives of them all—her life and Bentley's and his own. No, not Bentley's. Her kneeling
there for him, then, was something beyond understanding. She could not be lying. That was the sort of
thing which could not be imagined. It was one of
those strange things people really did—too strange to
be understood.

He believed that the men knew something of his
affair, and Bentley's connection with it. Potter, or
perhaps Bentley himself, had given them a hint of it.

But what did it all matter? He put the sheets of
paper aside and drooped into a melancholy survey of
the war. What he called his cowardice—his incom-

petence, even in his small job as corporal, and his innate complete inability to secure respect for his small orders—had for a long time now convinced him that he must throw in his stripes. What, to anyone else, would have been nothing, apart from the loss of extra pay, to him was a bitter humiliation. And yet his conscience reproached him for having held on to them so long when he was unworthy. For him it was indeed a matter of conscience—a momentous issue between right and wrong.

When, the day after they had commenced their rest, he conveyed his decision to Lieutenant Skipton, instead of being relieved in mind, he found his bitterness was only increased by the officer's too-ready acceptance of his resignation.

Artie Fethers became a full corporal and Blue McIntosh was induced to take the single stripe of the lance-jack.

Artie and Blue noticed, when Skipton called them to him and informed them of approval of their promotion, that he was put out by something. It took something to perturb that work-a-day equanimity, and Blue made no bones of asking him what was up.

"You'll find out this afternoon. There's to be a battalion parade. You'd better warn the men to hang about."

Skipton, indeed, was visibly distressed and at the same time angry. So, when the company drew up on one side of the battalion square, the interest of the platoon was on the quick. It was evident from the intent faces of others that they too had an idea that they were to be notified of something of special importance. Looking about the lines, now that the battalion was drawn up in mass, the weakness of its strength was appalling. Yet it was not to be withdrawn, but would be sent in again, or else, the men argued, it would already have been moving to the rear areas.

Colonel Gilderoy, the little spry adjutant, and the lean R.S.M. Grant, and the quartermaster, occupied the centre of the square. The officers stood in front of their respective companies. The sergeant-major stood the men easy. Gilderoy's face was hard, and his voice vibrated hoarsely as he read the orders.

Owing to the losses which had been sustained, and the absence of reinforcements, an amalgamation of the battalions had become necessary, and the Nth was to be dissolved and absorbed by the other battalions of the brigade.

After the first startled movement there was a spontaneous mutter from the troops which Gilderoy did not attempt to check. To the orders, he added, on his own account, only one sentence, "Boys, this is to be the end of the old Nth."

He was almost weeping. The parade was dismissed, but the troops collected in little groups of platoons. Dissolve the old Nth, their battalion! It was a personal affront to them. They found it hard to express their feeling, these men, who were not given to making a display of emotions. In the groups that gathered during the rest of the day there gradually arose a desire to resist this infamous order. The next day it was much the same, except that certain of the men, and lesser ranks of the N.C.O.'s, began to take the lead in the expressions of resentment and injured pride. Leaders—or ringleaders, if you like—emerged in the persons of Bill Batten, Artie Fethers and Ginger Fogarty.

At four o'clock a message went around the battalion. There would be a meeting in half an hour.

At the appointed time, the battalion drew together in the spot where the previous parade had been held. They grouped themselves again in a square of companies, taking up their ordinary positions in the ranks. No officers were present, but the sergeants formed a group outside the square. Batten, Artie Fethers and Fogarty and a few others stood in the centre where the colonel had stood. Ginger Fogarty, who had a recognised gift of the gab, took the stump. They had heard what was proposed—the old Nth was to disappear. What right had any bastard of a general to give an order like that? It was their battalion. He had been with it since Egypt, and was he going to be sent away into some other crowd after all the stunts? And their cobbers who had been with them and were gone—it was their battalion too. Who, living, had a right to destroy the battalion of those men who were wounded and those who were dead? What did they think about it? Were they going to stick that? Other battalions, too, were going to be cut up. Were they going to stand for it? The murmur of denial was loud and determined. But what was going to be done? How could they stop it? Go on strike? The more turbulent acclaimed up the suggestion. Yes, strike. Others, who were shrewder, were more careful. Appoint a committee!

"—— committees!" Hooky James called out. "Going on strike's no good. Let's go on as we were, in spite of their bloody orders. If the officers won't stick to us, we'll get other officers. Who? Appoint our own. That was the idea. See the officers, and, if they won't stick to us, make our own. They appointed a committee of five, then, to see the O.C. that night.

They broke up, talking excitedly, while the committee squatted on the ground and went into session. That was the idea—go on as if nothing had happened. It was a good idea, that. It seemed excellent to everyone. After tea the men collected about fifty yards from battalion headquarters.

The battalion office was in the remnants of a building which had been restored and patched up by Fritz not long ago. The men waited patiently for the reappearance of the committee, and, when they came out, drew off with them to the open place where they had paraded. Batten announced the result of the deputation shortly. The colonel wanted as little as any of them to see the battalion dispersed, but the orders were firm. He had seen brigade, and brigade had spoken to division, but there was nothing doing.

The next day Gilderoy addressed them, but his heart was not in it and they could see it. He ordered the men to march. It was only formal. They stood still. When he left, the committee appointed Batten colonel, Fogarty his adjutant, and the commanders of companies, including Artie Fethers, to D. Each platoon appointed its commander.

Jim Blount was the platoon's choice, and finally they overcame his laughing disclaimer.

The idea was to carry on as if there had been no orders. It was an interesting feature of the affair that other battalions had each had the same happy inspiration, and they, too, began to appoint their own officers. The reaction of the men threw divisions and corps into an immense perturbation. Some of the staffs talked openly about mutiny and such nonsense, but a few of them kept their heads. To these, humour came in aid, for brigade, not knowing what to do with states, requisitions and reports signed by, for instance, W. J. Batten, Pte., Commanding Nth Battalion, A.I.F., sent them off to division, as if they were all regular and proper. The battalion officers, visited hurriedly by generals and staff majors and staff captains, had nothing to suggest, and the men ignored the presence of these visitors. It was futile —it soon became evident to the Heads—to expect anything of officers who objected, just as bitterly as the men, to the obnoxious order.

Even the most bigoted disciplinarian found it difficult to call men mutinous who were carrying on their training with an amount of zeal which they never would have shown under their ordinary commanders. The troops were adamant. They would not be dissolved. Force was impossible, for the other battalions heartily supported the mutineers, and any attempt to break them up by English troops would only have led, it was made quite plain, to armed resistance from the whole of the A.I.F. However, the idea of English intervention was perhaps only a furphy started by the committees.

So the strike or mutiny went on. The climax was reached when the time came for the Australians to move forward towards the Hindenburg line, of which, though they, of course, received no orders, the temporary commands were made aware by their sympathisers in other units. The men in the battalions

K

on strike stated plainly their intention to go into battle, if necessary, under their new officers. The Heads had to crawl down and a compromise was arranged to save the brass face. The battalions were not to be dissolved, but to be under orders of one of the other battalions, if necessary, when the occasion arose. The new officers vacated their positions and the old took over. The strike ended in secret laughter. In the minds, however, of the higher commanders there continued to exist a feeling of uneasiness. The laughter was at their expense. They were the joke. The mockery in the merriment only aided the feeling. By it the men emphasised the helplessness of the leaders confronted by this mass determination. It was just as if it were made plain to them that their power depended, not on the inherent authority of command, but on the tolerance of the men themselves. What had happened once might happen again. This was a spirit, disruptive of the whole hierarchical system in which authority was presumed to flow, through the rubber stamping or printing of the Commission, from on high downwards. It was the sudden manifestation of an independent will in the gun fodder, all the more dangerous because discipline had not been lacking, but had become tighter, and lit up by a subterranean enthusiasm. To the wiser of the Australian commanders, however, especially those who had been in personal touch with the troops themselves, such an outbreak occasioned no great surprise. They knew that in the A.I.F. there was a force of intelligent public opinion which could never be disregarded as this order had disregarded it. There may not have been even at corps an attempt to disregard it, but only an attempt, made in desperation owing to the lack of reinforcements, to override it, and, in the circumstances, the revulsion was only to be expected. Indeed, there were some who had foretold trouble.

Now that the affair was over, the censorship descended on it and sought to blot it out as if it had never been, which was perfectly futile.

The battalion commenced its small preparations to move to the Hindenburg Line, the approaches to which were being cleared by the two advance Australian divisions and some English. When he had put his things in order, Jim Blount shut the pocket volume of Shakespeare's tragedies which he had bought on on leave. He did it with an air of satisfaction, for he had just finished Macbeth. Before he finally put the book away in his haversack, he opened it once more and read—

"Come, reeling night,
  Scurf up the tender eye of pitiful day,
  And with thy bloody and invisible hand
  Cancel and tear to pieces that great bond
  Which keeps me pale! Night thickens, and the crow
  Makes wing to the rooky wood."

He shut the book and turned on his side, propping his arm on a stone. This, too, his last leave had given him—this, and the memory of Audrey Monson, the Tommy officer and the girl during the air raid, and that night, when, at a dead end, he had gone, as usual, to any theatre he first came to, and heard the British National Opera Company give Traviata, and, on his last night, Boris Goudounov. He saw life unfurling before him like a gorgeous tapestry wrought with wonders. He lay there thinking for some time before he rose and went up the hill. It seemed that the sun, when it touched the horizon, had burst and scattered jets and splashes of blood over the evening sky.

Standing there, Jim felt aloof from the war. Just then it didn't seem to matter. All the dead he'd seen were dead, and he, too, might soon be one of the bodies in the mud or the grass. He felt almost aloof from the world. He turned to look at the flickering light in the east, and imagined once again that that light presaged a new dawn. The dawn of a new sun at the very instant when that old one was sinking in blood and would rise no more. His lips quivered, for at that moment a glow went up in the light in the east, and that also was red.

The weather, which had been patchy for some time, seemed really to have broken, and it was like old times to be squelching, underneath a waterproof cape, through the mud. But it was only slippery surface mud as yet. It would take a month or so, ploughing of the earth by shells, before it reached its proper deep consistency.

CHAPTER XLIII.

TOWARDS the end of September four great blows were struck at the enemy. First the Americans west of the Meuse, second the French west of the Argonne, third the British, including the five Australian Divisions and two American at St. Quentin·

Cambrai, and lastly, the Belgians and some French and British in Flanders. Of these, the centre, to be launched by the British against the Hindenburg Line itself, was the most important. The corps under Monash, whose organisation and drive and civilian adaptability, and whose willingness to trust to the issue of battle, had stamped him as a leader of first-rate importance, was extended to include not only his Australian troops, but the two American divisions.

In Monash the troops had a certain amount of confidence. At any rate, he was one of themselves—not like the Tommies. With the recollection of Gallipoli, the Somme and Pozieres, Bullecourt and Fleurbaix, and the bloody mud of the last week at Ypres in their minds, the men distrusted the British generals and their staffs. Distrust is perhaps too mild a word to define their feelings.

The first enemy defences on the corps sector were connected by a trench system which ran in front of the villages of Bellicourt and Bony. The trench system was elaborate and protected by thick belts of wire, so laid as to gather and bunch the attackers under fire from the front line trenches. In this system were many deep dugouts and protected works, the villages themselves being skilfully and powerfully adapted for the defence. Near Bellicourt the Canal du Nord passed underground through a tunnel which, in its depths, was itself capable of holding many troops secure from the heaviest shell fire. Behind this line there were others, also protected by thick tactical wire as strongly constructed as those of the front itself. A second line of defence embraced, going north, Nauroy, Cabaret, Wood Farm and Le Catelet, and, beyond this, was another, connecting the latter town with Estrees and Joncourt to the south. All this comprised the celebrated Hindenburg Line, the magnum opus of the enemy's defensive genius, in which, with massed artillery and hundreds of machine guns, he now awaited what would be the crucial test. If ever the strength of a position could give confidence, Fritz might feel confident of holding his pursuers there. A successful defence would give him the right to a peace by negotiation.

In dull, showery weather the battalion, with the rest of the brigade, approached the left of Hesbecourt, where the platoon, with the others, took possession of a series of trenches in which it encamped. There were a number of balloons up on their side, and the German also, and a constant activity of aircraft. The visibility, however, was poor. From where it was situated, the platoon could see the Yanks moving up in detachments, and, intrigued by these new arrivals in numbers which they had not previously seen, some of the men went across to engage them in conversation. They started, usually, with, "Good-day, Yank." "Hullo, Digger," and continued sometimes, "You'll know better when Fritz has a crack at you."

The Yanks were a little awed by the occasion, for, though a couple of companies had been lent to the Australians at Hamel, nearly all of them were without experience of war. Standing about with their hands thrust in the top front pockets of their pants, the Australians regarded these innocents abroad with some commiseration. "Well, good luck, Yank." "Good luck, Aussie."

The platoon, having had a good meal, idled about.

Charl Bentley, Ikey Harris—with whom Charl had become more particularly friendly since Bill had been knocked at Peronne—Blue McIntosh and Fatty Gray squatted in the shallow trench playing euchre. Frank Jeffreys, making his way moodily along it, did not notice Charl's outstretched leg and tripped over it.

Charl looked up and demanded "Why the —— hell don't you look where you're going?"

When he had seen who it was, his voice had acquired a nasty snarl, as if it had only needed this trifling accident to set fire to the whole train of his resentment against his enemy. As well as personal feeling, there was, beneath the ordinary demeanour of each of them, the same nervous tension that stressed them all in common. It had been noticeable even in the manner of that game of cards. Unable to forget the bitterness of the disillusionment of his love affair, Charl's temper leaped out openly.

His question provoked the irritable, almost shrill, report, "You shouldn't have stuck your damned leg out. What do you mean by taking up the whole trench like that?"

Charl straightened his back and knelt on his knees. "Who the hell are you talking to? You're not a —— corporal now."

"Perhaps I'm not. That's got nothing to do with it."

Charl stood up, while the others looked on silently.

"Hasn't it. By Christ it has, Jeffreys. You—you miserable bastard. You—you bastard—you crawling cur. I know you. You crawled over to England after my girl. She was not much better than a ——

whore, anyway; but you crawled after her, you mean
skunk. Went and tried to hook my sheila.''

It was as much a push as a blow that Frank, white
and trembling, made at the leering, ugly mouth of the
boy, but it was enough to produce a savage blow above
his nose.

They commenced to fight. The other three urged
Charl with their encouragement. The bastard Jeffreys
had been mean enough to try to do Charl out of his
bit of skirt—something, in their opinion, indescribably
base, putrid.

The narrow walls of the trench hindered the men,
making them come straight towards each other.
Frank Jeffreys, his arms flying wildly, kept uttering
quaint, harsh cries. It was beastly, but the others
would do nothing to stop it. It was worse than
that. Because it was human it was obscene.
For some minutes Frank's fury made an equal
fight of it, but then his devitalised physique
collapsed. Weak and faint, so that he could hardly
stand, he was soon almost helpless, and Charl's fists
struck into his face one after the other, again and
again. Suddenly the end came. Jim Blount and Harry
Mullane jumped into the trench and held the two men.

"God, what's this for?" cried Jim, looking at the
others while he supported Frank in his arms. "You
shouldn't have let them do this, Blue."

Blue nodded gloomily at Frank. "He pinched young
Charley's tart."

Jim helped Frank along the trench and let him down
on a place where he could sit. For a moment he stood
there and looked with a troubled gaze down at the
bent head, and then turned slowly away. A sob, and

then another, shook Frank's body, wrung from the darkness of his soul. Blood from his broken mouth trickled through his fingers.

A silent cry echoed in his brain, "God, O God." All at once his stomach heaved and he vomited. "God, O God, have mercy upon me," from the dark abasement of his soul.

He sat there where he was, until, towards morning, Sergeant Burke, after an uncomfortable look at the crouching figure, roused him. "Better be getting your equipment on, Frank; we may move forward a bit soon."

Frank got up in a dazed fashion and went and got his gear together. He did not put it on, nor had the others, for there was no need as yet. The night was dark and cold, and the platoon stuck close together, shivering themselves warm. There was a low rumble along the front. About nine, Jack Skipton came along with Lairey Ridley and told them what was to be done. The two American Divisions were to attack first, the one on the north towards Bony, and the other on their own front across Bellicourt and the tunnel area. Their division would pass through the Americans with thirty-four big tanks and eight whippets. One piece of luck, the brigade would be in reserve. Captain Ridley and Jack Skipton left to attend a meeting of officers at battalion headquarters. Gilderoy was nervous about the Yanks, not doubting their willingness, but their experience.

Once again the men commenced the dreary and desolate period, full of boreboding, which preceded the zero hour, though that feeling was not by any means so keen now that they knew they were to be in reserve.

They got their extra rations, which was something to do. And there was an extra issue of bombs, the bombers being given an extra haversack each, which they filled.

It was some little time before daybreak when the artillery really let itself go, and, towards six, the noise was appalling. A constant shattering bang. These men stood up to look at the light along the line, which, now in one place and now in another, glowed and flared up above the general flicker. Frank Jeffreys did not go on top, but sat with his back against the trench. His eyes were wide open and his body limp. The old spasm of terror which the gun fire used to produce had left him, but that gave him no comfort.

Nine o'clock. By now the advance brigades would be crossing the line, and in an hour there might be some news. The chaos of the guns continued, undiminished. Overhead there were many planes, but the visibility was poor, so that they were of little use to the artillery. After a while the troops saw a number of scattered Americans coming back. Word came through from brigade that the battalion was to hold itself in readiness to move at a moment's notice. The battle had become confused. The few reports from the attacking battalions indicated that something had gone amiss. The Australians, advancing over the ground of the Americans, instead of having a clear path, had had to fight their way forward. What, then, had happened to the Yanks? Where were they? It seemed that they had gone over, indeed, with great spirit, but, ignorant of war, they had neglected to mop up, and there were far more enemy underground than on the surface. Those emerging from the tunnel and the deep dugouts not only took the Americans from the rear, but made a line of resistance to the advancing Australians, who met parties of Americans escaping back through the German posts. These had had enough of the war. They knew that there was something wrong—that was all—and were taking care to remove themselves out of a business they did not understand. One thing, they had nothing to eat; and it passed their comprehension how they were to exist without food. As the day drew on, the weak Australian battalions, pushing on little by little, discovered small groups of Americans maintaining themselves here and there. Their divisions were cut to bits and hopelessly disorganised, and, before long, their numbers would have been almost all annihilated or made prisoners, this being prevented by the arrival of the Australians, who gathered up a few of the remnants as they went on, their firm purpose and control and leadership being hailed by the rescued as deliverance from the bitter despair of complete failure. Because the Australians had got up, the Yanks felt they had not failed entirely. Parties of these Yanks were actually discovered maintaining a tenacious hold on the outskirts of Nauroy when the first Australian reached the town.

Towards dark, on the 29th, the Australians held a line beyond Nauroy, stretching north along the Le Catelet system, then bending back west to the Tunnel, which was held for a short distance, and then bending back to include Quennemont Farm, Gillemont Farm and the Knoll.

At about the time the work of consolidation of this line commenced, Gilderoy received orders to lead

his battalion forward with the rest of the brigade.
They advanced slowly in single file, keeping some
distance to the left of a deep communication trench,
the sides of which were protected with wire, and along
which Fritz shelled heavily to hinder the advance of
the reserves. The night set in quickly—darker and
colder than the previous one—and the platoon stumbled
forward blindly, each man following the man in
front, and trusting to their leaders for direction. It
passed south of Hargicourt, finding it difficult to keep
touch there in the trenches and fragments of wire,
and north of Villayet, where it encountered another
confusing system of trenches. Though the march to
the position, where it halted in the first of the trenches
on the near side of Bellicourt, was only about three
and a half miles, in the darkness and confusion of
trenches and old wire it took close on three hours
before the brigade assembled on the new position and
settled down to wait.

The battalion was not called on to move much during the rest of that day, but lay low where they were,
troubled only now and then by occasional shells. The
others in the brigade, however, became involved in
confused fighting in the neighbourhood of the Tunnel
to the left of Bellicourt. At noon the platoon had a
good meal, which was shared with odd parties of
famished Americans, whose commissariat, owing to
their general confusion, was out of commission.

Towards the evening, Blue McIntosh and Fatty
Gray went scouting about a bit for what they could
find. Going down a little slope, they saw an amazing
sight—a mule with festoons of wire about it, and,
alongside, snoring peacefully, a signaller of one of

the advance brigades. The cause of his slumber was
not not hard to guess. There was a demijohn beside
him, and it had been opened. Blue put it to his mouth,
raised his eyebrows, and took a long pull, and handed
it then to Fatty, who did likewise. Rum!

"Cripes," said Fatty excitedly.

They regarded the recumbent signaller.

"Let's give him a start," suggested Blue.

They disentangled the donk, and, while Fatty held
it, Blue shook the signaller awake.

"Eh, what yer doin'?" he expostulated.

"They're waiting for you up there with the rum."

"My Gawd, yes."

He staggered up. Between them, Fatty and Blue got
him astride the donk and gave him a firm grip on the
mane. Rolling drunk as he was, the man could stick
on. He seemed to have an idea that the rum was
packed up with him, and he grinned and nodded, "All
s'rene, dig."

Blue gave the mule a slap with his bayonet and it
started off, its swaying burden raising his voice in
song.

The platoon welcomed that rum. They felt they
needed it. Only Frank Jeffreys refused his issue.

Some time in the morning they were set tramping
forward again, their way leading them through Bellicourt. On the other side of the village the battalion
took to a trench, the platoon bringing up the rear as
usual. It was just as well they were keeping a good
distance between each man. A shell lobbed on the
top of the trench, blowing part of it in. Charl
Bentley staggered back against the man behind. He
was not hit, but in the bottom, half covered with earth,

a figure twisted and groaned. Jack Skipton came back, and together they bent over Ikey Harris. How bad he was they could not say, but two stretcher-bearers behind wedged their way along and lifted him up. The rest went on.

The battalion, following along the trench, came soon to the left of Nauroy, and, striking a small body of the brigade, turned to the left around the station. Slowly the officers ranged the men in their starting line. The other two battalions were on the right. A conference of the officers in command was held, and it was decided that the main line of attack must be up what was called Mill Ridge, running half right up to Joncourt, which would give a more commanding position, while Gilderoy's battalion should go forward towards Estrees and provide a flanking movement to the main attack in case the left brigade were held up.

The platoon sat down and waited together with the rest of D company which, all told, numbered thirty-eight men. Jim Blount squatted between Harry Mullane and Frank Jeffreys and wrapped his scarf more warmly over his chest. This, he believed, must be their last stunt. The battalions could stand no more. They would cease to exist. Fritz also must be about fed up. It wanted, then, just good luck for the next day or two, and perhaps it would be all over. After the four years—just those two or three days to go. His imagination ran on to the days beyond them when the experience he had gained would discover a new life amazingly enriched.

Charl Bentley moved and coughed. He had been feeling wretched ever since his fight with Frank Jeffreys. At first he had been inclined, as a cover for his deeper uneasiness, to strut a bit, but now, in that strange dark hour before the dawn, lit by the customary flickering dim light of the intermittent battle, there was no strut in him. The thickening coarseness and carelessness which was encrusting his youth was now flaked off. Remorse kept pricking him for that ugly affair. It took the form of a persistent suggestion that he ought to do as the formal code of his school laid it down—offer to shake hands upon it. He was afraid, too. His two mates, Bill Potter and then Ikey Harris, were gone. He remembered, "Let not the sun go down on thy wrath."

At last he could stand it no longer, and got up and went over to where Frank Jeffreys was sitting. Glad of the darkness, which concealed his hot face from the others, he put out his hand and said, adopting the old style of address, "I'm sorry, corp."

Frank looked up. Take the physical firmness of the hand, like a ghost's, in the dark, he could not. He did not even think of it, but he could not rebuff the boy altogether. "It's not your fault," he admitted, and then went on slowly, "Not mine either. I am sorry too." His head dropped forward again. But Charl was still unsatisfied. He felt, now that he had started, he ought to clear up everything—for Jeffrey's sake.

He said, awkwardly, "I don't know whether you really thought she's dinkum. I sort of felt you might, when I've been trying to think, all along, you knew she isn't. If you did, I wasn't to tell you . . ." he stammered. "It's true I got all I wanted. I suppose you did too. I reckon we need'nt, either of us, worry about her any more." Charl picked his way back to Blue McIntosh's side, feeling quite relieved now that he had done what he knew a good sport should. In a glow of self-righteousness he was thankful he had not let the sun go down on his wrath. It would be all right now.

Frank looked after him and then saw Jim Blount regarding him. A slight moaning sound issued from Frank's lips.

"Perhaps he's right. Don't hold it against the boy, Frank. He told me something about it. He says she's no good."

Frank bent his head again and muttered, just loud enough for Jim to catch the words, "I loved her."

Jim felt that it was beyond him and said nothing more. That confession imposed its hopeless agony on him also, and he, too, now bore it as if it were his own. The blind chance idiocy of the fate which had overtaken Frank began to trouble his new confidence and tranquillity. Harry Mullane, too, had heard it all. He looked at Frank's dark figure with a sort of fear. A feeling of doom oppressed him, before which he was helpless as in a nightmare.

With the first glimmer of dawn, the hastily-improvised barrage commenced, weak enough as a barrage, as the waiting troops noted, although the whole of the enemy front was being subjected in depth to a heavy incessant fire. The men prepared themselves for the hop over. Ridley, his tin hat at an even jauntier angle, and Jack Skipton, took the left wing forward, with Gilderoy a hundred yards away on the right. The platoon had hardly got started when Skipton noted Lorry Swift slip down. He knew at once the boy was not wounded. A few months ago he would have yanked him up in an instant, but now he couldn't

do it, and let him lie. Not so long ago the boy had
been as good as any. Let him lie there. Some inkling
of the boy's misery must have dimly touched the
lieutenant's pity. Answering the barrage, the enemy
shells, including some shrapnel, were now fairly thick,
but most of them were going over. Frank walked on
like a sleep walker as if unconscious of the wailing
roar and rattle, the pitching shells and the unheard
threading of the machine gun bullets. Breaking
through a piece of shattered wire, the company availed
itself of the protection which a short contour of the
ground afforded.

While the left of the battalion was thus somewhat
protected, the right had come under heavy fire from
the neighbourhood of a farm to the left front, marked
on the map as Folemprise. From this place a minor
trench system ran south-west and then south.. It was
the southern end of this which the left of the battalion was now approaching. Realising the danger
to his flank which might lie in these trenches, Gilderoy
now came along and ordered Captain Ridley to push
up them for a while, and, establishing himself
there, to block any attempt of the enemy to debouch
from them. This movement, he hoped, would also dis-
tract some of the fire which was enfilading his centre
and right companies.

D company therefore turned half left, two platoons
entering the left, and the other two, Nos. three and
four, the right supporting trench. The trenches they
were in were wide affairs—nine feet wide in parts,
not properly looked after, and fallen in in places—
so that in places three or four men could meet abreast.
The company had not proceeded far before it

encountered some of the enemy in a short communication trench. The occupants of the trench were
killed, and D company formed a thin line along it.
Immediately after this, the group at the left, on the
junction of the main trench, and No. 4 platoon, at
the junction with the support, became involved in a
desperate encounter with the enemy, who began to
come down the trenches in considerable numbers. A
general melee commenced with bomb and rifle and
bayonet, mostly in the trenches, but occasionally on
top also. In the communication trench, Blue, kicking his toes into holds, got his head up. He and Fatty
with the drums. He knew they would be saying, as
they used to say when they heard the gun, "Blue's
got his head up." And by God he'd keep it up. It
took some keeping up, specially when Fatty rolled
back. The air, paled with breaking day, crackled with
the sharp sounds and acrid smell of the detonations,
with oaths and shouts and groans. The little groups
of Australians, combining a cunning advantage of
their position with a ruthless ferocity, not only held
the enemy for five to ten desperate minutes, but forced
him to withdraw up the trenches beyond the bombs.
In the supreme moments of those short minutes the
minds of these men became white and glowing, and
their condition a sort of ecstasy, in which courage and
fear were fused into one.

Frank Jeffreys was standing beside Jim Blount
behind a curve in the support trench, where Jack
Skipton and Jim had met, with their bayonets—for
the officer had armed himself with a rifle—the second
charge of the foe. In the breathing space which the
enemy's retreat afforded, Jim drew himself up out of

the trench to look around. Against the weak green
and yellow light of the east he perceived a little mob
of Fritzes collecting—about twenty or so. He touched
Frank on the shoulder with his boot and pointed. He
had seen in a flash that if this group should come
down on the flank of the survivors of the company, it
was doomed. Frank hauled himself half up out of
the trench to look in the direction of Jim's arm, and
found a foothold. An ironical smile played for a
moment on Jim's lips. The Germans were only thirty
yards away and drawing in. He stood straight up,
and, with a magnificent effort, flung a bomb which
burst in the front of them. Then he charged them—
alone. Alone, for Frank dared not. He saw the running, springing figure throw again, and then he sank
back into the trench, his nerves and muscles helpless.
All at once there was a cessation of the shots along
the trenches, and the sounds of another engagement
a hundred yards ahead. Fritz, caught by a party of
the flank brigade, and a tank which had come from the
direction of Cabaret copse, was retreating. The danger
to the battalion was over, and the remains of D
company, relieved by this advance, not only held
its trench in security, but wiped out the nine or ten
Fritzs who were cut off between them and the frontal
attack. The platoon gathered back to the line of the
communication trench, where Jack Skipton shep-
herded those still standing together. They were seven
—Bentley, Jeffreys, Mullane, Hecht, McIntosh, Johnny
Wright and Thomson. The latter had a deep cut across
the back of his left hand and was useless, so that
Jack told him to get Johnny to dress it and then beat
it, which left six. Sergeant Burke was dead in the

communication trench, and so was Fatty Gray. Jim Blount was missing, Darkey Lansdowne wounded in the mouth, and Dopey Kendall in the shoulder, were lying in the support trench. They would do well enough, but Artie Fethers, who was at the corner, was hopeless. A shot, or several, had taken him in the chest and he was bleeding from the mouth. Every few seconds his drowning lungs would heave up and a fresh flow burst from his cluttered lips. The others, with the exception of Frank Jeffreys, who, with closed eyes, leaned his head against the moist wall of earth, looked on with almost intolerable anguish. If Artie would only die. But his life lingered as though obstinate to depart until the last flow of his blood, and of his life the occasional heave of his chest was the only sign.

The one glance of Artie Fethers, his eyes opened sightlessly for a moment, touched no emotion in Frank Jeffreys. He kept thinking of Jim Blount's lonely sacrifice. Jim Blount, the best of all of them, who, unnoticed by the others, had scattered alone the impending charge. Alone, while he himself had not dared, but played the coward, deserting his mate. Always in the past he had succeeded in commanding his shrinking flesh to its duty, but now he had failed. His head sank down on his chest.

He was aroused by the plaintive voice of Harry Mullane, who was demanding of them what had happened to Jim, for he, shoved into the communication trench, had lost sight of him. With an effort Frank overcame his first fearful impulse to say nothing, and he stammered that he had seen Jim get up on top and run, he nodded, over there.

"Let's go and see," demanded Harry, and propelled Frank out of the trench.

They went together to the spot, forty paces or so away, where the enemy had collected. They found Jim lying on his back on the wet trampled grass. There were four dead Germans about him—one of them an officer. Others, too, Jim must have wounded, for one, left, no doubt, for dead, was sitting up with a broken jaw, on the side of which was a contusion black with blood.

Kneeling down by Jim's body, the two men regarded his face. It was untouched. Only a little blood and mucous had trickled from the nose and mouth. Then Harry bent forward and undid the scarf and tunic at the neck. When he saw that the dead meat tickets, one of black paper mache and the other of shining metal, hung, as usual, by their leather cord, he did up the buttons again. Then he rose and, having picked up Jim's rifle, stuck it straight up, driving the discoloured bayonet into the ground to the hilt, and put the tin hat, which he recovered a few yards away, on the butt.

At that moment he caught sight of the white eyes of the wounded Fritz, and stepped across to him to say, with a sort of grin, "I wouldn't stay here if I were you, Fritz." The German understood that look and got to his feet. He went off hastily with his hands up. Returning to where Frank still knelt by the body, Harry pondered a few moments, and then bent down on one knee. He opened the sticky breast pockets for papers, and found only a wet pay book, which he left. The haversack, which he got at with difficulty, for the body was heavy, contained a half-

eaten biscuit, the extra tin of bully, a holdall, pair of
socks, and a book, across the leaves of which he
whirred his thumb, and then slipped it into his side
pocket. That was all. They rejoined the others and
Harry went to talk to Lairy Ridley and Jack Skipton.
The captain had a slight wound in the arm. Frank
Jeffreys sat down quietly without a word. Meanwhile, some stretcher-bearers of the A.A.M.C. had
come up and were taking care of the wounded. It
was bad luck for the Fritzes, for there were no
prisoners to carry them, and not enough stretcher-
bearers. Every now and then there came, from somewhere along the trenches, a groan or a gurgling cry.

Gilderoy arrived. It was necessary to push on.
Progress now was easy, and the company, with the
remainder of the battalion, approached the village,
from which the rear guards of the enemy withdrew,
now that they, having seen the progress of the Australian attack up the ridge to Joncourt, were
threatened from the front.

A dead calm had settled on Frank's spirit as he
tramped up through the wet grass towards one more
ruin—dead. Though he thought nothing—Mary being
there in his mind, but there just like a dead shadow—
it was all settled. Something was settled. He did not
ask what it was. He knew that something was.

The village was occupied without much trouble, and
the line established on its further boundaries. The
Hindenburg Line was pierced right through, and here
it became quiet, while, on the left and right, the battle
also moved slowly eastwards.

Frank Jeffreys sat down a few yards away from the
rest of the platoon, who occupied a post in a trench

behind the rubble of one of the further houses in
Estrees. The weary day was mounting towards its
noon, and, now that the air was clearer, a view could
be obtained over the grassy patchwork of the countryside beyond some wire and trenches towards the village of Beaurevoir. One thing, firstly, the platoon
prayed for—immunity from counter-attack, and then
to be relieved, to get out before they were all
stonkered. They did not want to be wiped out
altogether. They feared that counter-attack. It was
a possibility well enough, because they could see Fritz
was holding the group of farms just along the road.
They spoke hardly at all, but chewed at their bully
beef and swigged at their water bottles. Frank, too,
ate his bully and had a drink. His broken lips were
painful. When he had finished, he shut up his clasp
knife and wiped his mouth with the back of his hand.
He knew now what this inevitable thing was. This
agreed-on thing of which now what he was to do was
but the final settlement.

None looked up when he walked off along the shallow trench out of their view beyond the broken wall of
the house. He leaned his rifle against the trench and
stood, with his face upturned to the sky, lean, haggard, the dark, fretful eyes now calm at last, lost
in the cavities beneath their brows. One thing he
knew. He shirked nothing now because for them—the
Australians—the war, of necessity, was about over. All
around him Death had stalked in gusty and fantastic
shapes, but beneath the various masks there was only
one face—one real and true face. All the others were
masks to frighten people. The real face was tranquil,
with the immobility of stone, inscrutable and pro-

foundly peaceful. He could see that real identity now as he took the last Mills bomb from his pocket.

With fingers which did not tremble, he drew the pin and let the lever spring off. Straightening his shoulders, he stood stiff, as if on inspection at parade, and held the serrated bomb with both hands at his heart. Jack Skipton, when, after the explosion, he came along to look around and saw the body in the trench, imagined that a small sudden shell had got poor Frank when he had gone off for a crap.

He called to Harry Mullane, who came around the corner and stood alongside his officer. They were both upset and visibly distressed. The body was very much mutilated. The chest was torn away and the head half off. When Harry's eyes wandered for a moment, they caught sight of the lever of the bomb. With a casual seeming movement he covered it with his foot and ground it into the mud. He knew that it was his memory of the feeling with which he had looked at Frank at the station, the remembrance of that foreboding there, which had caused him to peer around expectantly. And yet what could he have done then? Nothing.

The officer bent down over the body and then stood up. He, whom Horace Calverley had called "that iron man," was trembling like a jelly.

"One more of us gone, sir," whispered Harry hoarsely.

"Yes, and my God I hope we are relieved soon or there'll be no more of us. Poor old Frank. Poor old Frank."

"Do you think we ought to bury him?"

"Yes. His discs are gone."

Between them the survivors made a cross for the grave, on which, as there were no identification discs, Harry carved, "Frank Jeffreys, Corporal, Nth Bn., A.I.F. Killed in action."

L'ENVOI—THE ARMOUR IS PUT OFF

CHAPTER XLIV.

THE platoon had fought its last fight. The battalion was relieved that night of 1st October, and commenced its straggle back, dragging one foot after another, slow, in the urgency of its haste, for weariness and pain. Bit by bit those who were left emerged out of the zone in which the shells were falling, and came, beyond the line of the tunnel, at last back to its old position near Hesbecourt. After twelve hours' rest, the whole brigade moved back still further along a side road to another main road, where, in the dark, a fleet of motor lorries was waiting for it. Into one of these the platoon climbed together with others.

At last they were moving. Lying back with his head on his pack, Johnny Wright smiled. He knew, without being told, that they were going out the war for good—going back to some far village, and soon, perhaps, he would be in England—you never could tell. And then they would be going aboard the troopship and back to Australia, where they would be waiting for him coming home. Coming home. Barbara and the two kids waiting for him. "O, boys, we'll never get drunk any more, never get drunk, never get drunk any more." He imagined them as she had described them in her last letter, marching about, having begged a last respite before bed, in their pyjamas playing soldiers. He would be going back. He turned on his side, thankful that, in the black, covered darkness of the lorry, no one might see the tears which streamed from his eyes on the stiff webbing of the haversack. But in him, too, though more vividly still in Harry Mullane, was another thought. Harry, at the back of the lorry, gazed over the tailboard to the east. He felt, now, that it was almost wrong for them to be leaving that blasted land. He felt as if he were deserting those back there. Jim, old Jim. As if, almost, they all ought to go back and die there where they belonged. Perhaps they would be going home soon to mingle again with their own people in their own land. Some effect that return must have. They were a people. The war had shown that. The A.I.F.—was it not the first sign that they were, the first manifestation that a spirit had begun to work in the material mass? How long would it be before there was some other sign, some manifestations of a small creative ferment? Once he had read some speech of Pasteur's. Only by science, letters, art, can a people become great. Something like that. He kept looking out over the tailboard. It seemed, now that he was leaving the war and the old familiar landscape of death, that his life and the life of this generation was finished. They were the dung for the new flowering and fruit of the future.

Soon, in a few days, the other divisions—those who had relieved—were in their turn relieved, and all the Australian infantry were withdrawn.

What had they done during this last and culminating period of their history? The efficient soldier who was their leader sets it out as he would in a statistical fashion. From 8th August, the day, in Ludendorff's own testimony, called ''Germany's Black Day,'' to 5th October, the five divisions, weak to start, and

becoming weaker from losses, which there was no
flow of reinforcements to replenish, until at last they
were almost skeletons, captured 116 towns and villages, as well as hamlets, farms, brickfields, factories,
sugar refineries and similar groups of fortified buildings. One division had taken the impregnable Mont
St. Quentin from the Prussian Guards, another the
renowned fortress of Peronne held by the picked
volunteers of an Army, and yet another the ridge of
Bouchevesnes. They had thrust the enemy back from
the outer defences of the Hindenburg Line and pierced
through the line itself, after first meeting an unexpected and dangerous position in which two remnants of divisions had rescued two full American
divisions from the completion of a great disaster. During that period they had ejected the enemy from 394
square miles of French territory, and, during the pro-
cess, the Five had engaged 39 separate divisions—20
once, 12 twice, 6 three times, and 1 four times—each
engagement representing a distinct period of line duty
for the hostile division. Of these divisions, at least 16
had, by the time of the Armistice, to be disbanded
on account of their losses. From 27th March, when
their sangfroid and determination had saved Amiens,
to 5th October, the prisoners they had taken numbered
29,144, and the guns 338, apart from innumerable
machine guns and mortars. In March the five divisions
had represented nine and a half per cent. of the whole
of the other 53 British divisions on the Western Front.
Their captures, by the same comparison, were as follows:—Prisoners 23 per cent., guns 23½ per cent, territory 21½ per cent. of the whole of the British Army.
They had been the spearhead of the attack—the cen-

tral attack which shattered the German arms and inspired the others to north and south. Thus was written the last page of a record which commenced with Gallipoli.

And so the infantry of the A.I.F. laid aside their armour and became, what remains of them, just the sort of fellows you know—or so they seem.

Wholly and set up and printed in Australia by Periodicals Pty.
Ltd., King St., Melbourne.